'*Hello, Nancy,*' she whispered, brushing her thumb across the corner of the stiff yellowed paper. '*Why have I never heard of you before?*'

SARAH STEELE

THE
MISSING
PIECES
OF
NANCY
MOON

REVIEW

First published in 2020 by Headline Review
An imprint of HEADLINE PUBLISHING GROUP

1

Cataloguing in Publication Data is available from the British Library

Hardback ISBN 978 1 4722 7007 8

Typeset by EM&EN
Printed and bound in Great Britain by Clays Ltd, Elcograf S.p.A.

Headline's policy is to use papers that are natural, renewable and recyclable
products and made from wood grown in well-managed forests and other
controlled sources. The logging and manufacturing processes are expected
to conform to the environmental regulations of the country of origin.

HEADLINE PUBLISHING GROUP
An Hachette UK Company
Carmelite House
50 Victoria Embankment
London EC4Y 0DZ

www.headline.co.uk
www.hachette.co.uk

*Dedicated to the memory of
my dear and remarkable aunt Pam*

Prologue

Most journeys begin with a goodbye: to a friend or a loved one, often to a lover, and sometimes to a place. Goodbye sharpens the senses, reminds one of what might have been and excites one about what could be. It brings with it a little nostalgia, maybe some guilt or regret, hope perhaps, or even relief. Some goodbyes last merely for a few hours, but some will have to last a lifetime.

It was a muggy evening as they gathered for their own goodbyes, the end to one of those unexpectedly sultry days when city dwellers can't wait to get home and rip off ties and stockings, unbutton collars and loosen girdles and fling their heels across the floor, to open the windows of their flats and listen to the sounds of a city laid bare, finally free of the terrible smogs of winter. The wide glass canopy spanning the station platforms acted as a pressure-cooker lid, trapping the hot, dirty air in a cloud of noise and fumes mingled with the smell of several hundred damp bodies.

Who'd have thought you could get on a train at Waterloo station one evening, and arrive in France the next morning? From Wandsworth to Paris, just like that. She'd looked it up: it was only three hundred miles, the same as Wandsworth to Newcastle – although some Geordies had stopped her at Picca-dilly Circus the other day to ask directions, and she reckoned she'd have a better chance of understanding French. It was only for a couple of months, she told herself. London would still be here when she got back.

The platform was a chaotic tangle of passengers and sayers of goodbyes – family groups locked in tight huddles lest one of their young should break free, lovers exchanging one last kiss – and serious-faced businessmen marching towards their carriages, Crombies flapping behind them and trilbies pulled down over their eyes. She suddenly felt very English and unsophisticated in her hand-made dress, as she watched a Frenchwoman glide past on slim scissor legs, a long cigarette holder in one hand and a small dog tucked under the arm of her inverted-teardrop coat, while a porter scurried after her with her monogrammed suite of matching luggage. A couple of times she felt herself shoved as people hurried to find their carriages and get their orders in for dinner, but she barely noticed, floating above the melee and hearing the bland string of parting conventions that moved back and forth between her mouth and Peggy's as though through a partition wall. The words they both really wanted to say had no place in this public space, with Dorothy and Phyllis standing nearby, so instead they exchanged inanities, filling the last few minutes together with post-office-queue chitchat. The distant chug of the diesel engine did nothing to prevent conversation, even when there was nothing left to say: she missed the screaming of a steam engine gearing up to leave, the smuts floating in the air, that would have provided the perfect excuse for watery eyes. Instead, she looked down to pick at an invisible fleck on her sleeve.

She supposed she had secretly hoped that her parents would

come to see her off, and even if she wasn't surprised that they had stayed away, she couldn't help a sudden sad wave of disappointment, as she thought of Dad by now watching *Z Cars* on the new telly while Mum washed up the egg-and-chip tea they always had on a Monday. She was glad Peggy had come, even though she suspected it was partly to make sure she actually got on the train and didn't change her mind.

'All aboard, ladies and gentlemen. Last passengers for the boat train to Paris.' A uniformed guard bustled along the platform, chivvying the remaining stragglers.

'Well, I'd better be off, then,' Peggy said, and it seemed that one of those imaginary smuts had found her eye too. 'Better get back to Donald and . . .' Her voice trailed away. 'Well, you know.'

'I know.' She tried to smile, but none of the muscles she needed to perform this simple feat seemed to work.

Peggy hesitated, then gave her a quick Nina Ricci-scented peck on the cheek. 'You mustn't worry. Just have a nice time. And watch out for those Frenchmen, eh?'

She couldn't help but laugh. 'You sound like Dad. Now go on, clear off. I've got a train to catch.'

'I hate goodbyes. I wish you didn't have to go. I'll miss you so much.'

And before Peggy could reach into her pocket, Phyllis had appeared with a hanky for her, which Peggy blew into noisily. 'Here you go, Peg. Can't have you looking a state for your Donald when you get home. What'll he think?'

'You get off home, doll. Me and Phyl will wave her off.' She tried not to gasp as Dorothy wrapped an arm around her shoulders and squeezed hard.

Peggy could barely hide her relief. 'Are you sure? I probably ought to get back – Maddie's not been settling well this week, and I can't leave Donald to nurse her.'

'It's fine,' she said. 'Go, Peg. The girls will sort me out.'

'Clear off,' Dorothy said kindly. 'We can see her off from here.'

'Oh, wait!' said Phyllis. 'We ought to have a photo of us all. Where's your camera? You did pack it, didn't you?'

'Somewhere.' She pulled the brown leather case out of her overnight bag and opened it.

'Here,' said Dorothy, and grabbed a young man rushing to his carriage. 'Take a picture of us all, would you?'

He looked as though he wanted to say no, but as Dorothy leant her head on one side and pouted at him, he relented. 'As long as it's quick,' he said reluctantly.

'Here, bunch up, girls,' Dorothy said, pulling her three friends around her.

One quick smile and they were done. The man handed the camera back and hurried on his way, pausing only briefly to look back at Dorothy.

'I'd better get going too,' she said, putting the camera back. 'See you, then, Peg.'

They grasped hands and tried to find a few more words, but they were both spent, so Peggy squeezed her hand once more before turning away and walking briskly back along the platform. By the time the train pulled out, she would be on the number 44 bus back home.

As Peggy disappeared into the crowd, Phyllis and Dorothy positioned themselves on either side of her, and she wondered how comical they must look: Dorothy towering on one side in her high heels and equally high white-blonde beehive, and tiny Phyllis looking like a station pigeon on the other, dressed in office grey and balancing her buxom chest on spindly legs as her eyes darted around nervously.

'Don't you worry,' Dorothy said. 'Peggy'll be fine. They all will be. You just concentrate on that fantastic trip of yours. Wish it were me, lucky cow.' She nudged her playfully, but failed to raise the laugh she'd been hoping for. 'Come on, girl. You look like you're about to enter a workhouse, not go off to the Continent for the summer.'

Phyllis began digging in her handbag and muttering to herself.

'Phyl, what are you doing? You look like a bloody terrier after a rabbit.' Dorothy sighed, taking a bored drag on her cigarette.

Phyllis pulled out a small tin and a packet of custard creams. 'Here,' she said. 'Thought these might come in handy. If you get hungry.'

'They do have food over there, you know,' Dorothy said, rolling her eyes. 'She'll be eating the best snails, not corned bloody beef. Won't you?' she added, then laughed. 'Blimey, you've gone white as a sheet, darlin'!' Dorothy opened the handbag hooked across her arm and took out a half-empty packet of Pall Malls that she passed to her friend. 'Here,' she said, tucking them in her pocket and snapping shut the clasp on her handbag. 'This is more like it.'

'Whistle'll go in about two minutes, madam. Best get a move on now. Don't want to miss it, do you?' A fresh-faced young porter took her case and lifted it onto a trolley, gesturing for her to follow him.

'Come on, girl,' Dorothy said gently, dropping her cigarette on the ground and grinding it with the pointed toe of her black patent shoe, 'let's get you on that train.' She took her arm and pulled her along so that she found herself swinging in time with her friend's trademark sashay, Phyllis's quick little steps pattering close behind.

She almost tripped as she turned back to see if Peggy had waited for one final wave, but the space where she had stood was already filled with the ripple of passengers now hurrying to find their carriages, and there was no sign of Peggy's olive-green summer coat and strawberry-blonde hair.

Was that other face somewhere in the crush, coming to say goodbye, or to beg her to stay? Maybe he'd got the day wrong. Maybe she'd written it down wrong.

'No looking back now,' Dorothy said, seeing where her thoughts were leading. 'Onwards and sideways, eh?' She brushed away the porter's offer to help her friend into the carriage and pushed her up the steps in front of her.

'Onwards and sideways,' she echoed, looking down from the top of the steps. Even this old in-joke failed to bring the wished-for smile to her lips, however.

'You're sure there will be someone to meet you at the other end?' Phyllis said, almost biting her lip off with anxiety.

'Yes, Phyllis, for the hundredth time, they're picking me up at the station.'

The guard began to work his way along the long train, slamming carriage doors and shooing non-passengers away from the edge of the platform. She pulled the window down and leant out. 'Bye, then,' she said, clasping her friends' hands in turn as Phyllis blew her nose heavily into a handkerchief and even Dorothy seemed to have something in her eye.

The whistle blew and the heavy train ground into motion. Phyllis ran alongside it, waving frantically, until Dorothy caught up with her and pulled her back. There was still time to change her mind, she thought as she watched the receding figures of her friends blur into small dots: the train was going quite slowly, and if she jumped off now, she would land on what was left of the platform with nothing more than a red face and maybe a bruised knee.

And then it was too late: the last of the platform had melted away and the engine was cranking up its gears. She had no choice but to see this through.

'Stand back, please, miss,' said the guard, gesturing her aside and slamming the window closed. 'Don't want any nasty accidents now. Which compartment are you in?'

Her ticket was still scrunched into her fist, and she took it out and tried to flatten it. 'Here,' she said.

He peered at it over his half-moon glasses, then pointed along the corridor. 'Just on your left there. Someone will be along presently to sort out your refreshments.'

She picked up her overnight carpet bag and followed his directions, sliding open the heavy door of number 17, where she found her case waiting for her. The wood-panelled compartment, with its shiny brass and well-worn leather, exuded glamour. One of the girls from work had told her that the Duke and Duchess of Windsor used to travel on this night crossing when moving between Paris and London.

There was a gentle tap at the door, and a smart-uniformed steward who looked no older than sixteen poked his head through to ask if she required dinner in the dining car, or whether he could bring her a drink before she went to sleep. She had never been able to make the small decisions in life, so she declined dinner but requested a gin and tonic and a hot chocolate, to cover all angles. He nodded, his smart little boat hat bobbing up and down on his Brylcreemed head.

After a minute or two, she let herself out of the compartment, closing the door quietly behind her. She walked along the corridor, mesmerised by the swaying of the carriage and the thunderous rush of southern England disappearing behind them, and wondering who was behind each of the closed doors, their blinds pulled down and hushed voices from both sides of the Channel barely audible above the clickety-clack of the train as it raced towards Dover and the boat that waited there to carry it on to Dunkirk, then the Gare du Nord. Checking the guard was nowhere in sight, she tugged at the window at the end of the corridor, leaning her face into the hot rush of dusky air that carried the scream of the engine with it, oblivious to the instant damage to the shampoo and set she had paid a fortune for, as she watched miles of English countryside relentlessly eaten away and eventually dissolving into black night.

For a moment she couldn't remember which was her compartment, and panicked at the long row of identical doors, until she remembered the number printed on her ticket. While she'd been gone, the bed had been pulled down and made, the soft tartan blanket and crisp white sheet tucked neatly in on all sides, and the bright overhead lights swapped for a soft night light. She gulped down the gin that waited for her on a thick paper coaster embossed with the train company's logo, and quickly changed into her nightclothes, then took off her broad satin ribbon and brushed the wind out of her hair before settling herself onto the narrow berth.

Suddenly ravenous, she remembered the cheese sandwiches Peggy had made her for the journey, and ate all four in quick succession, washed down with the thick, sweet chocolate drink, only worrying afterwards whether she might lose them down the little toilet during the crossing. She'd never been on a boat before, apart from rowing on the Serpentine last summer, and had no idea whether she had sea legs or not. She'd find out soon enough, she supposed.

So this was it. She was on her way, her wardrobe made and packed with everything she needed for the next few months. She'd even brought her dress patterns with her; it had always been a bit of a ritual to collect mementoes of her favourite times wearing her dresses, and keep them in the original pattern packets. Mum said she was a ridiculous hoarder, but this wasn't hoarding: it was more like a diary, and one day when she looked through these packets and their contents, it would bring back memories of this trip more clearly than any photograph could.

There was no going back. Not for a few weeks, anyway. An amazing opportunity to see a bit of the world at someone else's expense. She had only once ever stayed at a proper hotel, so unlike the little B&B they always went to in Hastings for a week each summer, where you had to make your own bed and clean the communal bathroom when you'd finished with it. She couldn't imagine the French or Italians would kick you out after breakfast and not let you in again until tea, whatever the weather.

She pinned the ends of her hair into whorl-like curls and covered them with a fine-mesh hairnet, then, exhausted, she squeezed between the tightly made sheets of the narrow bunk. Although her body craved sleep, her mind flicked from vignette to vignette, refusing to let go. Eventually, though, even her worst anxieties could not resist the rocking of the racing train as it sang its metallic lullaby, and she spent her last short time on English soil sleeping as peacefully as a baby.

Part One

BRIGHTON

1

Flo wiped the last of Gran's teacups with the damp Fountains Abbey tea towel, putting it with its companions in the top-right cupboard. Not the middle one: that was for everyday crockery. The top-right cupboard was for visitors. And there had certainly been visitors today for the wake. Peggy would have been horrified if her granddaughter had brought out the old supermarket plates and royal wedding souvenir mugs today of all days. Instead, Flo had dusted off the Royal Doulton and made sure the matching sugar bowl and milk jug stood next to the cups on the sideboard, along with the best silver-plated teaspoons. She couldn't imagine that Peggy had ever needed twenty of everything – the only other occasion had probably been Flo's own christening, which she suspected her gran had most likely organised while Mum was away on one of her extended trips.

She rinsed out the dishcloth and wiped it across the table, rubbing at a speck of dried egg she'd not seen earlier. Not only had she forgotten to swap the faded oilcloth for a pressed embroidered linen one, but she had left the remains of what was probably Peggy's last breakfast at home for all the neighbours to see. If her grandmother's weak heart had not already surrendered its fight, she would surely have died of shame at this aberration. She gave the oilcloth a final wipe, so that the yellowed daisies sprinkled across it glistened briefly, then faded back into their dull beige background.

She jumped as she felt a hand on her shoulder, and turned to see Seamus standing close behind her.

'Right, Flossie, I'm off to drop a couple of old biddies home. Reckon I'll be safe?'

Flo did wonder: Seamus was a natural at funerals, and always had Peggy's friends eating out of his hand, with his perfect combination of pathos and humour and Irish blarney, and of course the killer floppy black hair and blue eyes.

He squeezed her shoulder, instantly taking his hand away as he felt her flinch. 'Be back in half an hour, if they've not kidnapped me and locked me in a cupboard.'

'Seamus?'

He stopped in the doorway. 'What is it, love?'

'It's fine, you don't need to come back. Why don't you get off home? There's not much more to do here except keep Dorothy away from the drinks cabinet.'

She spotted the whisper of barely suppressed relief. 'You sure? In that case I'll get us a takeaway on the way back, bottle of wine. Run you a bath if you're lucky.'

She wished he'd stop trying so bloody hard. He'd been so good all day, and she couldn't have asked for more, but it made it extremely hard to carry on being pissed off with him. 'I might stay here tonight, actually.'

'Really? What for?'

She didn't feel like explaining; she was virtually out of words. 'I just want a last night here, to say goodbye, I suppose.' And because I can't face coming home. Not to you.

He had the grace to take the excuse for what it really was, and dropped his gaze to the ground. 'Floss . . .'

'I'll see you tomorrow, Seamus.' She knew, as she turned back to the sink and began polishing a glass, that he was still there, watching her, willing her to look at him, but eventually she heard him sigh and walk away.

She listened to the raucous, affectionate goodbyes as he took his leave of the small wake and ushered his twittering charges out of the front door and into his car.

Apart from the chit-chat of the final few guests, the house was quiet again, drifting back into its default carpeted hush. Flo couldn't ever remember there being much noise here: Peggy and Donald were gentle, softly spoken folk, and in all the years she had lived with them, they had never exceeded a modest decibel count, not even when they were chuckling at *The Morecambe & Wise Show* or Donald had told one of his jokes he'd picked up from the chaps at work. There'd never been so much as a raised voice on the many occasions Mum had appeared on the doorstep with Flo and a little suitcase and a brief explanation, before disappearing to another airport and another continent. They had just quietly brought her in each time, Donald carrying her things to the little spare bedroom that eventually became hers permanently when one day they discovered Maddie would never be coming back for her.

And so Flo had found herself growing up in a sleepy coastal town whose average age never dipped below sixty-five, even after a colder-than-usual winter, and who remained indifferent to its brash London-on-Sea neighbour that she now called home. Peggy and Donald had lived at the top of one of many roads of identical bungalows that snaked around the contours of the town, fizzling out on the fringes. Through the net curtains, she saw the little green that had been built for children's games but that was home to a few dog walkers with their Yorkshire terriers, or occasionally an old lady or two, meeting to catch up on the news. She craned her neck to look at the sliver of sea, just visible beyond the television aerials and satellite dishes, the tired cafés and pebbled beach. Today the sun sparkled on the water, reminding the residents of this old-people's-home of a town why they had come here to quietly see out their days, rather than stick it out in the ever-changing and ever-expensive outskirts of a city they barely recognised and no longer understood.

'Anything else I can do, dear?'

She jumped at the intrusion, and took a second to acknowledge her grandmother's old friend standing in the doorway. 'You're fine, Phyllis. Thanks. You've been so helpful already.'

'Oh, I don't know about that. I seem to have spent most of the day keeping Dorothy off the sherry.'

'Trust me, that's helpful.'

The two women smiled at each other. In the distance they could hear Dorothy's raised voice regaling a captive audience with some no-doubt-raucous tale of her youth.

'Sounds like I failed, I'm afraid.'

'Don't worry. There's only Marco and Aunty Bean left in there with her.'

Phyllis sighed. 'Oh, your Seamus is a lovely man, Flo. He was a real tonic today. So funny, he is. There's something about Irishmen, isn't there?'

'You should live with him, Phyllis. You might not think so then.'

Phyllis put her hand to her mouth and giggled, misreading Flo's jibe as a joke. Flo could see why she and Peggy had been friends – they were so much alike in many ways. 'I'm sure that's not true. Such a kind, attentive man – your gran adored him.'

Flo wondered what Peggy would have thought if she'd known what a shambles her marriage had become. It hadn't felt fair to burden the old lady with any more than she'd already had to endure. It had been a tough time for all of them, with one thing and another.

She was aware that Phyllis was staring at her with exaggerated concern. She really didn't want to get into a feel-sorry-for-Flo conversation – Peggy's friends had been part of her childhood, and there was no kidding these old birds. She smiled brightly. 'Anyway, it's about time we got Dorothy to the station, isn't it? She won't want to be getting back to London too late. It's still so dark, these evenings.' She had a feeling that even into her early eighties, Dorothy was still a match for most self-respecting muggers, but the feisty old queen of Wandsworth was like family, and there was no way she would allow her to get home too late for her evening tipple in front of *EastEnders*.

Phyllis pulled her black cardigan sleeve up over her plump wrist and looked at her dainty gold watch. She had always had neat extremities – size three feet, tiny hands and delicate, pretty features – at odds with her waistline, which had grad-ually caught up with her bosom and expanded over the years in line with her unabated love of the ice cream that kept the family in business, and supplemented by the carbohydrate recipe book passed down to her by her Italian mother-in-law.

She had gone from Dolly Parton to Hattie Jacques in less time than it took to say tiramisu. 'Oh, I suppose it is getting on. Marco and I can drop her. It's on the way home. Or Aunty Bean might be driving back to London – we'll ask her.'

'Thanks, Phyllis. I appreciate it. You must be exhausted.'

As was Flo: suddenly overwhelmed by an urge for silence and solitude, and for an empty house. Today of all days, she could justify spending some time alone here before she locked up the little bungalow and travelled the few miles home along the coast to face the music.

From down the narrow hallway came the sound of Dorothy's hyena laugh. Flo smiled. 'It's definitely time to get her home! Come on, Phyllis, let's call it a day. Even Peggy wouldn't be able to find one more thing to wash up or wipe down here.' And it was true: everything had been put back in its allotted place. The dishcloth was neatly folded and hanging over the edge of the sink, tea towels pushed back into their sticky-backed rubber pegs, and Peggy's apron hung on the back of the kitchen door.

Phyllis tugged her black sweater down over her straining polyester skirt and brushed a few stray sausage-roll crumbs from the recesses of its pleats. 'Right you are, dear. If you're sure there's nothing else I can do?'

'No, really, you've all been so kind and helpful. Well, maybe not Dorothy, but she wasn't exactly made for labour.'

'Don't think she's ever so much as chipped a bit of nail polish off, that one. We love her for other reasons, though. She'd do anything for friends and family, our Dot.' Phyllis looked sadly at Peggy's limp apron. 'The four of us went back a long way, you know? Knew each other from babies to nippers to young girls and married women, we did.'

Flo had heard the old friends' recollections of their childhood scrapes on the streets of south London over and over again, but never tired of listening to the first-hand stories of a London that barely existed any more. She went over and hugged Phyllis, inhaling the cocktail of Silvikrin and Charlie that took her straight back to illicit ice-cream cones after school.

Phyllis stroked Flo's cheek. 'You're a good girl. Always were. Peggy loved you like her own daughter. Such a shame about your mum. She just had that wild streak – couldn't be tied down. Drove us all wild.'

Flo had a feeling that one of Phyllis's never-far-away tearful episodes was imminent. 'I was lucky. I had two mums in the end. Well, four, if you count you and Dorothy! Five with Aunty Bean.'

Phyllis's peach-powdered cheeks glowed as she pulled a hanky from her sleeve and dabbed at her eyes. 'Now, dear, you fetch your things and get yourself home too. We'll be fine.'

'I think I might stay here tonight, actually,' Flo said. 'Spend one last night in the bungalow.'

'Are you sure? Might be a bit lonely. Maybe Seamus will come back and stay with you?'

'Maybe,' she said, executing an unconvincing smile.

In the little sitting room, Marco was stretched out in Donald's chair, his tight grey curls pressed against the embroidered antimacassar and yellowed dentures on show as he snored gently, knocked out by the combination of stifling heat and Donald's best whisky and oblivious to the constant stream of invective coming from another third of the three-piece suite opposite him. His shirt collar had been unbuttoned and his black tie pulled loose, revealing a sprouting of curly greying hair that mirrored that on his head.

Aunty Bean was already in her coat, waiting patiently near the door. She saw Flo and winked, and they shared a quiet laugh unnoticed as Dorothy's monologue continued unabated. Flo loved Bean: she had started off as a lodger with Peggy's parents back in the sixties when she was a student, and ended up as a friend to the little network of Wandsworth families. Rumour had it that she had aristocratic blood, but Flo wasn't so sure: beyond the plummy vowels was a down-to-earth woman-of-the-people who wouldn't know a Barbour from a brogue, particularly in the corner of north-west London that she and her assorted dogs called home.

The heat from the gas fire had drawn out bright carmine discs on Dorothy's cheeks, matching the crêpey rim of dark-red lipstick around her constantly moving lips and the polished nails that pointed punctuation at the dozing Marco. She had never been one to halt her stream of consciousness just because her conversation partner was asleep – besides, they all knew Marco was a master of faking a nap when it suited him. Too many noisy women in his life, Phyllis always said, which was presumably why he had chosen the sweetest, quietest bride he could find.

Dorothy pulled herself up out of the chair and held her arms out. 'Come here, girl. Give us a hug.' Flo squeezed past the Ercol coffee table that took up most of the floor space and let Dorothy embrace her, the gold charms on her bracelet tinkling in her ear and the heavy gold hoops that always dangled from Dorothy's lobes pressing into her cheek. 'Don't you forget you've still got us, sweetheart. You're as much family to me as my own lot. Bloody useless bunch they are, mind you. Never visit me unless it's for food or money or somewhere to lie low for a day or two. You'll come and see me soon, though, won't you?'

'Of course I will. I'm sure to be up in London before long. I'll let you know, and you can bake me a cake.'

Dorothy laughed. 'Sod that, darling. You can have shop-bought like everyone else. But I might have a nice little bottle of something tucked away for special occasions.'

It was a well-known fact in Florence's family that you went to Phyllis to be fed and Dorothy to be watered. 'Perfect. I'll bring a lemon.'

Dorothy pinched her cheek, just as she had done when Flo was a child. 'That's my girl.' She rearranged her fitted black lace dress around her hips and shrugged her diamanté-studded cardigan back on. Even in her eighties, she hadn't let things slip. Flo had thought she was some kind of film star when she'd been a child – the Rita Hayworth of Wandsworth, with her proud bust and the platinum-blonde hair that now was more nicotine-yellow and came out of a bottle, defying the decades of gin and cigarettes that couldn't be denied in her complexion. 'Right, am I getting this train or not, young Marco?'

Marco, miraculously hearing despite his apparent deep slumber, shot upright and straight out of the armchair, rising from prostrate to his full height of five foot two in less than a second. He jangled his car keys in his pocket. 'Ready when you are, lie-ee-dies.'

'I'll drop you, Dot,' Aunty Bean said, brushing dog hairs off her shabby coat. 'It's on the way.'

'Bye, Aunty Bean,' Flo said as she hugged her, wondering whether she should mention that her ratty black cardigan had been buttoned up wrong all day. It amused them all that someone so chaotic in her own life had run a hospital ward like clockwork, and wouldn't tolerate so much as a scuffed shoe from her nurses.

'Take care, lovely,' Aunty Bean said as she squeezed Flo warmly. 'And bring that chap of yours to supper soon?' Flo nodded non-committally as the small party eased themselves out of the sitting room and into the salt-scented night.

'By the way,' Flo said, pulling Phyllis to one side as the others headed outside and started opening car doors. 'When we were in the kitchen, you mentioned the four of you. Not three: you and Peggy and Dorothy. Four. You said you'd known each other since you were babies. And Aunty Bean was a student when you first met her.'

Phyllis frowned, and Flo spotted a definite deepening of the rosy blush that always adorned her cheeks. 'I don't think so, dear. It was always the three of us. Why would I have said four?'

'You definitely said four. I remember it clearly.'

Phyllis squeezed her arm. 'You must have misheard, silly. Hardly surprising – you did just bury your grandmother today. You must be all over the place.'

Flo wasn't so sure, but she nodded anyway. 'You're probably right.' She gave Phyllis a peck on the cheek, transferring a residue of heavily scented powder to her own face.

'Now you're sure you'll be all right here on your own

tonight? And you'll remember to switch everything off when you leave? And check the oven's turned off? And Peggy likes to leave a key in the bread bin.'

'I'll be fine. I'll finish off the sherry and vol-au-vents and have a quiet one. It'll be good to have some time to say good-bye on my own.'

Marco clapped his hands together loudly. 'Come along now. Is getting late. Marco needs his rest.' He blew a kiss to Flo as he guided his wife down the drive and into his old Lancia.

Flo waved as first Bean's Golf drove away, then Marco's temperamental car hiccuped away down the hill. Finally she closed the door and let out a huge long breath.

2

Number 23 Seaview Avenue had always been the benchmark for bowling-green front lawn and polished brass door knocker. The white paintwork on its single-storey pebbledash frontage defied the lashings of the winter storms that blew along the old pier, then wound along the now-shabby promenade, past the bingo hall and the fish and chip shops, and blustered their way through the old Victorian then Edwardian streets, on up the hill until they reached the 1960s periphery of town.

Peggy and Donald had bought their bungalow long before their knees demanded it: they were planners, cautious custodians of their anticipated retirement, and having once been the youngest residents of the terrace, they eventually racked up a record number of years in this quiet corner of the south coast that seemed forgotten by all but the screaming seagulls and an unusually high number per capita of funeral directors.

To many teenagers, being sent here to live would have been akin to being buried alive, but to Florence it had been like coming home. It was in fact more home than any other place she had lived during her eleven chaotic years. She had waited patiently each time for her mother to become tired of dragging a child around Morocco or India, and to put her on a plane back to England, once she had proved her parenting credentials to whichever hippies or dropouts she had fallen in with. Sometimes it would be a peace camp, full of women who worshipped Mother Earth but weren't quite sure where a little girl fitted into their plans to save the planet for the children of the future; sometimes an ashram where she would be left to chase cockroaches with other children, who spoke many tongues between them but were able to communicate with each other only through the universal language of play.

The routine had always been the same: Donald waiting at the airport, ruffling her hair as he led her to his old Rover, then driving her back over the South Downs, whistling Perry Como all the way; Peggy opening the front door, releasing a waft of the sausage and chips she knew was Florence's favourite, before smothering her granddaughter in a bosomly hug that Florence never wanted to end.

As soon as she was in bed and Peggy had put all her belongings on a boil wash, she would hear them whispering through the paper-thin walls, their concern growing with each visit. Their questions began to chip away at her own anxieties: did girls her age go to school? Would Mum ever stop, and just find them somewhere to live? As Peggy drew her a long, hot bath, she'd look in the oval dressing-table mirror and see a wild thing with dirty fingernails and dreadlocked hair. Mum always laughed when Flo asked for shampoo or a hairbrush, or stared at the pretty hairclips and bangles and swathes of peacock-bright fabric in the souks or street markets, tugging her away and telling her not to be so bourgeois, whatever that meant. She had a feeling that Gran letting her order whatever she liked from her catalogue was bourgeois, as was Donald driving them into Brighton to buy T-shirts with glittery uni-corns emblazoned on them and eat knickerbocker glories on high bar stools, their shopping bags brushing against the soles of their shoes. When Mum eventually came back and took Flo to the next squat or caravan or cross-continental trip, they'd hide the worst offenders in the drawers that had unofficially become Flo's. Peggy always bought a few plain things that would pass under Maddie's radar, so that her granddaughter at least had decent underwear and clothes that fitted, until she next landed on the doorstep of number 23.

The worst moment, when she was about eight or nine, was when Gran had sat her down on the sofa and said she was tired, and would Flo read a bit of her Mills & Boon to her? Flo had taken the plastic-jacketed library book and opened it at the page marked by the leather souvenir bookmark they had bought together on one of their National Trust days out. She had stared at the intricate stacked pattern of tiny lines and curves, frantically trying to guess what Peggy wanted to hear, what this code was hiding from her, and knowing that she was failing the simple task. She had looked up at her grandmother in desperation, her cheeks burning, horrified that she had let her down enough to make the old lady cry.

The next day at 10 a.m. sharp, and every weekday after that for three hours each time, a bright-eyed lady with owlish glasses and a briefcase full of books arrived on the doorstep and sat at the dining table with her, until after a few weeks, the confusion of black noise on the page of Peggy's books cleared itself into letters, then words, and finally the secret language that she had always suspected was there. A couple of the kinder men who had drifted along in their wake had tried to show her, but Maddie quickly put a stop to anything that challenged her mothering skills.

And it was all still here: the dining-table schoolroom, the Bakelite-brown velvet sofa you could striate if you dragged your fingers against its pile, the ticking reproduction grand-mother clock in the hallway, the barometer hanging beside the gas fire, a thank-you to Donald for over forty years' service at the printing firm where he had first served as an apprentice, the little corner table with its silver tray holding his-and-hers bottles of whisky and sherry and his-and-hers crystal glasses.

Flo wandered into the little spare bedroom with the marsh-mallow-pink candlewick counterpane she used to rub her thumb along as she adjusted to set bedtimes, when you went to sleep with food in your tummy and a story floating in your ears and gentle hands stroking your hair until your eyes closed. 'Your mummy loves you very much, poppet. She really does. She knows you like being here with us, so she decided you can stay a bit longer this time. Now close your eyes and tomorrow we'll think of some nice things to do together.' And she'd drift off, trying to push away the guilty feeling that she ought to be missing Mummy, and wondering where she was, and hugging tight the little pink teddy she'd had ever since she was born, and which still sat on her pillow, one eye missing and its front paw worn away to nothing where she had stroked herself to sleep with its velvety-soft fabric.

Eventually, of course, it had been decided that she would be better off here on a permanent basis. Maddie's latest project, working in a Rajasthan orphanage, was far too important to give up – who would look out for all those poor little children otherwise? Eventually Peggy and Donald had started looking into schools for their granddaughter. Between their teaching her table manners and Miss Jones teaching her to read, they had done pretty well so far, but it wasn't fair on the poor little lassie, as Flo had overheard Donald saying quietly one evening when she tiptoed out to the bathroom. She needed stability, and no one else was going to give it to her if they didn't.

The next morning at breakfast, her grandparents had looked so worried as they tried to put their plan to her as delicately as possible, and Flo tried not to fling her arms around them both in gratitude. She never wanted to spend another night in a dirty hostel, or a tarpaulin village hanging off the perimeter of some military airbase. She wanted tomato ketchup, *Blue Peter* and school shoes, her own pencil case and her own bedroom.

To make her feel at home, Donald had bought her a fancy white dressing table with gold trim and a matching pink-velvet buttoned stool. Flo had loved sitting there, pinning postcards from her mother around the mirror, along with bits of ribbon left over from birthday-present wrapping, cinema tickets and eventually black and white photo-booth memories of Flo with the friends she finally made. And there it all remained, just as it had looked on the day when Donald had put on his best tie and helped her lift her bags into the boot of the old Rover before driving her to the darkest Midlands to start her student life.

Seated amongst the dusty bottles of Anaïs Anaïs and shiny black boxes of No. 7 eyeshadow was the rag doll that she had persuaded Gran to give her, still wearing the little gathered blouse and skirt Flo had made for it, two lengths of rickrack binding its thick two-ply woollen hair into stiff bunches. Flo had found it tucked in the back of a cupboard, wrapped in tissue paper and as spotless as the day it had been made. She'd shown it to Gran, who told her it had belonged to Mum once upon a time, made for her by a family friend. Maddie had never been one for dolls, but Peggy had kept it anyway.

Now Flo looked at the black button eyes and beautifully embroidered rosebud mouth, and wondered about the friend who had put so many loving hours into making this doll. She'd always imagined that one day her own child would cuddle this silly old thing that had meant so much to her. She felt salty tears burning at the corners of her eyes, and forced them back. Today was about Peggy, not the other soul she'd barely met.

She'd learnt to sew by making things for this old doll, asking Peggy if she could save up for a sewing machine, before Donald remembered that there was an old one in the shed somewhere. 'You can't let her have that old thing,' Peggy had fussed, when he appeared at the back door carrying a large wooden case by the handle and placed it on the table. Someone had engraved a couple of initials on the box: the second was almost completely worn away, and she couldn't tell if the first was a V or an N. Once Donald had unhooked the lid and lifted it away, and Flo had seen the beautiful gold filigree lettering and turned the wooden handle on the shiny, stiff wheel, run her hand over the embossed leather and silver plating set into the old oak base, there was nothing Peggy could do to separate her from it. Donald had spent the next two days taking the machine apart, oiling and polishing it until the needle bounced up and down almost silently and the cotton reel spun happily on its pin as Flo turned the handle.

That was probably the day she knew she wanted to make things. She started saving her pocket money to buy card wheels pierced with bright glass-headed pins, rainbow skeins of embroidery thread woven into wide flat plaits, fat quarters of fabric that became her new doll's wardrobe. Peggy had no interest in sewing – she was a non-stop knitter, whether they needed more knitwear or not – and so Flo had been left to work it out on her own. Eventually, when she outgrew the old biscuit tin she kept her sewing kit in, Donald had bought her a concertina sewing box, and she had sorted her haberdashery into the trays that opened up as she pulled the two sides of the lid apart: needles and pins in one, next to scissors and thimbles; buttons and fastenings; lengths of ribbons folded into neat bundles; embroidery hoops and threads and wide-weave canvas fabric; brightly coloured squares of felt, and finally little bundles of fabric scraps, laid neatly in the base of the box.

She had spent hours arranging then rearranging the contents of the box, and she couldn't remember now how something that had meant so much to her could have disappeared from her life. When she'd left for uni, she supposed there hadn't been space in her tiny shared student room, or maybe she had decided she wanted to keep it where it was, for when she came back down south between terms. She hadn't thought about that box in years, and now she wanted more than ever to open its folds, to bring back happy memories and help dull the sadness of the empty bungalow.

She'd thought she would enjoy spending a last evening here, surrounded by everything that had made this a home to her when she'd needed one so badly, but every Capodimonte ornament, every Len Deighton novel in the small bookcase, the coat rack still bearing the outer shells of her dear grandparents, made her lonelier than she had felt in a long while.

The minute Peggy and Donald had left these four walls, the house had ceased to be a home, and was merely a museum of their fifty years together. Long years had passed since Donald had sat in front of the gas fire with his crossword and his pipe, and it was a while since Peggy had been able to brandish her knitting needles in her arthritic hands, the clickety-clack of the cold metal pins punctuating her husband's tuts as he scribbled out wrong answers or muttered at the ineptitude of whichever government was in power. All the sounds that had been the gentle breaths of this home were now silent, and even the grandmother clock in the hallway had wound itself down without anyone to keep its heartbeat going.

Loneliness was a familiar state for Flo: during the years of travel, when she had felt like nothing more than her mother's accessory and had been moved on every time she found another little lost soul to gaze bewildered at the world with; her school days, when the other children stared at the strange girl who struggled to read or write; the terrifying undergraduate frenzy of fluid friendships, and then the comfortable void of home working, where she could create her online range of clothing without having to step into a meeting or eat her lunch in an office full of other people. Nothing, however, was like the loneliness she had known for the past twelve months, and yet still she had been able to come here and forget for a while, where no one asked questions: they just put the kettle on and sliced thick slabs of Dundee cake onto tea plates and talked about the weather or the neighbour's daughter's lottery win.

Flo suspected Peggy knew exactly what brought her granddaughter to the front door with increasing regularity, and saw straight through the unnecessary bags of shopping that always accompanied her. Peggy also knew that there was no making Flo talk if she didn't want to, even though at times she longed to tell her grandmother how unhappy she was, how lonely her marriage was, or to talk about the tiny person who was supposed to have made everything better but who had never made it to the pretty green bedroom in the sugar-pink house that was crying out for a family to fill it.

Flo's phone, with its rude reminder of the twenty-first century, broke into the decades-old freeze frame.

Seamus had sent a photo of a foamy bath surrounded by candles. *Bath waiting for you. Come home, Flossie. X*

She hesitated, her finger poised over the screen, then flipped the phone over and put it face down on the table. Disorientated by the swings in time that being in the little bungalow were bringing about, she struggled to identify what she instinctively knew to be home. Part of her longed to jump in the car and be back home with Seamus – the old Seamus, not the one that the last twelve months had carved out of the man she knew and loved, who had shattered the last few fragments of her; the old home that had framed the snapshots of their ten-year marriage, and not the reminder of what couldn't be.

She knew she was punishing him, and that she would only make things worse if she didn't reply – Seamus hated playing games. He was the one who insisted on talking about things, getting them out in the open, forcing her to spill her guts when all she had wanted for the past year was to crawl into a corner and nurture the pain that ate her from the inside out. She picked the phone up. *Staying here tonight. Tidying up to do and exhausted. See you tomorrow.*

As an afterthought, she added a small *x* and pressed send.

It was late, and although she knew she ought to get some sleep, she was still buzzing from the day, the sounds of so many voices ringing in her ears, from sharp London twangs to the softer version that had evolved as it moved southwards, faces new and old, and every shade of black fabric imaginable. She didn't want more noise, so resisted turning on the television and tucking up on the sofa. The house was spotless, and her grandparents' collection of paperbacks held little of interest. Maybe she should go home after all, she thought, if only for lack of anything else to do.

She tried to retrace her train of thought back to before Seamus's text had interrupted her, and as she rewound to the memories of the old sewing machine, she suddenly knew what she wanted to do. It must still be in the house somewhere, and there were only so many places Peggy could have tucked it away.

She quickly exhausted all hiding places in her own room – there was no space in the tiny wardrobe, and the divan bed allowed for nothing to be tucked beneath it. The hall cupboard was full of brooms and mops, its shelves crammed with cleaning products. Bar going out to the shed, the only place left to look was Peggy and Donald's bedroom. Flo's heart fluttered a little at the thought of trespassing on what had always been private territory, where she had only ever been when invited, or when she had tapped quietly at their door in the middle of the night, needing a distraction from her nightmares.

She pushed open the door, surprised at the strength of the residual intimacy of this shared marital space, with its embossed pale rose wallpaper and piped bedspread pulled neatly across the bed. Economical in their acquisition of property, her grandparents had needed little storage space in the small bungalow, and there was only one likely place large enough for something as bulky as the sewing machine. She squeezed through the narrow gap between dressing table and bed until she stood in front of the bank of doors that were the face of the built-in wardrobe Donald had constructed thirty years ago. If it was anywhere, it was behind one of these.

3

Peggy and Donald's wardrobes were testament to a tidy house and a tidy marriage. An invisible line divided the few hangers bearing Donald's wedding suit and work suit from the huddle of earthy-toned easy-wash frocks and slacks that had served Peggy through the decades. Flo ran her hand across her grandfather's thin shiny tweed and the age-yellowed shirts that Peggy had ironed to within an inch of their lives, then leant forward and closed her eyes while she breathed in the ghost of pipe smoke and tool shed. No wonder her grandmother had been unable to get rid of his clothes: maybe she too had wished that these garments could bring back the kindly old man.

She began to pull aside Peggy's coats and dresses, looking for a glimpse of the ark-shaped wooden box at the back of the cupboard. Each garment told of its decade, as the row of hemlines rose and fell, collars widened and narrowed, waists grew from tiny to elasticated. There was no doubting that Peggy knew what she liked, and Flo's eye alighted on the basket of vibrant beads and baubles, scarves and wraps that Maddie had brought back from her travels. Peggy had always politely thanked her, before putting the latest addition away with its companions, never to be worn. 'I'll save it for best,' she had always said.

Flo supposed these belonged to her now. It was doubtful

Maddie would come back, and she couldn't imagine her mother being interested in anything from the modest estate of Mr and Mrs Fielding. It had taken days for Maddie to send a cursory text explaining that it just wasn't possible to get back for the funeral, but feel free to add her name to any flowers Flo ordered.

She pulled out a garish beaded necklace punctuated with primary-coloured fringing, and remembered her mother haggling aggressively for this in a Moroccan souk, ignoring Flo, who tried to press on her a plain silver bangle. Flo had understood even then that Peggy would hate the necklace, and had asked Maddie for money of her own so that she could buy her grandmother something that would be enjoyed. She still winced as she remembered Maddie turning to snap viciously at her. She had put the bangle back, feeling the burning in her cheeks, and the soft-eyed stallholder had smiled and slipped her a brightly coloured key ring as Maddie marched away with the necklace stuffed deep in her shoulder bag. Flo had no desire to keep anything in that basket – let it go to a charity shop and do some good to someone else.

Her hand brushed against a zippered coat bag, and curious to see what had been so special that her grandmother had had it dry-cleaned and stored, she gently lowered the zip. Of course: Peggy's wedding suit. She knew it well from the photograph on the mantelpiece, but had never seen it in the flesh, assuming that Peggy, never given to bouts of sentiment about such things, had got rid of it. Ever practical, her grandmother had chosen a suit of light bouclé wool in a soft caramel colour that could be used again, but it looked as fresh as the day it had been worn, and Flo guessed it had been consigned to the 'saved for best' section of the wardrobe.

It was possibly the most stylish thing Peggy had ever worn, with its three-quarter-length sleeves and wide boat neck with slim lapels, its tiny waist giving way to a scalloped peplum and full skirt. Flo couldn't believe that she had spent probably a month's wages on something so exquisite. It had a two-tone pale peach and green silk lining, and hand-covered buttons, and the matching bow-shaped, net-frothed headpiece that had sat discreetly within her shampoo and set now hung from the silk-padded hanger in a little pouch. No wonder she smiled so radiantly out of the old silver frame as she clutched Donald's arm with one hand and a posy of lily-of-the-valley in the other. She could have been a film star – well, maybe more Ealing Studios than Hollywood, but she had probably never looked better.

Flo searched for a label at the nape, wondering where exactly Peggy had bought this clearly not off-the-peg cuckoo in the nest of otherwise workaday, practical clothing. Finding nothing, she looked inside the jacket, where a tiny label was stitched bearing simply the name *Nancy* embroidered in pretty italics and a small crescent shape.

None the wiser, she rebuttoned the jacket and zipped the bag closed, resisting the urge to strip off her funeral black and try the suit on herself. Whatever happened to the rest of the household contents, this family heirloom was definitely staying close by, even though she couldn't yet imagine a day when she wouldn't be too sad to wear it.

Hidden behind a pile of shoeboxes, she spotted what looked like the dark oak of the sewing-machine case. Her mood instantly lifted, and she pulled the shoes out and reached blindly through the curtain of polyester into the gloomy recesses of the wardrobe. The shape felt wrong: instead of the curved rectangular dome of the machine casing, her hands passed over sharp edges and a smooth, bare surface where she expected to find the old leather-covered carrying handle. She had always been banned from rooting around amongst Peggy's belongings – one of the few things her soft touch of a grand-mother had put her size-five foot down about – and she felt a fresh wave of guilt, but at some point someone was going to have to clear out the wardrobe, she told herself.

She dragged the box towards her, moving spare coat hang-ers and dusty hankies out of its path, until she tipped it over the lip of the sliding-door mechanism and sat it squarely on the deep sheepskin rug.

It was nothing special: probably just made of pine, but with a patina and network of scratches that spoke of a life-time of constant use. It was not much bigger than a shoebox, if a little taller, with a snug-fitting lid and a croissant-shaped carrying hole cut into each side, with which she lifted it and carried it back to her own room. She sat it on the bed, watched by the scruffy pink teddy, before climbing up next to the box and tucking her legs beneath her.

She lifted the lid away. Inside, stacked like record sleeves in a music shop, was a neat line of uniform-sized yellowed rectangular paper packets. There was no mistaking what they were: Flo herself already had a bookshelf full of them, but none like these, and none that was older than her own earliest attempts at dressmaking.

Her heart raced a little faster as she took the nearest one out, listening to the swish of the dry paper as she pulled it away from its neighbour.

McCalls 6673: Misses' day dress.

The hand-drawn picture on the front showed a perfectly coiffed woman with an impossibly long neck and acute-angled elbows and wrists, her white-gloved hands held in front of her to emphasise the nipped-in waist of her full-skirted, boat-necked gingham dress with its narrow belt. Just behind, her blonde friend wore the same dress, but with a slim pencil skirt and in midnight-blue evening fabric, her hands on her hips and chin tilted haughtily.

On the front of the packet were some scribbled pencil notes – *take 1.5" from bodice length. Waist to hem 25"* – and a few numbers that had been scrubbed out. She turned it around, scanning the sizing tables and list of notions: *22" zip, hook and eye, bias binding, interfacing.* A few numbers had been ringed, and mentally converting imperial to decimal, she quickly saw that whoever had made this dress was about the same size as she was, albeit with a considerably tinier waist. Curiously, three words had been written on the frayed paper flap: *London to Paris.*

She lifted the flap and began to pull out the tissue-paper pieces that were the key to turning a length of fabric into the beautiful dresses on the cover. Each had been cut out, careful scissor strokes neatly following the dotted lines that indicated the wearer's size-10 dimensions, and then refolded to match the original scores of the fragile paper.

She tipped the packet upside down, and gently shook it to release the last few pieces trapped inside. Along with the tissue paper, a few other items fell out onto the bed, including a swatch of white poplin, whose delicate pattern of green leaves and blue forget-me-nots was as fresh and clean as the day it had been bought.

A couple of photographs slid out with the pattern pieces, black and white with a broad serrated border. The first showed four young women on a station platform. Two looked near to tears, one was rubbing at a mark on her dress, and the fourth stood sideways on, as though a *Vanity Fair* photographer were behind the lens. Was that Peggy in the middle? And surely those two were Dorothy and Phyllis. She recognised their younger selves from photographs on the three women's mantelpieces over the years. But who was the fourth one, wearing a version of the primrose-yellow dress on the front of the packet? Even though she was standing at some distance from the camera, Flo spotted the intricate weaving of the foliage festooned across the swatch that she held in her hand.

In the second photo, the same young woman in the same flowery dress stood on a pretty iron-railed bridge. Her bouffant hair was pulled back from her face with a wide satin ribbon, its tonged tips ending in a bouncy jaw-length single upward curl, and she had a bewildered smile on her face. Flo looked closely, and saw that the woman wore only one shoe, the other held in her hand, and that her knees appeared scuffed. On the back had been written in pencil, *4 June 1962 – first day*. There was something familiar about her, too, the more Flo looked at the two images, but she couldn't place her, in the way that old photographs became more about their period than the real people within them.

She sifted through the rest of the pattern pieces and found a stiff paper coaster with an embossed logo on it, and a postcard addressed to 'Mrs P. Fielding', written in perfect fountain-pen copperplate.

Dearest Peg,

Mon Dieu, as they say here. I made it. Even though I felt so sick on the boat that I thought I'd have to send for the navy to fetch me home again. Paris is divine, and so far I haven't got lost, even though it was a bit of a drama finding the house – you wouldn't believe how I got there. Give Maddie a big fat kiss for me. I miss you all so much.

Will write again soon,
Nancy

Flo turned the card over to find a glorious Technicolor image of the Tuileries in Paris, looking like something out of a Truffaut film, the road in front of it barely recognisable with so few cars in sight. She knew it well, having spent a few of the most miserable months of her life in Paris working at an atelier on a student placement. Something tugged at her mind, but she couldn't think what it was, and instead she smiled at the thought of anyone daring to give Maddie a big fat kiss – Mum had never been one for displays of affection.

She carefully replaced the contents of the envelope, then peered inside the next one – this time a pattern for a shirt dress. Again a swatch of fabric had been stored with the paper pattern, and again there was a photograph, this time of the same girl at a Parisian pavement café. Another pattern was for a bathing suit, and this time a colour photograph showed the girl on board a large yacht, with a younger girl, the wind blowing her blonde hair off her lightly tanned smiling face. In the background stood two tanned, white-haired men in shorts and linen shirts unbuttoned to their waists, laughing together. On the back, the words *Nancy and Pea*. And again there was a postcard – Capri this time.

As though faced with a mountain of profiteroles, Flo was desperate and yet reluctant to open all the packets for fear of gorging herself, but glanced at the next few as they stood in the box. Day dresses, evening dresses, swimsuits – each packet containing mementoes of this summer journey, and each in order, according to the date written on the back.

By the time she reached the end of the row, she had been to the South of France, the isle of Capri, to a Venice that had no idea how its beauty would become its downfall; she had seen photographs of beautiful people in beautiful places wearing beautiful clothes, and at the heart of it all, Nancy.

She went back to the photograph of the girl at the station, surrounded by her friends, her smile seeming to jump straight off the paper, making Flo return the gesture as though they were face to face. She scrabbled around in her recent memory, trying to think why the name Nancy nagged at her, finally recalling the label stitched into Peggy's wedding suit. Had this Nancy made the beautiful two-piece in which Peggy had married her Donald? Surely the same hand that had made the suit had catalogued this collection of 1960s outfits that had travelled the Continent.

As she put the last of the pattern packets back in the box, she noticed a larger photograph lying face down beneath them, a photographer's stamp advertising an address in south London. She pulled it out gently, not wanting to scratch it, and on turning it over, recognised it instantly.

Even in black and white, the caramel suit was unmistakable, as were the beaming faces of her newly wedded grandparents. It was almost identical to the photograph that had sat in a silver frame on their mantelpiece for fifty years, except this one included a trio of smiling bridesmaids. Petite and nervous-looking, then tall and shapely, two of them could only be Phyllis and Dorothy, seemingly only a little younger than in the photograph taken at the station. Although they wore identical skater-style satin dresses, one of them would have looked at home at a school prom, while the other would have injected glamour into a Hollywood red carpet. The third girl stood close to the bride, their cheeks pressed together as they laughed at the camera. Flo had no doubt as to her name.

'Hello, Nancy,' she said quietly, brushing her thumb across the corner of the stiff yellowed paper. 'Why have I never heard of you before?'

4

It was nearly evening by the time Flo had finished tidying up at Seaview Avenue the next day and packed into the passenger seat of her Mini the box of patterns and the sewing machine she had eventually found buried deeper inside the wardrobe. She walked up the short path to the pink-stuccoed terrace house and turned the key, bracing herself for her husband's welcome. She was hit by the smell of cooking as she pushed open the front door, instantly exhausted at the thought of having to ingest a placatory meal.

'Seamus?' she called out, but there was no reply. Unkindly, she hoped he'd just cooked himself an early supper and gone out.

She felt the fuzzy edge of hangover-type exhaustion as she threw her carpet bag down at the bottom of the stairs, even though she hadn't drunk anything last night: the port and sherry she'd got in for the guests had been polished off long before the last stragglers left, and Marco had seen off Donald's whisky. She'd had a fitful sleep, a night to be endured with the knowledge that tomorrow the next sleep would come along and make it all right again. It had probably been two and a half decades since she'd last slept in the narrow bed in Seaview Avenue, and she had felt like a Goldilocks with poor judgement as she flitted between fear of toppling onto the floor and a half-dreamed montage of brightly coloured sunlit images of tiny-waisted, lacquered-haired women.

A croaky mewling announced the black cat that had sneaked up behind her. She was long past pretending to like one of the few remnants of Seamus's pre-Flo life. There had always been an understanding that they'd tolerate each other in Seamus's presence, but the gloves were off when he wasn't around. It watched her now with its one good eye, the other staring milkily at the feline hell that was surely not far off, while she imagined it assessing whether to piss on her bag or rub its arse against her new Wolford tights. What sort of cat lived to be nineteen anyway? She couldn't see the point of animal euthanasia if this mange-ridden fur ball was allowed to limp the planet. 'Bugger off,' she said, nudging it away with her foot and ignoring its rasping hiss.

She was still wearing the black dress and matching coat she'd worn to the funeral, and much as she loved their decades-old tailoring and timeless style, she couldn't wait to get out of them. Besides, they needed better coiffure than she was sporting today, yesterday's neat French pleat having melted into a messy blonde cascade.

There was a definite feel of spring in the air, and she threw open the bedroom window, letting in the scream of wheeling seagulls and releasing the stuffiness of a night's worth of sole male occupation: in all their years together, Flo and Seamus had never found a middle ground between their polarised ideas of nocturnal ambient temperature. She switched on the pretty curved French reading lamp, with its fluted peach-coloured glass shade, and folded back the duvet before picking up the books littering the floor and piling them neatly on Seamus's mahogany bedside table. James Joyce. She wondered why he wouldn't just admit defeat on that one; just because he was Irish, it didn't mean an innate understanding of *Ulysses* was in his blood. She smiled as she uncovered a Kate Mosse buried under the Colm Tóibíns and Edna O'Briens. What would his students make of that?

She cleared a path through discarded socks and T-shirts and opened the wardrobe door. Reaching out from the crush of her tightly compacted lifetime's collection, the sleeves of a couple of her dresses danced gently as the breeze from the open window teased them. Stiff floral poplin squeezed playfully against pastel-coloured silk georgette and broderie anglaise at one end of the rail, while at the other, Harris tweed and velvet mingled in an autumn palette crafted by skilled fingers long before Flo was born. For the first time in months, she went to the summer end of the wardrobe, pulling out a turquoise crazy-paved cotton pinafore that would not look too ridiculously out of season with thick tights and a cardigan.

As had become her habit over the last few months, she passed the closed door next to their bedroom without turning to glance at it, and managed to sidestep the cat, who had prepared an ambush for her at the top of the stairs.

Her heart sank as she walked into the kitchen to see the table laid for two, with pale pink roses stuffed into a china jug at its centre. He'd not quite managed a Debrett's-standard layout, but almost every bone-handled knife and silver-plated fork they owned had been carefully placed in formation, indicating a multiple-course dinner that would prevent her bolting her food and then bolting from Seamus. Ridiculously complex whirls of smoked salmon had been arranged on tiny side plates, decorated with sculpted wedges of lemon and clouds of watercress that belied her husband's shovel-like hands.

The front door opened and closed and Seamus appeared clutching two bottles of cold white wine. 'Chablis,' he said, holding them out for her inspection before putting one in the fridge and taking a corkscrew to the other. 'Your favourite.'

'Thanks,' she said, taking a dainty etched glass from him.

'Cheers, then,' he said, watching her carefully with his blue eyes as he emptied his own glass down his throat. 'Stupid feckin' tiny glasses,' he said, refilling it. 'Sit yourself down – food's ready.'

He pottered around, filling a jug with water and gathering salt and pepper, then slotted a CD into the machine and pressed play.

'Not this,' she said quickly, as the sound of the Divine Comedy filled the small kitchen with memories of their first proper date all those years ago.

'Oh,' he said, 'sorry, I thought it might—'

'I know. I just don't want to listen to anything, if that's OK.'

He looked hurt, and she knew she was spoiling the treat he'd planned for her in his attempt to make it right, make it better.

'Let's just eat, shall we?' she said, wanting to get both the meal and the inevitable conversation over with. She made an attempt to smile, and sat down heavily in the chair he had pulled out for her.

This house had been their home for twelve years, and yet she suddenly felt like a stranger in it, sharing a meal with another stranger. She wondered, as she sipped the cold white wine, what she would make of Seamus if she were sitting opposite him on some kind of blind date. Wild, curly grey-black hair that defied any barber's scissors; shabby, misshapen classic teacher jacket and faded seventies-band T-shirt; handsome, kind eyes that bore the scars of their shared pain and would melt the heart of any woman who listened to his story. At least the part up until six weeks ago.

Taking his lead, she emptied her wine glass then filled it to the brim.

He coughed into the silence of the kitchen. 'Flossie, I know what—'

'This is great,' she said, unfolding the petals of salmon and forcing a forkful into her dry mouth, then helping it down her tight throat with more wine.

He sighed. She almost felt sorry for him: catering was a big deal for Seamus, who had sprung from the loins of a County Wicklow matriarch of seven boys, none of whom was capable of more self-care than tying his own shoelaces or making a doorstep boiled-ham sandwich. This must have involved days of googling ingredients he probably had never even heard of. He cleared the first course away, and presented her with a pasty-shaped shiny grey entity on a plate, leaking pink juices into dark Bisto gravy.

'Come on, now,' he said, passing her a dish of lumpy mashed potatoes. 'It's beef Wellington, as if you didn't need telling.'

She poked at the gelatinous mass in the middle of the plate. She did need telling, and as she looked up and watched him attempt to swallow a mouthful, she almost laughed despite herself.

'Jaysus, this is shite.' He dropped his knife and fork on his plate, splattering the table and the front of his T-shirt with dark-brown specks. 'Don't feel you have to eat it.'

She gratefully set aside her cutlery. 'Sorry – I mean, thanks for making the effort.'

'I could go and buy chips?'

'You're fine. I'm not really hungry anyway.' She pushed the plate as far away as she could without it falling off the edge of the small Formica-topped table.

'Thing is, Floss . . .'

Oh God, they were going to have to talk. Why had she married an Irishman who insisted on bringing out the dirty laundry even when it wasn't wash day? Why couldn't she have chosen some uptight public schoolboy who would let the remains of the marriage fizzle away into silence and therapy fodder?

'Seamus, I'm not sure I want to do this right now. We only buried Gran yesterday.'

He leant forward and grabbed her hands. 'I know, love, and I also know your Gran would want us to sort this out. She'd want you to be happy.'

She snatched her hands back and pressed her fists into her lap. 'Happy? You think there's a happy ending to all this?'

'I made a mistake. A stupid mistake. Everyone makes mistakes from time to time. Even you, Floss.'

'Yeah, maybe, but my mistakes tend to be of the buying-the-wrong-milk variety, or putting diesel in a petrol car. Little mistakes that are bloody annoying but don't actually hurt anyone. So yes, everyone makes little mistakes, Seamus, sometimes even medium-sized ones. But not everyone makes massive great big blonde ones. That particular mistake is all yours. And every other pathetic midlife-crisis man who has to go one step further than a motorbike or a bloody guitar.'

Seamus closed his eyes and chewed on his bottom lip, and in the silence Flo heard the blood thumping in her ears. Hands slightly shaking, and shocked at possibly the longest, most furious and most eloquent outburst of her quiet life, she poured another glass of wine and downed it in one go. The volume of alcohol and the swiftness of its consumption was beginning to make her head spin, but it was certainly opening up a level of communication their marriage had failed to achieve recently.

Eventually he looked up at her and held his hands in the air, his huge palms facing her. 'You got me. There's no excuse, no reason other than opportunity and loneliness, no chance it will ever happen again. But it was one night, Flo. Just one stupid bloody night.'

'She was one of your students, Seamus.'

'Well, she was a postgrad, and technically . . .' he began, then had the sense to stop almost as soon as his mouth had opened.

'I can't forgive you, Seamus. And I don't want to. I want to hang on to how much I hate you at the moment, because I never want to forget what you did to me. To us. After everything I'd been through.'

A bitter laugh erupted from his lips. 'You see? That's exactly it. Everything *you'd* been through. Not us. Not me. You. Only you. Poor bloody Florence.'

'I don't seem to remember it was you lying there pushing

your heart out, all for nothing?' She knew she was crying now, but she couldn't stop.

'She was my daughter too,' he said quietly. 'And you never let me grieve.'

She stared at him. How could he? While nature had slowly repaired her body, she'd needed space to come to terms with the heavy, painful breasts that cried bitter drops of undrunk milk, the stomach that deflated a little more each day until, finally taut again, it barely bore more than a few faint stretch marks to remind her of the precious cargo it had carried for seven short months. If she'd needed to be alone, hadn't felt ready to give her battered body back to him, who could blame her? If he'd only waited, eventually she would have been ready.

'I want us to mend this, Floss. With all my heart. I want you back. I want *us* back. I'll never hurt you again. Please know that. I'm an eejit, but I'm not stupid.'

Seeing the tears in his eyes, she wanted to relent, to forgive him and feel his huge bear arms wrapped around her again, but she knew that for the rest of their lives, there would be a pretty blonde ghost in the corner of her eye. Or maybe one day a brunette. Who knew?

'I'm sorry, Seamus. I just can't.'

'But I thought the other night—'

She felt the Chablis bring a hot rash of shame to her cheeks. Ever since that night, she'd tried not to think about what had happened, how she'd let her guard down and forgotten to hate him. 'That was just nostalgia sex. I was upset about Gran and we'd drunk too much.'

'Nostalgia sex? That's what it was to you?' He rubbed his hand through his hair. 'Jaysus, Floss. And I thought it was a married couple expressing their love and comforting each other.' He sighed deeply. 'Maybe it was better when we didn't talk stuff through. At least I might have been able to pretend for a little longer.'

There was nothing she could say. She'd expelled more words in the last five minutes than she had in the last nine months, and she was exhausted.

He emptied his glass, then took a deep breath before continuing. 'I wasn't going to mention this tonight, because I hoped we might find a way around this fecking nightmare.'

'What?' Surely no more revelations – she really couldn't take any more.

'Don't worry,' he said, raising a hand. 'Nothing like that. It's a work thing.'

'What, they're sacking you for shagging a student?'

'Ouch. Thanks, Floss, but no. I've been offered a sabbatical – great opportunity. Would be mad to pass it up, but I've told them I need to think about it, and to talk to you.'

'What is it?'

'It's away. A long way away, in fact.' He cleared his throat. 'I've been asked to go to Columbia for six months.'

'Colombia South America or Columbia New York?'

'New York. I'm a lecturer, not a drug baron, Floss.'

They stared at one another for a moment, until Flo couldn't bear it any longer. 'We always said we'd go to New York together one day.' It was one of those trips they'd put off – waiting until there was enough money to do it in style, waiting to get the results of the latest tests, waiting for spring, waiting for the dollar to go down in value. 'When do they want you?'

'As soon as possible really. With things the way they are at work, after . . .' He paused. 'Well, you know. Next week, if I want it.'

'Next week? But that's no time.' She began to panic. She'd thought this would be a long-drawn-out severance, where they divided CDs and photo albums, not that he'd be on the other side of the Atlantic Ocean within days.

Seeing her reaction, he rallied slightly. 'Anyway, I was going to say no. I still want to say no, but only if I think you want me to.'

She stared at him, angry that he was pushing her into a corner. Had he asked her whether he could have an affair? How come her opinion was suddenly so important? 'What, so I have to tell you whether to go or not?'

He placed his hands flat on the table and looked directly into her eyes, and she didn't think she'd ever seen him look so sad. 'No, Flossie. You have to tell me whether to stay.'

5

'So that's it?' Jemima stopped trying to thread the needle she'd been fighting with for the last five minutes and stared at Flo.

'I guess so.'

'Seamus is going to New York without you?'

'Like I just said, Jem.' Flo was struggling to maintain her equilibrium this morning. She'd spent the first hour chucking up the remains of the salmon and Chablis, and was only here in the shop thanks to a massive dose of Nurofen and vitamin C.

'Look, tell me it's none of my business if you like . . .'

'It's none of your business.'

'. . . but you know that once he's there, he might not come back. It's how these things work.'

'Yes, I do know.' Flo lifted a limp flannel shirt out of the sack and sniffed it, recoiling instantly. 'Who wears this stuff?' she asked.

'Teenagers, my lovely. One man's duster is another's coolest thing ever. And their parents will pay through the nose for it.' Jem tipped her head in the direction of the pile of rank-smelling clothes in the corner of the shop. 'Wash, not rag.'

Flo held the garment between thumb and forefinger and delicately dropped it with the rest of the pieces waiting for a good laundering. 'Looks like something off the *Deliverance* wardrobe rail,' she said, going back to the sack and peering in before reaching for the next piece.

'And what if he doesn't come back?' Jem mumbled, bright-nibbed pins protruding from her lips. One by one she pulled them out and jammed them into the black velvet skirt spread across her knees.

'Look, it doesn't matter any more. We've reached the end of the line. Marriage over.'

Flo held up a pair of ripped Lurex leggings. Jem grimaced and nodded towards the rag bag. She had an eye for quality vintage clothing, and Queens of Vintage had a reputation for stocking timeless pieces crafted by skilled tailors and seamstresses, from lacy Edwardian bed jackets through to classic geometric-print wrap dresses from the seventies. The flannel-and-denim rail was there solely to buy Jem's core customers a little more trying-on time while their offspring nailed the dirtbag look.

'Shit. Bloody thing.' Jemima sighed and slammed the skirt down on the counter. 'I give up.'

'Want me to have a look? I'm good with zips.'

'Would you?' And as Flo moved over, Jemima slid out from behind the counter and turned her attention to a floor-length cornflower-blue taffeta gown hanging from the changing-room rail, pulling out the creases and fanning its train across her open palms as she scrutinised it forensically for evidence of parties long gone by.

Flo pulled away the uneven stitches Jemima had begun to weave into the heavy fabric, unpicking the threads securing the zip until it came free enough for her to recalibrate the stiff metal teeth, then carefully and invisibly, with tiny, even black stitches, sew it back into place.

'You're wasted here. You know that?' Jemima said, unhooking the gown and holding it up against Flo to gauge its size. 'You have strange and magical powers when you get a needle between your fingers. You really ought to start your business up again. You can't hide in this old time warp for ever.'

Flo took the dress from her and walked across to the mirror, pressing the bodice against her chest and turning sideways on to watch how the fabric moved slowly to catch her up. 'I love this,' she said, ignoring Jem.

'It loves you.'

'I think I want the life that goes with this dress.'

'Then you shall have it. But not on what I pay you two days a week.'

She put the dress back on its hanger. 'And not on half a heavily mortgaged house either. I guess it will have to be sold. That's what happens when people divorce, isn't it?'

'Who said anything about divorce? You should both just treat this as a break – a bit of space. You might feel differently in six months. It's a long time.'

'I don't think so. You can't undo what's been done, and I'm not sure I can ever trust him again.'

She was surprised Jem didn't instantly agree. Seamus and Jem had been for a couple of drinks over the last few months, were even friends of sorts when he stopped trying to wind her up, and although neither of them let Flo in on their conversations, she knew that he had been clutching at straws in asking Jem to help him save his marriage.

'Don't rush into anything,' Jem replied quietly, to Flo's surprise. 'You've had a lot to deal with recently, and you need your people around you, not to be sending them to the other side of the world.'

'Too late. He'll be gone this time next week.' Flo picked up an old Hermès scarf and began examining the rolled hem closely, hoping she could distract herself from the tears that threatened to break loose.

'Well, this could be a blessing in disguise, you know?'

'How do you work that out?'

'Look, babe,' Jem said brightly. 'These things happen. Take me: got over men and got myself a good woman.'

'I don't want a good woman. I want . . .' She trailed off, and wondered suddenly what she did actually want. Over the last few months she had begun to feel as though she were wearing the wrong clothes – Flo the mother, Flo the wife, Flo the businesswoman – and now that they had fallen away from her, she felt naked.

The bell made them both jump, as a customer pushed open the door, letting a blast of cool air into the stuffy shop and dissipating briefly the musty cloud of old perfume and mothballs. A worried-looking young girl with rainbow hair and torn tights looked at them both. 'Hi.' Her black-kohled eyes widened at the sight of the two women glaring at her. 'I just wondered whether you had any, like, shirts? Like, tartan? You know?' Her voice trailed away, and she stood still, ready to take flight.

'Sorry, sweetheart. Closed. Open again in half an hour.' Jemima put her hands on her dungareed hips in a manner that suggested there was no argument.

'Oh. OK,' the girl said, and backed away through the door. 'Cool,' she whispered.

Just before the door closed behind her, Jemima said, 'Wait.' She took the top item from the wash pile and threw it at the girl. 'Here. On the house. Needs a wash.' She looked at the girl's grubby T-shirt and torn denim shorts. 'Or not. Enjoy.' She closed the door, setting a rack of belts hanging from it jangling. 'So where were we? How about a cuppa to help you think?'

As Jemima clattered about in the small kitchen behind the shop, Flo absent-mindedly began to arrange pairs of shoes in size order. Placing the size fives in neat couples, she pulled out a pair in the softest cream kid leather. They were barely worn, their kitten heels only slightly scuffed, the leather soles barely grazed. Made in Italy. She tried to imagine the workshop where they had been crafted by one of a family of shoemakers, a rough dark hand gently moulding the toes into perfect points. These shoes were not for buying fish in the market, or hanging out the washing. They were the shoes of debutantes and dames.

'Try them on if you like.' Jemima appeared bearing two mismatched cups and saucers on a tray.

'Nah, can't be bothered to take these off,' Flo said, looking at the battered old brogues she had lived in all winter.

'So what are we going to do with you, honey?' Jemima set the tray down on the counter and moved a pile of sweaters off the chesterfield that was meant for customers' partners but invariably ended up covered in a mountain of garments waiting to be sorted and hung. 'Come. Sit.'

Flo sat herself down with a deep sigh. 'I have no idea.'

Jem passed her a cup and saucer. 'Extra sugar in it. Thought you needed it.'

'Thanks.' Flo made a space for it on the counter, then watched Jem rearrange her Land Girl-style scarf around her head in the floor-length gilt-framed mirror. 'What am I going to do? I've got nothing but a sewing machine and a Mini with career issues, and half a house at the wrong end of town that's probably worth less than my wardrobe.'

She began winding a lock of hair around her finger, and let her gaze drift to the window, hearing voices on the pavement outside. A young mother passed by, wrestling a buggy and a little boy who escaped her grasp as she bent over to rearrange a blanket. He stopped to push a little truck on the pavement, carefully navigating it around cracks and paving slabs, until he realised she had moved on a couple of paces without him, and launched himself at her legs. She scooped him up, kissing him before putting him back down on the ground and ruffling his hair, his hand held in hers.

'You OK?' Jem said carefully, as Flo kept vigil on the family scene outside the window.

'Mm?' She turned back to look at her friend. 'Yeah, sure.' She suddenly felt her stomach lurch as a spasm of tears caught her unawares. Tea slopped from cup to saucer to lap, creating a puddle in the broad grooves of her old corduroy skirt.

Jemima rushed over and took the cup from her. 'Look, I know it's tough at the moment. And you're feeling shit. But maybe in time this will seem like a new opportunity.'

'Jem, I'm thirty-eight. It's nearly too late for some opportunities.'

'Not necessarily. Look at me and Clare. Three years ago

I was married to Mr Shithead, and now I'm living with a woman I love and her two great kids. Things can happen.'

'They call you Dad, Jem. And they take the piss out of you behind your back.'

'It's affectionate. Teenage humour.'

Not wanting to start something, Flo leant behind the chair for her handbag. 'Where are those bloody tissues?'

Jemima looked at her and smiled. 'You'll be fine, Flo. Look at you: even with a shiny red nose and leaky mascara, you're lovely. And that's without your amazing eye . . . you can make 1970s M&S nylon and a pair of Lionel Blair flares look stylish.'

Flo frowned at her.

'Well, maybe not the nylon thing. But you get my point.' She reached over and rubbed Flo's shoulder. 'You're a babe, and even if Seamus has gone – which I'm not convinced about, by the way – you'll be just fine.'

Another customer peered through the curtain of belts and bags on the back of the door, trying to work out whether they were open.

Flo looked at her friend, seeing the anxiety at turning another customer away, and realised she had asked too much for too long. Jem was her friend, not her therapist, and she had a business to run.

'Do you know what?' Jemima said, and Flo braced herself, realising that she was staring at the frayed end of her friend's tether. 'I know this is all a pile of shit, and I know he's hurt you. But you have to stop feeling sorry for yourself and do something constructive, babe.'

And there it was. Flo was momentarily shocked by Jemima's words. For the last year, she'd known only quiet sympathy, people keeping their distance, treating her with kid gloves. Poor Flo: first the baby, then that husband of hers, then Peggy . . .

Obviously worried that she'd gone too far, Jem babbled on, 'I'm sorry, Flo. Just a bit stressed at the moment. Bloody builders have been in and told us there's asbestos and that we're going to have to move out. And stepchild number two got caught shoplifting last week. And I keep having hot flushes. Too young, my friend, I'm too young.'

'I'm such a shit friend, Jem. When did I last ask how you are?'

'Ah, forget it – it'll pass.'

'You know you can all come and crash at mine if you need to?'

'What, even the Godzillaettes?'

'Sure,' Flo said uncertainly.

'Anyway,' Jem was saying, 'I was hoping you'd let me have a poke around Peggy's wardrobe. I bet she never threw a thing away. It must be like a museum in there.'

Flo sat bolt upright. 'Oh my God. How could I have forgotten?'

'Forgotten what?'

She carefully pulled a small manila envelope out of her handbag. 'This.' She stood up and pushed the teacups to the side of the counter. 'Look. I found it at Gran's.'

She laid out the pristine black and white photograph, as clear and untarnished as the day it had been printed. Jem peered closely.

'That's your gran, isn't it?' she said, pointing to one of the bridesmaids.

'No, Gran's the bride.'

'Flippin' close likeness, then. Who are the others?'

'That's Phyllis and Dorothy.'

Jem snorted. 'I should have known. Trust Dorothy to outdo the bride.' She peered closer. 'She looks like Diana Dors. I never knew she used to be so good-looking.'

'She was a proper Marilyn in her day, our Dot. Imagine getting on the number seventy-seven bus and having your ticket clipped by that.'

'Dot worked on the buses?'

'It's where she met her husband. But I think in her time she's been a few things,' Flo said, and they both laughed.

Jem picked up the picture and examined it. 'That has to be Phyllis – how that woman doesn't fall over, I'll never know. So who's the other one, then?'

Flo took the picture from her and stared hard at the smiling girl next to her grandmother. 'That,' she said, 'is Nancy.'

'Nancy who?'

'I have no idea, other than she probably made Gran's wedding outfit.'

'Seriously? That's a pretty good job, from what I can see. Probably made the bridesmaids' dresses as well, in that case. She must have been close to your gran, looking at them. How come you don't know who she is?'

Flo slid the photograph back into the envelope. 'Exactly what I've been asking myself.' She looked at her watch. 'Listen, I know I've only just got here, but would you mind if I knocked off early?'

Jem tried to look annoyed, but Flo could tell it would be a bit of a relief: her friend couldn't afford to turn people away, and Flo was about as much use as a chocolate teapot at the moment. 'No, hon, you go. Do what you need to do.' She lifted Flo's coat off the rack and held it out to her. 'Which is what, exactly?'

'I need to go to Wandsworth,' Flo said, shrugging the old tweed coat on. For the first time in months, she felt an unfamiliar frisson of something approaching excitement. 'Let's hope Dot's got the kettle on.'

6

Flo smiled as she pressed the doorbell. Surrounded by clipped box hedges, white-gravelled frontages and the entire Farrow & Ball swatch card, Dorothy's slice of Victoria Street was a hearty two-fingers-up to the gentrification of this corner of south London. The uPVC front door and ruched net curtains formed a perfect backdrop for the tableau of gnomes surrounding a miniature pond complete with cast-concrete Dutch windmill. The Big Ben chimes had hardly finished their synthetic pealing before the door opened and Dorothy appeared in fluffy slippers and full battle make-up.

'Well, this is a nice treat. Come on in, doll,' she said in a career smoker's growl. She ushered Flo into the dark hallway and past the little front room, where one of her grandsons was giving a zombie what for on the PlayStation. 'Don't mind our Parker,' she said. 'His mum's left him here while she's at work. We'll go in the kitchen, shall we?'

Flo tried to remember which of Dorothy's three daughters Parker belonged to. Or was it her son? Dorothy's family tree was large and complex, and ever increasing, and her many grandchildren all had surnames for Christian names, confusing Flo further: was Parker Taylor's brother? Or was Taylor Jackson's sister? She honestly had no idea any more. The tightly packed display of framed school photographs on the mantelpiece offered no help, the cloudy-sky backgrounds and identical school uniforms blending into one cheeky-smiled, gap-toothed amalgam of Dorothy's DNA. She leant her head through the open door and shouted a generic greeting, but it went unheard within the sound of machete chops and machine-gun fire.

'Cuppa?' Dorothy said, filling the kettle.

'Thought you'd never ask,' said Flo, taking off her coat and hanging it on the back of one of the kitchen chairs.

Dorothy pottered around, spooning tea leaves from a Silver Jubilee tin into the old brown teapot that Flo remembered from her childhood visits to Gran's old neighbourhood, and emptying a few fig rolls onto a plate.

Flo looked around the dark little kitchen, wondering how she had ended up here this afternoon. Back home, Seamus was packing his life into a couple of suitcases, and instead of stopping him, she was in Wandsworth on some wild-goose distraction exercise.

'Here you go.' Dorothy poured two large mugs, sloshing milk into them from the bottle, then passing one to Flo and taking a large sip from her own.

'I've never known how you do that.'

'What's that?'

'Drink it straight from the pot. You must have an asbestos mouth.'

Dorothy laughed. 'That's what your gran always used to say.' She smiled. 'We had a few cups of tea round this table, she and I. Course, it was my mum making the tea back in the day. Table's new, and it's Peggy's granddaughter sitting here instead, but Mum's old teapot's still going.'

'You must be the only one left on the road from the old days.'

'Suppose so. It's all poncey four-wheel drives and baby yoga and fifty-quid-a-tin paint round here now. Your great-gran and grandad wouldn't recognise it. Bless 'em.'

Flo had never met the legendary Stanley and Beryl Moon, but over the years she had accrued an arsenal of stories about them: how Stanley used to chase Peggy up the stairs with a rolled-up newspaper if she came in late, and how Beryl and Phyllis's mum took competitive front-step cleaning to a whole new level. She'd seen a few photos of them, of course, Beryl always with her arms firmly crossed over her housecoat, her face set equally firmly, and Stanley unable to disguise behind his thick-lensed glasses the impish sense of humour that had got him through one world war and fifty years of marriage to Beryl and the Nine Elms gasworks.

'If it's not estate agents trying to tempt me out, it's my own kids. When I've gone, there'll be one hell of a fight over this place, I can tell you.'

Flo wanted to disagree, but Dorothy's brood could start a fight over a paper bag. This house had heard more expletives over the years than the average East End boxing club, and the nicotine-stained kitchen walls bore dents that the trained eye could match to most of the pots and pans hanging above the oven.

Dorothy began puffing on a long black plastic vape, encrusted with diamanté studs that matched those on the neck-line of her fluffy black sweater. The blueberry-vanilla fumes made Flo slightly nauseous, but they were infinitely better than the Benson & Hedges that had been Dorothy's cigarette of choice for fifty years.

'Didn't know you'd given up,' she said, trying not to cough.

'Our Mikey got it for me the other day. Bloody 'orrible, it is. But I promised I'd give it a go. Can't see as there's any point in me giving up the fags at my time of life.'

Flo suspected the contraption would be in the bin by the end of the week. 'Maybe, but it's got to be better for the grandkids, hasn't it?'

Dorothy snorted. 'If you believe everything you read in the papers.'

Flo wondered what sort of hell Dorothy's GP must go through every time she walked in the surgery door. No NHS pension could be worth it, surely.

'Anyway, dear. How's things? You get all cleared up after the funeral all right? Sorry I couldn't stay and help – had one of my turns. You know what I'm like.'

Flo knew exactly what Dot was like, but just smiled. 'Don't worry. It didn't take long.'

Dorothy popped away at the vape, then looked at Flo. 'You heard anything from that mother of yours yet?'

Flo was acutely aware of Dorothy and Phyllis's unspoken feelings about her mother. With Peggy gone, she was Maddie's sole defender, but even she was pretty close to her limit now. 'I had a long chat with her a couple of days ago,' she lied.

Dorothy raised an eyebrow. 'Oh yes? She coming back for the reading of the will, is she?'

'Don't be like that, Dot. She was really disappointed she couldn't make the funeral, you know?' Flo got it – why couldn't anyone else? Mum loved the ashram, and every single woman she helped learn to read had a chance to change her life. It was amazing. Really. 'Gran would never have wanted her to come all the way back here just to sit in the crem then stand around eating cheese and pickle sandwiches. She's making a real difference to people's lives, Dot.'

'I'm sure she is. Listen, you don't have to defend her to me, girl. She's your mum, and you love her, I'm sure. Anyway, she's all you've got now your gran's gone. So I hope you do get to spend some time with her. She doesn't know how lucky she is to have a lovely girl like you. I'd swap two of mine for you, I would, any day of the week.'

'Don't be daft.'

'You think I'm joking?' And Dorothy began to chortle to herself between sucks on the long pen-like pipe.

'Anyway, she's not all I've got. I've got you. And Phyllis. And Aunty Bean.'

'Not forgetting that lovely fella of yours.'

'Not forgetting him,' Flo said quietly.

Dorothy squeezed Flo's hand with her own red-taloned one. Flo looked at the raised veins and large beige speckles that mapped themselves across the wrinkled skin, and tried to reconcile them with those of the blonde bombshell who had outshone a bride over five decades ago.

'Listen, Dot, I wanted to ask you about something.'

'What's that, love?' Dorothy said, pressing the teapot to check it was warm enough, then topping them both up with thick, treacly liquid – strong enough to stand a spoon up in, as Donald would have said. Flo placed the manila envelope in front of her. 'Don't tell me Peg's gone and left me her bungalow? She always wanted me to go down there with her.' She shivered. 'Not a chance. All them bloody seagulls and pensioners.'

Flo slowly pulled out the photograph, turning it to face the older woman. She didn't need to look at the image that sat looking up at them – it was already imprinted in her mind. What she needed to see was Dorothy's reaction.

Dorothy put her mug down and took the photograph in her hands. Flo watched as a range of expressions flickered across her face, from a slight smile to complete tight-lipped shutdown.

'Well I never,' she said quietly, then looked up at Flo. 'I'd forgotten what a lovely day that was. Reckon I haven't aged at all.' She passed the picture back, then glanced at the clock on the wall. 'I need to be getting our Parker his tea soon. You'll have to forgive me if I crack on, young Florence.'

She began to pull herself up out of her chair, but Flo stopped her. 'Wait. Just for a minute. Please. I haven't asked you the question yet.'

With a weary sigh, Dorothy sat down again and looked directly across the table at her guest.

'You want to know who she is, don't you?'

There are moments in everyone's life when things will never be the same again. It could be missing a train, then finding yourself on the next one, sitting opposite the man or woman you will one day marry. It could be seeing an advert for a job that takes you to a new land that becomes your home and a new language that becomes your second tongue. It could be ordering the red snapper off the specials board, only to have it bite back and leave you choking your last under the table while the maître d' tries to remember his first-aid training.

The moment when Dorothy broke her fifty-six-year silence and brought Nancy Moon back into the family fold was one of those.

Flo stood on the pavement across the road, looking at number 75 and trying to take it back in time. Was that Peggy struggling to open the front door, socks round her ankles and weighed down with her school satchel? Beryl scrubbing at the front windows with newspaper and vinegar until she could see her work-weary face in them? Phyllis and Dorothy scratching hopscotch squares on the road with blunt, dusty chalk? And who was the girl climbing out of the passenger seat of a shiny new sports car just as Big Ben chimed midnight, watched by her anxious father in the upstairs window as he wondered if she was too big to put across his knee?

It was almost impossible to strip away the bunting strung across the inside of the bow window, the matching bay trees that stood sentry on either side of the matte mole-grey door; to take away the Golfs and four-wheel drives and shiny motorbikes so that the road was left clear for games of football and kiss chase, for the rows of washing strung from one side to the other and dancing like wayward Tiller Girls in the breeze that blew in from the Thames, across the roof of the cement works and through the geometric maze of perpendicular streets.

Flo knew Dorothy hadn't told her everything, but she had told her enough.

The girl waved at the driver of the car, her elbow-length white gloves gleaming against the dull brick of the dirty London street. She straightened out the creases in her gold satin skirt and arranged the oversized black dinner jacket around her bare shoulders as she hummed a snippet of Frankie Vaughan to herself. Just before she put her key in the lock, she turned round, startled by something on the opposite side of the street, and Flo recognised at once the bridesmaid who had pressed her cheek so affectionately against that of her bride sister. 'Hello, Nancy Moon,' she said quietly.

She pulled her coat around her against the chill evening air, and headed back to the buses and betting shops and halal butchers and all-night grocers and the shiny white cars blaring drum and bass out of open windows. So lost in thought was she, trapped in the vast space between decades, that she never registered the journey from Wandsworth to Victoria, or the quickly abandoned attempts at conversation by the Uber driver, her thoughts instead fixed on the young woman whose existence had remained secret for over half a century.

Part Two

LONDON AND BRIGHTON

7

Nancy Moon started running away the day she could put one foot in front of the other. Everyone in Victoria Street knew the little blonde-haired toddler with the rosy cheeks and the smile that could melt the heart of the toughest docker, and if her big sister Peggy hadn't already chased out of the house and up the street looking for her, there was always a neighbour ready to give her a biscuit and take her home. Beryl said she had never heard of a child that could get through a pair of shoes so quickly, nor lose a pair so quickly if she didn't like them. Given that most of Nancy's shoes were hand-me-downs from her sister or one of the other girls growing up in the street, more were lost than worn out over the years, and long after she'd gone, it brought tears to an old man's eyes when Stanley dismantled the coal shed in the garden only to discover a stash of girls' shoes, from tiny Mary Janes to sensible school lace-ups, crammed into the gap between the shed and the brick wall dividing the back yards of number 73 and number 75.

Nancy knew from an early age that there was more to life than the world that comfortably held her friends and family. She soon lost count of the times she came home from school tear-stained but defiant at yet another dose of the ruler for staring out of the window. Teachers accused her of being stupid or rude – some even suggested that there was something not quite right with her – but they were all wrong. She was just bored. If she wanted to, she could recite her times tables backwards, tell you the capital city of any country, conjugate a Latin verb to within an inch of its life, but she just couldn't be bothered. She had better things to think about.

So what was going through Nancy's mind during those interminable lessons? What was she staring at, if not the high brick walls of the school playground outside and the slice of grey London sky above them? Where was Nancy while everyone else in the class chewed the ends of their pencils as they tried to remember the chronology of English monarchs?

Nancy was far away from the scratched wooden desks with their ink stains and carved initials, from the boys who pulled pigtails and the girls who pretended to hate it, from the bespectacled teachers who wondered how their university education had led them to this den of ungrateful, information-resistant urchins who couldn't wait for the bell to go so they could scramble over weed-strewn bomb sites or spend their few pennies on a handful of sweets.

She was in the pages of one of Dorothy's magazines: walking a red carpet, sunbathing on a yacht, watching princes play polo. The location didn't matter, nor who she was with – it was what she was wearing that filled her head. As soon as her sister's friend had finished each month's instalment and memorised the latest additions to Marilyn's wardrobe, she would pass it on to Nancy, who spent hours sitting on the wall outside the front of the house, scrutinising each photograph to see where Audrey's hemline sat that month, how Grace managed to turn a simple silk square into an accessory of infinite versatility and elegance, and how Sophia could weaponise a pair of black sunglasses.

Who wouldn't pity the parents of the bright child, the bearer of great hopes, who treats her gift casually and can't see the responsibility she carries? So, as other less able children in her class found themselves catapulted into grammar school, Nancy followed her elder sister into the gloomy corridors of secondary-modern education, free of expectation and challenge and to remain forever a stranger to the mystery of the quadratic equation. It made no difference to her which playground she tucked herself away in each break time with her magazine, as long as she was left alone.

What did make a difference to her, however, came about in her second week at the new school. The break-time bell rang, and Nancy rolled her magazine back into her coat pocket in the cloakroom, then followed the rest of the girls into a classroom that had tables instead of desks, and a bright-eyed teacher who looked barely older than her pupils, and who eschewed the tweed and twinsets of the other teachers for pretty dresses with matching shoes and satin hair ribbons.

If Nancy didn't quite fall instantly in love with Miss Nightingale and her florist's shop of a wardrobe, she lost her heart the moment she saw the long bench at the back of the classroom, with its line of workhorse-like black sewing machines. Each week, she looked forward to needlework classes – darning, embroidery, hemming, she hungrily practised these whenever she could persuade Beryl to give her a needle and thread – but it was the machines that she patiently kept her eye on. Only girls who had reached their thirteenth birthday were allowed near them, and so Nancy spent the rest of her eleventh year and all of her twelfth developing her needle skills to virtuosic standards, so that Miss Nightingale tried and failed to locate her invisible stitching in the petticoat she had worked on at home, and even her own mother, who was never one for expressing anything other than exhaustion, exclaimed at the neatness of the darned repair in Stanley's socks.

And so a few weeks before Nancy's thirteenth birthday, Miss Nightingale called her over during class and let her put aside her embroidery hoop before leading her to the back of the room. She sat Nancy in front of one of the machines, and crouched next to her while she showed her how to wind thread onto the bobbin, then drop it snugly into the bobbin case; how to take the end of the thread from the reel and pass it around and through hooks and levers until it could be threaded through the needle; and then how to keep hold of it while a deft turn of the wheel allowed the needle to pick up the bobbin thread. For the rest of her life, the smell of Blue Grass by Elizabeth Arden instantly took her back to the thrill and anticipation of that afternoon.

Nancy was ready to go. After a few trial runs on some fabric from the scraps bin, she was stitching beautifully straight lines, and judging perfectly when to slow the turns of the wheel in order to corner or reverse. There was no time for magazines at lunch any more: she spent all her break times in the sewing room, helping Miss Nightingale by tidying away reels and boxes of pins in exchange for more time at the machine.

Two months after that first introduction to the machines, Nancy presented her mother with a simple shift dress for her birthday, made from a couple of spare metres of soft green cotton Miss Nightingale had given her. Beryl had never worn anything other than brown, and although she humoured her daughter and wore the new dress for her birthday tea that evening, she told Nancy she would save it for best in future. Since best never existed in the Moon household, Peggy had found it still hanging, pristine, in the wardrobe not long after Beryl had given up all mortal need for clothing.

Once Peggy dropped out of the other end of the education system and got herself a job in the dry cleaner's on Wandsworth High Street, Nancy spotted an opportunity. There was not much either of the Moon parents could do to stop the two sisters taking the bus up to the West End on a Saturday afternoon, especially since Peggy paid for the fares out of her wages. Nancy was insufferable around the house unless there was a pile of mending to set to, and so Beryl and Stanley breathed a sigh of relief when the two girls disappeared up Victoria Street with their faces scrubbed and their hair brushed. Nancy knew they probably resembled a pair of ragamuffins as they wandered around in their best coats that looked fancy in Wandsworth but shabby next to the Bond Street shoppers in their finery and furs, but she never cared. She used to take a little drawing book, and copy the dresses and hats in Fenwick's window, while Peggy shuffled self-consciously by her side, asking continuously when they could go to the Lyons for a cuppa.

When Nancy's time to leave school came around, she already had her career mapped out: she wanted to be a fashion designer with her own shop, she told the family one evening as they sat together listening to the radio. Stanley put his newspaper down and laughed out loud, and Beryl said she had never heard anything so ridiculous. Only Peggy knew how hurt Nancy was – she'd seen that brave face many a time when she'd caught her sister being bullied in the school corridors. Nancy might have been pretending she didn't care, but she was crushed.

The very next day, Beryl marched her younger daughter round to the knicker factory up the road and demanded to see the manager. Mr Watkins instantly spotted the young girl's bright curiosity about the rows of machinists and the bolts of fabric lined up against the workshop wall, and knew that she wasn't quite as stupid as she tried to make out: the monosyllabic answers to his questions were aimed at the mother she sullenly refused to speak to rather than at him.

Stitching pants was not part of Nancy's life plan, but she got on with it: at least it gave her some experience, and it wouldn't be for ever.

Off she went to work every day, until one evening a year later Mr Watkins turned up on the doorstep. Why hadn't she been into the factory? He was worried about her. She was a good little worker and had never given him any trouble. He hadn't seen her for a week, and assumed she was ill. Was there anything he could do to help? Perhaps the family would like some assistance paying for a doctor for her?

If there was one sure-fire way to antagonise the mild-mannered Stanley Moon, it was by attacking his pride. When Nancy got home that night, he was sitting at the kitchen table waiting for her. 'Where've you been? And don't bother telling me you've been at work, because I know you haven't,' he said in the quiet voice he reserved for his angriest moments. Nancy could tell by the look in his eye that she wasn't too big or too old for the strap.

It turned out Nancy had been at work. Just not at the work Beryl had fixed up for her.

It wasn't that she didn't enjoy the job: Mr Watkins was a kind boss who treated his girls well, and never gave them any of the bother she'd been warned to expect by friends who worked in similar environments. And under the tutelage of Madge, the shop-floor manager, she'd become proficient on the big industrial machines in record time, turning out pieces at nearly twice the rate of some of the slower girls. No, it had been a year well spent, although she would never have admitted as much to Beryl, and she'd saved enough money to buy her own sewing machine, with a wooden case into which Stanley carved her initials.

Nancy's life plan did not, however, include a decade of making underwear for the masses until some boy round the corner buried her in a dreary marriage. And so one morning she had put on her smartest dress, a fitted navy crêpe that was probably the best piece she had made, with three-quarter-length sleeves and a tiny Peter Pan collar, at which she pinned an enamel brooch borrowed from her grandmother. As soon as she turned the corner at the end of the road, she took off her everyday coat, and pulled out of her raffia shopping bag a pair of kitten-heeled cream shoes Miss Nightingale had passed down to her, swapping them with her sensible lace-ups, which she stuffed into the bag along with the coat. By the time she got off the number 22 at Oxford Street and walked the short distance down Bond Street, she was sporting a slick of red lipstick, her hair pinned up just as Dorothy had taught her.

She hid the bag behind the box hedge next to the shiny black front door, and walked straight into the offices of Victor Belgrave, looking as much like a client as a prospective employee. It took all her persuasive powers and an impressive exercising of self-taught elocution to convince the smart young lady on reception to introduce her to Mr Belgrave's assistant, a highly strung Frenchman with round black-rimmed glasses and a satin-backed waistcoat over his cream polo neck, its lapels punctured by a line of glass-tipped pins. Nancy was wearing her curriculum vitae, and stood quietly while he ran his finger along the top-stitching on her collar and asked her to raise her arm so that he could see how the sleeve had been set in. She didn't bat an eyelid when he crouched down and checked the evenness of her hemline, and turned over the edge of the skirt to reveal the binding, its stitching invisible on the reverse.

She was in luck. One of the girls had called in sick, and they had a gown to prepare for a fitting that afternoon. Could she stay and help?

She could, and seeing how easily she fitted in with the other girls, and how she could turn her talented hand to anything he asked, keeping her cool even when he lost his, by the end of that day Monsieur Jacques had offered her a job.

At last Nancy felt at home. As she proved her worth with hard graft and impeccable workmanship, even on the most mundane of tasks, she gained the respect and then friendship of the other girls in the studio, and found herself progressing from sweeping the floor to working on the calico tulles of the signature House of Belgrave cocktail dresses and evening gowns.

She was happy. She loved her work and her new friends. At the end of each season, the girls were allowed to take home leftover fabrics, and Nancy's little wardrobe was soon bursting with satin cocktail dresses, silk day dresses and fitted wool skirts, all made on the kitchen table with her own sewing machine.

Of course she needed a lifestyle to match, and as her friendships grew at work, pretty, bubbly Nancy was top of the list for drinks parties, country house weekends, and private gatherings in smoky nightclubs. Many of the girls came from parts of London she had only ever been through on the bus – Chelsea, Kensington and even the Bohemian fringes of north London – but they absorbed her into their circle as one of their own, sharing the messy flats their parents paid for and the plum-vowelled, time-rich young men who fluttered around them.

As Beryl and Stanley watched Nancy checking her make-up and adjusting her hair in the hall mirror while waiting for lifts from a string of young men in sports jackets by day and slim DJs by night, they couldn't help worrying. This wasn't their world, they didn't understand these people, and bar grounding their daughter, they weren't sure how to protect her. At best, she might find herself the wife of a man who would give her a better life than Peggy could expect, now that she'd married Donald from the printing press on Putney High Street. At worst . . .

Stanley was worried. There was Peggy, for a start – it was hard to untangle Beryl's deliberately oblique euphemisms, but as far as he could tell, things weren't right in the baby department, and even a fool would wonder why, after three years of marriage, there was still no little one in the nursery he'd helped Donald decorate. He could barely get a word out of Peggy, and to be honest, he barely knew what to say. This was not his territory, so instead he and Donald talked about football, or who'd been in the Legion last night.

And now, even though Nancy couldn't stop talking every night when she got in, whether he and Beryl had the energy to listen or not, he worried he would lose his little girl too. She still sat for hours with that sewing machine of hers, and made with her own hands every stitch she wore. And as far as he could see, she was as close as ever to Peggy and the rest of the local girls, who now hung on her every word and snapped up the printed coasters from the Ritz or the books of matches from the Savoy Grill that she brought back for them. She was still their Nancy, with no airs or graces – she just led a different life to the rest of them once she shut the door of number 75.

Over a few weeks, he noticed that it was the same car coming to collect her each time, a shiny new Jaguar with a throaty roar he soon recognised as it pulled up outside the house, bringing a few of the menfolk to their front doors to get a better look before being ordered back indoors by their wives, who preferred to peep discreetly through net curtains. Bar Phyllis's old dad, who owned a garage and was the first in the street to buy himself one of the new Morris 1100s, not many round this part of south London owned a car, and certainly not one like this.

He only met the driver once. Nancy was usually ready to dash out of the front door as soon as it arrived, but this once, she was late, having popped round to Peggy's, and he opened the door to a tall young man straight out of the Bristol cigarette advert pasted to the billboards at Nine Elms, with his Sean Connery good looks and barbershop shave and expensive cologne. They barely had time to exchange pleasantries before Nancy came skipping along the road and kissed her old dad on the cheek before disappearing into the London night.

Stanley had been right to worry. A few weeks later, there were no more cars purring outside the house, no parties, no dizzy girlfriends. As the leaves in the London parks began to turn to gold and curtains across the city were drawn earlier at the end of each day, the flame that had brought people to dance around Nancy was blown out almost overnight.

8

'Nancy, it's me.'

Peggy knocked lightly on her sister's bedroom door, but there was no reply. She'd been back for five days now, and still no one could entice Nancy out of her room. The curtains remained closed and the trays of food Mum left on the landing for her stayed there until sandwiches curled, chops congealed in their own juices and custard grew a thick, rippled skin. She needed feeding up, but nothing offered to her made it through the locked door.

Truth was, no one knew what to do with her. The terrible gap that had been left by her absence over the last few months had not been filled by the shell of Nancy that arrived at Paddington station a few days ago. Stanley, who had always been free with the embraces he saved for his two girls, had greeted her on the platform with a hesitant pat on the shoulder, before picking up her pale blue suitcase and hailing the first taxi of his life. Beryl would be furious when they got back, he knew, but he couldn't make this pale, sickly girl sit on a bus for all to see. She didn't even seem to notice the gesture, staring blankly through the cab window, her eyes fixed on a point in the distance. And when Stanley pushed open the door of number 75 for her, she walked upstairs without a word and closed her bedroom door behind her.

Closed it had remained, and each evening Beryl tidied the landing of the magazines Dorothy brought round and the tins of shortbread and jam tarts Phyllis made daily.

Peggy picked up that morning's untouched breakfast, wondering whether she should hide the boiled egg that still sat in its little blue and white striped cup. Mum was becoming frustrated at the waste, and Peggy feared that the soft-footed allowances the household was making for its youngest member had a fairly short shelf life. Beryl had never been one to indulge frailty in her daughters, whether it came in the form of a nasty cold or measles. Her maternal love was expressed in three meals a day and clean linen once a week, and her patience was wearing thin.

Peggy laid the tray on the kitchen table and went back to the hallway. Inside the huge pram, the tiny little bundle was beginning to writhe within her pink-crocheted cocoon. She was three months old now, and her face had smoothed out until she resembled a little peach. Peggy touched her flushed cheek, worried that she was too hot. It was a warm spring, and her fast-learning but terrified mother wasn't sure whether she was at risk of hypothermia or suffocation. Beryl couldn't understand why Peggy didn't just tuck her up and leave her outside in the yard in her pram: it hadn't done either of her girls any harm, and everyone knew a blast of fresh air helped Baby sleep. But this baby was precious: long awaited and completely adored, Peggy never let her out of her sight.

Maybe she shouldn't have brought little Maddie here, but Mum and Dad were both out, and she couldn't leave Nancy alone, even if she refused to come out of her room. She picked up the little bundle and jogged her against her shoulder, lest her whimpers escalate and find their way under Nancy's door.

She shushed the baby along the hall and into Beryl's kitchen, where she managed to put a pan of water on the hob with one hand, and drop the rubber-teated glass bottle gently into the bubbling water. Upstairs, she thought she heard foot-steps disturbing the floorboards above her head, but it was hard to tell, with the baby burbling in her ear. Still jiggling on the spot, she tipped a few drops of the still-cold milk onto the back of her hand. She had just enough time to run upstairs to the new bathroom before the milk was warmed, knowing that Maddie could make a feed last an hour and that Peggy's bladder wouldn't.

She popped the baby back in her pram and bounded up the stairs two at a time. Oh, the blessed relief – it seemed impossible that only a couple of years ago she'd have been sitting on a cold seat at the end of the yard and washing her hands under the outside tap, instead of standing on the Marley tiles Stanley had fitted himself, waiting for hot water to work its way through the system and wash the Pears soap from her hands. Finally the plumbing spat scalding water at her, and she raced back down to the hallway, relieved that Maddie was still silent.

'Come on then, my sweet,' she said as she walked towards the huge-wheeled vehicle. 'Let's get you fed.'

She leant into the pram to pick up the infant, but where she had been lying, there was only a creased, warm impression on the soft terry pram sheet. Peggy's heart raced. Had she left the front door open? Had someone come in and taken her? Maybe it was just Beryl back early from work at the bakery. Think, Peggy, think. The blood rushed around her head so fast, and her heart pumped so loudly, that she didn't at first hear the quiet singing coming from the other end of the hallway.

She walked slowly towards the kitchen. There, sitting at the table, was Nancy, the baby in her arms, little Maddie gazing up at her as she sucked greedily at the bottle.

'Oh Nancy,' Peggy said, walking slowly towards her, then crouching next to her and easing the baby out of her arms. 'I'm so sorry,' and the two sisters embraced, the tiny child pressed between them.

As the days lengthened and the sound of birdsong competed with the clamour of trains and buses and trams around the city, Nancy gradually spent more and more time out of her room, often tucked up on the settee with a book, or working her way through Beryl's mending basket, until there wasn't a single sock or slip that had a hole or a tear in it. Beryl was quietly pleased to have her back at tea each evening. Since Peggy had married, it had been just the three of them sitting around the Formica-topped table, and while Nancy had been away, she had secretly missed her younger daughter's constant chatter, and wondered now why she had always been so quick to tell her to be quiet while they ate. Not that Nancy was back on form yet, and she no longer had a catalogue of stories or the appetite to share them. But at least she was there, and the colour was coming back to her cheeks. Beryl pretended not to notice that each evening her portions became a little larger, and that there was no longer anything to scrape off her plate at the end of the meal, and Stanley pretended not to notice how relieved his wife was.

He also noticed that Nancy never received a single visitor from outside a hundred-yard radius of the house. The bright young things in sparkly jewels and fur stoles who had sat in revving open-top cars, laughing and shouting at his daughter to hurry up, no longer slummed it across the river, but stayed in the SWs. He wasn't cross – far from it. Good riddance, as far as he was concerned. He had his Nancy back, although no one could guess for how long.

Peggy and the girls, however: they were a different matter. Every day, each of them popped in with a bit of gossip, or a book from the library, or a quarter of pear drops. He would sit in his armchair after work, smiling behind his open news-paper at the laughter and shushed imparting of important news that came from the kitchen table. It was like the old days, and even Beryl left them to it instead of shooing them out, sitting quietly opposite him knitting endless jackets and leggings for the baby. How one small human being could wear so many balls of wool was beyond him, and he watched in wonder as Beryl unravelled anything outgrown and turned it through some kind of alchemy into a whole new garment.

They had all worried about how Nancy would manage around the new baby, but they had reckoned without how much she wanted her sister to be happy. Although after that first time she never went near Maddie again, there was no reason to believe she was anything other than glad for the proud new parents. In time, maybe she could find another job: obviously there was no going back to Belgrave's, but there were smaller outfits nearer to home, where no one knew

Nancy and where her skills would be snapped up. And so everyone waited.

'What are you going to do, then, Nance?'

It had to be Dorothy who plunged straight in with the question everyone had skirted around for the last six weeks.

Nancy picked at a daisy, rolling it between her fingers then pulling at the petals.

'Best not go there, love,' said her friend, and Nancy threw the remains of the flower onto the grass just beyond the edge of the blanket.

The common was busy, as half of south London decided to get itself a breath of warm late-spring air. The four girls had found a quiet spot under a tree, where the pram could sit in the shade and they could keep out of the sun. Phyllis had developed a marshmallow-pink stripe across the back of her neck, just on the walk from home, and was fretting about where you could buy calamine on a Sunday. Dorothy, whose latest crush was Brigitte Bardot, had pulled her tight skirt up and was working on a knee-high French Riviera tan. You never knew whose ticket you were going to clip on the bus, and she was nothing if not ready for any opportunity.

Nearby a couple of dads played football with their lads, sleeves rolled up and sweating slightly in the matching father-and-son knitted tank tops they had been sent out in. It was a well-known fact that in this part of south London you could still catch your death even at this time of year. Their heavy leather ball bounced towards the girls, making Peggy leap for the pram, followed by a young short-trousered boy with muddy knees, who blushed furiously as Dorothy pretended to keep it, then threw it back with impressive strength and accuracy towards the dads, who seemed more interested in her than in the return of their ball.

Phyllis dug around in her handbag and pulled out a small paper bag. She held it out to Nancy. 'Jelly baby?'

Dorothy and Peggy glanced at each other, then Dorothy snatched the bag off her.

'Hey!' Phyllis said.

'Nancy doesn't like these.'

'Since when?'

'Since I said so,' said Dorothy.

Phyllis shrugged. She knew better than to get into an argument with her friend, especially over something as stupid as a jelly baby.

Dorothy crammed three in her mouth at once and handed the bag back to Phyllis. 'You shouldn't be eating these anyway. You want to watch those hips of yours, our Phyl. You'll never get yourself a husband.'

Phyllis instantly withdrew her hand from the bag and scrunched it up, throwing it into the nearby bushes. 'You're a bully, Dorothy. I hate you.'

'That's enough,' Peggy said, rolling the pram back and forth from where she sat on the blanket. 'We're here to cheer Nancy up, not listen to you arguing.'

'It's fine,' Nancy said. 'It's just nice being here with you all. I missed you.'

'We missed you too,' said Phyllis. 'And I still can't believe you missed Maddie being born.'

'I know. Just my luck.'

'It was so exciting, Nance. I wish you'd been here. Donald

was like a little boy whose birthdays had all come at once. Dad said he bought a round for everyone in the Legion, soon as he got back from the hospital. They wouldn't let us see her until she was home, but when we did, oh, it was just lovely. Clever old Peg, eh?' and Phyllis nudged Peggy's knee playfully.

Peggy mumbled something coyly, suddenly taking a huge interest in the little white knitted bonnet in her hand.

Nancy looked at her beaming friend. A husband and a baby was all Phyllis had dreamed about since she was a child, and the pleasure she took from seeing her friend live the dream was unbearably sweet.

The girls fell quiet as Mrs Barrett from number 6 walked past with her daughter Betty, best winter coat and thick stockings on despite the warm spell. She slowed slightly to stare at Nancy and nudge Betty, whispering something of a clearly salutary nature, judging by the girl's wide-eyed response and the offended tilt of her spotty chin as she marched away from the little party under the tree.

'Snotty cows,' Dorothy said a little too loud. 'Don't know where they get their airs and graces from. My mum could tell a tale or two about that one, back when they were younger.'

'Ignore them,' Nancy said, although she had to admit that since she had come out of hibernation, it had been hard to face the stony faces of the Victoria Street matriarchs and the leers of their menfolk, and she knew from Dorothy that Beryl had found herself at the sharp end of veiled comments in the queue at the butcher's, or in the changing room at work. She hated to think that she had caused her parents even a moment's embarrassment. Perhaps it would be better if she just cleared off and let them all get on with their lives, now she was feeling stronger.

'Anyway, what was it like? You never told us,' Phyllis said. 'At the sanatorium,' she added when Nancy looked blankly back at her. 'Did everyone else there have TB? Were you allowed to talk to anyone? It must have been so lonely.'

Dorothy raised her eyes heavenward. 'Nancy doesn't want to talk about all that, do you, Nancy?'

Nancy shook her head. 'Not really. I'd rather forget it, if you don't mind, Phyl.'

Phyllis frowned. It was so easy to say the wrong thing these days, and she was increasingly beginning to think the others were keeping something from her.

Nancy patted her friend on the knee. 'Onwards and sideways and all that, eh?'

'Onwards and sideways. It's just nice to have you back.' Phyllis smiled brightly. 'So, have you heard from that fancy boyfriend of yours since you came back? Mum reckoned he looked like Gregory Peck.'

Dorothy picked up her cardie and threw it at Phyllis. 'For Gawd's sake, Phyl. What's the matter with you?'

Phyllis looked ready to cry, so Nancy leapt in. 'It's OK, Dorothy, you don't have to protect me. I won't be seeing him again, Phyl. Or any of that lot.'

'But what about your job? Your friends there?'

'That's finished. They let me go when I was ill.'

Phyllis was indignant. 'That's terrible. They can't sack someone just because they're poorly. You were brilliant at it.'

'They can and they did. It looks like I'll have to find something else to be brilliant at now.'

Peggy looked at her sister. How brave she was – she knew she could never go through what Nancy had and come out the other side. With her own little tragedies over the last three years, she had imagined that each would be the one to finish her off. She held Maddie's soft muslin cloth to her nose and breathed in the intoxicating smell of her daughter, her little miracle.

She opened her eyes and saw Nancy watching her, and turned away quickly.

'Hey, Dorothy!'

Relieved at the interruption, Dorothy waved back at the man walking past, his jacket hung over one shoulder and sleeves rolled up to reveal muscular black forearms.

'How you doin', petal?' he said, sunshine beaming through every lilting Caribbean inflection.

'Doing good, Denzel. Doing good.'

If Nancy hadn't known Dorothy better, she'd have thought that smile girlish, and was that a blush on her cheeks?

'Gonna come for that drink with me some time, girl?' he said, his head tilted shyly.

'Maybe, maybe. Now leave us alone,' Dorothy said, the broad grin on her face at odds with the hand that shooed him off. 'We've got girls' stuff to talk about.'

'In that case, I'll leave you to it. Good day to you all, ladies.'

He took a little bow, and carried on up the path away from them with dance-like steps.

'Dorothy?' Phyllis whispered, nudging her friend.

'What?'

'Who's that?'

'Denzel? He's one of the drivers at work. Looks good in a uniform, I can tell you.'

Phyllis chewed her lip. 'You're not going to go for a drink with him, are you?'

Dorothy stared at her. 'Why ever not?'

Phyllis looked at Peggy and Nancy for support. 'Well, he's . . . you know, he's . . .'

'He's what? A cracker? A gentleman?'

'No, he's . . . I mean, what would your mum say?' She leant closer. 'You going out with a black man?' she whispered.

Dorothy knew exactly what her mum would say: me next, that was what. 'You're pathetic, Phyllis. You know that? You sound just like your mum.'

'Well, at least my mum—'

'Phyllis doesn't mean any harm. Do you, Phyl?' Nancy said pointedly. She could see that things would escalate if they weren't careful. More and more friends and families had fallen out over the last few years, as some struggled to accept the changes to the city they'd been born into, and others relished the new cultures that gave fresh life to the tired post-war London streets.

Phyllis just shrugged and began making a little pile of grass on the blanket.

'Anyway, we were talking about Nancy, weren't we?' Peggy said, folding the muslin cloth and pressing it against her lap.

Dorothy lit herself another cigarette and blew the smoke towards Phyllis, who batted it sulkily away. 'You're right, Peg.' She flicked Nancy's leg. 'What are we going to do with you, girl? We need to find you a job. What about the knicker place again?'

Nancy laughed. 'I don't think so. Probably burnt my brassieres there. Anyway, it's a bit close to home.' She noticed Peggy watching her anxiously. 'Whatever I do, I think it needs to be away from here.'

'Over the river again?' said Phyllis, who found even the concept of Peckham bewildering.

'No,' Nancy said. 'I think it's best if I get right away.'

'Out of London?' Phyllis's jaw nearly hit the plaid blanket.

'Phyllis, they've just sent a man around the moon. I think I can manage life outside London for a while.'

'Peggy, you can't let her go!'

Peggy appeared not to be listening to the conversation, however, and was completely absorbed in jigging the pram back and forth.

'There's nothing for me here – apart from all of you, obviously,' Nancy added quickly, seeing Phyllis's face fall. 'You can't give me a job and a new life, though, can you? I need a change of scene.'

'I agree, doll.' Dorothy lit a cigarette from the packet of Pall Malls lying next to her, and drew hard on it until it glowed and crackled, then tipped her head back and let out a long plume of smoke that disappeared into the branches above them. She watched Peggy get up and pull the baby from the pram, Nancy's eyes glued to them both. 'The further the better,' she said quietly.

9

Nancy pushed the magazine across the kitchen table. 'What about this one?'

Peggy finished scratching at a patch of dried Farley's Rusk on her skirt, then turned the magazine around and looked at the advert Nancy was pointing to.

'"Live-in housekeeper, Scottish estate",' she read, peering over her winged horn-rimmed glasses. 'You'd spend your whole time hanging venison and gutting fish.' She shuddered. 'And it'd be freezing cold ten months of the year. You hate cold weather.'

'Hmm, I suppose so. It's a good long way away, though,' Nancy said, flicking to the next page.

Peggy noticed that her sister's fingernails had been filed, and shone with a coat of clear varnish. This was a good sign, even if it made her own hands, dried and reddened by the chemicals in the nappy bucket, look like she had more than just a five-year lead on Nancy. 'You don't have to go to Scotland, you know.'

'At least no one would stare at me there, and I wouldn't have to—'

'Here,' said Peggy brightly, looking at the magazine. 'What about this one? "Companion required for elderly gentlewoman, Home Counties." That sounds all right. Bet she's no bother, and she might leave everything to you in her will.'

Nancy snorted. 'Bet she's a cantankerous, incontinent old crow who's already made her will out to the cats' home. Thanks, Peg, but it's not really me.'

'What is this magazine anyway?' said Peggy, turning it over. '*The Lady*? Never heard of it. Where did you get it?'

'Phyllis, of course. Her mum buys it to look for jobs for her. They paid all that money for her to do a fancy secretarial course, and she just wants to work for old Mr Harris at the timber yard up the road.'

They both laughed. Poor Phyllis: she was so out of synch with her mother's aspirations. Never had anyone been quite so happy to live out her entire life within ten streets of where she'd been born.

Nancy took the magazine back. 'Hey, this sounds interesting.'

Peggy picked up her mug of tea and held it in both hands. 'Go on.'

'You sure you've got time, Peg? I don't want to keep you from getting Donald his tea or anything.' With Mum and Dad out at the matinee, she'd lost track of time. Stanley had been looking forward to that new film about the Arabs – said it would remind him of his days in the Desert Rats. Beryl hadn't been keen, but went along to keep him company, even though Nancy had caught her staring at a feature about Peter O'Toole in her magazine and suspected she had her own interest in seeing the film.

'You're fine. He's got bread and jam to keep him going, and Maddie's been fed. I think he quite likes having her to himself sometimes. Until her nappy needs changing, that is.' Peggy laughed, then took a big swig of the weak tea, a throwback to the ration-book years. 'Sorry. Go on, Nance.'

Nancy lifted the magazine up and read aloud. '"Assistant required for family on two-month European summer tour. Daughter aged seventeen. No experience required. Start June." What do you think?'

'Europe? Well, I suppose it could be exciting.'

Nancy saw her biting her lip. 'What? You don't seem keen.'

'It's just . . . do you really want to be looking after children all summer?'

'There's only one, and she's almost grown up. She's only eight years younger than me.'

'I suppose so.' Peggy looked less than convinced.

'June,' Nancy said thoughtfully. 'That's only a few weeks away.' She looked at the advert again. 'There's a PO box number here to write to. I think I'm going to apply, Peg. It says I don't need experience, so there's no reason why I shouldn't get it.'

'Of course you'll get it. They'll love you. Everyone does.' Peggy looked at her sister: even wearing an old sleeveless navy shift dress she'd made a couple of years ago, and with her blonde hair scraped into a ponytail, Nancy still looked a million dollars. It was like a bird of paradise had landed in their little nest of sparrows, with her big blue eyes and creamy skin and the long legs that were made for dancing rather than fetching coal from the back yard. Peggy couldn't bear the thought of life without Nancy to light it up, but they couldn't keep going like this, and Nancy deserved to get out and enjoy life again, even though Dad would have kept his little girl locked away from the big bad world for as long as he could, given the choice.

'Well, in that case, I have to. It might be fun, and you know I've always wanted to travel.'

'You should do it, sis. Onwards and sideways?'

The two sisters clinked the old sludge-coloured Hornsea mugs together.

'Onwards and sideways. Now where does Dad keep the writing paper?'

Nancy smelled as though she'd been at a Red Lion lock-in all night. The bus had been packed with commuters chain-smoking their way to their desks and shop counters, and she'd had no choice but to let the smoke settle in her hair and creep into the fibres of her linen suit. Her party dresses had been given away in a wardrobe purge exercised by Beryl in her absence, but her simple pale blue shift dress and match-ing jacket with three-quarter-length sleeves had survived, and was a safe bet for an interview. Peggy always said she looked like a blonde Jackie Kennedy in it, although maybe she was overdressed for today: they wanted a dogsbody, she suspected, not a First Lady, and so as she turned the corner, she quickly unclipped the diamanté flower pin on her lapel and tucked it in her pocket.

Carlton Row was a pretty crescent of three-storey houses hidden away behind its taller, slightly more fashionable neigh-bours, its wide pavements studded with dainty trees whose blossom was just giving way to a bloom of pea-green foliage. Nancy was sure she had visited this corner of Kensington in her short-lived former life: maybe for a party, or a stop-off to collect a friend. She couldn't remember – it was a lifetime ago, a tiny little lifetime.

She worked her way along the street, past identical ivory stucco frontages, until she found the Cavendishes' house. Number 20 was remarkable for the damp autumnal debris still collected around its iron-railed steps, and the dust-filmed windows that remained in night mode, their curtains closed to the world. Whereas the other mirror-like black doors in Carlton Row looked as though they had been sprayed in the Rolls-Royce paint shop, the sun-bleached portal to number 20 had a bad case of dermatitis, and Nancy tapped uncertainly with the dull brass door knocker. She was almost relieved when there was no response: maybe she had misread the address. This didn't look like the sort of household that would employ anyone. She pulled the letter out of her handbag, and was checking the instructions for the seventeenth time when the door opened and a gruff 'Yes?' made her look up in surprise.

A tall man stood leaning in the doorway, a pipe hanging from his lips and arms folded across his open-necked shirt as he squinted at her in the bright spring sunshine. His sandy-blond hair fell untamed over his forehead, and she couldn't help but notice the paint splashed across his bare forearms and ingrained around his fingernails.

'I'm sorry,' she said, 'I must have the wrong address.' Clearly the family who lived here had vacated while the decorators took over. 'I'm supposed to be at an interview.'

'Let me see that,' he said, taking the letter from her and pulling a pair of tortoiseshell glasses from his shirt pocket.

Now worried that she was late for her appointment, she was torn between tackling this man, whose accent certainly wasn't that of a decorator and who looked as though he had slept in his clothes, and risking missing her interview entirely.

He handed the letter back to her, then turned his head indoors and shouted along the dark hallway. 'Caro, for you.' He stood back and held the door open. 'You'd better come in. Looks like my wife's expecting you.'

It wasn't too late to walk back down the steps, to claim a sudden illness, a sick relative, a train to catch, but what was the point? If she didn't go through with this, she would only have to find something else. The worst that could happen would be that the job didn't suit her; the best, that it surprised her. She took a deep breath and stepped through the doorway.

He ushered her into a dark sitting room, gesturing for her to make herself at home. Nancy waited until she heard his footsteps pad back upstairs, then pulled the curtains open, the stream of dusty light revealing a high-ceilinged room packed with shabby furniture that had worked hard through generations of use, its walls crammed with oil paintings of all sizes and all centuries, dark, sombre portraits sitting beside crazily coloured landscapes and brutal, unfathomable abstracts. Where the Moon family would have been ashamed at the worn arms of the overstuffed sofa and the bare patches on the Oriental rugs, here their patina was worn with a quiet sense of ancestry.

Nancy picked up a black and white photograph, its tarnished silver frame leaving a slender rectangular imprint in the dust on the mahogany side table. Half a dozen chiselled faces peered back at her, their champagne glasses forever filled, the white bow ties and perfect teeth of the gentlemen as pristine and gleaming as the diamonds and long white gloves that adorned their partners. Judging by the mirrored walls and chandeliers, this was some party, she thought as she tried to make out the details of the ladies' dresses.

'Savoy. Ten years ago.'

She quickly put the picture down and turned around. 'I'm sorry,' she said. 'I didn't mean to be nosy.'

The woman closed the door behind her and stood looking at Nancy, her hands on slim hips that were accentuated by her black cigarette trousers and oversized cashmere sweater. She picked up a silver cigarette case off the coffee table and pulled one out, offering them to Nancy. She shrugged as Nancy shook her head. 'Suit yourself.'

Nancy took her hostess's lead and sat in one of the armchairs.

'I believe you just had the pleasure of meeting my husband.' She nodded towards the photo. 'Of course he looks a little different in a DJ. And I suppose we've all changed since then.'

Nancy couldn't imagine the perfect complexion sitting opposite her ever betraying a single year's ageing, and realised she would be hard pressed to say how old her hostess was – anything between twenty-five and forty-five could be true.

'Ah yes. I'm afraid I wasn't quite sure when I arrived here . . .' What? Whether your husband was a workman? Whether the house had been taken over by squatters? Nancy chose to let her sentence tail off.

'You have to excuse him. He's an artist – doesn't quite do the social niceties thing, you know?' the woman said, her clipped accent suddenly betraying a transatlantic hint that Nancy had detected but struggled to place.

'Of course,' Nancy replied, although she didn't know at all. She'd never met an artist, and had no idea what was normal and what was just rudeness.

'Anyway, why don't we start again? I'm Caro.' The woman smiled, and held out a smooth, slim bejewelled hand straight out of an Avon hand-cream advert.

'Nancy,' she said, shaking the proffered hand.

Caro sat back and ran her hand over her helmet of dark, shiny hair, her feet tucked beneath her on the lumpy sofa. 'You must excuse us. We're between help at the moment.'

'Which is why I'm here?'

'Which is why you're here.' She leant forward and lit her cigarette with the large mother-of-pearl lighter that acted as paperweight to a pile of bills and letters. 'You see, Nancy, we have a big trip coming up. A very important one for Peter. He'll be meeting lots of people who might want to buy his paintings, or want to commission one from him. Obviously we want to bring our daughter, but Peter must be allowed to get on with his work. We need someone who can keep her busy but who can fit in with the family and with our friends overseas. She might have to take Pamela to the beach one morning, then accompany us to a cocktail party later the same day. Do you understand?'

'Absolutely. You need someone versatile.'

Caro pointed at her and narrowed her eyes. 'Exactly.' She glanced appraisingly at Nancy's suit. 'And someone who won't look out of place at the right parties. I can already see you fit the bill in that respect.'

So the blue suit had been a good choice after all.

Caro pulled from her pocket the letter Nancy had written

only a few days earlier, and studied it briefly before looking up at her. 'And you seem to have ironed the south London from your voice. Good girl. I do think a regional accent lets one down.'

Nancy wasn't sure what to say, but suspected that a lot of work had gone into the anglicisation of Caro's own vowels.

'I seem to remember from your letter that you've worked before – Belgrave's, wasn't it?'

'That's right.'

'And how is darling Jacques?'

Nancy couldn't imagine her volatile firework of a former boss being anything approaching a darling, but she smiled and said, 'I believe he is well.'

'Excellent. I've always thought how much fun it must be to work with one's hands.'

Nancy had a feeling that Caro had never done a day's work in her life, but then she surprised her by reaching for a magazine at the far end of the sofa. 'That's what I do,' she said, opening the old copy of *Vogue* at a dog-eared page.

Nancy looked at the simple black and white photograph of a gamine model wearing a Givenchy bridal gown. 'It's you,' she said.

'Few years ago now. Of course I don't work much these days.' Nancy suspected that Caro's indifferent shrug belied a bitter battle to hold her own amongst the incredibly young models who were everywhere these days. 'Life is so busy.'

'I imagine being a parent takes up a lot of your time,' Nancy said, then, seeing Caro frown, continued in her best business-like voice, 'So tell me more about the trip.'

Caro took a long drag on her cigarette and blew the smoke

slowly out, so that it created a veil between her and Nancy as it caught in the dusty beam of light streaming through the dirty window. 'We'll be visiting Paris, the South of France and Italy, and staying with friends of the family as we go along. A friend of Peter's will be with us for some of the time – he has all sorts of connections over there, and they're such good chums, those two.'

'And your daughter? May I meet her this morning?'

'Pamela? God, no. She's away at school until next month.' Caro laughed, but seeing Nancy's surprise, she went on, 'Ignore me – people find me a little too direct sometimes. It's the brash American in me, I guess.'

'I find you just fine, really. So tell me about her. Your daughter.'

'Pamela's sixteen. Or is it seventeen? It keeps changing – I can't keep up. She's not actually my daughter, I should add.'

'Oh.'

'She's my stepdaughter. I married Peter when Pamela was two years old. Her mother had passed away, and the poor little mite was being brought up by her father's old nanny in the stately pile. Miracle the child didn't die of consumption in that mouldy old place.'

'How awful. But lovely that he met you,' Nancy added.

Caro smiled. 'Pamela's a little quiet, like her father, I guess. Feisty like her grandmother – she was a suffragette, you know? She has yet to bloom, but we'll make something of her, I imagine. She's probably not much younger than you. You might even become friends.'

'Oh. You make it sound like I've got the job.'

'I do rather, don't I? The thing is, Nancy, I know instantly whether I like someone or not, and I have a feeling you and I will get on famously.'

As long as I know my place and don't try to compete with you, Nancy thought wryly.

'Well, do you want it?'

Nancy heard her father in her ear, warning her to make sure she wasn't rushing into anything. 'Of course, it would be good to know the terms before I agree to anything,' she said, wondering whether this sophisticated creature would take offence at such vulgar behaviour.

'Fair enough. We will travel out ahead of you with Pamela, and you'll meet us in Paris. Your train will be booked and your tickets delivered to you – you just have to turn up at Water-loo on the right day, and Peter will meet you at the station in Paris. I'd suggest packing at least three evening dresses, and you might want to bring a swimsuit or two for the South of France. Unless you're prudish about such things?'

Nancy shook her head vigorously – she knew from Caro's impish expression that she was being tested. She'd have to lay off the lardy cake for the next few weeks, but her figure was already pretty much ready for the swimsuit she instantly brought to mind.

'Splendid. You'll probably also have to pick up a few clothes for me when we're in Paris. I've worked with a lot of the big labels over there, and they usually keep a few pieces back for me. Apart from that, what do you need to know? Your food and board is covered. You eat with us, you live with us, you're like family. Except you get paid five pounds a week.'

It didn't seem a lot compared with what she had been

earning at Belgrave's, but she'd have no expenses, no rent, no food to pay for. She would be mad to say no.

Caro stubbed the cigarette out in the marble ashtray and looked up at her. 'So what's it to be?'

Nancy smiled. 'It's to be a yes.'

'In that case, welcome to the family, Nancy Moon.'

10

'Seamus?'

Flo flung her coat on the hall stand and wandered into the kitchen, dropping her bag on the table. No sign of culinary activity, thank goodness, although everything was strangely tidy and she was relieved that for once she didn't have to spend her first twenty minutes at home clearing up the detritus of Seamus's prandial day. There wasn't so much as a dirty mug lying around.

'Seamus?' she called again, leaning on the banister and watching for signs of movement upstairs.

He was probably still at work, with so much to finish up before he left next week. Marking to do, a desk to clear, goodbyes to say . . . She chastised herself – what was the point of punishing him now? He was going. Bye bye, ten years of marriage.

It was a relief to have the house to herself. Their little slice of Willow Terrace had been a pressure cooker for the last few months, and now that Seamus had finally given up all hope of reconciliation, and had begun pointedly and noisily packing for his new life in the States, the lid was well and truly off.

She put the kettle on and went upstairs to run a bath. She was covered in a film of London dirt, and aching from the hour and a half crouched in a noisy cubic metre of between-carriage hell. She tipped liquid jasmine into the frothing stream of hot water, then remembered the box of ridiculously expensive essential oils Seamus had bought her as a last-minute Victoria station I-didn't-forget-your-birthday-after-all present. She opened the bathroom cabinet to look for it, and was surprised to see the sticky rings where Seamus's rarely used bottles of aftershave and shaving foam usually stood, her own collection of curl-control and age-bashing creams huddled tightly at the opposite side of the half-empty cupboard, as if cowering from an invisible enemy. A quick search found her toothbrush dangling alone in its holder, and a lack of reading matter within arm's reach of the toilet.

She turned the tap off and went to the bedroom. The wardrobe yawned widely at her, its doors gaping open, disgorged of shabby jackets and ill-advised flowery shirts. Her usually crushed collection of prints and textures had breathed out to fill the space. Although a few stray socks had escaped and lay abandoned on the floor, the drawers that had held Seamus's most intimate clothing were empty, his bedside table drawer cleared of coins and contraband emergency tobacco and papers. All that remained of his huge presence was the copy of *Ulysses*.

A folded note sat propped on her pillow, Seamus's unmistakable black, inky scrawl forming the letters of her name.

Flossie, I think it's best I just go. This has been the longest, most horrible goodbye ever, and I need to get out before my heart breaks completely.

I hope you find something or someone who will make you happy. I just wish it could have been me.

I'll always love you, curly girl.
Seamus x

Grief overwhelmed her like a steam train as she hugged the note tightly to her chest, hot, stinging tears streaming down her cheeks and her neck, soaking her collar. She heard herself howl, an animal noise that she had never even known was in her repertory, one that had been waiting to escape her stoically pursed lips for months.

She had no idea how long she lay curled on the bed, Seamus's pillow pressed into her belly, but eventually her body tired and her breathing settled and she became aware of the world around her: the birds singing their dusk songs, cars edging into spaces and neighbourly banter tossed from one side of the street to the other. Everything was carrying on as normal, as though the end of Flo's world were just one ephemeral episode in the complex soap opera of life. And somehow she too would have to find a way to carry on as normal, once she had worked out what her new normal would be.

A scraping, guttural sound made her sit up, in time to see the cat swagger through the bedroom door, its toothless mouth open as it yowled at her, offering her the opportunity to make a start by feeding it.

'Great,' she said. 'I've still got you. Thanks, Seamus.'

As the days lengthened and spring began to have aspirations towards summer, Flo found herself in a limbo, her world outside growing smaller, until it was limited to work or supermarket. She refused invitations from friends to go to the pub or the cinema, and only saw Jem and Clare because they stayed over a couple of times to escape the worst of the building work that was ravaging their house. Telephone conversations with Dorothy and Phyllis were kept as short as possible, as she evaded their concern with flippant comments about being fine, nice to have a bit of space, blah blah blah. They were no more convinced than Flo herself, however, and continued to threaten visits if she needed help.

She found herself residing almost exclusively on the sofa, taking a perverse pleasure in the decor of dropped crisp packets, their contents like miniature crazy paving under her bare feet, brown apple cores bleeding onto the glass coffee table, and smeared spoons glued to empty ice-cream cartons. How could she have spent so many years fussing around the little house that was now no more than a brick box full of fabric and wood and carpets?

Did she miss Seamus? Maybe, but her martyred solitude suited her for now, and while she missed his suffocating hugs, and how he made her smile with the slightest inclination of one rascally eyebrow, she didn't miss what they had become. Even the company of the cat was preferable to the glacial void that neither of them had the stomach to attempt to cross any longer.

Two or three weeks into her self-imposed exile, she was ensconced in her cushioned nest in the sitting room, wrapped in an old kimono and scraping the last of a Waitrose cauliflower cheese out of its microwave container in front of the episodes of *The Crown* she had promised herself. It had been a beautiful evening when she'd come home from work, and she'd gone around the house opening windows, allowing the breeze to carry birdsong through the little house, and awakening a primal instinct in the cat, who paced the windowsills looking for prey. In an attempt to drown out the repeated banging of a door upstairs, Flo turned the television up, but still it seeped through the sumptuous pomp of the soundtrack.

With a loud sigh, she made her way upstairs and along the landing, past her bedroom and the closed door next to it, which she had successfully managed to avoid opening for months now. Directly in front of her, the culprit tapped intermittently against its frame, and Flo went to close it. The small bedroom at the end, overlooking their handkerchief garden, was her refuge, a perfectly organised workspace where she lost herself in the reels of cotton arranged in rainbow rows of colour on a spindled display board on the wall, in the neatly ordered shelves of button boxes, bobbins and bias binding.

The room smelt fusty, so she opened the window, setting the curtains trembling and disturbing the magazines and cuttings that sat on her dusty work table. She picked up one of the neatly cut-out squares of quilting fabric that were laid out like a jigsaw on the table ready to be pinned, all in pretty shades of primrose. A tiny bow-tied teddy smiled out at her, and she stared back at it for a moment before scooping up the pieces into a messy heap and stuffing them into one of her drawers of scrap fabric.

She looked around the room. It was months since she had last been in here properly, and a cushion cover sat trapped within the teeth of the sewing machine, as though a three-minute warning had gone off halfway through the seam. Despite herself, she began to feel the satisfying calm that always filled her when she worked in here, where she could spend hours that felt like minutes, and where her old dress-making dummy could go from naked to best-turned-out over a weekend.

Her sewing room would have pleased any professional, with its racks of little drawers, and shelves loaded with folded colour-coded lengths of fabric that she had collected over the years. Some had been sifted from the boxes of roll ends in Liberty, some were left over from long-finished projects, but many were pieces of vintage fabric she had been given or had found at car-boot sales and markets. Whereas she battled a natural chaos in much of her life, in this room there was a quiet industry, a respect for her craft that had been drummed into her as a student.

She took the pile of magazines in her arms and straightened them, ready to put them back in the bookcase where they lived, but as she turned, she stubbed her bare toe hard. She knew every corner of this room, so was surprised and irritated to be caught out by the box tucked next to the work table.

She crouched down. Of course. Nancy's box. Ever since she'd placed it there after Peggy's funeral, she'd meant to look at the patterns again, but she'd been in a complete fug since Seamus left, swept along on her own tsunami of misery, unable to concentrate on anything, driving Jem mad at work and sliding from day to day in an insomniac blur that she couldn't shake off. It was almost as bad as that dreadful time all those months ago, except now she had lost Seamus too. She looked at the box and couldn't believe that something that had excited her so much, the thrill of discovering the mysterious Nancy, had been so totally eclipsed by her grief. Finally distracted, she felt the weeks of misery, the dark cloud of Seamus's departure, begin to dissolve a little, leaving a little Seamus-free space in her mind.

It seemed like months, not weeks, since she'd looked at the patterns, and it was as though she were opening the box for the first time as she lifted off the lid and pulled out the first one, the thrill at seeing them no less than it had been first time around. She stood up and laid the packet on the work table, pulling out the neatly cut-out pieces of tissue paper and unfolding them one by one, then taking the photograph of Nancy and her friends and propping it up at the back of the table.

As she smoothed each piece, she realised they were all marked with pencil jottings – a dart made larger here, seam allowance taken in there – so that the dress must have been a perfect fit. With her finger she followed the dotted cutting lines on the side front bodice panel, and although she and Nancy were both a size 10, she suspected that Nancy's waist was probably smaller than her own. Too many times she had tried on a vintage dress in her own size only to find that there was a huge difference in the proportions of women fifty years apart – poor nutrition, Jem claimed, although Flo wasn't entirely sure which end of the time frame she was talking about.

The packet told her that the dress required nearly five yards of cotton fabric, half a yard of interfacing, a 22" zip and a hook and eye. The last few she knew she had somewhere, and she cast her eye over the shelves of fabric, holding the little forget-me-not swatch between her thumb and forefinger and comparing it to her own collection. Something caught her eye. It wasn't exactly the same, but it was a beautiful vintage piece with stylised lilac flowers on a bed of lime-green leaves, and was probably around the same age as the pattern. She pulled the bundle out and threw it open, a waterfall of blossom cascading from her hands and across the floor, then uncoiled her tape measure and held it along the edge of the fabric, length by length, until she reached the end. Four metres eighty. Perfect. It seemed a lot, but looking at the drawing of the dress on the packet front, the pattern cutters had not stinted on the fullness of the skirt. She stretched the fabric across the long table, smoothing any creases with the palms of her hands, and began placing the pieces of tissue across it, along the fold where required, checking that the pattern always ran in the right direction.

It was a long time since she had felt the buzz she always got when ironing the sharp fold lines out of pattern pieces, gently pushing pins through paper and fabric, and hearing the rasp of her shears cutting through the entire layer cake. Her heart beat a little faster, even though she knew she had checked and double-checked that each piece was correctly positioned. She allowed herself a little more on the bodice seams, widening each one slightly to fit her modern figure, and knowing that it would be easy to play with the gathering on the skirt when it came to fitting the two halves of the dress together.

She threaded a lilac reel onto the machine, and one by one the pinned parts of the dress came together, Flo opening out each seam and ironing it flat before moving on to the next. Her dummy was set to her exact measurements, so it was easy to pin and correct each pairing before committing it to thread. It wasn't long before the entire bodice was completed, the darts perfectly positioned and the shoulder seams sitting flat on the dummy. She gently eased the short capped sleeves into place, pinning and then carefully tacking each joining seam before machining them.

The skirt was easy to put together in comparison: six flared panels with long side seams that the machine stormed through with ease, until she had a wide tube that she gathered at one end with two matching rows of neat running stitch, evening out the tiny pleats as she went along.

She was oblivious to the hungry mewling of the cat, barely remembered switching on the lights in her workroom, ignored the rumbling of her stomach as the long-finished ready meal was digested and her body called for another feed. She remembered to pull the curtains closed only because the reflection of her work lamp in the darkened windows distracted her from the task in hand.

By the time she had joined the bodice and skirt together and worked her way around the bottom of the skirt with a neat hemming stitch, the church clock at the end of the road was chiming the early hours. It was the work of twenty minutes to secure the zip in place and stitch the hook and eye that would prevent it coming undone.

She slipped her kimono off and stepped into the dress, pulling it up carefully in case any pins had been left in the seams and slowly zipping it up. It was a perfect fit: snug against her torso but with enough room to breathe and to move around, the waistband positioned exactly an inch above her belly button and giving way to a voluminous skirt that swished as she turned her hips. She glanced at the photograph of Nancy wearing the original dress. Maybe it was the late hour, but she felt her great-aunt was smiling directly at her, rather than at the anonymous photographer.

She walked over to the floor-length mirror. There, despite the straggly hair and lack of supporting underwear, was the girl in the photograph. With a little imagination, a good hairbrush and a neat Doris Day bob, it could have been Nancy standing in the little back room of 12 Willow Terrace.

'You look amazing.'

'Really?'

'Sure. You say you ran that up last night?' Jem shook her head. 'I don't understand how you can go from couch potato to dynamo just like that.'

Flo swung the skirt around, then grabbed a thick belt from a basket next to the counter and fastened it around herself. 'Hmm, too much?'

'Perfect.' Jem smiled. 'You've got colour in your cheeks and fire in your belly at last, babe. Never thought I'd see the day. So this is one of the famous dresses, then?'

'The first one. London to Paris. Nineteen sixty-two.'

'Sixty-two? Good year. Everything about to change, but Grace Kelly elegance was still key. Year that Marilyn died and the Beatles were born, I think.'

'The year that Nancy Moon went travelling.' Flo showed Jem the photo from the station.

'She looks so like you. I can see your gran, too. Beautiful.' She returned the picture to Flo. 'And she never came back?'

'Not as far as anyone knows.'

'Wow. Nor did the dresses, I suppose?'

'Trust you to think business when I'm telling you my family history.'

Jemima shrugged and held out the packet of biscuits. 'Can't

blame me,' she said, taking one herself and pulling it open to reveal the cream inside, then cramming both halves into her mouth at once. 'What happened to her, anyway?'

Flo slipped on the pair of cream shoes that no one else had yet had the discourtesy to buy, and wondered whether she should treat herself. They went so well with the dress. 'I'm not sure. I don't think Dorothy or Phyllis really knows either. Once she got to the end of that summer tour, it's a complete dead end.'

'So who was it she worked for?'

'Dorothy couldn't remember the name. All I know is that he was a society artist, married to an ex-model, and Nancy was there to keep their daughter company.'

'Is that all you've got?' Jemima frowned. 'There were lots of that set down in the South of France after the war. The Mitfords, the Churchills, then of course the Hollywood crowd. There are loads of books about it – maybe you'll be able to find something out.'

It would certainly make a bit of a project, Flo supposed.

Jem picked up the pattern packet that Flo had brought to show her. 'This would look amazing on you too,' she said, studying the drawing of the leggy girl in a knee-length sun-dress.

She was right. If Flo had that dress, she would live in it.

'What's this?' Jem said, pulling out the postcard tucked inside.

'There's one of those in every packet.' Flo leant across and looked at the picture, which showed a sunny St Mark's Square.

Jem looked up at her. 'That's it. You have to make this dress, and you have to wear it in Venice.'

Flo laughed. 'That's mad. What would I do in Venice?'

'I dunno. Look for Nancy? Find out who she worked for?'

'Don't be daft.'

'I'm not.' Jemima smiled at her. 'Listen, I don't want to get rid of you or anything, but seriously, you should get away. You need a break. This is perfect.'

'But what about my house? That bloody cat?'

'Clare and I can house-sit. It's going to take a month to get the asbestos out at our place, and we've got to move out while they do it, so that would be perfect.'

Flo wondered how the cat would cope with two teenagers sharing its home. Maybe they'd scare it off. The plan looked better and better.

'Come on. It's time to do something new. Get your confidence back.'

'But what about money?'

Jem snorted. 'If I know your gran, she'll have made sure there's something put aside for you.'

Flo didn't know what to say. She'd left Peggy's affairs in the hands of her solicitor, and had thought no more about it, but in all probability there would be a little windfall coming her way, and she had a few savings to keep her going until then.

'It's time to be more Nancy. Take a step outside this stupid town and see a bit of the world.' Jem stopped suddenly. 'Oh my God, that's it,' she said, staring Flo straight in the eyes.

'What's what?'

'The dresses, the tour, Nancy . . . You should recreate it. Start from the beginning, and work your way through.'

'Wearing this dress?' Flo said, looking down at the lilac blossoms.

'Oh no,' said Jemima, her face breaking into a wide beam, so that Flo could see the lipstick stain on her front teeth. 'Wearing *all* those outfits. You, Flo, are going to make them all, and you're going to take them everywhere Nancy took them.'

'What? On my own?'

'On your own.' She put her hands up as she saw Flo about to protest. 'I know, but you'll get used to it – it's good to travel alone sometimes.'

'For you maybe . . .'

'I know it's a huge step, babe, but what's the worst that could happen? You get homesick and jump on the next Ryanair to Stansted?'

'Maybe . . .' Flo felt her heart flutter, whether from nerves or excitement, she didn't know. This was a crazy-stupid idea. She'd never been anywhere without Seamus or her mother. She was not a natural traveller, despite, if not because of, the years on the road as a child.

'Didn't you say the first one was Paris? I've got a mate there. I'll put you in touch – it'll be someone to have a drink with. An ex of my sister Mel's, but don't hold that against him.'

Flo laughed. Back in her heyday, the then glamorous Melanie had got through quite a few hapless hopefuls before surprising everyone and settling for building-society Derek and post-baby jogging trousers. 'I think I like him already!'

'Actually, he was the one she stood up at the altar. I mean, literally at the altar. Remember that?'

'Oh God, yes. Poor guy.' Flo did remember now: it had been awful. Mel had simply changed her mind and disappeared with some ex who had shown up a week earlier.

Jem shook her head. 'Such a shame. Ben's a nice guy; all he ever wanted was to get married – well, egged on by his bloody mother. Think he's changed his mind now, though.'

'Didn't he ever meet anyone else?' Flo asked.

Jem looked up at the ceiling. 'Hmm, let me see. Well, there was the nutter who kept a wedding dress under the bed, just in case . . . the one he met at a karaoke night who ended up on Z Factor or something and dumped him for a soap star—'

Flo winced. 'OK, I get it. I promise to be nice if I meet him.'

'Just don't let his mother know you're having a drink with him, or she'll buy a bloody hat.'

Flo laughed. 'Don't worry – he'd be safe with me. Last thing I need right now is an entanglement. And anyway, I haven't said I'll go anywhere yet.'

'Aw, come on,' Jem said. 'It would be amazing to take those clothes back in time, wouldn't it? Paris, South of France . . .'

'What, like a sort of Nancy pilgrimage?' Flo said, as her mind worked itself around the idea of following in her great-aunt's footsteps.

'Exactly like a Nancy pilgrimage.' Jem put her hands on Flo's shoulders and stood face to face with her, her red lips widened into a huge grin. 'Go for it, my friend, and follow Nancy Moon's Grand Tour.'

Part Three

PARIS

11

McCall's 6673: Misses' day dress

Nancy let herself be swept along the platform, wondering at the similarity between two stations a stretch of water and three hundred miles apart, except there was no Peggy or Dorothy to meet her here. The vast arc of glass and steel was the same, the shrieking guards' whistles identical, people just as anxious to reach their destinations with as little human interaction as possible, and the magazine covers stacked up in newspaper booths showed the same faces: Marilyn, Jackie, Brigitte. The differences were in the details: the newspaper headlines shouted the same news, but in a different language; the skirts were a little tighter and shorter, the hair a little smoother, the heels a little higher, the hats a little larger; the booming tannoy announcements were still indecipherable, but with different inflections, and the station staff's uniforms were sharper, shinier, more military.

She was suddenly self-conscious in her home-made dress, its blue and white forget-me-nots like wallpaper against the sea of black and grey worn by everyone around her: black fitted suits, black shoes, huge black handbags draped over wrists clad in long black gloves, black bucket hats, and every woman hidden behind impenetrable black sunglasses. It was as though the sunny Paris day trying to break through the glass ceiling had been consumed by the most glamorous funeral ever seen. Her own dress looked like a bridal bouquet that had been ordered instead of a wreath.

She stopped outside a little concourse café, the smell of roasting beans awakening a craving for a cup of what Beryl called 'that stinking foreign muck'. She hesitated at the doorway, but one of the line of men drinking tiny cups of coffee and brandy shots at the long steel bar turned and spotted her, winking as he shouted a gruff greeting. She had learnt a little French over the last few weeks, but suspected that his vocabulary was rather different to that taught at the night school on Wandsworth High Street.

Flustered, she bent down to pick up her case again, and walked slowly onwards, trying to work out where the main exit was. She nearly lost her balance as a long-legged young man in a flapping hip-length mac and thick-rimmed glasses knocked into her, muttering angrily and waving his hands at her.

How hard could this be? All she had to do was find her way outside and get into the car that was waiting for her. She brushed a hand over her hair and straightened the creases in her skirt, then lifted her chin and followed the stream of people, who all seemed to know where they were going.

She could do this. She had no choice: there was no place for her at home any more and nowhere else to go.

Unbidden, an image flashed through her mind of a picnic, a riverbank way out of London, and the fear and disappointment in his grey eyes as she had spoken the words she knew would change her life for ever.

She was jolted back to the present as a pigeon swooped past, missing her cheek by inches and ruffling her hair in its slipstream, and found herself standing still no more than a hundred yards from the train she had just left.

Outside, a string of cars looped in and out of the vast station concourse. Dazzled, she reached for her sunglasses and looked around at the scores of shiny black cars with cherry-red roofs and taxi signs that flickered on and off as people climbed in and out of them. There was no sign of the car she had been told to expect. Maybe she had the wrong day. But she couldn't have – her train journey had run seamlessly, and her cabin had definitely been waiting for her. Maybe the traffic was bad, maybe the car had broken down. Maybe they'd forgotten.

Her confidence drained away, and the image she had carefully crafted of Nancy the intrepid traveller melted into a puddle not dissimilar to that left on the pavement behind her by the large poodle being yanked along by its owner.

She waited, and waited. She sat on her case and crossed her legs in what she hoped looked like a deliberate I-want-to-be-sitting-here-actually pose. She took the letter of confirmation from Caro out of her bag and read it for the thousandth time. There was no doubt about it: *Peter will meet you at the front of the station*. She had been nervous at the thought of a car journey alone with the gruff man who had opened the door to her back in Kensington, but now she would happily have driven from Land's End to John O'Groats with him if he would only appear.

Her slim leather-strapped watch told her that half an hour's wait had stretched into an hour already. Maybe no one was coming. Maybe she should get a cab. But she had no idea how much that would cost, and whether she had enough francs on her. And what if she didn't, and no one was there at the Marais address to pick up the bill for her? What if the whole thing was a mistake?

She thought of her friends at home, and how they would be wondering what sort of glamorous start to the day she was having. They wouldn't imagine her sitting on a suitcase being stared at by a dirty-faced tramp and shooing away the pigeons that threatened to soil her new shoes.

Suddenly she was overwhelmed with exhaustion and heat and anxiety and a desperate need to empty her bladder. Until a year ago, Nancy had always been the one in control, skipping her way through life and carrying others along in her wake. Where was the girl who had marched into Belgrave's and demanded a job? The girl who drank aperitifs at Claridge's and nightcaps at dawn? Who slept on Chelsea sofas and had men dangling from the tip of her pointy-toed shoe?

She took off her sunglasses and wiped a reluctant tear from her eye. A quick look in her compact mirror showed minimal damage, and she thanked her new Yardley mascara for its tenacity. She sponged a little powder across her nose and slicked some Rose Blush across her lips, then clicked the compact closed and dropped it in her handbag. Done. Nancy was back.

Now she had to decide on the best course of action. If she wasn't being collected, and she couldn't take a taxi, then she had no choice but to walk. She had a little Paris guidebook in her handbag, and the map allowed her to work out a route that surely couldn't take too long.

'Onward and sideways,' she said quietly to herself, pushing

her sunglasses back up her nose and levering herself off the suitcase.

By the time she had reached the far side of the concourse, sweat was prickling her back. Already her new shoes were pinching her feet, but on she continued, along the wide tree-lined road leading south from the station, her suitcase bumping along behind her as she passed people in earnest conversation around the little tables lining the pavements, while white-aproned waiters in bow ties and waistcoats slipped amongst the rattan chairs with trays delicately balanced on fingertips. She avoided the stares of the close-faced Algerians who watched her with curiosity as she in turn eyed their long embroidered robes fluttering around their legs, and kept away from the edge of the pavement, where cars drove terrifyingly close to her in the wrong direction.

Surely she must be nearly there. The road seemed to go on for ever, an interminable tunnel of tall balconied facades, a vortex for the hot city smells that rose from drains and doorways, broken only by the occasional sweet smell of roses crammed into tall buckets outside picture-book florists' shops.

She stopped at one of these olfactory oases to look back at a bunch of impossibly beautiful pink-green blooms, but felt her lower body continue on its path then stop with a painful jarring of her knee as her heel caught in a metal grille. The rest of her followed, and Nancy found herself rather too intimate all of a sudden with the hot, dirty Parisian pavement.

'Hey, miss. You OK?'

A long, shiny car had pulled up beside her, denuded of its roof, its engine thrumming quietly as the driver leant his tanned arm on the spotless powder-blue door and looked at the pile of girl and fabric and luggage splayed on the pavement, reflected perfectly in the mirrored sunglasses that hid his eyes from her.

'I'm fine,' she said, not fine at all. Nowhere near fine, in fact. Her heel had snapped clean away from the shoe, and the palms of her hands and her knees were embedded with grit and she dared not think what else.

'Don't look it, honey.'

Trust her to end up having her first conversation in Paris with an American. And a slightly smug-looking one at that. She stood up and brushed dirt off her skirt and her knees. 'Really, I'm fine.'

'English, huh?'

'Well guessed,' she said, wishing he'd just leave her to her humiliation in peace. Already the sight of his fresh-out-of-the-showroom car had stopped a few pedestrians in their tracks, and she was becoming the main protagonist in a drama she had no interest in being part of.

'Need a ride somewhere?'

'No, thanks.' She gathered her things and hobbled on, aware that he was slowly reversing his car to keep pace with her.

'Sure about that?' he laughed as she nearly tripped again.

She felt herself wavering. The only thing she was sure about was that there was no way she would make it to the Marais on one and a half shoes.

He jumped out of the car and took her case for her. 'Come on, honey. I won't bite. We'll have you there in no time, and then you'll never see me again,' he said, giving her a crinkly smile that she couldn't help but return.

She sighed as she let him drop the case onto the back seat of the car and open the passenger door for her. He seemed a decent sort, his clean, preppy look straight out of the Kennedy family Cape Cod holiday album, and he was probably not much younger than Dad, now that she saw him properly. She felt bad for being so rude. He was only trying to help, and all she'd done was dismiss him. She showed him the Cavendishes' address on her map, and he did a quick calculation, then swung the car around and headed south down the boulevard.

'So what's an American doing in Paris?'

He laughed. 'Nice one, lady.'

She wasn't sure what she'd said, but he was still smiling as he continued, 'I'm a musician.'

'Must be a good one to drive a car like this.'

'Oh, this isn't my car. It's just borrowed for a few days while I'm here.' He pulled a match out of a packet on the dashboard and began chewing on it.

'So what kind of musician are you?' she said, trying to see past the sunglasses in case she recognised him, but all she could make out was the reflection of the Paris streets mirrored in them.

'I guess you could say I'm a singer,' he said through closed teeth as he moved the matchstick around his mouth. He turned on the car radio as he wove through the traffic, instantly tapping his hand against the outside of the door in time to the music, and humming along to the bouncy tune in a pleasing voice.

She let the fresh, warm air brush her cheeks, and turned her head to watch a crocodile of small children being led by two teachers in smart navy suits and matching kitten-heeled shoes, the girls wearing adorable little straw hats and the boys culottes and floppy bow ties. Everywhere people seemed to be smiling and exchanging waves, whether from a bicycle or from behind one of the many flower or newspaper kiosks dotted along the streets. As she watched a young couple embracing in the doorway of a cinema, she reflected that the city was living up to its reputation already.

'First time in Paris?' her rescuer said, spinning the huge leather-covered steering wheel with one hand as he took a sharp right turn.

'Can you tell?' She knew she must look like a child paying its first visit to a sweet shop, craning her neck every time they passed a famous landmark.

'Hey, listen, kid,' he said. 'Tell me to get lost if you like, but how's about I show you my favourite spot in this city? It's only a few minutes from here, and I kinda get the feeling you'd like it.'

She'd already got into a strange man's car, so there was no longer any point in being cautious. Besides, she liked him. There was something familiar and a bit avuncular about him, even though she couldn't see him properly behind his sunglasses. 'OK, but then I have to get to the apartment, or they'll think something's happened to me.'

'This won't take long, princess,' he said, and as they turned a corner, she had her first view of the Seine. He drove for another few hundred yards, the river running beside them, then pulled up on the opposite side of the road. 'Here you go, kid. Now tell me you're not glad you said yes.' He hopped out and held her door open for her. 'You got a camera in that case there?'

She leant in over the back seat and popped open the clasps on the case, rummaging around until she found the Box Brownie Dad had given her.

The bridge was the most beautiful she had ever seen. Its broad feet leapfrogged the wide river in perfectly balanced cat's cradles of iron thread, punctuated by tall street lamps. To either side the Seine disappeared into the distance, tall town houses paddling at its edges.

At one end of the bridge, a young boy sat hunched over an accordion, squeezing out the very essence of Paris with his medley of forlorn love songs and age-old folk dances. As she passed, Nancy dropped a few centimes in the black beret that sat at his feet, and he acknowledged her with the barest nod of the head as he continued uninterrupted in his lonely recital.

She leant over the delicate filigree railing, watching a small tug boat chug towards the bridge. She waved at the skipper, who lifted his cap to her and smiled, before shuffling further down into his pea coat and disappearing beneath her.

'Here,' the American said, relieving her of the camera. 'I'll take your picture.'

Nancy leant against the railings, and as she took in the Paris air, she couldn't help but smile. She heard the camera click. The accordion stopped, and the young boy stared at them, watching wide-eyed as the American led her back across the road and into the shiny car.

Just a few minutes later, they were on the pavement outside the Cavendishes' apartment. 'See ya, kid,' he said as he handed her case to her and climbed back into the car, revving the engine. He pushed his sunglasses up on his head and smiled at her, and at last she had a proper view of his face.

How could she not have seen it? The rest of his features fell into place as he smiled at her with his piercing blue eyes, straight off the front of one of Stanley's cherished LPs.

'Hey, you're—' she began to say, but the car was already pulling away. 'I'm Nancy, by the way,' she called after him as he disappeared off up the road with a scream of tyres and a one-handed wave. How on earth would she tell the girls about this? No one would believe who had just dropped little old Nancy Moon home.

She sat on her bed in the little attic room, its tiny window trapping an oval of the night sky. The rattle of the train and the endless sea crossing seemed weeks rather than hours ago, and the euphoria of that morning had dulled into flat exhaustion. She was now bored rather than anxious at having found the apartment empty of her new employers, who had still not appeared. There was nothing more she could milk from the book Peggy had lent her; she'd been gripped by the story of Marnie a few days ago, but tonight had no interest in whether the heroine married the hero, or whether the heroine was even a heroine at all. She was just tired.

Her thoughts drifted back to London, and she wondered what they'd be doing right now. Mum and Dad would be dozing along to the evening play on the radio, Mum's knitting dropping slowly out of her hands and Dad's eyes closing as he tried to stay awake long enough to fill in his pools coupon. A few streets away they'd be sitting in front of the new black and white television that Donald had bought, Peggy with one ear open for her daughter's cry. Maddie would be tucked up, hopefully asleep, maybe beneath the patchwork cot quilt that

Nancy had made for her, or wrapped in one of the little white nightdresses she had embroidered with tiny blue forget-me-nots and pink roses.

She got up from the bed and stretched, distracting herself by picking the discarded dress up off the floor and hanging it in the wardrobe. She ran her hands along the rail of dresses, thinking through the next days' clothes and wondering what each one would see. She stopped at a plain cream shirt dress, a demure knee-length with a narrow lapel and covered buttons – that would do for tomorrow. Not too fancy, and it would dress itself up or down according to what she did or didn't accessorise it with. She had nearly thrown the wretched thing out of the window when she made it, the mechanism jamming on her sewing machine every time she reached a particularly intricate seam, until Dad could bear no more of the cussing and oiled it back to functionality so that peace was restored and he could go back to his newspaper undisturbed.

She sat down next to her suitcase and riffled through the pattern packets until she found the pattern for the day dress with full skirt and boat neck. McCall's 6673.

She tucked the coaster from the train inside, along with the postcard she had bought for Peggy earlier that day but hadn't posted. She could do that tomorrow, when she'd found a stamp. Once she'd had her camera roll developed, she could add the picture from Waterloo station and the one taken on the bridge. She folded the flap back over the top of the packet and picked up her pencil.

London to Paris, she wrote.

12

Butterick 2237: Ladies' summer shirt dress

'I'm so sorry about yesterday, by the way.' Caro drank down the last of her black coffee and placed the cup on the breakfast table. She tilted her head in what might have been a gesture of contrition or challenge, Nancy wasn't sure which. It was going to take a while to work out her new boss.

'Don't worry about it. I'm here now.' Already she was becoming accustomed to the high-ceilinged apartment that would be their base for the next few days. Owned by a friend of Caro's from her modelling days, it was one of the most beautiful homes she'd ever seen, stuffed with antiques and treasures and ceiling-height mottled mirrors, and smelling of floor wax and fresh lilies.

'Friends turned up and dragged us out,' Caro said. 'You know how it is. Lunch turned into supper, and before we knew it, it was late and you were tucked up asleep.'

Nancy had been tucked up but far from asleep. She had lain between the cool linen sheets for hours, avoiding looking at the huge, gaudy painting of the Madonna that hung on the wall opposite her, her sad eyes aimed at a cloud-filled sky and her baby's head lolling at an angle that would have filled Dr Spock with horror. She had heard the sound of voices downstairs, and known that the note she'd left on the table was enough to reassure them that she had arrived safely.

She finished the rest of her own coffee, enjoying the kick to her tired metabolism, and toyed with taking another croissant. She was still starving after what had essentially been a day without food. Although the maid had let her into the apartment, mealtimes had passed by as she waited uncertainly for her employers. Too tired to face walking the streets looking for something to eat, and worried she'd not be able to get back in again, she'd spent the day in her room. The maid had left a cold supper on the table before she left, but by that stage Nancy had been beyond food, and the garlicky smell of the sausage had made her nauseous. She hadn't thought Phyllis's custard creams would come in handy quite so soon into her trip, but she had blessed her friend as she sat on the edge of her narrow bed and demolished half the packet.

'Second on the lips . . .' Caro tutted, seeing her eyeing the basket of buttery pastries.

'. . . lifetime on the hips.' Pamela finished her mother's sentence and smiled ruefully at Nancy.

'Quite so, Pamela.' Caro stood up and smoothed the creases in her pale blue shift dress. 'And now I'm going to leave you two girls to get to know each other.' She walked around the table and planted a kiss on the top of Pamela's head. 'Be nice, darling. I've got things to do here today, and Peter will be working, so you two will need to keep out of the way. You can pretty much please yourselves until tomorrow evening, in fact. We're all going out together – won't that be fun?' She looked at Pamela. 'You could take a leaf out of Nancy's book,' she said, appraising Nancy's shirt dress with its fitted bodice and tiny lapels, and skirt falling in soft pleats beneath her narrow belt. 'Maybe you can find something together for Pamela to wear tomorrow while you're at it? Perhaps without a waist.' She passed Nancy a sealed envelope. 'She could do with a few decent summer clothes. Use this – there should be enough francs to keep you going.'

Nancy averted her eyes as the young girl's florid blush broke through her thin veil of indifference, and watched instead as Caro picked up the copy of French *Vogue* that sat on the table, her little cashmere cardigan balanced across her shoulders as she headed in a catwalk-straight line towards the door.

'Did you need me to collect anything for you?' Nancy called after her, eager for the opportunity to peek inside the doors of one or two of the big Paris ateliers.

Caro frowned. 'Like what?'

'You said you might need some clothes picked up.'

'No, I didn't,' she snapped back.

'But . . .' Nancy backed down, confused but unwilling to challenge her new employer's memory.

'Just keep Pamela busy. That's what we're paying you for.'

The door slammed closed behind her, and they listened in silence to the click of her heels disappearing down the hallway.

'So, it's nice to meet you at last.' Nancy turned and smiled at Pamela, who was chewing for dear life on a nail.

The girl whipped her head round. 'I don't need a babysitter, you know. I've no idea why you're here.' She glared at Nancy, then went back to gnawing on the end of her finger.

This wasn't going to be easy. Nancy sighed. 'I'm here because your parents hired me.'

'My parents are idiots.'

'I'm sure they're not.'

'Actually, they are. Well, Dad is. Mostly. She's just mean. And she's not my mother. My mother is dead.'

Nancy wasn't sure what to say. Based on their two meetings, she had to agree that perhaps Caro wasn't the easiest of people; Peter she was still embarrassed to have mistaken for a labourer and had yet to form an opinion on. However, she'd never heard anyone speak of their elders in this way and not have their backside slippered as a result.

'We didn't see friends yesterday, by the way. She just forgot you were coming.' Seeing that she had not managed to drag from Nancy the reaction she was hoping for, Pamela pushed further. 'We all did, actually.'

Nancy stared back at her with wide, innocent eyes. The girl was clearly hoping the new help would crumble before her, but she hadn't mastered her stepmother's ability to disarm, nor had she the physical presence to carry it off. Her thin-blooded aristocratic looks were a direct gift from her father, but whereas his sandy hair and ruddy complexion gave him a shabby charm, on his daughter they combined with volatile skin and lanky locks to create an unappealing look that was not helped by her choice of oversized hand-me-down knitwear and pleated A-line skirt. Nancy had a feeling that the whole look was designed to infuriate Caro – in which case, she had been wholly successful.

Over the last year, Nancy had let herself be pushed around and let her heart be broken, and although she loved the idea of this job, she was prepared to give it up rather than be bullied by an overprivileged, hormone-riddled child. She had to nip this in the bud and establish her authority quickly if the next few weeks were not to be intolerable.

'Listen, Pamela, whether you like it or not, I'm going to be around for a while. I don't expect to become your best friend, and I certainly don't expect you to become mine, but we might as well rub along together, since we're stuck with each other, don't you think?' She glanced at the door. 'It's me or Caro for company, let's face it. For all you know, I might actually turn out to be all right. And I have a feeling you might be quite nice under that grumpy exterior. What do you say?' She reached out and picked up one of the remaining croissants, taking a large bite from it before passing the basket to Pamela, who hesitated, then took one and wrapped it in her napkin, stuffing it into her skirt pocket.

'That's settled, then,' said Nancy, dusting crumbs from around her lips. 'We're going out.' She stood up and pushed the delicate-backed chair under the table. 'I'm going to get my things together, and we'll meet back here in ten minutes.'

'Fine, but I'm not going shopping,' Pamela shouted after her.

Using Nancy's guidebook, they walked through tree-lined parks where groups of bereted old men clustered around stone benches under boughs weighted down with foliage, watching each other roll shiny metal balls along gravel strips on the ground. They worked their way slowly along the Seine, Nancy stopping to admire the view from time to time as she waited for Pamela to catch up. The girl seemed determined to walk ten paces behind her all the time, so she decided to go along with it and enjoy the fact that she didn't have to make conversation and could lead the way without argument. At least Pamela had taken that awful sweater off, and although she appeared to be wearing her school PE shirt, she was a little more dressed for the weather.

They passed the bridge that the American had taken her to, and she dropped a few centimes in the upturned hat at the feet of the young accordion player, who gabbled excitedly when he recognised her.

'What was that all about?' Pamela said, forgetting to be grumpy for a moment and skipping to catch up as Nancy waved goodbye to the man and carried on.

'He remembered me from yesterday. I got a lift from an American when no one showed up at the station, and he took me to this bridge.'

'An American? You never said.' She sounded almost impressed.

'You never asked.'

Pamela sniffed and brought out a handkerchief, rubbing it vigorously across her nose. 'Who was he?'

'Just a singer.' There was no point saying more; the girl wouldn't believe her anyway.

Pamela was clearly caught between maintaining her determination not to like Nancy, and a child-like curiosity. From what Nancy could glean, she had spent most of her young adulthood locked in a boarding school in deepest Sussex, where stories of Americans with fancy cars would have provided gossip fodder for weeks on end. Stubbornness prevailed, however, and they carried on walking in silence, the subject dropped for now.

They crossed the river, stopping to watch the pleasure

boats pass beneath the bridge, passengers jostling to catch the beautiful view of Notre-Dame on their cameras, then wandered around the flower market tucked within the great cathedral's shadow.

'I'm hungry,' Pamela said, idly popping fuchsia buds while Nancy buried her nose in a raspberry-rippled rose.

'Then let's find something to eat.' Nancy had looked after Renee Walker's toddlers at number 17 enough times to know how to handle tired, truculent children, and she had a feeling that Pamela would respond to the same treatment. She led the way, even though she had no idea where she was going, or what on earth they would manage to find for lunch.

As they ventured deeper into the little streets behind the cathedral, it was as though a different city lived here. Gone were the tight skirts and high heels; in their place the women wore their hair short and their shoes flat, and despite the weather, a unisex uniform of black polo necks pervaded.

They soon came across a pretty café on a street corner, sheltered by trees and with a clientele of Gauloises-smoking academic types either in animated conversation or with their noses buried in books. A waiter pulled out chairs for them at a little round table and left them with a couple of menus.

'So what would you like?'

Pamela was busy playing with the camera she had pulled out of her bag, and took no notice. Nancy looked around to see what other people were eating. Everyone here seemed to exist on caffeine and wine and erudite conversation, and so she scanned the menu to see if there was anything she recognised.

The waiter reappeared, his pen hovering impatiently over his notepad as he waited for Nancy to order.

'Er, *bonjour*,' she said, realising that this was the first time she had tried out her rudimentary French in public. Whether he didn't understand or whether he couldn't be bothered to reply, she wasn't sure; he just tipped his head and frowned at her impatiently. She had no idea what to order, so gestured at the two glasses of milky liquid on the table next door, and pointed to the only thing on the menu that she hoped she had a chance of getting right. Surely you couldn't go too wrong with a salad? After a minute or two of exasperation as the waiter claimed not to understand, he eventually wrote down her order.

'*Deux Pernods et deux salades de gésiers?*' he said.

She glanced at Pamela, who was no longer disguising her amusement at Nancy's discomfort. '*Oui?*' she said quietly.

Pamela sighed and took the menu from her, launching into an alternative order, given in perfect French, at which the waiter nodded and smiled, joking with her at what Nancy knew was her expense, before moving on to the next table.

'You speak French. Why did you let me make an idiot of myself?'

'Because you just ordered gizzard salad for me.'

As Pamela went back to playing with the camera, Nancy watched the stream of people passing the café: students, mainly, with piles of books under their arms. The girls all wore cropped trousers and pixieish short hair, while the boys seemed to be growing theirs, some way past their collars.

A loud click made her turn back, just in time to see Pamela pointing the camera at her.

'Pamela! Stop that. You can't just go around taking people's photographs.'

The girl just shrugged.

The waiter appeared with a tray bearing two glasses of squeezed lemon juice, accompanied by a carafe of water and a bowl of sugar, which he deftly placed on the table, and two plates balanced on one arm.

'Salade Niçoise,' Pamela said, watching Nancy poke at the olives and raw onion that garnished her plate of bright ruffled lettuce leaves. 'It's very French. Do you want some ketchup with it?' she said sarcastically, then poured water into her glass and mixed in a small spoonful of sugar, stirring it vigorously.

Nancy followed suit, adding more sugar when the first sip made her eyes water. 'Where did you learn to speak French so well?' she said, tapping the long spoon from side to side in the glass.

Pamela shrugged. 'They send me to Switzerland every summer holiday. With all the other rich kids whose parents have other plans.'

'Oh, I'm sorry.'

'Don't be sorry. At least I'll never have to eat a gizzard salad.'

Nancy couldn't help a laugh escaping, and for just a moment, Pamela joined in, until she remembered she was not meant to be having fun and folded her arms defensively across her chest.

'You still can't make me go shopping, you know.'

13

Vogue 5727: Evening dress, cowl neck, tie waist

'There. You look perfect.'

Nancy finished clipping the diamanté brooch in Pamela's hair, then stood back and let her see herself in the full-length mirror.

Two of the most tortuous hours of her life had paid off, and the fleeting then quickly extinguished surprise on Pamela's face told her that she almost agreed too.

In different circumstances, Nancy would have loved exploring the department store that made Fenwick's look like the Co-op on Wandsworth High Street. The customers here wore perfectly tailored cocoon coats and boat-necked, tight-skirted suits in ice-cream pastels. And the hats: huge cloches, sweet boating hats, turbans, all balanced by oversized handbags that could have contained a spare pair of kitten heels, a litre of Chanel No. 5 and half a dozen pairs of stockings. It had been more theatre than emporium, and Nancy had expected an orchestra and chorus to appear at any moment from within the lavish wedding-cake layers of the opera-box galleries.

Pamela had been less impressed, merely asking incessantly where the toilet was and when could they go, and shying away from the expressionless black-suited stick insects who attempted to spray her with perfume.

The patience of the young woman who brought them every shade of every fabric of every style of cocktail dress and day dress was beyond saintly, and Nancy had tried to explain, in the face of Pamela's sudden inability to speak a word of French, that her charge was in turn tired, hungry, ill. By the time they left the store, she would have thrown herself happily under a guillotine.

The dress suited Pamela well, even though it added five years to her, and with nowhere for her to hide in the fitted peach-pink bodice and gently tapered tulip skirt, Nancy had been surprised to see what a pretty figure was hidden beneath the oversized armour of Aertex and twill.

'I don't see why I have to wear this.' Pamela turned from side to side, examining her unfamiliar reflection. 'I look like a flower fairy. In fact, I don't see why I have to go out. Why can't I stay here?'

'But it'll be nice to spend the evening with your parents.'

'I don't want to go to some stupid nightclub. I want to go . . .' She hesitated.

'Go where?' Nancy asked as she smoothed the French pleat into which she had fought to mould Pamela's freshly washed hair.

Pamela dug the toe of her new shoe into the little rug at the foot of Nancy's bed. 'Nowhere,' she said quietly.

Nancy took her bare shoulders and looked her in the eye. 'I know you must miss your friends at school, but you'll be back there in a few weeks, and think of the stories you'll be able to tell them.'

Pamela snatched herself away. 'You don't understand, do you? I'm not going back to school. They've taken me out, and I'll never see my friends again.' Tears welled in her eyes, threatening the mascara that Nancy had persuaded her to try.

'Don't be silly now,' Nancy said calmly. 'I'm sure you'll see them again. And you have your parents here, don't you?'

'I'm not being silly.' There was an edge of hysteria to Pamela's voice. 'What would you know about my family anyway? They're nothing like your stupid boring lot, who'll be waiting for you in your stupid little terraced house when you get back, hoping you've brought them a stick of rock from the Eiffel Tower. You've probably got a stupid boring boyfriend waiting for you too—'

'That's enough,' Nancy said. 'You don't know anything about me. Or my family.' She knew the girl was just lashing out, but she couldn't keep the sharpness from her voice. She'd done such a good job of keeping everything in check, of focusing on the job and not on home. She didn't need a spoilt brat hurling abuse at her life. She reached for her compact in her handbag and dabbed powder on Pamela's raging cheeks, refusing to make eye contact as she did so. 'I don't want to hear any more about it, all right? I won't insult your family if you leave mine alone.' She stood back and looked at her charge. 'Now go and show them what a charming young woman you are, and I'll be down in a moment.'

Pamela stuck her tongue out, then silently picked up her evening bag, shrugged on her jacket and left the little attic room.

Nancy sat down heavily on the bed. Come on, she told

herself. You're about to paint Paris red. You are so lucky. You have so much.

She saw herself in the mirror, and sat up straight. What *did* she have? Good looks and an eye for an outfit? What was she, even? There was nothing of the south London girl staring back at her, but she wasn't fooled by the champagne-coloured shantung silk and long white gloves, the immaculate beehive and flawless skin. She might look like the rest of them, but she knew from bitter experience that she could never be one of them, and how it felt to be thrown out into the cold.

What was he doing now? she wondered. Who was driving around town on his arm?

Not you, Nancy. Not you.

She stood up and checked herself one more time in the mirror, arranging the folds of her draping cowl neckline and the wide pleat at her hip, and adjusting the tie belt so that the ends hung in exactly the right place. She clipped on the cold, heavy drop-pearl earrings, which tapped against her bare neck, then leant forward and painted her lips with the new lipstick she had treated herself to that afternoon. She pouted, then pressed a tissue between her lips, so that the dark red was softened to a just-kissed deep pink.

'Onwards and sideways, Nancy,' she told herself.

They spilled out of the taxi onto a rain-slicked pavement that sparkled with the reflection of a thousand bright lights, changing from white to gold to red in time with the illuminated board above the inauspicious entrance tucked halfway along the Champs-Elysées. Before so much as a drop of rain could dampen dinner jacket or lacquered hair, a bevy of doormen appeared with umbrellas and guided them across a red carpet and through the doors of the Lido de Paris.

'Well, I must say, I'm a very lucky chap to have three such beautiful women with me this evening,' Peter said once they were inside, as uncomfortable with the forced flattery as he appeared to be in his slightly ill-fitting suit. It was clear where Pamela's dress sense had come from. 'Pamela, you look quite the young woman,' he said, chucking his daughter's chin and ignoring her embarrassment as she turned away from him. 'You make your parents feel terribly old, doesn't she, Caro?'

Caro raised her perfectly painted eyebrows. 'She's not twelve, for God's sake, Peter.' She turned, allowing him to take her short fur jacket from her bare bony shoulders, revealing an exquisite strapless black dress with frothy net skirt that Nancy was sure she recognised from the Dior catalogue from a couple of years ago. In Nancy's world, shoulder blades that could slice a Sunday joint and a spine you could play with xylophone sticks would have had the doctor crying malnutrition, and although she could see that most of the other women in the room seemed to survive on cigarettes and eau de cologne fumes alone, she couldn't help being shocked at the sight of Caro's skeleton laid so bare. The strings of giant pearls wrapped tightly around her throat looked heavy enough to crush her.

'I feel sick,' Pamela said, looking the picture of health. 'I want to go home.'

'Don't be ridiculous.' Caro took a cigarette out of her handbag and held it to her mouth, waiting for Peter to produce a slim gold lighter from his breast pocket, then blowing smoke out of the side of her mouth, away from the rest of the group. 'You're perfectly fine, and you had better be nice to the Hendersons. They have a charming grandson, I hear.'

'Let me take your coats,' said Peter.

'Nancy can do that.' Caro looked idly around the foyer, examining the buzz of people swarming beneath the immense chandelier.

'Really, darling, there's no need.'

Nancy had already taken Caro's fur from him, however, and was now trying to prise Pamela's hip-length gold jacket from her. Her charge was quite determined not to let go of the garment, and had folded her arms to prevent it being taken.

'It's fine,' Nancy said, giving up the fight and leaving Pamela sheathed in her outerwear. 'I'm here to help, after all.'

As she headed across the foyer, she looked around her, taking in the diamonds and furs, and marvelling at the boredom on the faces of many of the clientele. Perhaps it was not 'cool', as she'd heard some of the youngsters back home say, to show enthusiasm in this city. Even on Bond Street and at some of the smarter parties she sometimes found herself invited to, she had never seen money wear itself so subtly and yet so blatantly. There was not a pair of shoes walking across that marble floor that had not cost at least a month's salary at Belgrave's, and Peggy and Donald could probably have bought their little house for the price of the ensemble worn by the woman arguing with the young man at the main reception desk. And yet she could never have imagined that money would make people so miserable: not one of the glittering guests here so much as smiled as they drew hungrily on their cigarettes.

She could see her entourage in conversation with a dinner-jacketed man with a trim moustache, and was aware that Caro was watching her, so she turned back and hurried towards the cloakroom.

'Oh, I'm sorry, ma'am.'

One moment she had had the coats in her arms, the next they were piled on the floor, and all she could see of the man who had bent down to pick them up for her was the top of his head, with its glass-smooth black hair.

He glanced up. 'Wasn't looking where I was going for a moment there. Pre-show nerves, I guess.' He stood up straight. 'Hey, I know you, don't I?'

There was no mistaking her knight in shining chrome.

'You saved me yesterday,' she said, looking down at her lightly grazed knees.

He laughed. 'The English damsel in distress.'

Nancy became aware of people staring at them, including Caro, whose gaze was even more intense than before. 'I ought to go. I have to take these . . .'

'You watching the show tonight?' he said.

'If I don't get sacked before it starts, yes.'

He laughed. 'In that case, I'll look out for you in the crowd. Hey, kid, what did you say your name was again?'

'Nancy.'

'Nancy,' he said slowly, and nodded. 'Good name. I got a daughter called Nancy. Say, I gotta go, but it was swell meeting you again.' He handed her the coats and gave her a quick kiss on the cheek. 'See you around, kid.'

A flash and a pop behind her made her jump, and she turned to see a photographer taking their picture, before he moved on to snap other guests as they milled around.

Anxious not to hold the rest of the party up any longer, she hurried over to the cloakroom and checked in the coats as quickly as the young boy behind the desk could manage. Young enough to be of school age, he could barely see over the counter, but he still managed to stare open-mouthed at Nancy.

'I'm sorry about that,' she said as she reached the others, only to find Peter and Caro speechless, staring at her with the same rapt attention as the coat-check boy, the man who had joined them barely hiding his laughter.

'Do you know him?' Caro said incredulously, her accent suddenly slipping far to the west of the Atlantic.

'Of course. Well, only a little. He gave me a lift yesterday.'

'He gave you a lift?' Peter broke into the first smile she had ever seen cross his lips.

'I must say, you two, you know how to hire a nanny,' their friend said, appraising Nancy. 'You don't need me, Peter, old chum. This young lady seems to have better connections than I do.'

'She's not my nanny.'

'Oh, do be quiet, Pamela.'

The young girl quickly recognised that Caro was not to be crossed, and went back into silent sulk mode.

The man held his hand out. 'Tony Scott. Pleased to meet you, Nancy. You must introduce me to your friend over there.'

'Oh, he's not . . .' Nancy held out her gloved hand. His handshake was firm, and there was something of a David Niven sparkle about his eyes, even if they did seem to be laughing at her.

He loosened his grip and held his hand up. 'No need to

explain. A girl's entitled to be discreet. Especially one who looks like you.'

'Tony is an old family friend, Nancy,' Peter explained quickly, earning Nancy's gratitude as he covered over her discomfort. 'We went to school together. Don't take any notice of him.'

It seemed an unlikely friendship: Peter, so reserved and almost reclusive, and Tony, whose flamboyance was evident even in the short conversation they'd had.

'You'll have to get used to me, I'm afraid. You'll be seeing a lot of me this summer.' Tony nudged Peter. 'And I hope to see a lot of you, Nancy. Eh, Peter?'

Peter had the grace to ignore the comment, but Nancy knew that look, and had brushed it off plenty of times and from plenty of equally silly men. Still she felt uncomfortable under Tony's gaze, and under the accusatory stare she was receiving from Caro. She wished someone would change the subject.

'We're staying with Tony in . . . where is it . . . Antibes? I never remember.' Peter knitted his eyebrows.

'Because you never pay any attention when we're down there, darling,' Caro said, brushing her husband's arm with her black-gloved hand. 'You're always too busy bloody painting.'

'Perhaps now you've got this one in tow, you'll join in a bit more, eh?' Tony said with a chuckle, gesturing towards Nancy, who was beginning to wonder whether she should take a leaf out of Pamela's book and cry sick. In any case, if she looked any longer at the residue of Tony's supper nestling in the far-left corner of his spidery moustache, she wouldn't have to feign illness.

'Tony, you're dreadful and I hate you.'

'No, you don't, Caro. You love me.' He grabbed Caro by the arm, kissing her on the cheek and surprising Nancy by making her employer blush girlishly, then offered his other arm to Pamela. 'Come on, dumpling,' he said. 'It's showtime.'

'Don't call me that,' Pamela muttered, ignoring the proffered arm.

'Don't mind Tony,' Peter said to Nancy as they followed behind, heading towards the gold-curtained entrance to the bowels of the nightclub and the bank of ushers ready to escort the Lido clientele to their tables. 'He's a good chap. Just a bit brash sometimes. You'll get used to him.'

Nancy rather hoped she wouldn't.

It was the early hours by the time they arrived back at the apartment.

'Nightcap, anyone?' Peter said, heading straight to the whisky decanter and pouring himself a large shot.

'I'm going to bed,' Caro said, kicking off her slingbacks and dropping her jacket on the sofa before disappearing through the ornate doors towards the master bedroom.

'Me too.' Pamela did in fact look quite sick now, having drunk the three glasses of champagne that Tony had forced on her.

'Maybe I should sleep in your room with you, Pamela?' Nancy said, worried that the champagne might make a reappearance during the night. She couldn't imagine Caro being ready with a bucket when it did.

Pamela just shrugged. 'If you want.'

'I'll get my things.' Nancy went to follow her up the stairs to the little attic rooms, but Peter called after her.

'Stay and have a drink with me, Nancy. You a whisky lover?'

She hesitated, but Pamela had already gone on, and wouldn't want to be disturbed while she was undressing. 'Yes, occasionally.'

Peter poured another drink and held it out to her.

She supposed it wouldn't harm. 'Thanks,' she said, and took the glass from him.

He gestured to the sofa, inviting her to sit down, and sat in an armchair opposite.

'We've not really talked properly, have we?' he said, turning the crystal tumbler around in his hands. 'I'm afraid I was rather rude when we first met. I get like that when I'm working. Nothing personal, you understand?'

Nancy smiled and took a sip of the smoky liquid. Donald was partial to a whisky, and had talked her through her initial dislike of the amber liquid until she'd come through the other side and become rather a fan, to the surprise of those who expected young ladies to go for a sherry rather than straight for the hard stuff. 'Of course. You didn't know who I was and I didn't know who you were.'

'You're very generous.' He inclined his head and smiled. 'Tell me, did you enjoy the show?'

Nancy had never seen anything like it in her entire life: dancing girls, dancing dogs, and then of course the main act. Every guest at every one of the candlelit tables had stood in his honour, and Nancy had wanted the ground to swallow her up when he sang one of his numbers directly at her.

Peter laughed. 'I still can't get over how you met him.'

Nancy was becoming tired of the attention her little adventure had provoked, so instead asked, 'And how did you enjoy the evening?'

He groaned. 'I think I'd have preferred a quiet dinner somewhere, but it was good of Tony to get the tickets.'

'It was lovely to meet your friends.'

'Ah, the Hendersons. They're actually pretty awful, especially the wife. But he wants a portrait painted of her, so I'm going to have to get used to looking at her, I suppose. And work out how to make that nose look a little smaller. Caro has got it into her head that Pamela would get on well with their grandson. Although from what I've heard, he's pretty dull.'

'You were very good at pretending to like them.' Nancy smiled.

'Part of the job, I'm afraid. Although I'm not sure my heart's in it these days.' He went back to the decanter and refilled his glass. 'Need a top-up?'

She shook her head and he came back to join her. 'Caro tells me you were a seamstress. Must be wonderful to put together raw materials and create something out of them.'

'You could say that's what you do, though.'

'I suppose so. In a way. A portrait's not much bloody use to anyone, though, is it? Except as a mirror to one's vanity.'

She laughed, realising that for the first time since she had arrived, she was actually feeling at ease, in the company of this gentle man. 'I'd love to see some of your work some time, if you wouldn't mind?'

His face brightened. 'Really? I've only got sketchbooks here at the moment, but once we get to Venice, you'll see some of my work at an exhibition there, and of course there'll be the studio.' He laughed. 'Sorry – I'm so used to Caro and Pea being bored to tears if I talk about work.'

'I promise not to be bored.' And she meant it: she had always wanted to build on her scant knowledge of art, fuelled by the trips to London galleries that seemed such a long time ago now, where she loved watching the shifting colours in a Monet, or the sombre beauty of the Dutch miniatures. She knew nothing about them really, but perhaps this was her chance to learn more.

He waved his glass in the direction of her dress. 'I suppose you're going to tell me you made that?'

She tipped her head in a gesture of modesty and smiled. 'Yes, actually.'

'Clever girl. I hope you don't mind being here with us too much. Must be a little unchallenging for you.'

'Not at all. I needed a change.'

'I shan't ask why, but I'm very pleased you did, and I hope we won't be too much trouble for you. I think you'll be good for Pamela. She seems to like you.'

Nancy was surprised. She wondered how Pamela treated those she didn't like. 'And I like her.' Was she lying? Actually, she thought not. It would take a while, but she suspected that once the layers were peeled away, there was a very sweet girl underneath.

'It's not been easy for her, losing her mother so young, and then being away at school.'

Nancy had picked up a few snippets of information about poor Alice Cavendish, who had developed complications after a difficult delivery and left her doting husband and newborn daughter only days after the little family was formed. Peter's parents had stepped in and brought the old nanny back into the fold so that he could get back to London and to work without worrying about the tiny infant, who broke his heart every time he visited Sunberry Park to see her. When he met Caro and reclaimed his two-year-old daughter, she screamed the Kensington house down, yelling for Nanny, who was quickly installed in the attic and peace restored.

'She's a good sort when she's not pulling faces or winding Caro up. And I'm afraid I've probably not been much of a father. Too busy, you see.' He took a large sip of the whisky and rinsed it around his mouth. 'Not always sure it was the right thing to send her away when she'd only just got used to us again, but Caro knows what young girls are like, and she'd have been bored to pieces at home.'

'Well, hopefully you'll have plenty of time with each other this summer.'

'That's the plan. Although after that . . .' He tapped the glass thoughtfully. 'Well, we'll see. Anyway, I suppose you must be missing your own family?'

Like someone has cut my right leg off. Like someone pulled out my heart and put it in a paper bag and left it in Waterloo station. 'Just a little.'

The combination of champagne and whisky and the late night and the overstimulation of the evening suddenly overcame her, and she was afraid she might do something silly like telling him her life story. 'I think I'd better check Pamela's all right and get to bed. Do you mind?'

'Good plan,' he said. 'We're off in a day or two. It's a long way down there – catch up while you can.'

She stood up and studied him as he stared into his glass, and he looked as close as she to tumbling over a precipice. She'd better leave him to his thoughts and let him fall in peace, as she wanted to be left to hers.

He barely noticed as she put her glass down next to his and tiptoed out, closing the door gently behind her.

14

So here she was, and as Flo surveyed the Gare du Nord, she was hard pushed to imagine a less romantic welcome to the Continent. She looked around at the strings of jabbering summer-school students and the commuters shouting into telephones, a chocolate-coloured stain bleeding into the sprigs of lilac on her skirt. All around her, people were dressed in black – anoraks and parkas, jeans, heavy boots; even the large dogs on chain leashes were black – and she felt like an extra off a Doris Day set.

How different had it looked to Nancy as she emerged from this station in 1962? Flo imagined the concourse in bold Technicolor, stripped of the diesel-pumping cars, people going about their business through the sugar-coated lens of a fanciful Paris long gone, but the truth was, she struggled to see past the pitiful souls huddled in damp sleeping bags in doorways, and the grubby hotel signs and fast-food concessions that lined the broad street in front of her.

It wasn't too far to her hotel, but she was exhausted, and her ill-advised suitcase was already proving cumbersome, so she hailed a taxi and allowed herself the luxury of letting go of responsibility for ten minutes or so. She'd hoped to watch the view go by, but her driver clearly thought he was at Le Mans rather than in the streets of Paris, and so it made for a much more endurable journey to close her eyes to the near misses and terrified stares of pedestrians.

She allowed her thoughts to wander back to the long journey that had brought her here. With no one to wave her off at St Pancras, she'd averted her gaze from the statue of the parting lovers, realising with irritation that she wished Seamus were there, and marching with manic vigour to find her train.

She'd found herself squashed onto a table with a young mother, one of whose children watched a continuous string of noisy cartoons on an iPad while her brother kicked Flo's shins sporadically all the way to Lille, laughing as she spilled her carton of chocolate milkshake and asking his mother loudly if that lady was an alcoholic when Flo brought back a much-needed G&T from the buffet car. Never had a journey passed so slowly, until daylight finally streamed through the train windows and they were through the other end of the tunnel.

The car stopped violently as they arrived at the hotel. '*Ici*,' the driver said, opening the door for her, then pointing into the open boot at her suitcase.

'I'll be getting that, then?' she said, vowing not to tip him as he leant indifferently against the car, and then paying him an extra five euros.

The hotel wasn't quite how it had looked on the Internet, but all she needed was somewhere to sleep at night. As she walked through the lobby, however, lined by silent men who looked up briefly from their smartphones to check her out, she wondered whether she had booked herself into a minicab office masquerading as a brothel. She was about to turn tail when a tall eastern European woman appeared behind a desk and motioned her over. Flo hesitated, with no time to back out inconspicuously before the woman had pressed a key into her hand and pointed towards the door that led to the guest rooms.

Why hadn't she spent the extra money? she wondered, as she poked at the hairs in the sink with a pencil and swept the crumbs off the worn armchair before putting her case down. For a little more, she could have had a hotel just a few streets further south with a welcoming bar and vintage furnishings, instead of rooms by the hour and enough polyester to self-combust.

She opened the case and pulled out the first packet, sliding her hand inside until she found the photograph of Nancy on the bridge. Who had taken it? she wondered. The black fuzzy fingermark in the corner of the picture gave nothing away, but she could see what looked like a chair and some kind of musical instrument to her right, as Nancy stood there smiling, her dress lifting a little in the breeze and exposing marks on her knees. There were only so many bridges spanning the Seine, so it couldn't be too hard to find.

She flicked through her guidebook, working through each geographical section until she found a photograph straight out of a honeymoon catalogue, showing a view through fili-gree railings of the Seine, its watery bulk split in two by the majestic prow of the Île de la Cité, and illuminated by strings of lamps bordering its banks. Even though the photograph had been taken at night, there was no mistaking it: this was the bridge where Nancy had smiled happily at her anonymous photographer.

*

The heat of the Parisian afternoon was ebbing as she arrived at the Pont des Arts, the breeze from the water helping to ease an incoming headache. She took a moment to listen to the young man standing on the corner, singing operatic arias to the crowds of tourists who crammed onto the bridge, his backing track obscured by the constant passing traffic and the amplified commentaries of the sightseeing boats shuttling up and down the river.

So here she was, wearing dress number one, even if it was already a little tired after its trip across the Channel. She forced her way gently through the throngs of teenage couples posing in front of their selfie sticks until at last she found herself next to the railing. Except it wasn't the railing that Nancy had known: it was a mass of padlocks, consuming every spare inch of the delicate filigree like a rampant metallic cancer, weighing down the beautiful bridge with the promises of thousands of lovers whose gesture had probably outlasted their relationship.

She leant out over the water, drinking in the view. So much must be unchanged since Nancy had stood here: to the left, the Eiffel Tower reaching up out of the dense mat of grey roofs, and in the distance Sacré-Coeur a white beacon at the tip of Montmartre.

The singer was packing up now, the void he left revealing a musical layer she'd been unaware of. Sitting at the far end of the bridge, bent almost double on a chair that looked as old as he did, an accordion player coaxed the essence of Paris out of his instrument's huge bellows and yellowed keys. She took the picture of Nancy out of her bag and looked closely at it.

Now she knew what she was looking for, it was obvious that the instrument in the photograph was an accordion.

'Excuse me, monsieur?' she asked the old man.

He slowly lifted his head, turtle-like, squinting into the lowering evening sunshine, his curled arthritic fingers pausing over the shiny buttons and worn keys, surprised to find himself spoken to.

She held out the photograph. '*Ma tante. La reconnaissez-vous?* Do you remember her? She was here in nineteen sixty-two.' She held up fingers to help him understand which year she meant.

He took it from her, rubbing his stubbly salt-and-pepper chin while he looked at it. Suddenly he chuckled and pointed to the accordion. '*C'est la mienne!*'

'Yes, I thought so. *Et la femme?*'

He looked at her. '*C'est vous, n'est-ce pas? C'est la même robe, non?*' And he waved at the skirt of her dress.

'No, it's not me. Although it's almost my dress, you're right. It's my aunt. *Ma tante?*'

Suddenly he smiled. '*Ah, je me souviens. La belle dame et le chanteur.*'

'*Chanteur?*' Flo felt her heart quicken. 'What singer?'

The man beckoned her closer. '*Americain.*' He waited until she was inches away from his face and she could smell the sweet, liquorice Ricard on his breath, and then sat back and laughed. And laughed. Until Flo thought he might fall off his chair.

Jesus. She was going to get nothing out of him, she could tell. What a wasted lead.

She straightened up and thanked him, but he was already back at his instrument, churning out a melancholy version of 'My Way' that sounded more suicidal than triumphant. What had she expected? The man had been sitting here for over half a century, and there was probably more pastis than blood running through his veins.

She sighed. It hadn't been the best start to the trip, but at least she was here. She headed back towards the hotel, stopping at a little supermarket to buy a cold supper to eat in her room. She'd take it easy this evening, and let a good night's sleep work its magic.

Flo didn't so much wake as resign herself to the dawn and the end of what was possibly one of the worst night's sleep she had ever endured. Although her bedroom was four floors off ground level, that was no protection against the raucous nightlife, early-hours belligerence and caterwauling, then the dawn raids by the city's refuse collectors.

She was tired, overwhelmed and ravenously hungry, and not feeling remotely in the mood for another day in the city. Come on, Flo, she told herself. Get dressed, get breakfast and get out there.

Following Nancy's lead, she pulled out the poplin shirt dress that had nearly cost her sanity, and heeding the cry of her aching feet, paired it with her favourite Converses. With a thick leather belt and a smear of Jemima Red on her lips, she might get away with it as a 'kooky' look, although she wasn't sure that what worked in Brighton would sway it in Paris.

She held the dress up: the lapels actually looked pretty good. Had Nancy too nearly ripped the thing up in frustration?

Unpicked seams and trimmed selvedges and ironed in rippled interfacing until she wanted to weep? She slipped the dress on, and carefully did up the buttons that ran from top to bottom, pleased she'd managed to find vintage ones that took the newness of the dress away. Then she looked at herself in the mirror. To her surprise and relief, the narrow notched collar of the dress lay beautifully flat and wide on the shoulders, a flattering cut that was as stylish today as it was when Nancy wore it, and the pinched-in waist led down to a gently pleated skirt that sat just on the knee. Flo had almost matched the crisp cream-coloured poplin swatch that had been kept with the pattern, but had a feeling that Nancy was made of tougher stuff when it came to footwear and that the original model was probably worn with something slightly more feminine. Her scrub of blonde curls was definitely not very 1962, but she wasn't going to a *Mad Men* tribute weekend.

She was ready for the worst that any Continental breakfast could throw at her, and was about to leave her room when her phone pinged. Jem.

Here's Ben's number. He's expecting to hear from you. He's a bit daft, but good company. For a bloke. Just don't let his mum know you're meeting him.

Flo sighed. The last thing she needed was a blind date, but it would be nice to have someone to have a drink with, since drinking cheap red wine in her room wasn't exactly how she'd seen her time in Paris panning out.

Well, she had learnt yet another lesson, which was never to ask for tea on the Continent, and that it was always possible for low expectations to be exceeded. With half a rubbery croissant and a glass of acid-coloured fruit juice inside her, she was ready to go.

Packet number two had revealed a photograph of Nancy at a pavement café. There was nothing written on the back, but Flo surmised from the logo on the envelope of matches that had been tucked in with it that this had been taken at a well-known café on the Left Bank, once famously frequented by the intelligentsia of Paris.

She packed her tiny concertina map of the city, and headed south towards the river, dodging mopeds and bikes hired by the hour, and leaving behind the mobile phone repair shops and neon-lit nail bars. Instead, tucked within the Belle Époque shop facades, discreet homeware emporiums displayed anything along the colour scale of ivory to mole. Across the river, the shop windows were full of cellophane-wrapped hardback books with black and white photographs of serious old men with equally serious eyewear. She paused outside a patisserie, its polished slopes of glass displaying glistening strawberries and peaches, and lengths of chocolate nestled in upside-down paper petticoats.

Eventually she found herself opposite the Café de Flore. Its green and white canopy, topped with a fringe of opulent window boxes, and the pavement tables and chairs flanking each side of the apex formed by its position on the corner of two roads were straight out of a French romcom.

She sat at a table outside and ordered a coffee, and feeling suddenly conspicuous sitting there on her own, pulled a leather-bound notebook out of her handbag. She'd wondered whether she should bring it with her, but it was only the size of a large purse. She let her pencil hover over the page for a moment, and looked around, spotting a young mother in black pencil-pleat trousers and expensively scruffy T-shirt. With a few lines of her pencil, she sketched the folds of the T-shirt, the angle of the woman's chin. On a whim, she added a jacket slung over a shoulder. Suddenly she was back at college, sketching live models, or sitting in her studio space with a tray of watercolour pencils. Funny how you never lost it, she thought as she held up the sketch and eyed it critically.

'Espresso?' The waiter returned, and lifted a tiny cup and saucer from the tray, placing a carafe of water next to it.

'*Merci.*' She closed the book and dropped it in her handbag, and spotting the dress packet sticking out, pulled out the photo of Nancy sitting outside the café. '*Monsieur?*' she said, as he glided away from her, but he was already taking another order, and had deactivated his customer radar. She wasn't sure what she wanted to hear from him, really. His parents probably hadn't even been born in 1962, and there was no reason the picture of Nancy would mean anything to him. There was most likely nothing to be learnt from this stopover, but at least it had given her the first decent cup of coffee she'd drunk since she left home.

Her thoughts drifted to Nancy's next dress: the shantung silk cocktail dress. And whereas Flo was quite happy floating around on her own in a day dress, a cocktail dress needed an evening setting, and it needed company.

She picked up her phone and scrolled through her texts, noting sadly that the last message Seamus had sent was now far down the list. He would be well settled in by now, too busy with his new life to miss her. She hoped he was happy – well, a bit happy.

She replied briefly to Jem, thanking her for the number, then wondered how to compose a text to a complete stranger. What had she got to lose, apart from her dignity, as she sat in some swanky bar all dressed up with no one to go to?

Hi, Flo here, she typed with one finger. *Jem's friend in Paris. Fancy a drink?*

She finished her coffee, off-setting it with a glass of cold, sweet water, then left some change in the saucer with the bill. She had an afternoon to kill: perhaps she'd do some shopping. It was a pleasant walk to Galeries Lafayette, and she hadn't been there for years. Maybe she'd treat herself to a new lipstick.

'Can I get you another?'

Flo drained the last of her cosmopolitan and pushed the glass towards him. 'Why not?' Although at fifteen euros a pop, there was every reason why not. It was her last night in Paris, however, and his round, and it seemed a shame to spoil a perfectly pleasant evening with a dose of common sense. Despite her reservations about meeting a virtual stranger, she was having a surprisingly nice time. Ben had far more about him than Jem had led her to believe, and she could almost forgive him his slightly *Top Gear* suit jacket and jeans.

She popped a few salted almonds in her mouth and watched as he swivelled on his stool and gestured to the bartender to top them up.

'So you're an old friend of Jem's?' she asked, fighting to be heard against the rattle of crushed ice. Why did every man think he was Tom Cruise the minute he got a cocktail shaker in his hands?

He frowned. 'You know I used to go out with her sister Mel years ago? Former life and all that,' he added quickly, although Flo could see that his throwaway dismissal masked a hurt that still pained him. 'I always liked Jem better really – I'm glad we were able to stay in touch.'

Flo had met Melanie a couple of times, and couldn't quite picture the tired and overweight mother of three small children with this well-turned-out and, yes indeed, pretty man. Ben definitely belonged with the younger Mel, who had eaten boyfriends for breakfast. As far as she could see, it was Mel's loss, not his.

'Have you been in Paris long?' she said, taking the fresh glass of cranberry-coloured liquid, a curl of wafer-thin orange peel threaded onto a cocktail stick and balanced across its salt-frosted rim.

'Couple of years now. Needed a fresh start, you know?'

She nodded, stirring the thick liquid with the needle-like cocktail stick. 'I'm impressed. Not easy moving to a foreign city, I guess?'

He shrugged. 'Not at first, but I worked on my French, made myself go out, made a few friends. It's fine. I like it on the whole, but maybe I'll move on and do some travelling eventually. It's too easy to get comfortable, isn't it?'

Flo laughed. 'I think I'm done with travelling – well, apart from this trip, obviously. Perhaps I'll tell you about my childhood one of these days.'

He looked hopefully at her. 'I'd like that.'

'Gone native, I see.' She pointed to the packet of Gauloises poking out of his jacket pocket.

'When in Rome . . .' He shrugged, but hadn't quite captured a fully Gallic version of the gesture. With his blond hair and blue eyes, he would never quite blend in. 'You could certainly pass for Parisian in that dress,' he said. 'Far too chic to be English. Rock chick, almost.' Almost as soon as he had said it, she sensed he regretted it. A mortified blush washed across his cheeks, and he lifted his glass to disguise it.

Flo bit back her instinctive dismissal of his compliment, and decided to enjoy the tiny thrill that came from being noticed for the first time in what seemed like years: just for one evening she didn't have to be the cuckolded wife, or the woman who worked in the shop, or the woman crying in the nappy aisle in Tesco. She smiled. 'Thanks,' she said, and was pleased to see his instant relief.

Chic was possibly an over exaggeration, but Flo had to admit that she was pleased with the dress, which fitted perfectly and looked good. As the weight had melted off over the last few months, she'd avoided looking at the body that had let her down so badly. Tonight, however, she realised she was actually enjoying being dressed up, and loved how the wide neckline of her dress, which had looked so strange when she'd cut it out, fell in soft folds once it had taken its place with the rest of the bodice parts. Having never lived a cocktail lifestyle, she had paired it with her scuffed old fitted leather jacket. The last thing she wanted was to look like an Audrey Hepburn tribute act, although she wasn't sure that rock chick was quite her thing either. From the look on Ben's face as he peered nervously at her from behind his cosmo, and the swept-back Sting circa 1988 shoulder-length hair and designer stubble, she had a feeling it was his, however.

'So what is it you do out here?' she asked, carefully lifting the fully loaded glass to her lips and taking a sip of the viscous bittersweet liquid.

'Journo,' he said semi-casually. 'It's not as glamorous as it sounds. Unless you ask my mother about it,' he added, and rolled his eyes. 'In which case, I'm John Simpson. Speaking of which . . .' His phone pinged and he pulled it out of his pocket, checked the text message and sighed. 'Sorry,' he said. 'That's her. Again.'

Flo smiled. 'It's nice that she takes an interest.'

'Trust me,' he said. 'It's really not.'

'Well, if your mother doesn't mind, maybe you can help me,' she said, 'Mr Simpson?'

His eyes brightened, and she could see instantly how easy it was for women to take advantage of his openness and puppy-dog enthusiasm. 'Happy to,' he said, then frowned as he lowered his voice to a more casual baritone. 'What can I do?'

'I'm trying to find out what happened to my great-aunt. She was here in nineteen sixty-two – well, all over the place – and I'm kind of tracking her down. You must have lots of contacts here.'

He deflated a little in front of her eyes, suddenly turning down the self-importance dial, and she found herself liking a little more the slightly ordinary man who was hiding behind his self-constructed advertising hoarding. 'I'm not sure they'll be much help,' he said uncertainly. 'I'm more, like, property journalism. But I can see.'

Flo smiled: she'd had a feeling he wasn't working the Paris news desk at Reuters.

The time disappeared as quickly as their drinks, as Flo explained her pilgrimage and the barman replenished their empty glasses for a second time. She took out of her bag the battered programme from packet number three and placed it on the bar. A few sheets were missing from the middle, but it still made an interesting artefact.

'Wow,' he said, turning it over and examining the tasselled red thread that held the leaves of the little booklet together. They laughed at the stylised drawings of dancing girls with impossibly long legs and gravity-defying scanty costumes, and at the black and white photos of spectacular Busby Berkeley-style show numbers. 'When was this?'

'Fifth of June nineteen sixty-two,' she said. 'My aunt was there that night.'

'Oh yes?' He pulled out a photograph. 'Which one is she?'

'Bloody hell. I'd no idea that was in there.' Flo snatched the image from him, wondering how she had missed it. It had obviously been taken by the official Lido photographer, and showed a table of bow-tied gentlemen and ladies in heavy jewellery. For the first time, she saw her own dress, looking as expensive as every other gown around the table, worn by a polished Nancy with perfect French pleat, long white gloves and a delicate smile.

'That her?' he said, leaning closer. 'She's gorgeous. Must be in the genes,' he added, coughing to cover his embarrassment.

A girl of around sixteen or seventeen sat to Nancy's left; Flo assumed this was her great-aunt's charge. It was impossible to see her face clearly, as it was partially obscured, her elbows on the table and her chin cupped in the palms of her hands. Her boredom was unmistakable, however, the challenge of Nancy's workload apparent for all to see. To her left, a light-haired man who looked as though he were being strangled by his own bow tie gurned awkwardly at the camera, and to *his* left, a beautiful racehorse of a woman had her back to him as she smiled and listened to a slick-haired man with a moustache straight out of a black and white war film who was whispering into her ear. The final dinner companions were an elderly couple who seemed to be held in place by stiff pokers, transported directly from a 1930s country-house dinner party.

Flo turned the photograph over, and found a diagram of names to match the positioning of the guests around the table: *Colonel Henderson, Mrs Henderson, Tony, Caro, Peter, Pamela, Nancy.*

Pamela. So that was the artist's daughter who Nancy had looked after. It felt like an enormous step, and Flo knew that two of the other faces around the table had to be her parents. There were no surnames on the back of the photo other than those of the Hendersons, who were clearly far too old to have a teenage daughter. That left Tony and Caro, the amorous couple next to them, and the sandy-haired man.

She turned to Ben. 'Drink up. It looks like we're going to the Lido.' She hesitated. 'If you've got time, I mean. You haven't got to go on anywhere else?'

But before she had even finished her sentence, he had jumped off his stool and was ready to go.

The rain had started by the time the taxi pulled up on the Champs-Elysées, and Ben held his jacket over Flo's head as they raced across the pavement and through the doors of the nightclub.

'Show's started. Sorry,' the uniformed man inside the lobby told them, as Ben shook the rain from his dark-grey pinstripe jacket, having quickly processed their appearance and found them to be English.

'Thank God for that,' Ben said as he found a leaflet and showed Flo the ticket prices. 'I can eat for a month on that.'

'It's fine, we don't want to see the show. We just want to ask about a show here a few years back.'

The man shrugged. 'You could ask at reception?'

Flo headed over to the desk, shimmering with a thousand tiny gold discs that fluttered in the aggressive air conditioning.

'*Bonsoir*,' said a girl with a robotic smile and perfect white teeth.

'Is she a hologram?' Ben whispered in Flo's ear.

'*Bonsoir*. I'm hoping you might be able to tell me something about a show here a while ago.'

'I'm afraid the show has started. Would you like to book for tomorrow?' the girl said, her voice prettily accented.

'No, I want to find out about a show back in nineteen sixty-two.'

'We have seats available in the balcony for tomorrow, madame?' She continued to smile at Flo.

'Thank you, but I don't want seats for tomorrow. Or the day after. I'm looking for some information.'

'We have very good availability for next week. Would you prefer afternoon or evening?' She tilted her head on one side, and her shiny dark helmet of a bob tilted with her.

The arctic air in the empty foyer was chilling Flo to the damp bone by now, the warm glow of vodka and Cointreau fading along with the last of her patience.

Ben leant over the desk and smiled at the young woman.

177

'We'd just like to ask someone a few questions if that's possible, please?' he said quietly.

The girl's head jolted upright once more. 'Of course, monsieur,' she said, pressing a bell and locking her eyes once more on the entrance.

'I hate that,' Flo fumed. It always happened when she was out with Seamus, whose charm and lopsided smile rendered her invisible to other women. Ben wasn't quite in Seamus's league, but he too had trumped Flo.

'Forget it,' he said. 'Anyway, you might be in luck. That fella looks at least as old as your programme.'

A door opened on the far side of the desk, and a small elderly gentleman in dinner jacket and bow tie appeared. 'May I help you?' he said through a thick Parisian accent.

Resisting bending down to talk to the man, Flo pulled the programme out of her handbag, along with the photograph, and handed them to him. 'This is my great-aunt,' she said. 'She was here on June the fifth nineteen sixty-two.'

He took the picture from her and frowned as he examined it, his lips moving silently.

'Do you know who these people are?' Flo said.

He shook his head. 'I've been here for many years and seen many people pass through this place. I was the coat-check boy before I became the manager, you know,' he said proudly.

Flo sighed inwardly. Fascinating though this piece of information was, it shed no light. It had been too much to hope that anyone would remember Nancy after all these years.

'Wait,' the man said, chewing his lip. 'Fifth of June, you say?'

'Yes, why?'

He handed the programme back to her and laughed. 'Wait here, please, madame, monsieur,' he said and scurried back through the door.

Ben nudged her. 'See?'

The man reappeared and placed an old scrapbook on a little coffee table. 'Come, sit,' he said, inviting then to join him on the richly upholstered armchairs.

The scrapbook was in a pretty desperate state, but there was no mistaking the copperplate inscription on the front: *1962.*

'I began keeping this when I was still a boy working here,' he explained, carefully opening the book and occasionally chuckling at a photograph, or smiling at an autographed coaster. 'I was fifteen in nineteen sixty-two. Can you imagine?' Suddenly he stopped. 'Here,' he said, turning the book around and pushing it towards Flo.

She picked it up and looked at the yellowed scrap of newspaper, and the grainy pixelated photograph of a pretty blonde woman being kissed on the cheek by an older man. *Qui est-elle?* the headline ran, and with Ben's help, she translated the text that ran alongside it.

Guests at the Lido de Paris were delighted to get a glimpse of Mr Sinatra as he made his way through the crowds before his performance last night. And it seems one lucky lady certainly caught the eye of the American star! Ol' Blue Eyes gave a thrilling show last night, and had the crowds smiling as he sang all the old favourites, finishing with a moving rendition of 'Nancy (With the Laughing

Face)'. Was it dedicated to his daughter, or to the mystery lady in the audience? We can't decide. But look out, Mrs Sinatra!

Flo and Ben looked at each other.

'Well, blow me down,' he said eventually. 'I think you just found your aunt.'

'I think we did, Mr Simpson.'

Flo wasn't sure where those first three days had gone, as she loaded her belongings back into the suitcase. Her feet told her they had been spent pounding the streets of Paris, and her dwindling supply of euros told her she ought to rein it in a bit – she had already seen off the best part of two weeks' wages. Her heart told her it was now three months since she had seen Seamus. Her head told her that she was spending too much time with Ben, and that she needed to make the next move on her own.

She and Ben had both agreed, after some vigorous googling on Ben's phone, that the singer was a red herring, albeit a happily married, entertaining one, and so Flo was no further in her quest, and there was no Sinatra love child hiding behind the scenes.

They had also agreed that Tony and Caro had to be Pamela's parents and Nancy's employers, and that the next step was to find out their surname.

It was time to move on, and she looked forward to pulling out of the Gare de Lyon and leaving the city behind her as she headed south for the next leg of the journey and the next phase of Nancy's wardrobe.

She was also looking forward to leaving behind the awkward confusion over the botched cheek-kiss in a taxi at the end of the evening. To be fair, she had nothing to lose, and maybe one day down the line she'd consider looking at someone else, but it was unlikely to be for a while, and she was nowhere near ready to let anyone replace Seamus. Ben was sweet, and she enjoyed his easy company, but he was almost as fragile as she, and she didn't want his next heartbreak to be on her conscience. She had, however, agreed to let him research the other members of the party: with his schoolboy enthusiasm and ability to make her laugh, it would be nice to hear from him when a few days had passed.

For the time being, she needed to focus on finding Nancy and discovering more about the artist Tony. She wasn't sure what she expected to unearth next, but the trail was a relatively short one. It began here in Paris, and ended amongst the canals of Venice.

'Right, Nancy,' she said, zipping the case shut and slinging her handbag over her shoulder. 'Let's see where else you've been hiding.'

Part Four

ANTIBES, CÔTE D'AZUR

15

McCall's 6372: Bathing suit and beach dress

Nancy closed her eyes and let the heat of the sun wash over her bare legs. She slid further down in the low-slung deckchair, reaching to dig little holes in the sand with her toes. The sand was hot and fine and white here, a far cry from the cold, murderous pebbles at Eastbourne, which twisted your ankles and dug into your back if you were foolhardy enough to lie on them. Here you only had to worry that you might burn the soles of your feet, and she could see why so many people wore the canvas and rope espadrilles that could be bought all over town for a couple of francs.

A light breeze rustled the fringing of the parasol that shielded the rest of her body from the burning rays, and she opened her eyes to watch the white tassels shimmer and sway against the cloudless blue sky. No wonder they called this the Côte d'Azur, she thought: she couldn't remember ever seeing an English sky so very blue, although the vivid turquoise of the sea surely had as much right to lend its name to the sweeping coastline of arc-like beaches and rugged cliffs.

She was close to sleep, but couldn't switch off from the chatter of her fellow bathers, their laughter and conversation rising and falling along with the gentle swish of the waves that brushed against the sand. Every so often a child would run past, laughing as its adult failed to keep up, or a song wafted from a transistor radio, serenading her with Charles Aznavour or Ricky Nelson.

'Can we go yet?'

She lifted her head and looked around. Pamela was sitting on the sand next to her, tracing circles with a stick then scrubbing them out again.

'We've only just got here.'

Pamela sighed. 'I'm bored.'

So it was going to be one of those days. Nancy braced herself for a repeat of the train journey down from Paris, when she had had to field the 'when will we be there?' question on average every ten minutes throughout the length of France, and Pamela had needed feeding constant snacks in order to stave off her boredom. Nancy had wished there'd been space for the girl in her parents' compartment, and that she herself had been left in peace to enjoy the beautiful fields of endless sunflowers that morphed into gauzy swathes of lavender as the train sped down through Provence and towards the coast. She could also have done without apologising to their fellow travellers every twenty minutes when Pamela got up and shuffled around the compartment like a caged bear.

They had arranged to fly down, but Peter had changed their plans after the awful air crash at Orly airport a couple of days before Nancy arrived in Paris. Ten days later, terrible pictures of the crash site still dominated the front pages of newspapers everywhere she looked: being trapped on a train with a bored teenager was as nothing compared to what some had gone through, she realised.

'And it's too hot,' Pamela added, when Nancy failed to react. She pulled the towel closer around her shoulders.

Nancy patted the empty deckchair next to her. 'Why don't you sit here? It's much nicer in the shade.'

'I don't want to sit there. I want to go back.'

'And what are you going to do when you get there?'

Pamela shrugged. 'Read a book?'

Somehow Nancy doubted that.

'You must be tired. Lie down and have a rest.'

'I'm not tired.'

Of course she wasn't.

'Well, why don't you take that camera of yours and see what's around? We could have a walk along the beach.'

'I don't want to go for a walk.'

'Bloody hell, Pamela!' She sat up and turned to find the girl pointing her camera at her, and with a click, Nancy's irritation was captured for eternity.

'You wanted me to take some pictures,' Pamela said, smiling sarcastically as she wound the film on.

Nancy growled at her, and for a moment or two they sat in simmering silence until, to her surprise, Pamela quietly got up and lay next to her.

It was just as well, since Nancy had had a bad night's sleep and was at the very fringes of her temper. She and Pamela had been put in the maid's cottage in the grounds of the villa on the hill, and whereas the main house had state-of-the-art air conditioning, their box-like dwelling was a fiendish heat trap. The choice between open windows and being mosquito food was a difficult one, but in the end Pamela's outbursts against her tormentors won through, and so Nancy had suffocated while her companion slept in peace.

She looked at the angry red and white bumps all over Pamela's legs and felt a rush of pity for the girl hiding under the large towel: she just wanted to be queuing up at the tuck shop with her friends or charging around the lacrosse pitch. She could see how out of place she felt, surrounded by tall, lean bodies that only served to emphasise the plumpness and Englishness of her transitional form. Nancy's own limbs were almost as pale, but their length and slimness made it a feature of them, rather than a failing, and the grazes wrought by the Paris pavement had now faded to near invisibility.

'Here, why don't you borrow this?' she said, passing Pamela the pretty sleeveless beach cover she had made to go with her swimsuit.

Pamela looked unsure at first, but put on the little flared hip-length coat with its gently ruffled hem, and did up the four oversized white buttons that matched its scrambled-egg yellow and white gingham. She looked down at it. 'This is really pretty. Where did you get it?'

'I didn't get it. I made it.'

Pamela looked across at her. 'You *made* it? How?'

'Scissors, thread, sewing machine, magic sewing pixies . . .'

Pamela chucked a handful of sand across Nancy's thighs. 'No, really.'

'It's not that hard,' Nancy said, brushing the sand off where it clung to her suncream. 'You just need to know what you're doing.'

'Did you make your swimsuit, too?'

Nancy looked down at the white halter-neck suit, which had miraculously forced the last of her flabby belly into a tight skirt-like girdle that skimmed the top of her thighs, hid her ugly stretch marks and gave her back her twenty-five-inch waist, a small price for her impeded breathing. 'Yes,' she said. 'In fact I made all my clothes for this trip.'

For a moment, Pamela was lost for words, and stared with unrestrained admiration at her companion. 'Would you make something for me one day?'

'If you like.'

She nodded. 'Thanks.'

'I can show you how to do it yourself, too.'

'Really? I've done a bit at school, of course. We made aprons. And did some embroidery. I wasn't very good at it, though.'

'What *are* you good at?' Nancy closed her eyes, hoping that her feigned inattention would draw the girl out of herself.

'Me? Not much really. I can't paint, can't sew, can't play the piano.'

'But there must be something you like doing. Everyone has something.'

'I had a pony when I was little. At my grandparents' house. I used to ride around the estate on my own when I went to stay with them in the holidays, as long as I was back in time for supper. I liked riding, but there's no opportunity any more.'

'Why not?'

'Well, they died, then Uncle Cecil took it over, but he was pretty hopeless. And when he died, everything had to be sold. Even Fudge.'

'I'm sorry.'

Pamela shrugged. 'I never really liked Uncle Cecil. He always smelled of whisky.'

'I've met a few of those,' Nancy said, and they swapped a brief smile. 'So if you can't be a top showjumper, what are you going to be?'

'Me?'

'No, that waiter carrying drinks over there.'

'Hmm.' Pamela fiddled with a loose thread on the deckchair. 'Ma thinks I should get married as soon as I'm old enough.'

'But you're only seventeen.' Nancy sat up and turned to face her. 'Really?'

Pamela sighed. 'Might as well, I suppose. And I'm nearly eighteen, actually. Granny was married when she was nineteen. Anyway, I'm not good for much else.'

'Don't be silly. Everyone's good for something. What would you do if you could choose anything?'

'Anything?' Pamela looked out to sea. 'You'll think I'm mad if I tell you.'

'No, I won't,' Nancy said, slicking suncream onto her legs and passing the bottle to Pamela, who sniffed at it and turned her nose up.

'All right. But you mustn't tell Ma or Pa.'

'Promise.'

She took a deep breath. 'I'd be a nurse.'

Well, she hadn't seen that one coming. And a more unsuitable bedside manner it would be hard to find.

'You think it's funny.' Pamela glared at her.

'I don't. I think it's admirable. I'm just surprised.' Pamela was blushing, so she added quickly, 'I think you'd be a very good nurse, actually.'

'No, you don't. But I'm nicer than you think. You just don't know me.'

'I don't think you're not nice. But I'm not sure I can see your mother letting you look after the great unwashed. Have you told her?'

'Once.' Nancy didn't need to ask more: the expression on the girl's face said it all. 'I had to promise I wouldn't mention it ever again. Don't tell her I said anything, will you?'

Their attention was suddenly torn away by a hubbub a little further along the beach, as a petite blonde woman in a tiny bikini and a deep suntan walked down the steps and along the row of loungers and seaweed-green parasols, her fluffy ponytail bouncing on top of her head. The posse of men following her with cameras were shouting at her to smile, to pose, to pout.

'Did you see who that was?' a man's voice said close by.

They both turned, to see a figure outlined against the bright sunshine, his white linen shirt hanging open over swimming shorts.

'Don't be so provincial, Tony.' Caro appeared at his side, her high-waisted black bikini serving only to accentuate the skeleton too close beneath the surface. 'You'd think you'd never seen an actress before.' She looked at Nancy. 'I suppose you're going to tell me *she's* a friend of yours too?'

'Why are you here?' Pamela said to Tony, whose smile suddenly dropped beneath the pencil-thin moustache. 'I thought it was just going to be girls this morning.'

'Don't be rude, darling,' Caro hissed.

'Where's Pa?'

'He's gone for a walk to do some painting. He wanted a bit of peace and quiet, so we headed over here, didn't we, Tony?'

'Certainly did. So,' he said, rubbing his hands together and pulling off his shirt, 'who's up for a swim with Uncle Tony? Nancy? Shame to let a swimsuit like that stay hidden under a brolly, eh?'

'Oh, I'm fine. Thanks, though.' There was something about Tony that made her want to put more clothes on; besides, she was receiving strong invisible signals from Caro.

'Pamela?' Caro tried to get her daughter's attention. 'Why don't you go for a swim? Get rid of a bit of that puppy fat before the party tomorrow?'

'I don't like swimming.'

'Don't be ridiculous. Everyone likes swimming.'

'Why don't you go, then?'

It seemed as though the whole beach fell silent as Caro worked out what to do about her daughter's insolence before deciding to file it away for another, less public time.

Pamela, realising she had overstepped the mark, saw an opportunity to escape, and flung off Nancy's coverall, letting Tony drag her away by the arm as he shouted, 'Last one in's a dumpling.'

'There's no hope for that girl,' Caro said, sliding herself into Pamela's lounger and helping herself from the bottle of lotion.

'She's just a little tired. It's been a busy few days.'

'Don't make excuses for her, Nancy. She can't behave like a child for ever.'

It struck Nancy that Pamela probably hadn't had much opportunity to behave like a child during her seventeen years.

'What's the matter? You look like you just lost a pound and found a farthing.'

'Nothing. I expect I'm just a little tired too.'

'Aren't we all, darling.' Caro lay back with her eyes closed, one knee lifted and leaning against her other leg.

Nancy looked out at the masts bobbing about on the sparkling sea, the speedboats roaring back and forth around the pine-covered cap to the next beach or the next party. Behind them the palm trees lining the medieval walls of the pretty town swished in the warm Mediterranean breeze.

'So,' Caro said. 'We've not really had a chance to chat, just the two of us, have we?'

'I suppose not.'

'You must be missing home.'

Nancy hesitated. There was no way she was going to recount the terrible night she had had, when her body ached to be back in Wandsworth, her stomach cramping and her breasts painful against her light cotton nightie. Or to say how close she had come to packing her bags and walking to the nearest airport, however far away it was and however much she dreaded the thought of flying.

'Not really,' she said.

'No young man waiting for you back in London?' Caro said teasingly. 'Pretty girl like you must have a few admirers.'

'There was someone, but not any more.'

'Plenty more fish in the sea,' Caro said, patting her arm.

Nancy watched Pamela outlined against the shimmering horizon, arms folded, feet in the water as she gazed out to sea, oblivious to the children splashing around her and the nut-brown professional beachgoers wandering slowly along the shoreline, showing off their tans and the swimsuits that would never get wet. Tony walked amongst them, greeting a few of the women and chatting with the men. He never seemed to stop making connections, and she wondered how someone so brash could be friends with someone as quiet as Peter.

'She's a worry,' Caro said, breaking into Nancy's thoughts.

'Pamela? I don't know. She's got her head screwed on.'

'Perhaps. I'm not so sure – she's probably been away from us too much, but she's like a fish out of water over here. I'd hoped she might fit in, meet some people, get an idea of what she wants from life . . .' Caro sighed. 'She really is her father through and through. Perhaps we need to find some farmer for her. Someone with horses who won't mind his wife dressing like the groom.'

Nancy laughed, but she sensed the disappointment that crept through the older woman's smile. Pamela and Caro really couldn't have been more different.

'Have you thought about her maybe getting a job, or going to university?' she said hesitantly.

Caro lowered her sunglasses and peered at her. 'Pamela? A bluestocking?' She shook her head. 'Neither of our families is exactly what you might call the academic type. Apart from Peter, I suppose, if the Slade counts as a university. He was the first Cavendish in generations to actually work for a living. Quite shocked his parents.'

'Pamela told me they passed away. And then her uncle? I'm sorry. It must have been hard. She was obviously very fond of them.'

Caro pursed her lips. 'Cecil died two years ago now, just a year after his parents. All the blue blood in the world couldn't rescue that family or their godforsaken rotting pile. Cecil was a pisshead and a gambler, so I wouldn't shed too many tears there. Poor Peter: he's the only normal one in that nest of inbred relics.' She reached for her bag. 'They only tolerated me because they thought I'd bring a magic pot of dollars with me across the pond. An American marrying a baronet's son? The horror! We'll be infiltrating their precious royal family next.' She laughed, and lit a cigarette, cupping the flame of her lighter against the sea breeze. 'Not Peter, though. He wouldn't know a pot of gold from a pot of soup. Bless him. He's a good sort, that one. I was lucky.' She turned to Nancy. 'So, from one outsider to another, how do you manage, with your British class thing? Working-class girl and all that. It must be difficult to fit in.'

Nancy looked at Caro, unsure whether her employer was having a dig at her or was just curious. Until she had said those words, Nancy hadn't given a thought to the differences between the Cavendish background and her own. She was just Nancy. She'd always felt at home wherever she was, although she knew she spoke very differently at the kitchen table in Victoria Street to how she spoke across the river. Dad was more traditional, she knew: a firm believer in people sticking to their place in life, and that trying to be something you weren't would never make you happy in the end. Had he been right? She wasn't sure, but he had a wisdom no education could buy, and he was usually on the button. Undoubtedly, if she'd stuck to her own kind, things would have turned out differently. Maybe she was kidding herself, and she'd always be the outsider in this world.

Things were changing, though, she was sure: youth and talent were becoming the new aristocracy, and anything and anyone went. Girls like her would have opportunities that Beryl's generation could only dream of.

She smiled thinly at Caro. 'I don't know about that. If working-class girls and Americans can find themselves sitting on a beach together in the South of France, then maybe the world is moving on.'

'Let's hope so, sweetie.'

Nancy stood up, stretching the stiffness out of her limbs. 'I think I'll get Pamela back to the house before she has too much sun.'

'Good idea,' Caro said. 'We don't want her looking like a lobster at the party, do we?'

Nancy began packing her things into her beach bag, picking up Pamela's sandals and towel and waving to get her attention. As Pamela saw her and began walking slowly back through the sand, Nancy turned round to say goodbye to Caro, but she had moved off the lounger and now lay on a towel on the sand in full sun, her oiled face illuminated by the concertina-fan aluminium reflector placed below her chin, and her eyes closed. Nancy knew enough to let sleeping dogs lie, suspecting that this particular one would awaken like a Rottweiler if disturbed, so she quietly picked up the beach bag and padded away across the hot, prickly sand.

16

McCall's 6571: Misses' cocktail dress

As the car rolled along the gravelled drive and set down its passengers beneath a canopy of palm trees, the sound of music and muted laughter drifted across on the warm evening breeze, cutting through the insistent rush of waves on the rocks below.

The irritation between Caro and Pamela that had shrouded the journey along the narrow winding coast road was temporarily forgotten as they stopped to take in the view of the beautiful rose-pink miniature palace, transported from an Arabian kasbah to the Cap d'Antibes via an F. Scott Fitzgerald novel. Its balconied stucco facade deepened in colour as the sun began its descent below the cliff and the cicadas welcomed in the night, the last rays of light sliding over the frilled white castellation trimming the roof line of the mansion. As midsummer crept closer, the nights were beginning to feel like no more than the blink of an eye, and Nancy craved darkness and a rest from the dazzling Riviera skies.

She followed the others along the line of flaming torches that led to a terrace festooned with glowing candy-coloured paper lanterns.

'Peter, old chap,' she heard a voice say, as the Cavendishes broke through into the party. An older gentleman in a white tux grasped Peter's hand and patted him across the back, then kissed the fingers of Caro's gloved hand.

Caro had outdone herself this evening, despite an early near-fatal wardrobe malfunction, and looked beautiful in an oyster-coloured Grecian-style chiffon dress from the Givenchy back catalogue. No one would have known that only two hours ago there had been a crisis of international proportions as she found a huge rip along the front of the strapless bodice, where Pamela had secretly squeezed into the dress earlier that day, pushing the delicate fabric beyond its limit. It was potentially ruined, and Nancy had earned the eternal gratitude of her employer when at the eleventh hour she had whipped it away and, with the help of her sewing kit, turned the long sash into a wide halter neck that crossed over on itself, wrapping around the waist and tying in a bow at the base of Caro's bare tanned back.

'Will there be food?'

'I expect so, Pamela,' Nancy said.

Pamela had hung back, and was loitering at the top of the steps, waiting for her to catch up. She must be hungry, banished from having supper with the rest of them and refusing to eat the plate of sandwiches Nancy had sneaked over to the little cottage.

'Let's be polite and say hello to your hosts, then we'll get you something to eat.'

Pamela sighed, letting herself be drawn in as everyone exclaimed how much she had grown, how like her grandmother she was, and was she really seventeen? Goodness, time to think about what she wanted to do with her life. She really ought to meet their grandson. Did she know him? Very good-looking and doing marvellous things in the City. Yes, they'd arrange a dinner for all of them back in London. So much fun.

Nancy could only admire how Pamela smiled and rose above it.

'Now, Pamela, I want you to behave tonight,' Caro said as she led them away. 'There's a very good chance Daddy will meet some potential clients this evening. And,' she added, glancing at Pamela, 'it looks like someone's got herself a dinner invitation.' She ignored Pamela's rolling eyes and waved at a group of people next to the pool. 'I must go and say hello. Will you be all right for a moment?'

'Go,' Peter said, and turned to Pamela as Caro headed away from them. 'I'm sorry about that, Pea. She just wants the best for you.'

'She just wants to get rid of me.'

'It sounds like you might get a painting out of it, though?' Nancy said to Peter, trying to shift the conversation.

He sighed and blinked in the way she had noticed he did when he was anxious. 'I wish she would just give up. Really, no one wants portraits any more. Look at that new chap of Princess Margaret's. That's what they're all falling over themselves for: a fancy black and white photograph from a royal-about-town, not a stuffy old oil painting.'

'I'm sure that's not true.'

'I wish it weren't, Nancy, but I have to face facts.'

'But you're so good, Pa,' Pamela said, leaning against his arm.

He smiled. 'Thanks, Pea, but you're not exactly going to commission a portrait, are you?'

'If I had some money of my own, I would.'

'And if *I* had some money, I certainly wouldn't!' He tugged at his bow tie and grimaced. 'Who on earth expects people to wear these wretched things in this heat? I'm going to go and find a drink. Anyone want to come with me?'

Pamela grabbed his arm, and it broke Nancy's heart to see how eagerly she lapped up her father's attention, and how when left alone, the two of them were so easy together. It was the curse of the upper classes that they never allowed themselves to watch their children grow up; she had a feeling that Peter had missed more than he cared to or had chosen to.

'I'll stay here,' she said, wanting to give them some time. 'I could do with a bit of fresh air. I'll find you shortly.'

'Are you sure?' But Pamela was already dragging him away, and the pretty polka-dot underskirt peeped back and forth beneath her powder-blue spaghetti-strapped dress as she bounced along beside him, the hair that Nancy had spent half an hour pinning up already coming loose and falling on her shoulders.

Nancy wasn't in the mood for a party, and her conversation with Caro on the beach had combined with her general malaise to make her a less than perfect guest. She'd imagined that Caro had employed her because she would fit in, but maybe, as Pamela had told her in a fit of pique one morning as Nancy tried to brush her hair, it was because no one else was desperate enough to accept the paltry money on offer. She was cheap: that was all.

She decided to head away from the main bulk of the party; other than her employers, there was no one she knew here. She took a glass of champagne from a passing waiter and avoided eye contact with the other guests as she wandered the length of the pool and down to a lower terrace with an uninterrupted view out over the cliff edge to the crimson-fringed sea.

She leant against a low balustrade wall and sipped the cold champagne, thinking about the letter from home that had found its way to her earlier that day. Trust Dorothy to make the impossibility of the situation seem normal and easy. For a woman who claimed to have been bottom of the class at school, she could be incredibly clever, reassuring Nancy that all was well, without filling in details that she knew would torment her, and making her laugh as she recounted the date Phyllis had had with the lad who worked at the grocer's, and how her mum had gone mad when she found out. Poor Phyllis: it mattered little to her where her husband came from, only that he put a ring on her finger and gave her babies.

Nancy was homesick. That was the bottom line. One crabby teenager did not make up for the company of her friends, however fond she was becoming of Pamela. She wished Dorothy were here right now to laugh at all these pointless people with their fancy cars and jewels, the men who looked her up and down and the women with radar that spotted her as an imposter; she would have put them in their place. She missed Phyllis and her twittering and fussing, con-sistently and unwittingly Dorothy's fall guy. She missed Peggy and sharing a cup of tea over the kitchen table, or making jam tarts together; sitting on the stool in Dad's little shed while he tinkered with an old clock or the big Bakelite radio, asking her to pass a screwdriver from the neat rows of tools hanging on the wall. The simple things. Things she feared she might never enjoy again. And she missed Maddie: rosy-cheeked, milk-scented Maddie.

Behind her, she heard the band strike up, a gentle jazzy number she was sure she had danced to in the old days, thinking that she would be doing this for ever. The sweet and mournful tune floated through the cypress trees and across the rocky clifftop. She wondered if the yachts in the distance, their lights dappled on the inky waters, could hear the music, and whether a man standing on a deck would ask a woman to dance, and put his hand around her waist as they swayed to the decaying refrains of the old love song.

She closed her eyes and began humming along. *I've got you under my skin* . . .

The melody changed to something more upbeat, bringing her out of her reverie. She couldn't hide out here for ever, she knew, so reluctantly she packed up her thoughts and wandered back towards the party, stopping to smell the oleander and listen to the roosting of the last of the late-to-bed birds. She watched the crowd on the terrace, wondering which were the bankers, the writers, the countesses, the oil tycoons, the real deal or the hangers-on, but actually more interested in comparing brocade with bias cut, back-combing with bob, as the women vied for the attention of a selection of tanned gentlemen of all sizes and ages, whose attractiveness, she suspected, was based on their connections and their bank accounts.

'Hey, Nancy,' a voice called, 'come and join us.'

She turned to see Tony with an older woman, her black sleeveless shift offset with a diamond choker that hung loosely around her wrinkled neck, and the matching bracelet of Crown Jewels proportions making her look like Holly Golightly's grandmother. She eyed Nancy from head to toe, expressing with the tiniest inclination of one pencilled eyebrow her resentment towards the intrusion, and clearly disappointed not to find Nancy wanting in her knee-length Schiaparelli-pink silk dress with its voluminous skirt, wide V-neck and narrow shoulder straps. An ironed-out, younger version stood beside her, her thigh-high ivory A-line dress revealing tanned coltish legs straight out of a racehorse stud. Unlike her mother, she failed entirely to acknowledge Nancy, her eyes instead fixed on Tony, so that Nancy could stare unobserved at the intricate pattern of carefully pinned white-blonde curls and plaits on top of her head.

Tony put an arm around Nancy's waist. 'Nancy, meet Mrs Devere and her daughter Barbara. This little lady is helping Peter and Caro out over the summer,' he explained, to the complete indifference of the older woman and the mild irritation of the younger, who took her gaze from Tony and slowly turned towards Nancy. 'She's a complete sweetie.'

'Really. How interesting,' the older woman said in a gravelly Texan drawl, and casually flicked ash from the end of her cigarette onto the ground at Nancy's feet.

Her companion merely stared expressionlessly at the newcomer.

'Isn't she a doll?' Tony gave Nancy's waist a tickle, and she managed to pull away from him with a polite laugh.

Mrs Devere stretched the corners of her thin dark-red lips into an approximation of a smile. 'Quite the little Barbie,' she said.

'Quite the Barbie, Mother,' the girl parroted.

The older woman turned to her quickly and hissed, 'Don't call me that. Darling,' she added with a thin smile.

'Mrs Devere and I were just talking business. I'm trying to persuade her to get involved in my new film. Shouldn't mix work and pleasure, I know, but we're old chums, aren't we?'

Nancy was surprised to see the woman's expression soften a little. 'Please don't call me that, Tony,' she said, almost flirtatiously. 'You make me sound like my poor dead third mother-in-law. God rest her twisted little soul. It's Dolores.' And as Mrs Devere brushed Tony's arm, Nancy began to wonder about the relationship between the man who was probably only twenty years older than herself, and the American who could have been his mother. Barbara looked equally uncomfortable, and Nancy threw her a conspiratorial look, but not a thickly mascaraed eyelash fluttered in response.

'Can't say too much at this stage, but we've got a pretty big name signed up.' Tony smiled and looked around the group.

'You are clever, Tony. You know simply everyone.'

He bowed his head slightly. 'You are working with the right person, my dear Dolores.'

They all jumped as the party photographer leapt in front of them to capture their image, and for the first time Barbara's face automatically broke into a practised smile as Tony pulled Nancy towards him for the shot. The man ripped a photograph out of his Polaroid camera and offered it to the group. The Devere women scanned it quickly, but clearly finding their captured images not to their satisfaction, passed it to Tony.

'Here, you have it, Nancy,' he said. 'Nice little memento for you.'

'Oh, I'm not really sure . . .' she said, looking at the image of Tony's arm around her.

He took a slim cigar out of his top pocket, and was still patting ineffectually at his jacket when Dolores held out a little gold lighter, its flame flickering in the breeze. Tony cupped his hands around hers as he leant into the flame and worked the cigar into life.

Nancy sighed, and tucked the picture into her clutch bag. 'Well, it's been lovely to meet you both, but I must go and find Pamela,' she said, more as a way of escaping the strange tableau than out of genuine need to look for her charge.

'I'll be after a dance with you later,' Tony called as she turned away. She pretended not to have heard him.

'Nancy, Nancy!'

Pamela stood waving at her from the veranda. The crush of people was much denser near the house, and Nancy had to twist sideways to work her way through the crowd. Finally she reached her charge, who was standing with Caro and Peter and bursting with news.

'You'll never guess what?'

'You're right, I'll never guess.'

'Well, two things really. Pa, you should say your news first.'

Peter tilted his head modestly. 'Well, it's not really news until it's definite. Don't count your chickens, and all that.'

'For goodness' sake, Peter, have some faith.' Caro lit a cigarette and inhaled deeply, then let out a stream of smoke that was illuminated briefly in the lamplight before it diffused into the night air. 'I'm going to find Tony,' she said. 'I'll leave you to it.'

Pamela looked across at the drive, where the shiny black car was making its final turn before disappearing out of view. 'He said yes.'

'He said maybe,' Peter added.

'It's a friend of Uncle Douglas's,' Pamela said. 'He's at the embassy in Paris and on holiday down here.'

'In that case, it's in the bag, I'm sure,' Nancy said as Peter shook his head in exasperation at his daughter. 'I'm thrilled for you. So what's the other news?'

'Oh, this is even better,' said Pamela.

'Princess Grace has invited you for tea?'

Pamela laughed, her cheeks a little flushed, and Nancy wondered how much champagne she'd drunk. Given the fact that the girl hadn't eaten for hours, she hoped it wouldn't mean she was in for another long, miserable night.

'Don't be silly. It's better than that. Cousin Charlie's coming to meet us in Capri!'

'Well, I'm sure that's lovely.'

'I'm going to tell the others,' Pamela said, and disappeared off into the crush, heading for the barely visible figures of Caro and Tony standing close to each other on the far side of the pool.

Peter watched her go, a wistful look on his face. 'Dear Pamela. She adores Charlie. He was always very sweet and tolerant of a rather annoying young child. He's like a big brother to her.'

Nancy suspected that Pamela had been not so much annoying as desperate for attention, but she simply smiled. 'Is he much older than her, then?'

Peter frowned, and took his pipe from his pocket, tapping

it, then stuffing sweet-smelling tobacco into its bowl. 'It's hard to remember by how much, but he's probably about the same age as you. You might even get on with each other. Be nice for you to have a pal of your own age around, rather than us old fogeys.'

She watched him as he squinted through the pipe smoke and the strings of lanterns as he tried to locate his wife.

'So who *is* Cousin Charlie?' she asked, taking a sip of her now warm champagne.

He turned back. 'Charlie? Oh, not really a cousin. Son of friends of mine – father's a lawyer. Think they're rather hoping he'll join the family firm, but he's got other ideas. Wants to be a writer,' he said, laughing. 'Poor chap. He'll grow out of that, I'm sure!'

Nancy felt the champagne hit an obstacle in her throat, and struggled to release her next words. 'Really?' she said quietly. 'What's his name? Maybe I already know him.'

And as Peter spoke the familiar words, Nancy felt her knees crumble and her carefully constructed walls come crashing down around her.

17

LONDON, 1960

It had been Diana's birthday. They were going to go back to her Cheyne Walk flat after work to drink champagne and make spaghetti and plaster their faces with creams while they watched *The Avengers*. 'Absolutely no boys,' Diana had said as they walked out of the workshop and into the car parked in the street outside Belgrave's, an early birthday present from her parents.

Nancy was more than happy with that: they'd been out twice this week already with Diana's brother and his friends, and although she loved a night out on the town, she needed a quiet one. It would be fun, just the two of them: Diana was hilarious, even if she was a bit of a madam sometimes, and could take off just about anyone from work. Her impersonation of Monsieur Jacques was so good that one of the new girls had thought he was actually ordering her, from behind a partition, to go and buy tartan thread for the workshop.

She really ought to go home tonight, she knew: she'd slept more on Diana's put-you-up than in her own bedroom this week. Dad's jokes about dirty stop-outs were beginning to feel slightly less jokey every time she put her key in the door of number 75, and Mum had long since replaced her 'treat this house like a hotel' rants with the silent treatment.

She'd go back tomorrow, and maybe buy them all fish and chips and a few bottles of Dad's favourite beer. Perhaps Peggy and Donald could come over, if her sister was feeling up to it. Should she have spent more time with Peggy? she wondered. It was hard to know where the line was between being a support and getting in the way, and she had no idea how to begin comforting her heartbroken sister and quietly stoic brother-in-law. No one could really know what they were going through again. She made a mental note to buy Peggy some flowers. Before she went to the chippy. And the offie.

They clattered up the stairs to the flat, throwing their coats on the sofa and their shoes on the floor, before Diana disappeared into the kitchen to fetch a couple of greasy wine glasses, filling them from a bottle straight from the fridge, the condensation on the heavy cold glass nearly causing it to slip from her hand. Nancy was always amazed at the contents of Diana's little fridge, where the ratio of champagne to sour milk was at least six to one, and the only foodstuffs were dried-up lemon halves and a pot of Gentleman's Relish. 'Cheers,' she said, handing Nancy a glass. 'You hungry? We could just go to the Stockpot.'

'It'll be closed by now.'

'You're right. And it is a bit working-girl, isn't it? All those shepherd's pies. Boarding school all over again.' She shuddered. 'I forgot to go shopping, so there's not much here, I'm afraid.'

Nancy did wonder if Diana ever ate. She'd never seen her friend consume more than the lettuce out of the middle of her lunchtime sandwich, or the lemon in her gin and tonic.

'I could go and buy chips?' she said, although she very much doubted there was a chippy in Chelsea.

'Chips?' Diana laughed and slapped her friend gently on the thigh. 'Oh, you can be so quaint sometimes, Nancy. I do adore you.'

Nancy smiled, resisting the temptation to slap her friend back. Sometimes she felt that her role in their relationship was as Diana's pet working-class friend, and she was sure she had overheard Diana taking off her south London accent. Was she there simply to enhance Diana's social status and ease the little chip that sat on her friend's shoulder, burrowing away at the lowly origins of the vast family fortune? You couldn't buy class, Nancy knew that, but she wondered how many generations had to pass away before muck was washed from brass.

A car horn sounded in the street outside, and the two girls rushed to open the sticky old sash window.

Below them, two young men in dinner jackets stood on the pavement, looking up at the window. 'Happy birthday,' shouted one of them, who Nancy recognised as a friend of Diana's brother.

Diana quickly smoothed her glossy chestnut bob and told him to go away.

'Come on. At least let me buy you a drink on your birthday?' he wailed.

She pulled herself back from the window. 'What do you think, Nancy? Fancy it?'

Nancy wasn't sure. Maybe she should let Diana go on her own, and head back down to Wandsworth. She could go and see Dorothy after tea and find out how her new job on the buses was going. Or help Mum with the mending pile.

Diana blinked chocolate-brown puppy-dog eyes at her. 'Go on, it'll be fun. It is my birthday. Besides, I can't go on my own. Henry's brought Charlie with him, and he'll end up being the gooseberry.'

Nancy saw there was no way out of this, even though she really didn't fancy being left with another tedious public-school bore who spent the whole evening talking about Mummy. 'All right. But I've nothing to wear.'

'Yes, you have. You left that gold dress here a couple of weeks ago. And you can borrow some of my shoes.' Diana disappeared into her bedroom, and Nancy watched her fling clothes from one side of the floor to the other.

So that was where it had gone. Nancy loved that dress: with a couple of metres of eye-wateringly expensive heavy gold satin Monsieur Jacques had let her have off the end of a roll, she had crafted it into a perfect copy of a Givenchy dress worn by Audrey Hepburn a few months earlier. She hoped it hadn't spent two weeks scrunched up in a pile of discarded stockings.

Diana came back with the dress and a pair of pale cream slingbacks. 'Here,' she said. 'No excuse.'

'Thanks.' Nancy took the crumpled dress from her, noticing a couple of marks that definitely hadn't been there when she'd last worn it.

'Last one ready buys the drinks,' Diana said brightly, and promptly locked herself in the bathroom.

Funny how Nancy always seemed to be last, she mused, and that those with the deepest pockets never put their hands in them.

*

She sat on one side of the curved banquette watching Diana and Henry perform body-language foreplay as the waitress brought one bottle after another and the mood of the music changed from lively to time-to-go-home. If Diana fiddled with his bow tie one more time, Nancy would rip it off and wrap it around her friend's long, slender neck. Yes, Henry was handsome – even the most aesthetically challenged man looked good in a dinner jacket – but there was a vacuity about him that bored Nancy rigid. How Diana had maintained such a rapt interest in his rowing triumphs and hunting-field exploits, she had no idea. She was almost grateful for the intermittent raising of champagne glasses as they chirpily toasted Diana's birthday for the umpteenth time.

'I'm afraid you're finding this terribly dull.'

She had switched off to such a degree that she'd almost forgotten Charlie, the fourth member of their party, and the lighting in their little booth was so subtle as to make it hard to see anyone else around the table.

She turned around. 'Is it that obvious?'

Charlie shrugged. 'If it's any consolation, I was just considering gnawing on my leg for a little light relief.'

She laughed, feeling bad now that she'd practically ignored him ever since they'd arrived at the little private club in Soho. 'I know how you feel. I was just eyeing up my arm for the very same reason.'

He smiled at her as the waitress arrived with fresh candles for the table. As they glowed into life, she saw him properly, and realised he had the palest grey eyes she had ever seen, all the more dramatic against his thick black hair, which did its best to defy his hair cream. It was like looking at Tony Curtis's younger brother: she half expected Jack Lemmon to appear at any moment wearing a flapper dress.

'Nancy?' Charlie said. 'How about we leave these two here and go and get a drink somewhere else? I don't think they'll notice, do you?'

Nancy watched Henry nibbling the ends of Diana's fingers and quickly picked up her handbag. 'What are we waiting for?' she said, and they slipped out from behind the table without so much as a glance from their friends.

They walked through the streets of Soho, and he draped his jacket over her shoulders as the November chill made her shiver in the sleeveless dress. They chatted, about this and that, and she laughed as he described how Diana had worked her way through just about everyone in her brother's year at school.

He'd come down from Oxford a couple of years earlier and wanted to be a writer, he told her, if only he could persuade his parents not to make him take up law. Nancy had never met a writer: the men she'd grown up around worked with their hands, and those in Diana's set seemed not to have any work at all, nor to need any. She was curious, and a mere couple of streets into their meanderings, she had forgotten that only a short while ago she had been prepared to take several buses across London just to get home.

'So tell me about you, Nancy,' he said as a tired-looking waitress placed their hot chocolates in front of them, her deep sighs making clear her disgruntlement at being forced to serve people at this time of night.

'Me?' she said, stirring the thick brown liquid. 'Oh, I'm not very interesting.'

He smiled at her, a boyish beam that stopped her spoon in its circling. Of course she'd met plenty of young men, and had seen a few off when they got fresh, but not one had drawn her in like this, nor caused the slight flush she could feel creeping up from her neck as he looked at her with those wide glacial eyes. Was it the hot drink that made her heart beat a little faster? Or the Frankie Vaughan song playing on the radio in the tiny café?

'I don't believe you,' he said quietly. 'I think you're actually very interesting. And perhaps once you've decided I'm not some kind of sex maniac or a ghastly cad, you'll let me take you for dinner one evening so I can find out more about you.'

Later, as he dropped her in Victoria Street, she wondered whether she'd ever see him again. Boys like Charlie didn't go out with girls from Wandsworth, and the fact that half the street was peeping from behind their net curtains as she climbed out of his car proved how different their worlds were. He took her hand just as she was about to walk away, stroking the soft white of her elbow-length glove, then letting her go and roaring away into the night. She thought she could hear the last of the midnight chimes from Big Ben, and looked up just in time to see Dad stand back from the upstairs window. She'd pay the price for this in the morning.

She pulled her key out of her handbag, humming as she did so, then hesitated, sensing for a moment that someone was watching her from the other side of the road. She waited for a moment, but it was just the shadows, and she turned the key slowly in the lock and slipped silently through the front door.

*

Two nights later, he was waiting for her outside number 75, engine thrumming and Petula Clarke playing on the car radio as he chatted with Geoff from 56 and Doug from 71, who paced around the car, examining the wheels and checking the finish on the dark red paintwork until their wives called them in and Nancy skipped the few yards between front door and the passenger door.

Four nights later, he was back again. Then five.

'It's fine, Dad, don't worry,' Nancy said, patting her hair in the hall mirror and kissing Stanley on the cheek. 'You should come out and meet him. He won't bite.'

'I'm not frightened of him, my girl. I'm just worried for you.'

'Well, you don't need to be. He's a gentleman, and you'd like him if you made the effort.'

Stanley shook his head, and Nancy felt a pang of guilt as she saw the sadness in his eyes. 'I'm OK, Dad. Really,' she said, kissing him on the cheek.

And she was: she was having a ball, in fact. She and Charlie were joined at the hip, whether they were wandering around the National Gallery, or dancing at the Flamingo, or lying under a tree in Green Park while he read his latest prose to her.

She had never been happier: she had her work, her family, her friends, and a man she adored.

Nancy listened to the rhythmic wash of the waves outside. She'd left the door between her room and Pamela's open, and could hear gentle snoring. The bonhomie of the evening had quickly deteriorated into truculence and bad temper as the champagne wore off, and she had struggled to get Pamela into her own bed and out of Nancy's, where she insisted she wanted to sleep. In the way that a puppy collapses into a deep sleep at the end of a crazy few minutes, however, Pamela had gone from stroppy to unconscious the moment her head hit the pillow. Nancy had sat beside her for a little while, stroking the hair away from her freckled cheek as she listened to the girl's breathing become deeper and steadier and watched her eyes flicker gently beneath the closed eyelids.

They were leaving tomorrow. It was time to pack again, and so she dragged her suitcase out from under the bed. She might as well get a head start so that she was free to help Pamela in the morning.

Capri. She should have been beside herself with excitement: it was the playground of billionaires and film stars and presidents. Peter and Caro were definitely not in that league, but they seemed to know everyone, and whoever they didn't know, Tony did.

She was puzzled by the three-way friendship. Tony was so different to Peter, and she couldn't imagine how they had ever become friends, but these were people who valued roots and were loyal to their family history. Maybe there was a side to Tony that she'd yet to see, but so far she'd found him to have less class than your average East End barrow boy, and she had the feeling Peter was embarrassed at his constant attempts to draw people into funding his new film. Then there was Caro, who seemed to spend more time with Tony than with her husband. There was something reptilian about the man, and Nancy couldn't see why Caro wanted to be even remotely near him. Did Peter mind? Or even notice? She had a feeling he did, and had seen him watching them on occasion, a sad expression on his face. She wondered if she would ever understand these people, who for all their glamour had a strange system of moral values.

And now there was Capri.

And Charlie.

She opened the suitcase and drew out a little drawstring bag hidden at the bottom, pulling the cord and reaching inside to take out the satin jewellery roll. With slightly trembling fingers, she undid the bow and slowly unfolded the fabric. This was the first time she had looked inside the hiding place for five months, and her heart leapt as she gently lifted the contents out and pressed them to her nose, then held them tight against her chest. She knew she should have left them behind, but she equally knew that she could never be parted from them. They were all she had now.

A cloud passed across the moon and a bright blue light was suddenly cast through the open window and over Nancy as she sat child-like on the cold tiled floor, her head buried in her chest.

18

OK, so she had failed on this one already. It was never really a goer, to be fair, and with all the will in the world, Flo hadn't had any intention of making a swimsuit. To want to make a swimsuit, you really had to want to wear one, and there it was.

'But you can't go to the South of France without a swimsuit,' Jem had said. 'Are you insane? What, you're going to sit on the beach in a two-piece suit? Or maybe a tweed coat, why not?'

To be honest, Flo had lasted most of her life without wearing a swimsuit. Oh, she could swim, that wasn't the problem; she'd learnt when she was very young, when one of the young men in their hostel had taken it upon himself to teach her. Watched by her mother, he had chucked her in the river repeatedly, dragging her out each time she slid dangerously beneath the surface of the dirty, leech-ridden water, until she eventually floated, tired and terrified but able to make her own way back to shore, to the whoops and cheers of the onlookers. And that was probably the last time she'd submerged herself in anything other than a hot bath. Peggy and Donald had tried to coax her into the cold, stinging water of the English Channel, but she'd always stood fast, shaking her little head and refusing to put so much as a foot in the shallows, so that they always relented and took her for an ice cream instead.

It helped that Seamus couldn't swim. She smiled as she remembered daring him to prove it, watching him creeping further and further out into the cold, grey water, a pale, screaming walrus, until she took pity on him and let him come back to shore. It had taken a hot scented bath, a bottle of Rioja and a massage before he'd forgiven her.

Besides, you needed an awful lot of body love to be able to put on a swimsuit. And, well, Flo and her body weren't quite there yet. They were capable of having a coffee together and passing the time of day, but that was about it. Flo's body had been through more than most, and she had every right to resent the combination of flesh and bones that had consistently worked together to deny her the one thing she wanted more than anything.

So no, she wasn't going to put on a swimsuit. She was going to sit on this sunlounger fully dressed and boil slowly to death, even if she had just paid seventeen euros for the privilege.

She was tired, having slept fitfully, prey to the bowl of mussels she had eaten for dinner at a little restaurant overlooking the old harbour, and her head filled with images from a book about the Côte d'Azur she had found at her Airbnb: glittering vignettes showing politicians, princes, Hollywood stars and presidents, all partying hard on the strip of land Nancy had visited all those years ago. At one point she had woken just as Wallis Simpson was handing her a tightly swaddled blanket, which she took from her only to discover a giant croissant nestled within.

Though many of the famous names were long gone by the time Nancy and Pamela found their way there, their legacy remained, and as Flo had climbed on board the double-decker train from Nice, she had made sure to sit upstairs on the sea-facing side of the carriage, so that as the train hugged the coast she could catch a glimpse of the chalk-white villas carved into the cliffs, with pools that had once been topped up with perfume and champagne, and where the sun had barely set on a decades-long party. Who owned these places, she wondered, now that Middle Eastern princes, Russian oligarchs and Chinese businessmen had displaced the bohemians and the baronets?

She suddenly remembered the little pot of ice cream she was still holding, which had cost as much as a bottle of Tesco wine and was now rapidly melting into a gelatinous orange gloop, but she was tired and hungry, and forced it down, even though she was feeling horribly bloated after five days of relentless carbs and a long train journey. She'd gone back to dress one, in the absence of swimwear, hoping that Nancy would understand, and that cheating the game wouldn't jinx it. Even though the dress had been made to measure, her recent croissant diet was taking its toll, and she felt the seams straining slightly.

She was exhausted and overheated, her metabolism all over the place. The excitement of Paris had dulled into an overstimulation hangover, and she was struggling to resist contacting Seamus, torturing herself with images of his new life. God, they'd love him over there; an Irishman, the life and soul, intelligent and good-looking, he'd have women all over him. Flo would be just an episode in his life – barely remembered, absorbed into the DNA of the next chapters but not part of them.

She closed her eyes, trying to shut out the sound of his voice as it spoke softly to her, listening instead to the shouts and laughter around the beach, the loud barks of long-limbed teenage boys as they chased chestnut-brown girls into the sea, the mash-up of music as transistor radios competed with each other, and of course the never-ending lapping of the mild Mediterranean waves on the soft white sand.

As her mind stilled, she let herself just enjoy lying under the wide raffia parasol as the gentle breeze tugged at the hem of her skirt. She sensed that this point of the journey would give her a chance to recuperate and recover from five days in the city while she dug a little deeper.

What was she hoping to find here in Antibes? She wasn't really sure; the contents of the next packet were sparse: the usual postcard, this time showing a harbour full of graceful sailing boats, rather than the modern-day multistorey floating hotels that blocked the view across the coast to the Monaco mountains, and a photograph she was surprised Nancy had kept. Her great-aunt had been snapped leaning out of a striped deckchair, and even though the photo was black and white, Flo could see the slowly emerging suntan contrasting with her white spaghetti-strapped swimsuit and the blonde hair that was whipped up into a loose knot on top of her head. In a wonderfully candid shot, the seemingly unflappable Nancy had lost her cool for a moment, and her cross expression was captured on film, even though the camaraderie with the pho-tographer was still evident decades later.

She flipped the photo over. *The beach at Antibes: Pea driving me mad!*

Who was Pea? She thought back to the photograph taken at the Lido, and the list of names scribbled on the back.

Pea . . . It must be a nickname. She pulled out her phone, seeing another text from Ben, the latest of many endearing promises of forthcoming information. He really was so kind, but she had to be careful there: Jem had texted to tell her jokingly that her old friend was smitten, and what had Flo done to him? This wasn't what she had planned for her trip, and she had to stay focused. Despite her feelings for Seamus and the fact that he was the first thing she thought about each morning and the last each night, there was an unmistakable flicker of something whenever she heard from Ben. It might just be her recently battered ego responding to the thrill of his increasingly obvious interest, or perhaps even the tiniest nugget of something reciprocal on her side, but she couldn't be side-tracked. This trip was about Nancy, not about Seamus or Ben or anyone else. She had to be selfish.

She tried to forget Ben and scrolled through her photos until she found a copy of the Lido image, squinting as she cupped the screen against the bright sunshine. *Colonel Henderson, Mrs Henderson, Tony, Caro, Peter, Pamela, Nancy.*

Pea . . . Peter maybe? She zoomed in on the man in the centre of the photograph. He looked kindly, artistic and slightly aristocratic, and was probably in his late forties, although she had watched enough old black and white films to know that it was hard to tell a twenty-year-old man of that era from a forty-year-old. But he certainly didn't look like a 'Pea', and she didn't think Nancy would have been on nickname terms with him only a week into the trip.

She moved to the right of the picture and the girl next to Nancy.

Pamela.

P for Pamela. Pea. It had to be.

Her stomach flipped as she looked again at Nancy's cross face, imagining Pamela laughing as she caught her unawares. It was her first real sense of connection between Nancy and her charge. This was the Nancy from Peggy's photograph; not the Grace Kelly-like mannequin of the first few pictures, but a real person who could laugh and be cross. This was the girl pressing her cheek to her sister's on her wedding day, who drove her father mad sewing through the night; the beating heart of the quartet of girlfriends who never saw her again once they'd put her on a train to France.

Flo knew that if she could get to the bottom of who Pamela and the artist Tony were, she had a chance of finding out what had happened to her great-aunt.

There was no point staying on the beach just to make the most of her seventeen euros, and she decided to pack up and spend a few more on an iced tea in the busy town square and watch the tanned boat hands and seasoned sailors as they stopped off to test their land legs. Tomorrow was another day, with another packet and more clues.

Flo took it easy during the afternoon, in preparation for hiking up the hill to the Villa du Cap Bleu, where Nancy had partied once upon a time, preserved for ever in the photograph that Flo looked at once more, Nancy's perfect copperplate on the reverse giving her the exact date and location of the pretty pink dress's debut. Now a hotel, in the sixties the villa had belonged to expats Douglas and Cynthia Aston, who had run the place as a non-stop champagne-fuelled party. She had googled them, of course, and found a semi-aristocratic family with artistic leanings and connections that stretched from Westminster to Hollywood, their address book reading like Debrett's.

If nothing else, she was looking forward to putting on the shocking-pink shot-silk dress that she had carefully unwrapped from its tissue and hung in the little wardrobe in her Airbnb. She'd done a good job on the tricky garment: the matching pink lining sat inside the bodice without so much as a crease, and the delicate straps tapered to exactly the same width on each shoulder as they curved upwards from the sweetheart neckline. The gathering around the waist was perfectly even, and Flo had constructed a net petticoat with a ruffled edge, so that the ballerina skirt opened like a ripe fuchsia. It was a dress to wear on a date, a dress to be admired in and to feel loved in.

Stop it, Flo, she told herself, feeling self-pity creeping in uninvited. She picked up her phone and hovered over her Facebook page, wondering whether just checking he was OK could be construed as stalking. She had enough dignity to know to stop texting him in the face of his digital silence, and so she was justified in finding other means of making sure he was OK. Wasn't she?

Heart racing a little in case she found something she didn't want to see, and secretly hoping that whatever was on his page would show her a miserable, homesick Seamus, she quickly clicked on his profile, but found it blocked and herself unfriended. Whatever that meant. He never used Facebook, so how come he'd worked out how to jettison her?

What was her problem? she wondered as she seethed. She

was the one who'd let him go. She should be pleased he was helping her cut the ties.

Her phone pinged and she snatched it up quickly, scanning the banner that told her a message had just come in.

Hey, Ben here.

She smiled. It said *Ben* right at the top of the message.

She read that he had a few days' leave and could book a flight down to the coast and be there by the evening if she wanted. Not to worry if she didn't. But he could be. Or he could meet her in Capri. Or Venice. Which would be better? And he had some information he thought she might like to hear. But it would be better first-hand . . .

Oh Ben. She forced herself to read through the next four paragraphs, wondering that a journalist could have so few editing skills, then hesitated before replying. It would be lovely to have Ben around, but she was nervous after hearing from Jem. The last thing she wanted was to lead him on, and she had nothing to offer him right now except her company. But if she made that clear, surely it would be OK to spend a few more days together? She was still a married woman, and he was just a friend of a friend. And there was no doubt they'd enjoyed each other's company in Paris.

Go on, then.

Go on, then, which? he texted back immediately.

Capri. Canzone del Mare, three days' time. See you there, Mr Simpson.

There. It was done. No point in worrying any more.

Mindful of the eye-watering prices in the little bars dotted around the narrow streets of the old town, and not keen to sit at a restaurant on her own in the unmissable pink silk dress, Flo ate at her apartment, with its stunning views out to the rugged cap and the lighthouse perched above its wooded slopes. She wolfed down a plate of baguette and fragrant peaches with sweet mountain cheese and cured hams that she had bought from the covered Provençal market that morning before going out, astonished at how hungry she was.

By English standards, it was quite late by now, but the little town was only just coming out of its early-evening hibernation, and gradually the yachts in the harbours emptied and the bars and restaurants filled with a selection of conspicuously expensive handbags, loafers and facelifts. The narrow streets around the ramparts and the main square became an ever-moving procession of slowly meandering families and couples dressed to the nines, the whole town bathed in a cloud of sickly perfume.

The forty-minute walk to the hotel across the cap was out of the question for the cream shoes Jemima had given her as a leaving gift as long as she promised to Insta a picture of them out on the town (whatever that meant), so she hailed a cab at the harbour, feeling self-conscious in the dress amongst the T-shirted yachting crowd with their deck shoes and mirrored wraparound sunglasses.

The car climbed the narrow, windy road, disappearing beneath a thick canopy of plane trees before the view suddenly opened out onto a sparkling sunset that shimmered on the still water. She was suddenly the star of every Riviera movie she had ever seen: she was Grace Kelly, Audrey Hepburn, Jean Seberg, although the taxi driver was certainly no Cary Grant as he hunched baboon-like into his seat and munched on his dentures in time with the tinny Europop leaking out of his car radio.

Eventually they drove through open wrought-iron gates and along a gravelled tree-lined drive. Flo nearly gasped as the greenery gradually parted before them to reveal a beautiful rose-pink villa with delicate decorative columns and ruffled crenellations, its filigreed features accentuated by subtle uplighting. She had never seen anything like it, and wondered how it had seemed to Nancy all those years ago: she must have thought she had walked straight onto the set of *The Arabian Nights*.

The driver slowed down to let her out, taking twenty euros from her and moving off before she had a chance to ask for her change. Immediately a young man in pristine white polo shirt and with knife-sharp creases in his matching trousers leapt to meet her, politely unfazed when she said she was just here for a drink.

'Of course, madame. Would you like to sit in the bar or on the terrace?'

She looked around. Much as she wanted to see the interior of the hotel, it was a beautiful evening, far too lovely to sit indoors, the blistering heat having given way to a balmy warmth tempered by a soft breeze. 'The terrace. Thank you.'

'Please. There is a table over there for you, madame. It has a perfect view of the harbour.'

She thanked him and ordered an Aperol spritz, and as he disappeared to fetch it, she wandered slowly along the terrace, the perfumed air alive with the sound of cicadas and discreet conversation, people sitting quietly in the shadows around small tables lit only by flickering hurricane lamps and the rows of tea lights that marked paths and boundaries. This was real money, which kept itself behind closed doors and thought nothing of spending the cost of an entire family's weekly food shop on one bottle of good wine.

She paused, leaning into a delicate waist-high balustraded wall that looked out over the emerald-green swimming pool, smooth as glass with shadows bouncing around beneath the surface as the beams of submerged lighting played with the water.

Why had Nancy's family come to this villa? Were they friends of the Astons? It seemed possible, although from what she had learnt from her reading, many of the hosts along this stretch of coast often didn't know the glittering guests who adorned their parties. Anyone might turn up to a lunch party or for cocktails, be it a prince, an actress or a Wall Street banker. No one cared, as long as the conversation was dazzling and the company beautiful.

It was likely that Caro and Tony, who certainly appeared dazzling and beautiful, were friends of the Astons, and Tony had probably even painted one or both of them. Flo had found an obscure portrait of Cynthia Aston online, its broad brush-work almost impressionistic, and taking no prisoners when it came to capturing her aquiline nose and high cheekbones, but no artist had been credited for the work, so she was none the wiser. Maybe Tony had been hoping for an introduction to a potential sitter that evening, amongst the probably stellar guest list.

The gentle tinkling of ice cubes announced the arrival of her drink, which was placed on her table along with a bowl of fat lime-green olives and a leather folder containing the bill.

'*Excusez-moi*,' she called to the waiter, who slid back towards her on soft moccasins. God, she had T-shirts older than this young Adonis.

'*Oui, madame?*'

In fractured French, she attempted to ask him whether there might be anyone working at the hotel who knew anything about how it had been back in 1962. She was trying to trace a relative of hers who had been a guest here, she explained.

'It's OK, I'm Swedish,' he said. 'English is good. I'm not sure I can help, though. I've only been here for a few weeks.'

'Oh.' She felt ridiculous: why on earth had she expected it to be easy? She'd been lucky at the Lido, but the intervening half-decade would have seen off many of the people who might have been able to help her, and who would have remembered something about the beautiful English ingénue who had partied here with the rich and famous.

He sensed her disappointment, and went on, 'I can ask my manager, if you like. He's certainly not old enough to have been here back then, but he may know something that can help you. He knows everyone around here.'

She smiled. 'That would be incredibly helpful. Thank you.'

He tipped his head. 'She must have been something pretty special for you to come all this way to find out about her after such a long time.'

Flo nodded slowly. 'I'm beginning to realise she was.'

He turned away, the tray tucked under his arm, then suddenly looked back at her. 'Your dress is beautiful, by the way,' he said. 'I wish more women still knew how to dress.'

Flo mumbled an embarrassed thank-you and looked down

at herself. The dress was indeed beautiful, its crisp silk skirt fanned around her and its bodice fitting perfectly, and there was no doubting that it made her feel more feminine than she had done in a long time. Maybe when she was home again, she would find more excuses to wear beautiful dresses – it felt good, and she definitely needed more good in her life.

As she waited, she took the Polaroid photograph out of her handbag. Despite her squinting at the flash bulb, the smile on Nancy's face was not that of the girl pressing cheeks with her sister on her wedding day, or posing on the Pont des Arts. In contrast, she looked distinctly resistant to the arm thrown around her shoulders – and who could blame her, considering the leering expression on the face of the man in possession of the offending limb? There was no mistaking Tony's millipede-like moustache, and this time the two of them were in the company of two women with staggeringly strange smiles, who looked like forty-year-apart versions of the same person and were presumably fellow guests at the party. There was no sign of Caro this time, or of Pamela. Or indeed the fair-haired man called Peter, who perhaps had just met them for the evening in Paris. The Hendersons, whoever they were, were also absent. There was a crush of people behind Nancy's group, but Flo couldn't make out any of the faces on the faded Polaroid paper.

'May I help you, madame?'

She looked up at the sound of the soft French voice to see a tall man of around her own age standing beside her, immaculate in white shirt and blazer, his collar-length dark hair brushed back just so. She sighed. Someone should open a style school for English men – and this man here would be a perfect tutor. 'I hope so,' she said, and handed him the photograph.

'I'm hoping to find out what happened to one of the women in this picture.'

'May I?' he said, indicating the seat next to her, and as she gestured for him to join her, he looked carefully at the faded image. 'This was taken here at the hotel?' he said.

'Yes, in June nineteen sixty-two.' She leant closer to him, inhaling the inviting cloud of expensive aftershave. 'This is my great-aunt,' she said, pointing to Nancy. 'And this is her employer. He was an artist called Tony. Do you recognise them? Or would you know anything about a party the Astons held here that night?'

He shook his head slowly. 'Of course I know about the Astons; they lived here for a long time. Everyone who grew up in Antibes, as I did, knows about them. But I don't recognise either of these people. I'm sorry. Your great-aunt is very beautiful – if I'd known who she was, I would definitely remember.'

Flo sighed. This was clearly going to be a very expensive dead end, once she'd factored in the taxi home. 'It was a long shot. But thank you for looking.'

As she went to take the photo from him, though, he held on to it. 'Wait,' he said.

'What? Have you remembered something about them?'

He shook his head. 'No, but I think I might know who this is.' He smiled and pointed at the younger of the two women standing with Nancy.

Flo looked closely at the picture. 'Really? Who is she?'

He laughed. 'Unless I'm mistaken, that is Madame Devere. Barbara, I think her name is. Of course she doesn't look like that any more, but she is well known around Antibes and used to come here a lot. Quite a woman in her day, I believe. An American heiress with so many divorces, she ended up using her maiden name to avoid confusion. Most of my male staff were terrified of her. She had quite an eye for the young men, you know?'

'You say she used to come here? Does she not any more?'

'Not for a long while now. She is pretty elderly these days.'

'So she's still alive?' Flo felt a spark of hope: maybe this anonymous guest from a long-ago party could shed some light on Nancy's story.

'I'm not sure, but I believe so. The last I knew, she was in some sort of private *maison de retraite*, like a hospital for the elderly, you know? Unfortunately a former member of my staff befriended her, and we had to let him go. It was an unpleasant business: taking advantage of an old lady, and a valued cus-tomer at that. But it happens – especially around here. There are only one or two of these homes near Antibes, so maybe it wouldn't be hard to find?' He shrugged. 'I don't know. And she may not even still be alive. She always said that when she couldn't make it up here for cocktails any more, she would give up on life.'

'Do you know why she stayed here in France? You said she's American?'

'*Oui*, from Texas, I think.' He smiled, light crow's feet creasing around his eyes. 'I think many women who have been beautiful at one time want to hold on to the moment when they felt at their best. Madame Barbara is probably the same.' He tapped the photograph. 'And no one could deny she was a beauty back then.'

Flo wondered if somewhere there was an elderly Nancy

clinging to the ghost of the beautiful young woman in her photographs. She could only hope so. 'You've been so helpful,' she said. 'Thank you.'

The manager stood and nodded slowly. 'It is my pleasure. I just wish I could have told you more.'

'You've given me more than I could have hoped for. Thank you. Here.' She took out her purse and began to fold a twenty-euro note into the leather wallet on the table, but he held up his hand.

'No, madame. It is beautiful that you have come all this way to our hotel to find your relative. Please enjoy your drink with our compliments.'

She smiled and thanked him, and sipped from her glass as he walked away. How much sweeter the drink suddenly tasted.

It was mid morning by the time Flo completed the steep walk up from the old town, the incredible view along the coast to Monaco opening out with every step until she had a clear view of the distant snow-capped mountains and the wide sweep of the yacht-littered blue bay. The manager at the hotel had been right: there were only two private care homes nearby, and a couple of complicated phone calls had eventually located the elderly American. Flo had written her a short note explaining that she hoped they might be able to meet and talk about the summer of 1962, and now found herself invited to visit the old lady at the Corbusian slab of elegant white-painted concrete perched on the brow of the hill straddling Antibes and Juan les Pins.

As the pristine glass doors opened automatically with

a barely audible whisper, she wasn't sure whether she had entered a French offshoot of NASA or the set of a Swiss skincare commercial. Soft music played discreetly as white-coated staff wheeled immaculately groomed residents across the polished concrete floor and around vintage pin-legged leather sofas and glass tables groaning under the weight of vast floral displays.

Flo explained to the terrifyingly chic receptionist that she was here to visit Madame Devere, and was directed to a day room at the far end of the long foyer, where Madame was expecting her.

The room took up an entire corner of the building, vast picture windows forming two of its walls, with bright Chagall-like murals echoing the vivid blues and greens of the landscape beyond. Clusters of armchairs were scattered around little tables bearing more flowers, along with books and magazines to cater for everyone from the retired sailor to the interior designer. There was a marked absence of the television that had dominated the day room in the care home where Flo had regularly visited Donald in his final weeks – who needed fabricated images when the whole swathe of the Côte d'Azur was laid out in front of you?

The sole occupant of the room sat in a wheelchair by the window, the air-conditioned silence punctuated only by the wheezing and clicking of the oxygen machine positioned next to her.

'Mrs Devere?' Flo said quietly, afraid that she might be disturbing a mid-morning nap.

'Who is that?' the woman said in a throaty Texan drawl, without turning her head.

Flo moved closer. 'It's Florence. I wrote to you and you kindly said I could visit.'

A gnarled finger pressed a button on the arm of the chair, and its occupant was slowly pirouetted around until she faced Flo. 'Ah, the Englishwoman,' she said slowly, drawing in shallow lungfuls of oxygen through the tubes that led from her nose to the heavy wheeled machine beside her.

Flo was instantly hit by a cloud of Dior Poison as she went to shake the papery hand offered to her, and tried not to look too surprised at the vibrantly patterned chiffon kaftan straight from Elizabeth Taylor's seventies wardrobe, matched with a tired blonde bouffant wig. 'Flo,' she said. 'Thank you so much for agreeing to meet me.' She had examined the photo of Barbara closely, but found it almost impossible to reconcile the image of the long-legged heiress with the elderly lady slumped in front of her in the wheelchair.

'Siddown,' the older woman said, waving towards one of the chairs. 'You make me feel like the goddamn Queen.'

Flo pulled a chair across and sat, trying not to look at the giveaway lopsidedness of a face that had had a fortune spent on maintaining its youth, only for the sudden blow of a stroke to undo decades of surgery.

'So what do you want to know?' Barbara said, her red-nailed hands fidgeting and fretting in her lap.

Flo explained about her great-aunt, and how she had been at the Villa du Cap Bleu in 1962, and instantly the older woman's face relaxed as she was carried back across half a century.

'Nineteen sixty-two, darling. Those were the days.' And as she forced out a rhythmic rasping sound that was something between a death rattle and a laugh, Flo marvelled at the irony of how the unaffected side of her strangely smooth face barely moved: decades of work had made it impossible for her to open her mouth properly, and her heavily rouged sallow cheeks remained immobile. As the coughing fit slowly subsided, she continued, 'That was my first summer down here. Mother brought me. I expect she wanted to find me a millionaire.'

'And did she?' Flo asked.

'No, she did not. I found my own a couple of years later, down in Texas.' She attempted to wink at Flo with one iri-descently blue-shadowed eye. 'The first of a few, I should say,' and she chuckled to herself. 'No, that summer I made my own entertainment. God, Mother would have killed me if she'd known.'

Flo leant closer, until she could see clearly the black smears of eye make-up and the thin wisps of silvery-yellow hair that peeped beneath the slightly skew-whiff woven cap of her wig. 'Was he very unsuitable?' she said, smiling conspiratorially.

Barbara waved her hand dismissively in the air. 'The worst: he'd steal his mama's egg money, that one. But we all got to start somewhere, eh? Good job Mother never found out: I think she had a soft spot for him too, not that it did her much good in the end.' She sat back and looked at Flo through rheumy eyes. 'So,' she went on, 'ask me what you want and I'll see if I can give you answers.'

Flo explained about the party, giving her the date, and told her that Nancy had been there with the family of an artist.

Barbara narrowed her eyes. 'June tenth, you say? Well, that's my birthday, so I ought to remember. Yes, I was here. Had a beautiful new white dress Mother bought me – cost the earth, it did. Yves Saint Laurent, I think. God, I wish I still had that dress. I looked as pretty as a pie supper in it.' She shook her head, as though looking for something and failing to find it. 'Say, you remind me of someone back then,' she said, looking closely at Flo, then drifting off into a world of her own, so that Flo had to prompt her to carry on.

'So did you meet the artist who was at the party that night?' she said.

'Artist?' The old woman frowned.

'Yes, that's who my great-aunt was working for.'

Barbara began coughing again, and Flo poured her a glass of water from the carafe on the table, holding it gently to her lips while she sipped from it, then discreetly dabbing the older woman's chin with a tissue.

'Did you meet him? The artist?' Flo repeated when she was sure Barbara was able to speak again. 'Or his family? His name was Tony.'

Barbara's tattooed eyebrows frowned. 'You sure about that?'

'Yes, of course. Why?'

She shook her head. 'There was a Tony at the party, but he won't be who you're looking for. He was my – how do I put it? – my distraction. He used to take me to the casino or out in his little boat, and, well . . .'

Flo smiled. 'It's fine; you don't have to tell me your secrets.' She reached into her handbag. 'Look, I have a photo from that night. And I think you're in it.'

'Me, honey?' Barbara chuckled.

'Here. Perhaps it'll help.' Flo pulled out the Polaroid and

held it in front of the old woman, moving it gradually closer to her face until she was able to focus on it.

'Well, blow me down and call me Mother if that ain't me,' Barbara said eventually, pointing to the girl in white on the right of the photo, her eyes glassing over with sadness. 'And there's Mama, looking like she's swallowed a wasps' nest.' She sighed. 'Better hope there's silver service in hell,' she said quietly. 'I could almost feel sorry for her: she lost her fortune and her daughter that summer, all to the same man.' She moved on to the figure of Nancy. 'And that has to be your great-aunt. My, you look alike. Mind you, she's quite a bit younger, I'd say. And slimmer.'

Flo chose to let that pass and instead pointed to the figure of Tony, his arm draped around Nancy. 'And that's the artist. Tony. Do you remember him?'

Barbara beckoned for Flo to hold the photo up again, then scrutinised it closely, muttering to herself and shaking her head. 'Well, if it isn't the devil himself. That's Tony, all right,' she said. 'My Tony. But he sure as hell was no artist – not of the type you're thinking of anyway. As my old mama's bank would tell you.' She looked up at Flo. 'Hope you're not planning on finding him,' she said, and shook her head slowly so that her long jewelled earrings trembled.

'Well,' Flo said, 'this was a long time ago. He's probably dead by now.'

Barbara laughed. 'Dead by now? My darling girl, Tony was dead not two weeks after that picture was taken.' Seeing Flo's inability to form a response, she went on, 'Plane crash, like all the best folks back in those days.'

'I don't suppose you remember his surname, do you? It would be incredibly helpful.' Flo looked at the old woman, and could see that her attention was slipping away.

'Devere. My surname is Devere,' she said irritably.

'No, I mean Tony's surname?'

'Who are you?' Barbara said sharply, as though seeing Flo for the first time.

'I'm Florence. You were about to tell me Tony's surname. From the party at the villa?'

The older woman's hands began twitching anxiously in her lap. 'I don't know who you are. And I don't know any Tony.' Agitated pinpricks of colour appeared on her cheeks, and Flo knew that her opportunity had passed. Unless she gave up, she would find herself being hauled out of the building by security, as Barbara repeatedly pressed a button on the arm of her wheelchair.

'I'm sorry,' she said. 'Thank you for meeting me.'

But already Barbara, exhausted and upset by the conversation, was looking around for the help she had just summoned. She stared once more at Flo, as though about to say something, then slumped as a young assistant appeared.

'Shall I take you back to your room now, madame?' he asked, and she instantly brightened a little.

'See, the young men are still trying to get me into bed!' she said weakly, as he smiled indulgently back at her, tucking the oxygen machine behind the chair and wheeling her away.

Flo watched their slow progress across the room, amused at how despite her years, Barbara couldn't stop herself from gazing up at the handsome young man and tilting her head coquettishly.

So it seemed she'd been on completely the wrong track, misled by the Paris photo, which had suggested that poor doomed Tony was Caro's husband, and not the man staring awkwardly at the camera, who, she could now see, was clearly the genetic origin of Pamela, with their shared sandy hair and fair skin. She took a last look at the Polaroid image, Tony grinning at the camera like a tomcat amidst the ill-matched trio of women, unaware that he only had two weeks left on this earth. She wasn't sure what he was to the small party, but the long-preserved look on Nancy's face suggested that she was not a fan. The beautiful and the damned, in the words of Scott Fitzgerald. It seemed that Tony had been damned; Flo could only hope that Nancy had been merely beautiful.

She stepped out into the midday sunshine, and for the first time in days, she felt chilled as a cool breeze swept in from the sea and set the pine trees rustling. The journey had taken a sombre turn, and she was ready to move on. Next stop was Capri, with a story slowly emerging and Ben to help her uncover it. The least she might find there was the surname of the artist who had taken Nancy away and never brought her back: any more, she dared not hope for.

Part Five

CAPRI

19

*McCall's 6291: Misses' two-piece bathing suit
and short beach dress*

How could she ever go home after this? She had asked herself this question often over the last fortnight, and as she became increasingly used to the heat, the cocktails, the people-watching, she knew Wandsworth would never be the same again. Unbidden, the waiter brought more iced water, placing it on the low table beside her sunlounger, and thus ruining her for the next pot of over-brewed tea served by a surly waitress in a gloomy caff.

So where would she go? She supposed there would be a place for her back in England somewhere. Obviously not in Victoria Street – in fact, south London was pretty much out of bounds altogether – and she was done with the West End. The West Country was out of the question, after Somerset, and any English seaside town would be a disappointment in comparison to this trip. She knew nothing about the north other than the Albert Finney and Alan Bates films that had done the rounds, portraying a bleak industrial world that held no appeal for her.

The one thing drawing her home was the one thing keeping her away, and although it tore her in two, she knew that at some point she would have to decide what to do.

What she did know, however, was that she adored the Mediterranean climate. No British heatwave had prepared her for how it invigorated her, how she loved the darkening of her limbs and lightening of her hair, even if the sultry nights were unbearable, conspiring with her tangled thoughts to keep her awake. What matter, though, when you could spend the next day lying in the sun, listening to the roar of distant speedboats and soothed by the smell of coconut oil and lemon groves?

People apart, what she missed most from home was her sewing machine, the sense of purpose in taking a length of fabric and then wearing it a few hours later. She missed the total absorption in the creation of something that had not existed before, and of having something to show for a day's work, other than a mildly pacified teenager. Their next stop after Capri was to be Venice for a whole month, and she wondered if she could get hold of a machine so that she could spend some of her time fruitfully, and perhaps help Pamela make something, as she had promised. It would be good just to feel like herself at last.

But first there was the island to enjoy, even if she was on permanent standby in case Charlie made an appearance. She would deal with that if and when she had to.

She was enjoying a rare moment of solitude, albeit in the company of a hundred fellow bathers, who splashed and paraded and watched tall brown Italians swallow-dive into the deep pool. Pamela had gone to lunch with Caro in the awning-covered café at the far end of the pool, leaving Nancy to sunbathe while Peter swam in the sea just below them. She raised her hands above her eyes, checking that they weren't looking for her, but all she saw was happily entertained punters, and a stunning view out to the three giant rocks that reached up out of the aquamarine water, small white speedboats slaloming around them.

She rearranged her bra top so that the little buttons securing it at the back didn't dig in, and shifted the waistband of the matching turquoise shorts to stop the zip, now blisteringly hot in the bright sunshine, from burning her. Her sunglasses were big enough to keep out the worst of the rays, and she tied a scarf around her floppy sunhat and under her chin to protect her from the fierce midday sun.

She dozed blissfully, the poolside noise actually helping her to switch off, woken by the occasional splash of cold water and lulled back by the rise and fall of chatter and laughter.

As a shadow blocked the light and cooled her skin momentarily, she pondered whether to acknowledge her neighbour or continue to slumber. She heard him fiddle about with pockets and mutter under his breath, before the smell of a British cigarette wafted across, making her suddenly nostalgic. She was on the point of sitting up to ask if she could have one when he called out loudly to someone on the far side of the pool.

'Peter, over here, old chap.'

She thought they had done well to avoid Tony. He had stayed back in Antibes for a few days, with meetings all over the place as he finalised the details of his film, and she was pleased to hear that he was staying in a hotel a small distance from their apartment, making it easier to avoid his unwelcome attention. She noticed that Pamela was also much more relaxed when he wasn't around.

A compulsion to cover her semi-nakedness battled with the desire to play dead and avoid attention.

'Tony. How are things? Haven't seen you for days.' She heard Peter shaking seawater from his ears and rubbing himself vigorously with a towel.

'Not bad. Few loose ends to tie up, but looks like we're pretty much there. Start shooting in a couple of months.'

'Excellent news. Caro will be pleased to see you.'

'Always a pleasure to see your womenfolk, Peter.' There was a pause, then he said, 'Nancy's out for the count.'

The shift in light told her that the two men were leaning over her.

'Sparko,' Peter said. 'Don't blame her. It's been a busy few days.'

'Must be nice to have her around. And not just for Pamela.' She heard Tony draw on his cigarette then stub it out in the ashtray next to her. 'So, old fellow, tell Uncle Tony: have you, er, you know, been tempted? She's a looker.'

There was no way out now. If she sat up, they would assume she'd heard, and if not, she would be forced to continue listening.

Peter sounded embarrassed as he tried to laugh off Tony's comment. 'You know me: bit of a one-woman man. But she's a sweetheart with Pea, and I must say it's been nice having her around.'

Tony laughed. 'Ha! Knew you'd noticed.' She heard a chair being dragged close. 'Here, sit with me for a minute, Pete. Got something I want to talk to you about.'

'I ought to see if the girls have finished lunch . . .'

He patted the chair. 'Won't take a minute.'

Peter sighed and sat down. 'What is it, Tony?'

There was a pause, and she sensed that Tony was checking

she was still asleep, before he went on in a much quieter voice, 'See, the thing is, it's about this film.'

Peter laughed. 'Who'd have thought it. I never had you down as a Hollywood mogul.'

'Well, not quite a mogul. Anyway, we've got the script, got the studio booked, director, lovely little actress, everything in place.'

'Sounds terribly exciting. Let me know if you need a set painter.'

Tony laughed. 'You'll be the first in line. Promise.'

There was a pause. 'But . . . ?' Peter said.

'Bit tricky, but we're just a few thou short of what we need. Got some bloody amazing investors: people who know a sure thing when they see it and know they'll get a good payback for their cash.'

In the silence, Nancy heard Peter breathing heavily. 'How many thou, Tony?'

'Twenty.'

'Twenty thousand pounds?'

'To make a profit of double that.'

'Tony, old chum, you know we're a bit tight at the moment. We've thrown everything into this trip, in the deluded hope that I'll get some work out of it. Truth is, though, it's not good. We shouldn't be here, it's insanity.'

'But what about the money from Sunberry Park? Surely you're the sole inheritor after Cecil . . .' He stopped.

Peter laughed. 'What money? My poor dead brother was a drunk and a gambler and borrowed a king's ransom against the place when the parents died.'

'But there must be something left from the sale?'

'Not the proverbial bean. The last of it went on his funeral. All we've got is a meaningless title and the Kensington house, which thank God I bought myself. But it's mortgaged up to the hilt.' He sighed. 'At least Cecil couldn't get his hands on that before he blew his brains out. We've had to take Pamela out of school, you know? God knows what we'll do with her now, if Caro doesn't manage to set her up with some ghastly oil baron. She'll have to get a job or something.'

She heard Tony pull another cigarette out of the packet. 'Well, maybe this is what you need. Come on, two old school chums helping each other out. You lend me what you can, and I guarantee I'll double it.'

Peter sighed. 'Caro would kill me.'

'Caro doesn't need to know.'

'I don't know, Tony. It doesn't feel right.'

'Listen, old chap, I'm telling you: movies are where the money is. Look around this place: movie star, movie star, movie star's husband, movie producer, scriptwriter . . .'

'All right, I see your point. I'll think about it.'

She heard a gentle slap of flesh on flesh. 'Good chap. Now, how about we go and have a drink with those girls of yours, and leave Sleeping Beauty to it?'

She listened to their bare footsteps padding away from her on the wet concrete, and lifted her head to watch them go: one tall and pale and unmistakably English, with white matchstick legs, the other blending slickly with the Capri crowd with his suntan and his confident swagger.

'Nancy, get your things together. We're going sailing. And bring Pamela's too while you're at it.'

Nancy stopped halfway up the steps out of the pool and looked up into the bright sunlight to see Caro silhouetted in front of her, her face obscured in the shadow of a huge black straw hat.

She quickly towelled herself dry and slipped her little beach dress over her two-piece, which instantly leaked a bikini-shaped puddle into the stiff poplin, darkening the pale turquoise and pink flowers by several shades.

She gathered their things into a large straw basket and looked around, spotting Caro waving impatiently from the stone jetty at the far end of the pool. By the time she had stepped into the leather sandals she had bought at the market, the rest of the party were already aboard the old blue-painted boat, squashed onto narrow wooden benches along either side while the shirtless mahogany-brown skipper stood at the back, his hand poised over the rudder and the little engine sputtering a cloud of filthy diesel fumes.

Pamela squeezed along and patted the bench next to her, allowing Nancy to fit into the tiny space at the end. She saw the girl staring at the ghost-like white lines sketched across her hips, and quickly pulled the dress down to cover them.

The old skipper tipped his dazzling-white sailor's cap at his passengers, and with a roar, the little boat shot away, its nose rising high out of the sea.

'Don't leave me alone when we get there,' Pamela whispered in her ear, eventually shouting when Nancy failed to hear her above the scream of the engine and the bumping of the shallow boat on the gentle swell of the waves.

'Why ever not?' Nancy shouted back.

In answer, Pamela nodded towards the young Italian beside

Caro, in whose sunglasses Nancy could see the two of them reflected, so that she couldn't tell whether he was looking at them or not. Whatever the case, he was paying little attention to Caro, who was talking in his ear, despite the impediment of her huge hat, which he batted away like an irritating mosquito.

The engine dropped a few decibels and the boat slowed as they approached a huge white yacht anchored a short distance away: a long, sleek white vessel that looked as capable of space travel as of cruising the Bay of Naples. Were all the men here beautiful? Nancy wondered as she watched the deckhand prepare to meet them, his tanned muscular thighs encased in bright-white shorts. He caught the rope the skipper threw to him, then held out a hand to help the passengers onto the narrow ladder leading to the deck of the *Alessandra*.

Nancy was the last to embark, laden with the family's bags. '*Signorina?*' the deckhand said, the embossed buttons on his liveried shirt-style jacket as dazzling as his toothpaste-advert smile as he took the bags from her then hauled her aboard. As she scrambled to stand up, she spotted a button that had been kicked into a corner, identical to the ones on the man's uniform. Magpie-like, she picked it up and popped it into her pocket. No one could miss a button, surely.

Unable to be heard above the noise of the little engine sputtering to full throttle as it headed back to the beach club, the man pointed Nancy towards the front of the boat, where a group of swimwear-clad guests clinked champagne glasses as they leant over the polished brass rails or oiled each other's backs. In the midst of this, Pamela sat miserably on a white leather bench, next to the young Italian who had accompanied them across the water, Nancy's yellow gingham coverall pulled tightly across her chest and her freckled white legs tucked out of sight.

Nancy waved at her, and Pamela looked feebly back, her already pale complexion now taking on a slightly green tinge.

'Gianni and Pamela seem to be getting on, don't you think?' Caro said, approaching Nancy from behind.

Nancy thought that Jack Kennedy and Fidel Castro would probably get on better if they were plonked on a bench together, but merely shrugged.

'Gianni's father Giacomo and I go back a long way. He owns a fashion magazine in Italy. As well as this boat. I met him when we did a Balenciaga shoot in Venice many years ago. The family used to come and stay at Sunberry before Peter's brother pissed the place away.' She sighed. 'Happy days. And now look at those two: he used to play hide-and-seek with her when she was a little girl and he was a teenager. They just adore each other.'

'I can see that,' Nancy said, watching Gianni checking his reflection in the window to his side. 'But isn't he a little . . .'

'What?' Caro said, pulling down her huge black sunglasses to peer at Nancy.

'Well, a little old for Pamela?'

'For God's sake, Nancy, they're only having a conversation. It's not like it's an arranged marriage or anything.' Caro watched her stepdaughter for a moment before pushing her sunglasses back up her nose. 'Mind you, he's rather handsome, don't you think? And the family's got pots of money. I'd like to think Pamela would be looked after if anything . . .' She stopped, and a rare flash of fragility briefly melted her mask.

'Anything what?' Nancy said.

'Nothing. You just shouldn't underestimate financial security. You and I both know that, don't we? Girls from the wrong side of the tracks, and all that.'

Nancy didn't know what to say. It was so hard to work Caro out sometimes.

'Anyway, you must excuse me. I need a lie-down. I have one of my headaches. All this sun is too much. Keep an eye on Pamela; you might have to take her back, looking at the colour of her. She'd better not throw up all over Giacomo's boat. I would just die.' She smiled thinly at Nancy, then adjusted the chiffon wrap around her waist and dabbed at her poppy-red lipstick before slipping through the low doorway that led below deck.

'Oh, help me, please,' Pamela groaned, staggering over and taking Nancy's arm. 'He's just awful.' Gianni was now mingling shirtless amongst the drinkers on the deck, surreptitiously admiring his well-defined stomach muscles as he moved around. 'Do you know, he used to be so mean to me. They came to stay at Granny and Grandpa's when I was little, and he locked me in a cupboard for two hours with a dead mouse. I hate him.' She puffed her cheeks and blew out slowly. 'I don't feel terribly well,' she said. 'When do you think we can go?'

'All right, dumpling?' Tony said as he passed them. 'Look a bit green about the gills, if you don't mind my saying so. Best thing is to jump in the sea,' he added, grabbing Pamela around the waist and pretending to throw her overboard. Nancy had heard enough play-acting in her time to know the difference between squeals of encouragement and those that wanted to shut the game right down. There was no doubt that Pamela was not in the mood to play. Unfazed by his ill-received attempt at rough-and-tumble, he tapped the champagne glass in his hand. 'Just off to find a top-up,' he said. 'Can I get you anything?'

They both shook their heads, and let him pass by and on down to the cabin below.

Across the deck, someone had turned on a radio, and the breezy beat of generic European dance music started a small pulsating wave of movement amongst some of the female guests, as suntanned girls began to shimmy in their tiny bikinis. Leather-faced older men with receding hairlines and forests of grey chest hair sat back on the white leather armchairs dotted around and watched, puffing on enormous cigars.

'There are so many people here,' Nancy said. 'Do you know many of them?'

'Not really. Look, there's Pa. Perhaps we can persuade him to let us go home soon.' Pamela looked longingly back at the shore. 'How long do you think it would take to swim?'

'Too long,' Nancy said, ushering her towards Peter and wondering whether Pamela's jumping overboard might not be a bad idea after all.

'*Formaggio!*' a voice behind them said, and they turned to find Gianni pointing a brand-new shiny black and chrome camera at them. Pamela just had time to stick her tongue out before the shutter clicked and he wandered off.

'Hello, Pea,' Peter said, pulling his daughter towards him and placing his arm around her shoulders. 'I say, you look a little off colour. Are you all right?'

'I'm fine,' Pamela said, resting her head against his white linen shirt while he stroked her hair.

'Aren't you going to say hello to Giacomo?' he said,

waving his whisky glass towards one of the men he'd been chatting with.

Nancy watched Pamela's face turn a little greener as the older man leant forward and kissed her hand. '*Una rosa inglesa*,' he said as he stood back and smiled at the girl. 'And who is this?' he asked Peter, his eye landing on Nancy.

'This is Nancy. She's helping us out this summer.'

The Italian laughed and nudged him. '*Bellissima, non?*'

Peter looked down at his tatty old deck shoes. 'Er, yes, absolutely. Well, anyway, Giacomo is rather interested in my painting his portrait. Isn't that so?'

'*Si, si.* It would be an honour to be painted by such a fine artist.'

Pamela managed to stand up a little straighter. 'Pa is brilliant, actually. He's absolutely . . .' They all watched as she began to sway slightly. 'He's absolutely . . .'

And then suddenly the caprese salad she had had for lunch landed all over Giacomo's immaculate cream calfskin loafers.

Peter sat Pamela down under the shade of an awning, while deckhands appeared from nowhere in a well-practised routine with buckets and mops, and Nancy ran downstairs to look for a glass of water. The boat was bigger than it appeared from the deck, and she couldn't find the galley, which she supposed was located deeper within it, but there had to be a bathroom with running water somewhere nearby. The wide dining area at the base of the stairs gave way to a narrow corridor leading towards the bow of the boat, lined on each side with polished mahogany doors with bright brass handles. Surely one of these must be a bathroom, she thought, as the acrid fumes from the splashes that had landed on her legs began to make her retch. She tried a couple of the closest doors, but one led to a wood-panelled study, and the next to a dressing room. The third door was a little stiff at first, as though something were blocking it from the other side, but she pushed firmly until it gave way and she found herself standing on the threshold of a stiflingly hot bedroom, whose bed was a writhing tangle of sheets and clothing and tanned body parts. She stood trans-fixed as two sets of limbs disentangled themselves from one another, and the dishevelled faces of Tony and Caro stared up at her.

She stepped back quickly, almost tripping as she slammed the door closed behind her. 'Pretend it never happened,' she said quietly to herself, reversing back along the corridor. 'You imagined it.'

'Imagined what?'

She gasped as she felt herself collide with another body, then whipped around, almost fainting on the spot as she came face to face with him.

They stood staring at one another for what felt like long moments.

'What's up, Nancy?' he said eventually, smiling at her. 'You look like you've seen a ghost.'

20

McCall's 6653: Misses' capri pants

Breakfast had been a strange affair. Pamela, ravenously hungry after her clear-out of the previous day, had silently set about consuming everything on the table, for once without the admonition of Caro, who instead drank cup after cup of coffee between cigarettes, the toe of her right foot tapping rhythmically against the table leg, her eyes fixed on a spot beyond the terrace, and her lower jaw tensing so that the tendons in her long neck flexed.

Nancy was beyond any kind of breakfast. Unsure which of yesterday's events to process first, she had chosen none, and merely stared at the bowl of waxy lemons that sat at the centre of the table, the fresh warm roll on her plate untouched and the slivers of cheese and ham gradually sweating as the temperature rose and the sun crept through the dense vines of the pergola above them.

To his delight, Peter had got hold of an old copy of *The Times*, and was muttering intermittently about Cuba and the cricket. It was hard to tell which vexed him more. Eventually he placed the crumpled pages on the table and looked around, as though surprised that anyone else was there. 'So,' he said. 'What's the plan today?'

Caro turned to look at him. She sighed and recrossed her long legs. 'Lunch with Giacomo and Alessandra and some friends of theirs,' she said, flicking away a fly that had landed on her white linen shift.

Pamela groaned. 'Do I have to go?'

'Yes, you do,' Caro snapped, and for once Pamela had the sense to recognise when an argument was over.

Peter looked disappointed. 'Oh, well, that'll be lovely, I suppose.'

'Meaning?' Caro said, pouring herself a refill from the chipped blue enamel coffee pot.

'Only that it would have been nice to have the day to ourselves, just the four of us.'

Caro looked as though he had suggested they spend the day begging in the Piazzetta. 'What on earth for?' she said, lighting a fresh cigarette from the one she had nearly finished.

'So we can have some family time?' he said.

Pamela had stopped eating and was watching the scene intently, a huge hunk of bread and jam halfway to her mouth.

Caro laughed.

'What is the matter with you? It's not funny, Caro. I could take Pea sketching. And Nancy too, if she wanted. Or maybe you girls could go to the shops and we'll meet for lunch afterwards? There are some nice little boutiques down by the square.'

'With nice little prices. Anyway, we're already having lunch. At the Cavellis', remember?'

Peter sighed. 'I'm not sure I fancy it, Caro. I could do with a day off from all of this.'

She stood up, the table shaking as she pushed her weight

against it. 'Well, I'm not sure I fancy it either, Peter, but there it is. We're going. And you're going to be very charming to both of them until they agree to a commission.'

'What about Uncle Tony? Is he coming too?' Pamela said.

Nancy looked away quickly, trying to dismiss the image of Caro and Tony's interlaced bodies. She hadn't been surprised when late last night there had been a little tap at her door, and she'd padded out of bed to find Caro standing there, a glass of brandy in each hand. She'd offered one to Nancy, who declined politely, quickly reassuring her that she'd not really seen anything, and that it wasn't her business anyway. She'd had a feeling that Caro wanted to talk, and that the brittle armour was falling away, but she had no desire to acquire any more information than she already reluctantly possessed, and had politely excused herself so that she could go back to staring at the ceiling and trying to absorb the second shock she'd had that afternoon.

Pamela waited for an answer, but the only sounds to break into the silence were the squeaking of the little house sparrows pecking at the crumbs around their feet, and the first of the speedboats roaring out of the harbour below.

'Tony's had to go back to Paris,' Caro said eventually, and Nancy detected a crack in her voice that made her wonder whether she should have offered more than just silence last night.

'Paris?' Peter said. 'Whatever for?'

'He's catching a flight to South America. Chile or some-where . . . I can't remember. Something to do with the film, I think.'

Nancy dared to look up, and saw that Peter had suddenly

lost all the colour he'd built up over the trip. 'He's leaving? When did he tell you this?'

'Oh, I don't know. Last night, maybe. What does it matter?'

Peter cleared his throat quietly. 'And when's he coming back?'

'Pamela,' Nancy whispered, 'let's go and pack your things for the day, shall we?' But her charge was rooted to the spot, and resisted Nancy's gentle pull on her arm.

'How am I meant to know? I'm not his wife, am I?' Caro snapped, then snatched her sunglasses from the table, creating a rosemary-flavoured cloud as she brushed past the herb border and headed back towards the house.

'Well, it's someone's time of the month,' Pamela said quietly, reaching across for another glass of fresh lemonade.

Eventually Nancy found herself alone, the headache that had excused her from lunch only partly invented. Pamela had threatened to stay with her, but then remembered that Charlie was joining them. 'You should come, Nancy,' she'd said. 'You and Charlie could catch up properly. How funny that you know each other!'

How funny indeed.

Nancy sat on the swing seat and flicked through Caro's magazine, one foot tucked beneath her as the other occasionally pushed against the ground to maintain the gentle rocking. The magazine described a parallel universe to that of Peter's newspaper, fears of Russian missiles eclipsed by speculation about presidents and showgirls, and paparazzi shots of a yacht spotted a little further north from Capri, where the two stars of *Cleopatra* had been spotted canoodling, sending a ripple of excitement across the Bay of Naples.

She swapped the magazine for a little piece of fabric she'd been embroidering, and was instantly soothed by the in and out of the needle, the reassuring pull of the thick silk thread as it wove through the fragile linen, even though her fingers were beginning to sweat in the late-morning heat. She had finished the intricate pale-pink initial, and was now decorating it with interweaving rosebuds and soft-green tendrils. She tied off the thread into a knot, squeezing it between her thumb and the fabric as she pulled gently, then snipped the end with her little travel scissors and threaded the needle a couple of times through the fabric so that she wouldn't lose it. She held the finished piece up, pleased with her handiwork. Maybe she would wander down into the village and find a post office. Peggy would be so excited to open a package that had come all the way from Capri.

She folded the fabric and put it back down beside her. Who was she fooling? She'd never send it. Like she'd never send all the postcards she'd bought. She'd only written on the first one, from Paris. What could she say, after all?

She stood up to stretch, tightening the loosened ties at the waist of her sleeveless shirt and smoothing the creases in her trousers. The white capri pants were a triumph, worth the painstaking measuring and constant trying-on. They flattered her tiny waist, flat stomach and long legs, and allowed her brown ankles to peep below the shin-length hem. If nothing else, the passage of time had given her back her figure.

The stray dog that hung around the dirt road leading to the

little houses on the hill began barking. She heard the gate open and close, and a man's low voice chide the creature gently.

'Who is it?' she said.

He stood uncertainly at the opposite end of the terrace, clutching a bunch of tissue-wrapped hot-pink hibiscus.

'I thought you were having lunch with the others,' she said.

'I thought you were. I wouldn't have gone otherwise.'

'So how come you're here?'

He shrugged. 'Pretended I had to be somewhere else.'

'And do you?'

He scuffed at a pine cone on the ground with the toe of his pale suede loafer, then looked up at her with his grey eyes.

Why had he come? They'd said everything there was to be said a year ago, and despite how it had seemed at the time, she had survived; the world had not ended when Charlie Blake walked out of it.

'Charlie . . .'

He held out the flowers, but she folded her arms, so that he had to place them on the table. 'Please, Nancy. Can we just talk? I've missed you.'

Even though she had heard not so much as a breath from him in twelve months.

'I haven't missed you.'

He tilted his head and gave her the sideways smile that had always got him his way. 'Not even a little?'

'After the way you treated me?'

'I know, and I'm sorry. My parents . . . well, you know how it is.'

'Do I? I have parents too, you know, and they would never

let me treat anyone the way you treated me. How do you think they felt?'

'I'm sorry. Please?'

He looked genuinely upset, and she felt herself cracking, just a little. 'I don't know. I have a headache.'

'No, you don't.'

'Do too.'

'Don't.'

Despite herself, she fell into the old pattern, and put her hand to her mouth to disguise her treacherous smile.

He dared to take a step closer. 'Have lunch with me. And I promise to tell you about Diana running away with her mother's gardener.'

Nancy's eyes widened. 'No!' she said, forgetting briefly that she was meant to be resisting him.

He took a set of car keys out of his pocket and jangled them in front of her. 'Take you for a spin after?'

What did she have to lose? It was just lunch.

Damn it, Nancy, say no. Tell him to go away. No. No. No.

'All right,' she said.

It was so easy to ignore the voices in your head when you were driving along clifftop switchbacks with the roof down and the Mediterranean sparkling below. Nancy closed her eyes and leant her head back, thinking how strange and yet natural it felt to be in the passenger seat with Charlie at the wheel.

She listened to him humming along to the radio in that horrendously toneless way that had always made her smile, and was transported back to the happy time, when everything was still ahead of them.

'Nancy?' he had said to her one day last April, as they sat on a bench in Green Park during her lunch break.

'Mmm?' she murmured, her head tipped back to enjoy the heat of the spring sun.

He'd hesitated, and she suddenly panicked, wondering if this was to be the moment when he realised she really wasn't terribly interesting and was about to tell her he wanted to move on.

'What is it?' She had sat up, blinking slightly as her eyes adjusted to the bright sunshine, and his face slowly came into focus.

He had begun playing with the bangle on her wrist, turning it this way and that. 'Well, we've been seeing each other for a little while now, haven't we?'

It hadn't seemed possible, but it was already a few months since Diana's birthday, and Nancy couldn't imagine life without him. 'We have. Why?'

He blushed, and she laughed. 'All right, I'll just ask . . .'

'What, Charlie?' She waited impatiently for an elderly couple to walk slowly past.

'Nancy . . . would you spend the night with me?'

She didn't know what to say. Of course she'd realised that at some point their relationship would take a new turn, and she hadn't imagined herself begging for a ring before it did, but still, it was a huge step.

'I'm sorry. I've spoiled everything. You're cross with me.'

She'd squeezed his hand. 'Of course I'm not cross.'

'But you must know how much I want you. You're perfect, Nance. And I'm not saying that to get you into bed.'

She'd smiled at his obvious awkwardness. 'And I think you're perfect too.'

'You look unsure. Are you one of those girls who wants to wait until she's married? I mean, it's fine if you are.' He stopped, flustered, then went on, 'Not that I want to get married. Not yet, at least. You do feel the same, don't you?'

Marriage had never occurred to her, even though Phyllis quizzed her incessantly about it. She had a life to lead, a career to build, and the last thing she wanted right now was to be tied to a husband and a couple of babies. No, Charlie was right. Anyway, it was 1961, not 1921: why shouldn't they, as long as they loved each other and were careful? Dorothy knew all sorts of tips to stop a girl getting pregnant; it would be fine.

'So?' he'd said, leaning closer.

'So . . . yes.'

Yes. Such an easy word to say.

They had lunch at a little café in the crowded Piazzetta, eating oozing slices of pizza as he talked of his writing, their friends. Everything but the one thing that sat between them. As the blue and white ceramic clock overlooking the square marked the time they sat together, she watched his face as it grew animated, then grimaced at the sickly yellow limoncello, remembered how his slight stutter had made her heart yearn for him. She looked for a reminder in those grey eyes of how she had felt about him, but it was as though she were looking through a veil.

Afterwards they sped off along the coast road, his tanned arm leaning on the car door, until they reached a little lay-by and climbed out, perching on the metal rails that divided the road from the sheer drop down to the wave-splashed rocks below.

He looked over at her. 'I'm sorry, Nancy.'

She didn't want to see his expression, which was a year too late and served only to emphasise the awfulness of what had happened.

'I let you down.'

She turned to face him. 'You let us all down, Charlie.'

'I know. I was pathetic.'

'How could you have left me like that? You said you loved me.'

He went to take her hand, but she folded it in her lap. 'I did love you, Nancy.'

'Just not enough.'

'You don't understand. It was very difficult. Father was—'

'And how do you think *my* father was, Charlie?' she said, pulling away from him. 'My family couldn't just walk away from it like yours did.'

They sat in silence for a while, the lost months between them a huge chasm filled by the screech of the cormorants nesting in the cliffs below.

'So what happened after . . . ? Did you . . . ?'

'So you're interested now?' She shook her head. 'You're something else, Charlie Blake.'

He turned to her, and she was shocked to see his eyes welling up. 'No, *you're* something else, Nancy. I was an idiot.'

He leant closer, and just in time she turned her face, so that his lips only brushed her cheek, close enough that the scent of him chased through her blood.

He pulled out his wallet and took out a photograph, handing it over to her. 'Here. I found this,' he said.

She took it from him. It showed the two of them on a beach, faces glowing in the fresh spring air, him standing behind her with his arms wrapped around her chest and his cheek pressed to hers.

'Eastbourne,' she said quietly, and handed it back to him, but he shook his head.

'Keep it. Or throw it away. Up to you.'

She tucked the photo in her handbag and stood up, brushing the dust from the front of her trousers. 'I should get back,' she said. 'They'll wonder where I am.'

He opened the door for her, then held onto her arm just as she slid into the passenger seat. 'Nancy, can I see you again?'

She looked at him in disbelief. 'Have you no idea what I went through when you left me? You never even asked what decision I made.' She pulled on her sunglasses and looked away from him. 'Take me home, Charlie.'

He sighed and followed her into the car. 'I'll always love you, Nancy,' he said, his eyes fixed on the winding clifftop road ahead of them.

She trailed her arm out of the car, catching the breeze in the palm of her hand. In his absence, she'd thought she would always love him, but the last twelve months had diminished him, and as she looked at him, she knew that at last she was free.

Nancy was still on the swing seat when the others returned that evening, lit only by the hurricane lamps she had placed on the table. The bouquet of wilted hibiscus lay on the ground beneath her, apart from one flower, which she had put inside her book.

'Hello,' she called out, but Caro and Pamela marched straight indoors, one claiming her own headache and the other saying she was going to her room and not coming out again. Ever.

'How are you feeling?' Peter said, standing over her, his linen jacket slung over his shoulder.

'Better now. Thank you.'

'Better enough for a nightcap? Whisky, isn't it?'

She ought to get to bed, but she had been sleeping badly, and a whisky might help. 'Twist my arm,' she said, smiling at his candlelit silhouette.

The banging of doors inside the house gradually subsided, and as Peter reappeared with two chunky blue glass tumblers, the trilling cicadas and yowling street cats took over the night air.

'Bottoms up,' Peter said, clinking glasses with her. He found his jacket and pulled his pipe and tobacco from its breast pocket. 'Mind if I . . . ?'

'Not at all,' Nancy said, and watched the complicated ritual of tapping and tamping and popping before he took the first inhalation. 'What's up with those two?' she asked.

'Oh, Caro's been in a stink all day, and Pamela got the huff because she wanted to go to the Blue Grotto rather than some boring lunch. Can't say I blame her. Oh, and then Charlie disappeared God knows where.' He shifted in his seat, then suddenly exclaimed. 'Bloody hell. I've been bitten by some-thing.' He brushed at his trousers before spotting the piece of delicate fabric where he had been sitting, the long, sharp needle still attached.

'Sorry,' Nancy said. 'I should have put that away.'

'Did you make this?' he said, examining the intricate needlework. 'Looks like a baby's bib.'

She took it gently from him, folding it and tucking it beside her. 'It's for my niece. Maddie. She's six months old next week.'

'Lucky thing, having a clever aunty like you.'

'I don't know about that,' she said, reminding herself to hide it away in her suitcase with her other tiny treasures.

'I remember when Pea was a baby. Good Lord, that girl could cry.'

They sat in silence for a little while, sipping the burning whisky and rocking gently on the seat, lost in their own losses.

'Ever had the feeling someone's up to no good?' he said suddenly.

'What do you mean?'

'Oh, I don't know. I'm sorry. I shouldn't be talking to you like this.' He swirled his glass, the ice cubes ricocheting around in the whisky centrifuge.

'I don't mind. I'm very discreet.'

He sighed. 'Shouldn't talk out of turn, but I'm worried about Tony.'

'Tony?' Nancy said, trying to sound surprised, although from what Charlie had told her that afternoon, Tony had pretty much worked his way through his address book looking for investors in a film that everyone in London had serious reservations about. 'Inveterate fantasist', Charlie had called him.

'Probably something and nothing. There were rumours tonight that he's done a bunk. Police were at his hotel, apparently. All nonsense, obviously.'

'But I thought he'd just gone away to tie up some business?'

'In South America?' Peter shook his head. 'Only people who go to South America are old Nazis and people on the run. Pretty sure Tony's not a Nazi.'

'I'm sure there's an explanation.'

'Bloody hope so.'

'You didn't . . .' she wasn't sure how to be discreet, but carried on, 'well, invest anything, did you?'

Peter looked at her. 'No. Thank God. Came pretty close, though; had to call the bank to cancel the cheque. Don't tell Caro, whatever you do. Bloody Tony. What a fool.' He shook his head. 'Anyway, how was your day? Glad to have a break from us all, I should think.'

'Not at all.'

He sighed. 'Nancy . . .' She could hear the awkwardness in his voice as he struggled to continue. 'None of my business, but young Charlie . . . Well, I gather you know each other.'

'We used to, yes.' Was that her voice? It sounded like someone had tightened a scarf around her neck.

'It's just . . . I shouldn't speak ill, and the boy's my godson after all, but . . . friend to friend, I'd steer clear.'

She took a long slug of whisky in lieu of responding.

'He rather let a young girl down, you see. Not a nice business, and if he'd been my son, it would have been a different matter, but Charlie's father . . . Well, as I say, not my business, but I wouldn't want anyone else getting hurt. Not on my watch, anyway.'

How she managed to smile, she had no idea, but Peter seemed content as she reassured him that she didn't know Charlie that well, and was unlikely ever to see him again. And as she said the words, she knew they were true: Charlie was finally out of her heart, even if his legacy would haunt her for the rest of her days.

The next day, the small party piled into the motor launch headed to the mainland, where they would catch a train across the calf of Italy and over to the lagoons of the Venetian gulf. There the apartment belonging to the family of Peter's old tutor awaited them. No one spoke as they raced across the water, and neither Nancy nor her companions looked back to the beautiful island whose Sirens had once enticed Odysseus, where emperors had bathed and where racing drivers and millionaire playboys cavorted along the beautiful but dangerous coastline.

21

It was a relief to have the sea air blast into her lungs as she stood at the prow of the hydrofoil racing across the Bay of Naples towards the huge slab of jagged rock that breasted the smooth blue water. Her only previous visit to Italy had been to Milan, which had seemed like a warmer, more sophisticated version of London compared to the chaotic sprawl of Naples, with its graffitied streets and stray dogs and weeks' worth of uncollected refuse.

Flo was exhausted by the time she climbed the hill from the ferry terminal to the apartment she'd rented above the little square already teeming with day trippers. She took a watery cup of Lipton's tea to the little white table on the terrace. It was so peaceful up here, the sounds of the boats chugging backwards and forwards down in the bay drowned out by the rasping of crickets and the rustle of darting lizards, and the canopy of bougainvillaea shading her from the sun's powerful rays.

She looked at the two packets on the table in front of her. She was intimately familiar with the patterns they had contained, of course, but had resisted looking at the other contents since that first night she had discovered them, not wanting to move on any further than her predecessor. What would be the point of taking this journey if she were just to gather all the information at once and google the answer?

She pushed aside the bowl of huge dimpled lemons and tipped the contents of the first packet out in front of her. She had felt less nervous about this beachwear: it was really just a pair of shorts with a bra top, and a pretty hip-skimming tunic, and so she had taken the plunge and followed Nancy's lead, although she'd had to allow for a slightly larger cup size than her great-aunt. Where Nancy had used a beautiful turquoise linen, and for the dress a poplin with huge pink and turquoise flowers on a white background, Flo had managed to find some pale blue linen that did the job, along with a piece of fabric with a definite sixties feel to it, with its bold daisy pattern.

Alongside Nancy's swatches and the pattern pieces, Flo found the postcard she had known would be there, as well as a photograph and a time-tarnished brass button. The postcard was of a beach club and hotel, owned back in those days by Gracie Fields, who had made her home on Capri. Nancy must either have stayed there or spent a day enjoying the facilities, and Flo would make a day trip there to do the same.

The photograph had dropped out of the packet face down, and Flo turned it over. Nancy looked more tanned and her hair a little blonder as it fought against the pins holding it loosely on top of her head. Flo thought for a moment that she could see something of her own mother in Peggy's sister, in the narrow chin and wide eyes that Flo and Maddie shared, and that had bypassed Peggy, who had been Beryl through and through, whatever she did to her hair or make-up and whatever she wore. Nancy's flowered tunic had dropped off one shoulder to reveal the wide straps of the little bra top beneath, and she was full of smiles as she turned affectionately to the other face in the frame, its freckled nose scrunched as it stuck its tongue out at the photographer. Pamela. The thick ponytail and straight fringe were without a doubt those of the girl sulking at the Lido de Paris. The two faces were bound together not only by a contract of employment, but by a growing friendship.

The two of them had been photographed on board a boat, and in the background Flo made out a few figures in swimwear and a white-uniformed waiter. She thought she could see the man with the fair hair from the Paris photo, which she quickly found on her phone. There he was, and she couldn't believe she had failed to notice the family likeness: the long, equine features and impossible hair.

She picked up the brass button, and as she rubbed at the decades-old layer of dirt, yellow Braille-like splashes appeared, until she was able to read the single word embossed on its surface. *Alessandra*.

'Hey.'

She sat bolt upright, knocking her copy of *I Love Capri* to the floor, which in turn took out her glass of iced fresh lemonade.

'Mr Simpson at your service, madam. Sorry. Wasn't sure whether to wake you.'

She shielded her eyes against the sun. 'Hi, Ben.'

'You hadn't forgotten I was coming, had you?'

'Of course not,' she said. In fact she'd been more than a little preoccupied about his arrival, worrying that she had made a mistake in inviting him, and worrying about her motive for that invitation. And now that she saw him, standing in front of her in immaculate white linen shirt and perfectly worn-in tailored shorts, she began to realise that she might just be interested in more than his sleuthing abilities.

He visibly relaxed. 'Phew. Wouldn't want to be in the way.'

'You're not in the way, Ben. It's good to see you.' And it was true: she had missed his company in Antibes. Sitting around in bars on her own had been pretty lonely, and she suspected Barbara would have told Ben anything he wanted to know. He was just her type.

He gestured to the empty lounger next to her. 'Mind if I . . . ?'

'Sure.' She put her sunglasses on and surreptitiously watched him trying to adjust the height of the lounger, muttering under his breath as the contraption outwitted him. He actually looked much better in shorts and an old shirt than he had in his Clarkson jeans and jacket, and had he had a haircut? She deliberately called to mind as many images of Seamus on holiday as she could, trying to eclipse Ben's obvious charm with memories of her husband's ratty swimming trunks that he wouldn't let her throw away, the mashed-potato whiteness of his ever-chunkier torso, and of course the sock–sandal combination that he insisted was acceptable when abroad.

Ben frowned at her. 'What are you laughing at?'

She smiled. 'Nothing. No one. I was just remembering something.'

'OK,' he said uncertainly. 'Because I can actually manage to do this without losing three fingers, you know.'

'Why don't we get some lunch?' she said, seeing that the sunlounger was probably about to prove him wrong. 'I don't know about you, but I'm starving. There's a café at the end of the pool there.'

They found a table overlooking the three giant dragon's teeth reaching out of the sea, and watched as the waiter brought them two huge plates of wagon-wheel blood-red tomato alternating with slabs of creamy white mozzarella and pungent basil.

Flo was surprised at how excited she was to describe to Ben the Antibes photos from the beach and the party at the Villa du Cap Bleu. She told him about Barbara, stretching out her heyday in the town where she had loved and lost one of Nancy's companions, and still sharp as a pin when it came to the night in June 1962 when she had been photographed with her.

'And Tony was dead two weeks later?' Ben said, his salad suddenly forgotten as he peered at the photo of the party.

'Plane crash apparently. But I've no idea where or how. Maybe if we can track him down, we can find out more about Peter. It can't be so hard to find a mid-century portraitist with that name, can it? At least we now know who Nancy's boss was.'

Ben reached inside the man bag tucked on the seat beside him and handed her a couple of sheets of paper. 'I did find this for you.'

Flo took the printout, glad that Seamus wasn't there to make his usual unreconstructed jokes about men's handbags. She read a short obituary of Lady Sybil Henderson, published twenty years ago, of little interest to anyone other than those who followed hunting, the charity-dinner circuit or the history of the British Raj, other than that it named her sole surviving daughter. Ben had tracked down Tabitha Pennington, née

Henderson, to a large corner of Berkshire, where she was happy to take half an hour out from organising the Pony Club summer fete to chat with him and take him on a brief tour of the house and its contents, which included a portrait of her mother from 1962. She wasn't sure of the artist, but she was terribly fond of it, even though it was rather unkind in its portrayal of her mother's nose. She'd allowed Ben to photograph the work, including the indecipherable signature on the bottom right of the canvas. Flo scrutinised the scrawled letters, which definitely began with a P, although it was impossible to read any more.

'This is amazing, Ben,' she said, handing the pages back. 'It must be Peter. We just need his surname.'

'Once we've got that, and we've got your man Tony nailed, you'll be closer to finding Nancy, I'm sure. Barbara couldn't remember his surname?'

Flo shook her head. 'I asked her, but she was quite confused by then.'

The waiter came to take their plates away, and she smiled at him, asking if he wouldn't mind helping them.

'*Si, signora?*' he said.

She pulled the little brass button out of her handbag and held it out to him. 'You don't know what this is, do you?' she said.

He took it from her and frowned. 'It looks like is from a uniform. A boat, maybe?' He held it closer and peered at the writing, then turned a huge smile on her. 'Is the *Alessandra*,' he said.

'And what's that?' Flo asked, trying not to shrink back as the young man knelt down close beside her.

'It was a yacht. Was kept here in the nineteen sixties. Lots of parties, lots of scandals,' he said, laughing.

'Do you know who owned it?' Ben cut in, to the annoyance of the young man, who aimed his response at Flo.

'I not know,' he said, shaking his head, 'but you could ask my uncle. He worked on all the big yachts when he was young.'

'Really?' Flo saw him smile as her eyes widened. 'And can we meet your uncle? Is he still on the island?'

He nodded. '*Sì*. He is quite old now, but he has his own boat: he does tourist trips to the Blue Grotto. Here . . .' He scribbled a phone number down on a napkin and held it out to Flo. 'This is him. Alberto. Tell him Andrea gave you the number.' He took the napkin back and wrote another number beneath the first.

'What's that?' Flo said, taking it from him.

He smiled as he stood up. 'That,' he said, 'is my number.'

Ben watched him walk away. 'Tosser,' he said quietly, stirring a large lump of brown sugar into his coffee.

'Yeah, but a helpful one.'

'You're sure you don't mind me tagging along? I've booked my own hotel and stuff, so I won't be in your way.'

Flo hadn't been sure about Ben joining her, but after the last few days, it was good to have some company and someone to throw ideas around with. And there'd been no awkward-ness so far: Jem had probably just been exaggerating his interest in her, stirring it up as usual. Flo was unused to solo travel, having always been away with Seamus, and even if Ben didn't make her laugh out loud like her husband did, he was good company. He drank considerably less, for a start, and was unlikely to get down on one knee and sing old Gaelic love songs to her after a whiskey too many, whether they were in the pub or the privacy of their own home. Or present her with bunches of flowers harvested from neighbours' gardens after the pub had closed. And anyway, she realised, as she caught Ben looking at the curve of tanned shoulder peeping out from the sleeve of her floral beach tunic, it was nice to be noticed.

The good news was that Alberto was happy to talk to them for half an hour. The bad news was that it would cost them fifty euros each to hire him and his boat. Everyone's got to make a dollar, Flo supposed, as she and Ben sat on the quayside waiting for him to appear.

It was scorchingly hot, even with the breeze that drifted ashore. The white capri pants were struggling to work for her, the waistband digging into her sweatily uncomfortable girth, and something up with the way she'd fitted the zip, which scratched furiously on her left hip. There had been no photo of Nancy in the trousers, only a swatch of white sateen, which must have been a bugger to keep clean, Flo thought, as she narrowly avoided dribbling the last of her chocolate ice cream down her own version.

Ben, in contrast, looked positively native as he leant back, tanned legs stretched in front of him and arms spread along the back of the bench. She did like a man who eschewed the T-shirt in favour of a natty linen shirt, something she'd never been able to persuade Seamus to adopt. She wondered whether it was as hot as this in New York: she'd checked her weather app from time to time, and knew that her nearly ex-husband was basking in something of a heatwave across the Atlantic.

She hoped he'd remember to use sun cream without her there to nag him – with his pale Irish skin and distrust of potions in bottles, he was an inveterate burner. Maybe he already had someone else to rub cream on his shoulders, she thought sadly. She looked across at Ben, humming Ed Sheeran to himself, and smiled. It was good to have someone to distract her and keep her self-invented visions of Seamus's beautiful new life at bay.

'Here, that must be him. He said he'd be wearing a red cap.' Ben pulled Flo to her feet. Across the harbour, a small blue boat chugged towards them, an elderly man standing aboard looking around for his two passengers.

He rowed the last few lengths, then held out a wrinkled mahogany-brown hand to help Flo across the short plank that reached from the harbourside to the little *gozzo*.

She moved along the bench so that Ben could sit beside him, and as they awkwardly shifted their thighs out of touching distance, the old man tugged at the thread on the outboard motor until they were drenched in diesel fumes and he could steer them out of the crystal-clear waters of the Marina Grande and along the coast.

It was impossible to talk above the motor, so they sat back and watched the cliffs zoom past, candy-coloured houses perched on their flanks and firework-bright spatterings of pink bougainvillaea splashed in between the scrubby patches of olive and gorse that clung perilously wherever they could find a foothold.

Eventually they slowed down, and found themselves in a gently bobbing queue of similar boats, all waiting to enter a tiny fissure in the rocks.

'So,' the old sailor said, switching off the engine and sitting opposite them. 'You want to talk to me?'

Aware that they were already a third of the way through their allotted half-hour, Flo quickly reached into her bag and pulled out the button, plus the photo of Nancy and Pamela and the Paris photo of the whole entourage.

The man lifted his red cap and scratched his head. They waited in silence while he looked from one picture to the other, then smiled as Flo passed him the button.

'Nineteen sixty-two, you say?' He pointed at Peter and shook his head. 'I no know him.' He paused as his finger traced across the image of Tony in the nightclub, comparing it with the photograph from Antibes she took out of her bag and showed him. 'Him,' he said, looking up at Flo and shaking his head.

'What is it?' Flo asked.

He rubbed his thumb across his forefinger. 'He take money from the *Alessandra*. We all get blame, you know?' He leant closer. 'I find him in Signor's office. He try to pay me to be quiet, but I an honest man,' he said, holding his hand to his heart. 'If I take you money, I tell you first.' And he pointed at Ben and Flo and laughed.

'So what happened?' Flo asked.

'My boss, he say he call the police. Then Mr Tony disappear,' his fingers burst open, 'like magic.'

'And can you remember Mr Tony's surname?' Ben asked.

The old man shook his head. 'No, but I remember the date. Maybe that help? It was June thirteen: the Festival of Sant' Antonio: Signor gave us all the evening off so we could go to the procession. You want to know how I remember?' He waited for them to nod before smiling broadly. 'It was the day I met my Giulia.' He leant forward and nudged Ben. 'I hope you as happy with your lady.'

'Oh no, we're not . . .' Ben said.

'No, God no,' Flo added.

The old man sat back and folded his arms, smiling at them both. 'Maybe Sant'Antonio, he not agree.'

Flo needed to change the subject. Fast. 'So, Alberto, your boss, the owner of the boat, what was his name?'

'The signor? Giacomo Cavelli – the richest man on the island back then.'

At a shout from across the water, Alberto picked up the oars, splashing them around until the boat turned and they found themselves heading for the tiny gap in the rock. He grabbed the chain that ran along the edge of the cave, pulling the boat alongside it before suddenly yelling at them to lie down. They fell backwards, their heads just missing the jagged entrance to the grotto, and as they were briefly plunged into darkness, their bodies pressed together and neither of them had time to register the proximity of their lips, which gently brushed before the boat emerged into a huge cavern, its deep waters glowing with the most remarkable bright-blue phosphorescence. Flo struggled to pull herself away from Ben's sleepy brown eyes and the kiss she knew was waiting just a breath away, and that she suddenly wanted more than anything. She couldn't let it happen: everything would change, would become complicated and messy and hurtful. And there had been enough of that already. So she pressed her hand on his smooth cheek and smiled sadly as she pushed herself away from him.

As the two of them sat up, staring silently in opposite directions out of the sides of the boat, Alberto laughed and launched into a soulful Neapolitan love song, and Flo didn't know whether to cry out of embarrassment or disappointment.

'Well, that was interesting,' Ben said.

Flo knew he was watching for her reaction to his flippant comment, that whatever she said would determine how she felt about what had so nearly happened between them on the boat ride. Cowardice being her preferred course of action right now, she chose to say nothing, instead taking in the view before her and waiting for Ben to look away.

They were sitting at the table on Flo's terrace, watching the last of the daylight being replaced by the twinkling of lights of the little town below.

A light ping interrupted the peaceful symphony of cicadas and distant mopeds. Ben picked his phone up and sighed, switching it off and putting it back down on the table.

Flo smiled, relieved at the change of subject. 'Mother?'

He rolled his eyes and nodded.

'Your mother needs a new hobby. Or a job,' Flo added, glad that Ben's mother's interest in his new friend had become a standing joke rather than anything meaningful.

'My mother is unemployable.'

They laughed awkwardly, and Flo pushed the bottle towards him. 'More wine?'

'Thanks.' Ben topped up his glass. 'Good stuff, this.'

'Grown in the shadow of Vesuvius, apparently.' She watched him sniff the dark red liquid, not taken in by his forced jollity. 'Ben . . .'

'It's OK, Flo.'

'What's OK?'

'You know. What nearly happened. In the boat. We'll just forget it, shall we?'

'Oh. Yes, probably best.' But was it best? She barely knew any more. With the amount of sun she'd had that day, coupled with the bottle of wine they'd already finished, and the complete absence of Seamus everywhere, she was feeling a little dazed and confused.

He didn't reply, but looked down, concentrating on pushing a dried leaf around with his bare toe. She wished he'd say something else. Did he really want to forget it? With Seamus, there was never any doubt what he was thinking: if he was angry, he yelled; if he was sad, he cried; if he wasn't sure what she thought, he asked. It was blissfully simple, if annoying. But with Ben, she couldn't tell. Maybe life had taught him that it was better not to ask, in case you got the wrong answer. She wished she could go over to him, give him a hug and tell him it was all going to be fine; that they were just good friends and nothing had changed.

As the sun went down, she started to feel a little chilly. 'Listen, I'm just going in to get a sweater. Do you want anything? A blanket? Something to eat?'

He was still wearing only his thin shirt and shorts, and looked as cold as she. 'Sure, maybe a blanket. If it's not too much trouble.'

'No trouble,' she said, and rubbed his shoulder as she walked past. It was so warm, so solid.

She came back a few minutes later with a plate of cheese

and bread, plus the blanket. Ben seemed to have cheered up, and smiled at her. 'Thanks,' he said.

'I thought we could look at these,' she said, placing the next packet on the table.

He wrapped the blanket across his knees and shifted his chair closer to hers as she carefully took out the contents.

'This is Nancy again?' he asked, looking at the photograph of a British beach scene. Flo nodded. 'Looks like your great-aunt had a great love,' he said, pointing to the smiling pale-eyed man standing behind her, his arms wrapped around her chest.

'So it does,' Flo said quietly as she turned the photo over. 'Eastbourne, April nineteen sixty-one. Charlie and Nancy.'

'Isn't that the year before her trip?'

'Yes, and we haven't come across this fella before.' Flo saw the bright glow in Nancy's eyes, the wide sparkling smile. This was a young woman in love. 'So who do you think he is?'

Ben sighed. 'Well, obviously I'm no expert – in fact, my track record with relationships is pretty dire – but as far as you remember, there wasn't an Uncle Charlie anywhere?'

Flo shook her head. 'I don't think so. But then I didn't know I had an Aunt Nancy.'

'True. But if she'd married him, they'd have been part of the family, don't you think? And a year later, there she was, travelling around Europe as a single girl. Girls who were engaged or married back then didn't disappear off without their man.'

Flo frowned. 'I suppose not. She might have been escaping from the relationship. Maybe they had a bad break-up? It still doesn't explain why she didn't come back.'

'No, and to be honest, he looks nice enough. Good look-ing, well dressed, but not your classic love rat.'

'So what about the other things?' Flo passed him the deli-cate dried flower, its colour almost drained away across the years.

'I don't know. Memento of a nice day out? Maybe she just liked flowers.'

'Possibly. And this?'

Inside the packet was a slim brown envelope from which she pulled a piece of yellowed fabric.

'What's that?' Ben said.

'I'm not sure.' Flo opened it out, worried that it might break along the fragile folded edges.

'Is that a baby's bib? And what's that on the front?'

She picked the bib up and held it close to her eyes, strug-gling to see in the fading light. 'It's embroidery. Looks like a letter. And some flowers.'

'What's the letter?'

'It's an M.' She looked up at Ben. 'M for Maddie. It must be. Nancy made it for Mum.'

She ran her hand over the immaculate stitching. So much love had gone into this bib, but why had Nancy kept it and not sent it on to Gran? She remembered how much she herself had invested in the unfinished quilt that should have been ready for its tiny owner's arrival, each stitch a declaration of love and hope.

From nowhere, she suddenly thought of the little toy Seamus had tried to make for him. 'But you've never made anything in your life!' she had exclaimed, watching with amusement his fat-fingered attempts to carve a figure out of a lump of wood. 'What is it anyway?'

'It's a . . . thing. I'll tell you when it's finished,' he'd said defensively, as he cursed and hacked at the ever-shrinking lump of wood, the chimera that evolved day by day according to how much he accidentally shaved off it. It had touched her more than anything he had ever done, which said a lot about a romantic man prone to expansive expressions of love.

'Hey, are you OK?'

She looked up. 'I'm fine.'

'Don't worry, we'll find out what happened to her.'

'It's not that . . .' But she had no words to tell him what was tearing at her heart. The words she'd had back then had been kept inside for so long, they had shrivelled away. 'Sorry, I think I might be a bit drunk.'

'It's OK, you don't have to tell me,' he said.

He moved his chair closer to hers, taking the blanket and wrapping it around them both.

'Thanks, Seamus,' she said sleepily, as she felt the wine dragging her towards oblivion.

Ben looked at her, seemingly on the point of correcting her, then sighed and sat back, leaving her to her thoughts.

They sat in silence, until the heaviness of night and the dark red wine closed her eyes, and Ben quietly led her to her room, covering her before turning out the light and heading downhill to his dingy hotel room.

The next morning, Flo awoke to the smell of coffee and fresh bread. She reached out across the bed, surprised, as she often still was, not to find the large, snoring shape of Seamus lying next to her. How long would it take to change the habits of a marital lifetime?

She wandered out to the terrace to find Ben waiting for her with a large cafetière and a bag full of fresh bread.

'Morning,' he said brightly, looking as though he had run five miles instead of waking up with the red-wine hangover that was seriously slowing Flo down. 'Hope you don't mind me bringing breakfast.'

'Are there any liver salts amongst that lot?' she said.

''Fraid not.'

'By the way,' she said as she sat down at the table and ripped off a corner of bread, 'I'm sorry about yesterday.'

'Which bit?' he said.

Which bit indeed? The almost-kiss in the boat, or getting drunk and calling him by her husband's name? Ex-husband. 'The drunk bit,' she said. 'Mainly.'

'Oh, OK.' He sounded uncertain, and there was a hint of optimism that she hadn't the heart to squash, and that she wasn't yet sure was completely unfounded. She had so much spinning round her head, it was hard to tell what was real and what wasn't. 'Here,' he said, pouring her some treacly coffee, 'get this down you and I'll tell you what I found out this morning.'

Apparently, while she was sleeping in, he had been up with the lark and spending some quality time with Google. He pulled a small laptop from his bag and placed it on the table. 'Here,' he said, typing quickly then pushing it towards her.

Flo peered at the smudged screen through bleary eyes, looking at an article about Giacomo Cavelli, a Neapolitan businessman and owner of, amongst other things, a movie production house and fashion magazine. As well as being known for his philanthropic work in his home city, he was also renowned for his high living and his many connections. The parties on his yacht *Alessandra*, named after his long-suffering wife, were legendary. An image showed Giacomo smiling at a camera, his arm around a dark-haired man with a pencil moustache; the article went on to describe the night Cavelli's close friend Anthony Scott narrowly escaped arrest by Italian police, who had raided the *Alessandra* and Scott's hotel room for evidence in their investigation into fraud. Cavelli, keen to distance himself from Scott's dubious business arrangements, had apparently tipped off the police about the Englishman, who had been caught with his hands in the boat's office safe.

'Ben, you're a genius.'

'That's not all,' he said as he took the laptop back.

Flo came to stand behind him, and together they read the newspaper article from June 1962 that described how Anthony Scott, a British national, was thought to be amongst the dead after the crash of Air France Flight 117 from Paris to Santiago. *All one hundred and thirteen passengers perished in the accident, and although it is believed Mr Scott was travelling with a female companion, her identity has not yet been confirmed.*

'Wow.' Flo sat down, and they stared at one another.

'You've got more of Nancy's patterns, haven't you?' Ben said. 'I mean, she couldn't be . . .'

'God, no. Surely not. There aren't many more, but she definitely went to Venice after Capri: the trail doesn't dry up until after that. She can't have been on the plane. It must have been someone else. Hang on, let me check the date of the last one.' She disappeared indoors and came back with the final two packets in her hands. 'Here,' she said. 'Eighteenth and twentieth of June. What date did you say the plane crash was?'

Ben scoured the article, then looked up at her. 'Twenty-second of June.'

'Shit.' This wasn't what she'd come all this way for. She'd hoped to find that Nancy had lived a long and happy life; nothing could extinguish that smile so brutally, surely? And anyway, why would she have got on a plane with Tony? Her loathing for him had jumped out of the photographs.

'Hey,' Ben said, rubbing her hand with his. 'I'm sure it's not her. The family would have known, wouldn't they? Why would they keep that secret?'

'I suppose so,' Flo said.

'Look, I'll keep digging. We'll find out who it is, but I bet you it's not Nancy.'

'I hope you're right.' Please don't let Nancy have been snuffed out on the side of a South American mountain. Please let it be someone else. She looked up. 'What if it's Pamela?'

'She'd have no more reason than Nancy to travel with Tony. But at least now that we know who he is, maybe we'll be able to find Peter's full name, and that will lead us to the others.'

'I hope so. They must have known each other from school or the army or something. We'll find him. And of course there's Charlie now.'

Ben frowned. 'You sure we can't cheat and look at the last packet?'

'No!' she said. 'Not in the rules.'

He shrugged. 'Fine, it's your game after all.'

'Ben . . .' she said, wanting to ask him something but needing to be sure of something else.

'Yes?'

'Well, I just wanted to be sure that we're OK. You know? Friends?'

He flushed slightly, but nodded his head vigorously. 'Oh yes, of course. Absolutely. Friends.'

She smiled, almost convinced. 'Good. Listen,' she went on, 'I don't want to twist your arm or anything, and of course there's no ulterior motive – and whatever you do, don't tell your mother – but, well, would you like to come to Venice with me? I've got a two-bedroom apartment, so there's plenty of space and you'd have your own room . . .' Was she mad? Was she encouraging something she might not be able to see through? But Ben was just a friend; they'd established that, hadn't they? She wasn't over Seamus, and Ben knew where they both stood. It would be fine.

He looked like a Labrador that had just been given the key to the larder, and Flo watched him try to temper his reaction, downgrading it to reluctant acceptance on the basis that it would help her out.

She held up her coffee cup and clinked it against his. 'Last leg,' she said. 'Here's to finding Nancy.' But she spoke with a little less confidence than she'd had only a short while ago.

Part Six

VENICE

22

Butterick 2308: Wide-necked sleeveless shift with matching three-quarter-sleeve jacket

'It stinks here.'

'For God's sake, Pamela. Is that the best thing you can find to say about Venice?'

'Well, it does.' Unfazed by the bite in Caro's tone, Pamela came back in from the little balcony overlooking the still, green water and began twisting herself inside one of the long brocade curtains that framed the huge French window.

Nancy couldn't help agreeing with her: the recent heat-wave had done nothing to dampen the aroma of drains and fish that wafted in from the old fish market a few hundred yards upwind of them along the canal, where crates of lagoon harvest were unloaded and eviscerated each morning, seagulls fighting over the bloody entrails sluiced into the deep murky water.

'Stop that,' Caro said, looking up from her magazine to see Pamela coiled inside yards of soft furnishing. 'You'll pull them down, you stupid girl.'

Pamela glared, then slowly pirouetted out of the thick fabric. 'Why has Uncle Tony gone?' she said.

'Mind your own business.'

'I heard Pa say he's in trouble with the police. Is that right?'

Caro pointed at her, her face suddenly betraying the exhaustion of several nights pacing around the house. Nancy was a light sleeper at the best of times, and had heard the back and forth of the creaking floorboards with sad recognition. 'It is none of your business, madam,' she spat. 'You shouldn't listen to grown-ups' conversations.'

Pamela flushed an angry scarlet and turned her back on the room, staring instead at the watery scene through the tall windows.

Caro tutted and lit herself another cigarette, then carried on reading the magazine she had already read ten times. It was strange to see her in just a dressing gown and without make-up, and Nancy realised that it was only her daily routine of cosmetics and products that kept her employer visibly, if not in fact, the right side of forty. She actually looked better without her usual thick mask; there was a girlish beauty about her that had probably improved with age and that sat well with her high cheekbones and huge brown eyes. She doubted Caro would agree, and had listened with half an ear as Pamela told her how her stepmother's work had dried up and how she'd been turned down by a couple of her favourite fashion houses when she called to ask for some pieces from their new collections. At least that explained the confusion in Paris, when Nancy had offered to collect them for her.

The remains of Pamela's picnic breakfast sat on the coffee table, and Nancy went to clear it away, assuming that they were now on minimal domestic-help rations. Neither Caro nor Pamela looked the slightest bit inclined to lift a finger, and Peter was happily ensconced in the attic studio where he had once been a pupil, and was to be left alone to work on his canvases. Caro had attempted to keep tabs on the portraits he was supposed to be sketching out, but he had become quite secretive about his work, and had imposed a complete ban on all females entering the studio.

'Make some more coffee while you're in the kitchen,' Caro called out as Nancy walked along the hallway, balancing the large tray and trying not to skid on the polished marble floor or be distracted by the stunning frescoes painted all over the walls and ceilings, the sunlight from the open windows glinting on the gilt paintwork that spread ivy-like over every surface.

To be honest, Nancy didn't mind a stint in the kitchen; it would at least give her a break from the grumpy torpor that had settled over the household ever since the water taxi had dropped them and their bags at the little jetty on the waterfront of the crumbling old palazzo a few days ago. Peter's private view at the gallery that evening would be a miserable affair if the mood didn't improve soon.

The atmosphere had rubbed off on her, and she felt more unsettled than she had done for a few days now. The combination of seeing Charlie, and Maddie's half-birthday tomorrow scratched at her, and she would have to work hard to keep going.

She rinsed the few dishes in the sink and left them to drain, then sat at the old oak trestle table that ran the length of the kitchen. She pulled Charlie's letter out of her pocket and looked at the inky scrawl smudged across the thick, textured headed paper, bearing the address of the house whose door had been barred to her. Did he really think they could be together? He was either a liar or a fantasist.

'I hate her,' Pamela said from the doorway, surprising her. 'I wish she'd never married Pa.'

'You don't mean that. You just don't like her very much at the moment. It's completely different.'

'What's that you're reading?'

Nancy stuffed the letter back in its envelope and scrunched it into her pocket. 'Nothing.'

Pamela leant in the doorway. 'Doesn't look like nothing.'

They stared at each other for a moment, both trying to look annoyed. Pamela was the first to succumb to the smile fighting to break out.

'I'm glad Uncle Tony's gone,' she said eventually.

'You shouldn't say things like that,' Nancy said, although she shared the girl's relief.

Pamela sighed. 'I've never liked him.'

'Why not?'

'He gives me the creeps. Too touchy.'

'He didn't ever . . . well, make you feel uncomfortable, did he?' Nancy said, suddenly alarmed.

Pamela stared at her, then shuddered. 'What, you think . . . ? No! Not with me, anyway. He was always all over Caro, though. I don't know how Pa put up with it.'

Nancy hoped Pamela had never had to witness what she had unwittingly walked in on during the yacht party.

'Anyway, I don't suppose we'll see him again. Apparently he owes money all over the place and that film he's making was just a massive lie. That's why he's going to Chile. So they can't get him.'

Nancy stood up and took her hand. 'Come on, let's go and

look at a gallery or something. We can't hang around here all day.'

Pamela kicked the door frame with her new Caprian sandals and sighed. 'A gallery? Do we have to?'

Nancy tried to look stern. 'Yes.' She smiled. 'And then ice cream. Go and get ready. I'll see you here in a minute.'

Nancy was enjoying her new-found fascination with art; encouraged by Peter, who was all too grateful for someone to share his passion with, she'd learnt so much about Vermeer and Titian and Rubens in the last few days, and if she took nothing else away from this trip, it would be her hunger to learn more. Only yesterday he had suggested a trip to the Gallerie dell'Accademia to see the Bellinis and Fra Angelicos and Veroneses, and she had been the only one to leap up and accept the offer, while Caro raised an eyebrow, suggesting they go to the Guggenheim instead: at least Peggy mixed a good cosmo. Pamela, however, had said she'd rather chew on her own leg, thank you.

Nancy had left her handbag and sunglasses in her room, and was just leaving the kitchen to fetch them when Caro came in and began searching the cupboards, muttering and cursing when she couldn't find what she wanted.

'I thought you and Pamela were going out?' she snapped.

'We're going in a minute. Pamela's just getting ready.' She watched as Caro tried to tie her dressing gown, her fingers fumbling as she fought with the heavy chinoiserie silk.

'Are you sure I can't help? Perhaps I can find whatever you're looking for.'

Caro stood up and laughed, the bottle of gin she'd been

searching for now firmly clutched in her hand. 'Somehow, sweetie, I doubt that very much.'

'It's not my place, but isn't it a little early?' Nancy said hesitantly, looking at the breakfast crockery still drying next to the sink.

'You're right, honey. It's not your place.'

This was a new Caro. Gone was the gentle sarcasm and in its place was a brittle woman. Nancy had overheard the raging row once she and Pamela had gone to bed last night, in which Peter had been a silent partner in the one-sided screaming match that had nearly brought the ancient plaster crumbling from the palazzo walls.

It didn't take a genius to work it out. Nancy knew only too well what it felt like to have someone you were close to disappear out of your life, and she had no doubt that the encounter she had stumbled on at the yacht party was not Caro and Tony's first.

Poor Peter. Poor Caro, she supposed. And of course, poor Pamela.

'I love him, you know?'

Nancy stared at her. 'It's not really—'

'It's not just a stupid affair.' She poured herself a glass of neat gin and drank it down in one mouthful. 'I love him. And he loves me.'

Of that, Nancy was not entirely convinced, but she remained silent.

Caro poured another glassful. 'I know you think I don't care about Pamela. But you're wrong.'

'Oh no, I would never think that,' Nancy protested, knowing that everyone had their own way of loving other people. Beryl, for instance, would never win the Cuddly Mother of the Year award, but that didn't diminish her love for Nancy and Peggy. She just showed it in different ways.

'It's OK, you don't have to pretend. I've been a terrible mother to that girl, although God knows I've tried. It's not easy loving someone else's child, you know? Especially when you can't have your own. But I do love her, even if it doesn't show. I'm the daughter of a terrible mother, and I suppose some things just stick. At least I didn't beat the crap out of her, like my mother did me. I guess that makes me better than her.'

'There's no rulebook, as far as I know. I'm sure you've always done the best you can. And Pamela's a really lovely girl.'

'When she wants to be. I don't know . . . This whole trip was about making sure she's got a secure future. Peter too. I just want them to be OK.'

Nancy felt uncomfortable: there was something strange about the way Caro was talking, a manic desperation to her unexpected intimacy.

'Is everything all right?' she asked tentatively, but Caro continued as though she had not heard.

'Poor little Pea,' she said sadly. 'She deserved better than me. Listen, Nancy. If you ever have a daughter of your own, you cherish her, right?' Her berry-red cheeks blazed feverishly, and Nancy was lost for words as she battled with her own emotions.

And then Caro said something that took Nancy completely by surprise.

'Look after her, won't you?'

Nancy stared at her, shocked to see tears springing to the older woman's eyes. 'What do you mean?'

Caro held up her hand, as though about to say something, but changed her mind, letting it drop limply to her side. 'Nothing. She just seems fond of you. They both do. I'm glad.'

'You all right, darling?'

The two women both looked up to see Peter standing in the doorway.

'I'm bloody marvellous,' Caro said, scooping up the bottle and glass and deliberately banging her elbow into him as she flounced out, the gown billowing behind her.

Peter scratched his head as they listened to the huge carved doors to the canalside sitting room slam shut behind her. 'Maybe best if you and Pea stay out of the way this afternoon until she's feeling a bit better. She'll be fine by the time we go out this evening.'

'Is she drunk?' Pamela stood in the hallway, looking from one to the other.

'That's enough,' Peter snapped.

'She's just not feeling well,' Nancy added.

'Do we have to go to that stupid party tonight if she's ill?'

'For a start, it's not a stupid party. It's a private view in Lorenzo's gallery, and some of my paintings are being exhibited. For once we are doing something that *I* want to do. And yes, you have to go.'

'I don't see why,' Pamela said.

'Oh grow up, Pea,' Peter said, raising his voice for the first time that Nancy could remember – and Pamela too, judging from the shock on her face. 'Nancy, please take her out before I say something I regret,' he added, before heading into the hallway and up the stairs. 'I'm going to do some work,' he shouted down from the top of the echoing stairwell, 'and I do not want to see another woman. For the rest of the day.'

Pamela waited until his footsteps had disappeared into the distance, then folded her arms. 'Raspberry ripple,' she said. 'Double.'

The atmosphere had levelled out by the time they convened ready for the private view. The gallery owner had arranged a water taxi to collect them, and Peter stood on the edge of the jetty, ushering Nancy and Pamela into the little boat.

'Where's Ma?' Pamela said, and Nancy felt a surge of warmth to see the girl looking so confident, even beautiful, in the dazzling emerald-green chiffon dress with its ruched bodice and tiny spaghetti straps. She had let Nancy curl her hair, which fell around her lightly freckled shoulders, and wore a hint of make-up, just as Nancy had shown her: a lick of blush-pink lipstick, and a lightly drawn black line defining her eyelids and swooping into a delicate wing. She was a pretty girl, there was no denying it, so far from the schoolgirl who had stamped her feet at Nancy, and as testified by the open stare of the boatman, who clearly hadn't seen such hair since Titian's models were in town.

'She's staying behind. Headache. There you go, Pea.' He handed her into the boat, then turned to Nancy. 'Madam?'

Nancy struggled to climb into the boat in the tight shift dress whose heavy gold brocade left no room for manoeuvre, but Pamela grabbed her arm and pulled her rather unceremoniously aboard. As they sat at the back of the boat, watching the crumbling facades of the centuries-old palaces race past, she was glad she had brought the little matching jacket: although it only had three-quarter-length sleeves, once she had done up the three huge buttons on the front, she felt protected from the cool breeze. This had been Phyllis's favourite outfit – 'Just like Jackie Kennedy would wear,' she'd said, clapping her hands together in glee as Nancy provided the fashion show they'd all insisted on – and had begged to borrow it when Nancy came back. If she came back.

The exhibition was being held in a room off the inner courtyard of one of the great palazzi along the Grand Canal. They walked through the colonnaded cloisters lining the courtyard, the early-evening air scented with the roses planted around the fountain at its centre. This was like no art gallery Nancy had ever seen before, its walls whitewashed and the tiled floor bare.

'It's so modern,' she whispered to Peter.

'I know. Bit of a change from the National, eh?'

Peter was immediately swept up by a man somewhat younger than himself, closer to Nancy's age than to his own, also wearing the standard uniform of pale linen suit. 'Pietro,' he said as they shook hands heartily. 'The star of my show.'

Peter fiddled uncomfortably with the back of his collar. 'Hardly, old chap.' He turned to see the two young women staring expectantly at him. 'Oh, I'm sorry. Lorenzo, you know Pamela, of course, and this is Nancy, who's . . . well, a family friend.'

Lorenzo bowed his head, then kissed Pamela on both cheeks. 'Lorenzo Vitari. Delighted to meet you, Nancy,' he said, and shook Nancy's hand. He was good-looking in the way that so many Italian men were to the English eye, but without the braggadocio that Nancy was beginning to find tiresome. Maybe it was the Atticus Finch glasses, or the shabbiness of his suit, or even the fact that he didn't instantly press his lips on her hand, but she was intrigued by this slightly shy Italian man, unlike so many others she'd met, who'd fixated on her hair and assessed her as though she were in a beauty contest. Unlike Charlie, too, she realised, always so perfectly starched, so sure of himself and of her.

'I knew Lorenzo's father Luigi a long time ago,' Peter explained, startling Lorenzo, who realised he was still holding Nancy's hand and dropped it quickly. 'He was a great artist, and I studied with him here after I finished at the Slade. In the very house where we are staying. They were happy times, weren't they?'

Lorenzo smiled. 'They were always interesting times when my father was around, God rest his bad-tempered old soul!'

Peter laughed. 'You could say that. Lorenzo now runs this gallery, and is a great supporter of my work.'

'On the contrary: I am very honoured to show your new work here. It is already causing something of a stir. Come, ladies, let me show you around.'

He led them past huge abstract canvases in bright colours that leapt from the bare walls, plinths bearing tall, spindly bronze figures in various states of anguish, and on to a small anteroom in which three square paintings, each the size of a tea chest, hung in a row. With her new vocabulary, Nancy could see they were impressionistic visions of a Venice far removed from that recorded by Canaletto. They were ghostly, brutal, their brave, broad brushstrokes describing a decaying city caught between two worlds.

'These are beautiful,' she said.

'They are extraordinary,' Lorenzo replied, and Nancy turned to see that his eyes were not on the paintings, but on her. He blushed, finding himself caught out, and cleared his throat noisily. 'Yes, quite remarkable,' he continued, staring intently now at the triptych.

'Is that meant to be a sheep?' Pamela said, peering closely at the central panel.

Peter rolled his eyes. 'You see what I have to put up with?' he said to Lorenzo.

'Who painted them?' Nancy asked.

'Why, your friend Signor Cavendish. Of course.'

She looked at Peter. 'I had no idea. I thought you did portraits.'

'I make my money through portraits, but I feed my artistic soul with this stuff.'

Pamela stood back and looked again at the paintings. 'You're quite good, I suppose,' she said, and sniffed.

'Thanks, Pea,' Peter said, frowning at the half-compliment.

'You really should forget about the portraits, my friend. As you know, it's all about photographs now. But this,' Lorenzo gestured at the trio of works, 'this is what you need to be doing.'

Peter sighed. 'I wish. But I need to make a living, you know. Daughters don't come cheap.' And he smiled as Pamela nudged him hard with her elbow.

'Seriously, Peter. I could have sold these ten times over this evening. Listen,' Lorenzo said, 'I've just bought an old place in Tuscany. About two hours from here. I'm planning on opening a gallery there, and having studio space for artists to work.

Why don't you come and stay for a while? All of you? And Nancy, of course,' he added, smiling at her.

Nancy felt herself blushing lightly too, and was almost relieved when Pamela dug her in the ribs.

'I don't know,' Peter said. 'There's the house in London. And I'm not sure I could bury Caro in the Tuscan countryside.'

'It doesn't have to be for ever. Just a few weeks, a few months. You could have a space to paint, an inspiring landscape on your doorstep . . .' Lorenzo adjusted his glasses, which had slowly made their way south, despite his strong Florentine nose.

'But I can't just come and stay and not pay you anything.'

'Then pay me by helping to work on the buildings.'

Pamela looked at Peter. 'Why don't you, Pa? You love it over here.'

'I know, but it's not just me, is it? There's you—'

'Me? I might as well be bored to death in the middle of Tuscany than bored anywhere else. It's not like I can go back to school, is it?' She looked at Lorenzo. 'Do you have horses?'

He smiled. 'There are plenty of horses out there.'

Pamela sniffed and began to examine the floor tiles; Nancy recognised the signs that she was working things through. A marvellous opportunity for Peter could be death by olive grove for his daughter, who already missed her friends, but it looked like the horses were swinging it for her.

Lorenzo turned again to the paintings. 'These really are your best work, Peter. My father would agree; he was so angry that you wasted your talent on vain aristocrats. Give it a try. What do you have to lose?'

Peter exhaled slowly, then grabbed a fresh glass of champagne from a passing waitress and downed it in one long draught. 'Potentially nothing, and potentially everything.'

As the boat slid across the black, brackish water, they all sat in their own bubble of silence, broken only by the phutting of the engine and the occasional laugh or shriek as the complex matrices of other people's lives broke through and drifted along the narrow alleys and across the water. Nancy was pleased to see that the worry furrows ploughed across Peter's forehead most of the time seemed shallower, and even if Pamela couldn't go back to her school life, she seemed happy with the idea of a temporary Tuscan idyll. There was still Caro, but maybe Peter could persuade her to spend the rest of the summer in Italy. There were worse ways of passing a few weeks.

As for Nancy . . . well, Lorenzo had extended his invitation to her too, but she couldn't impose for ever; she needed to make a plan of her own. It was tempting, though, for a city girl to spend some time in the Italian countryside, watching Pamela blossom in the fresh air and Peter able to dedicate himself to his work, and helping Lorenzo as he built up the Tuscan retreat. She had a feeling that this was one Cavendish family friend she would enjoy getting to know.

Something felt wrong as they marched back into the old house: a disturbance in the air, a displacement that Nancy couldn't identify. Peter called out to Caro, but his voice echoed unanswered around the hallway, twisting its way up the spiral marble staircase and through the cavernous reception rooms of the ground floor.

Nancy recalled the strange conversation she and Caro

had had that morning, and suddenly knew that they weren't looking for a person any more, but most probably for a letter.

And there it was, propped against a vase of lilies on the hall table.

'Peter?' she called. 'I think you need to see something.'

He came running back down the stairs, two at a time. 'What is it?'

Nancy pointed to the note.

'Damn,' he said. 'Listen, take Pamela upstairs for a moment, would you?'

'Of course.'

She found Pamela lying on the sofa, having picked up the book she'd bought at a second-hand English bookshop earlier that day, about nurses during the Blitz in London. 'Time for bed,' Nancy said.

'Where is she?' Pamela said, reluctantly getting up and turning over the corner of the page she had just finished.

'Not sure,' Nancy said, wondering how they could get through the hallway without Pamela seeing Peter reading the note.

'What do you mean, not sure?' She wandered over to the doorway. 'Pa?'

'Pamela,' Nancy said, 'just wait a moment . . .' Her heart was pounding, a hundred horrific scenarios playing through her mind. Caro had seemed off colour, but surely she wouldn't do anything stupid?

But it was too late. As Nancy stepped into the hallway, its wall sconces barely letting out enough light to illuminate the frescoed panels they were set into, she watched Pamela take the letter from her father and hold it close to her face as she struggled to read in the half-dark.

She walked over slowly and took the page from Pamela's hand.

I'm so sorry to do this, my darling. By the time you read this, I will be on the night train to Paris. Tony and I fly to Chile tomorrow. I love him, and I wish I didn't, but things are how they are. Please don't miss me, and please look after each other. I do truly love you both and I know you will be happy in the end.

  Caro x

23

McCall's 6261: Misses' sundress

They sat on a bench in St Mark's Square, Pamela periodically kicking away the flock of pigeons that besieged them.

'Do you think Pa will be OK?' she said.

Despite the drama of the previous night, Peter had seemed in good spirits that morning, if not more relaxed than Nancy had seen him in quite a while. She suspected he had been dragging the carcass of a dead marriage along behind him for some time.

'I think he'll be fine. He has you, after all, doesn't he?' She squeezed Pamela's sticky hand.

'I suppose they'll get a divorce now,' Pamela said, and looked down at her sandalled feet. 'I think it's my fault. I've never been the sort of daughter she wanted. She didn't exactly choose me.'

'That's where you're wrong, Pea. She did choose you. She chose both of you. She didn't have to marry your father, you know. Or become a mother to you. But she did. Because she wanted to.'

Pamela shrugged. 'Maybe if I'd tried harder at school, or made a bit more effort with my clothes and stuff . . .'

Nancy took her hand. 'Don't be silly. You're perfect as

you are. It's not your fault. You can be a bit annoying . . .' she waited for Pamela to return her smile, 'but she loves you to bits. She told me so.'

'Really? I've always thought she put up with me because I was part of the package when she married Pa.'

'That's not true, and you know it.'

Pamela spotted a drip of ice cream on her arm and licked it away. Nancy handed her a napkin, but Pamela shrugged it off, then sighed deeply. 'I wish you were my mother. I think you'd be a smashing mother.'

'I don't know about that. But I do know that if I had a daughter, I would want her to be just like you.'

Pamela said nothing, but she took Nancy's hand in hers and rested her head on her bare shoulder, her untethered peach-coloured wisps tickling Nancy's nose as they danced in the light breeze that blew in from the Grand Canal and snaked around the four huge bronze horses standing proudly over the entrance to the basilica, sending flurries of pigeons into the air and tugging at the hem of Nancy's dress.

'Are you really going to eat all that?' Nancy said, watching Pamela carefully work her way around the massive ice-cream cone so that it didn't drip down her short white cardie and pretty flowered skirt, which had already developed an interesting collection of jam and chocolate stains. They really must make a note never to buy Pamela anything white ever again.

'Uh huh.' She leant across Nancy to look at a tiny dog being dragged along by its white-haired owner in huge black-rimmed sunglasses.

'Hey, you've just dripped that all over me.' Nancy dabbed

at the yellow and pink blob right in the middle of the skirt of her dress.

'It'll be fine,' Pamela said, reaching over and rubbing it with her cardigan sleeve, so that they now both wore best Venetian gelato.

'You can be infuriating, you know?' Nancy said, a little too scratchily. Her head was thumping, and she was feeling overwhelmingly homesick, knowing that Peggy would invite everyone round for tea and cake that afternoon to celebrate Maddie's six-month half-birthday. Mum, Dad, Phyl and Dorothy . . . they would all be there to raise a mug of tea to the little girl who had transformed the family. All bar Nancy.

'Sorry. Is that one that you made?'

'Yes, it is.' And it was one of Nancy's favourites: a simple grey and white striped linen sundress with wide straps and an A-line skirt, a little self-patterned bow at the waist and a row of grey glass buttons running down from the neckline, positioned just off centre. And now it had a huge raspberry smear all over the front.

A young family walked past, the father leading the pack with his head buried in a newspaper, and the mother trying to hold onto her little boy and steer a huge bouncing pram at the same time, struggling to navigate the cobbles in her tight skirt and kitten heels. The boy was trying to shake off her hand and chase the pigeons, his other hand tightly clutching the string of a fat blue balloon that was equally keen to make a bid for freedom.

Nancy felt her hair flying away in the breeze, so she took a band from her pocket and tied it into a ponytail, enjoying the fresh air on the back of her neck.

She watched as the balloon suddenly wrenched itself free and bobbed across the heads of the milling crowds in time with the briney gusts of wind. The little boy slipped his mooring and escaped from his mother, his bright white shirt and little polished shoes quickly disappearing into the confusion of tourists and birds.

Still clutching the pram handle with one hand, the young woman looked around wildly, torn between searching for her child and leaving her baby. She screamed at her husband, who pulled his head out of his paper and looked up in horror.

Pamela dropped Nancy's hand and leapt up. 'Here, we'll help you,' she said. 'Won't we, Nancy?'

'Thank you,' the woman said in heavily accented English, and pushed the pram towards Nancy. 'You look after the baby and your friend help us look for our *bambino*.'

'Come on,' Pamela said, 'we'll fan out. He can't have gone far.'

'*Mille grazie*,' the woman said, tears in her eyes, and squeezed Nancy's hand.

And then all three were gone, and Nancy was left with the pram.

For a moment she just stood looking around, at the vast pencil-tipped bell tower, and the arches of the Doge's Palace, the cafés lining the fringes of the square. Anywhere but at the infant lying in the pram.

A gurgling chuckle brought her eyes to the little girl's face, watching with curiosity her new adult, her pretty chubby cheeks framed by a frilled bonnet similar to one that Peggy had bought for Maddie. She stiffened, staring at Nancy with huge brown eyes, then relaxed, her fists pumping the air, and her tiny feet in their white crocheted booties thumping against the pink ruffled pram blanket. She was about the same age as Maddie, who was probably also making burbling little attempts at conversation by now, and maybe blowing funny little raspberries like this tiny angel.

Nancy bent down and smiled at the baby, who instantly beamed at her. 'Hello, little one,' she said, stroking her peach-like cheek.

A loud bang nearby from scaffolders working on the facade of one of the palazzi in the square made the baby jump, and her surprise quickly turned to alarm. Her rose-pink bottom lip began to tremble, and tears sprang threateningly to her eyes.

'Hey, hey,' Nancy said. 'It's all right, poppet.' But the child was not so easily pacified, and she reached into the pram and placed her hands around the stiff, warm body, which was already convulsing with sobs. 'It's all right, sweetheart,' she said, and held the little girl to her shoulder. She closed her eyes as she pressed her cheek against the baby's hot, damp face. 'Shh, shh. There now.'

She jiggled the child, her hand cradling her head, and whispered soothing words in her ear. But instead of settling, the infant became more distressed, and her quiet sobs began to increase in volume.

'Don't cry, my sweet,' Nancy said, her eyes closed as she inhaled the baby's milky, fresh-laundry smell. 'Mummy's here.'

Why wouldn't she stop crying? Nancy couldn't understand it. It had worked before when she put her on her shoulder and held her tight, showing her that nothing could ever hurt her and that she was the most loved child in the world. So why was she still fretful? What had Nancy done wrong? Surely she couldn't have forgotten those few hours they had together, just the two of them?

'Nancy.'

A voice broke into the cocoon they had made together. Why couldn't it leave them alone? Didn't it know they had so little time?

'Nancy!'

Firmer now, and she opened her eyes, irritated at the persistent interruption.

Pamela was standing in front of her, an Italian-looking woman at her side holding out her arms to take Nancy's baby. She couldn't let them. Not again.

'No,' she said, and held the child tighter. Why was she crying even louder? Please stop, my angel, or they'll say I can't look after you.

'Nancy, you're being weird. Give the baby back.'

Pamela appeared frightened now, and as Nancy looked around the tableau of anxious faces in front of her, she grew confused. Who was this woman trying to take her child from her? And the man with the frightened face, whose little boy clung to his legs and stared at her? Where was she? It was so bright, so sunny, the buildings so beautiful. Where was the constant rain and the thick grey walls?

She lifted the baby from her shoulder and cradled it in front of her. Where had that black hair come from? And those dark eyes? Her baby had wheat-blonde hair and grey eyes the colour of an Eastbourne pebble. This wasn't her baby. Someone had taken her baby and swapped it.

In horror, she felt herself hold the baby out and place it in the hands of the other woman, who clutched it to her and sobbed Italian words of comfort into its ear as it gradually stopped crying and looked up at its mother, its creased face unfolding into a smile of love and recognition.

Never again had she thought she would feel the enormous cold void in her empty arms, and she barely noticed the man hand a card to Pamela as he thanked her for finding his little boy, nor felt Pamela's hand on her arm, guiding her away from the square and into the warren of narrow arteries that radiated across the city.

Pamela told Peter that Nancy was ill, that she'd had too much sun and needed to go to bed. Neither of them spoke a word of what had happened, and Nancy let herself be mothered by the young girl, who asked no questions but quietly washed the city dust from her skin with a cool flannel and made her up some warm, sweet milky tea. She helped Nancy change into her nightdress, and tucked her under the white linen sheets in the narrow bed, closing the shutters to the last of the daylight.

As Pamela eventually left her, Nancy lay watching the slivers of light through the shutters move around the room, the porthole of Venetian sky in her ceiling turning from blue to rose gold to the black-purple of a fresh bruise.

The noise of chattering waterborne tourists and their singing gondoliers gradually died away, and her mind replaced it with the sound of soft-shoed nuns and the mewling of newborn babies. The worst sound of all was that of a car arriving on the gravel drive, the click of expensive heels and leather-soled brogues on the steps leading to the old house, and the ululating cries of the grieving mothers when the same sounds were reversed hours later.

How could he have let her go through that? To have had her child taken from her before her physical wounds were even healed, while her breasts still poured hot milk and her womb bled? And now he had asked her to take him back. She felt under her pillow for his letter, looking at it only briefly before scrunching it up and throwing it into the corner of the room.

She thought back to those few dark hours together, hours that would have to last a lifetime. She had been so sure that she could do the right thing, but holding that little warm bundle had unlocked something that nagged and scratched at her, until her resolve wore away and she knew there was only one thing she could do, whether it was right or not.

Exhausted, she was eventually overcome by sleep, and drifted off clutching the little drawstring bag.

Nancy's fitful sleep was broken by an unfamiliar sound. She opened her dream-ravaged eyes to see the oval of sky now a dull grey, flecked with fat, heavy drops of rain. She reached across, patting the bedside table until she found her watch. It was still only 6 a.m., and she dressed quickly and quietly, pulling on yesterday's clothes, which Pamela had left folded neatly on a chair, as well as a sweater against the chill.

She closed the little wooden door onto the back street carefully behind her, choosing narrow, sheltered alleyways that hugged the canals as she criss-crossed the city, dodging the greengrocers' carts that were setting up, stepping over puddles that soaked her shoes and made them chafe her bare feet, occasionally stopping in a church doorway to shake the rain out of her hair. She knew from the pattern of left/right, that she would soon be there, and as the wide ribbon of the

Grand Canal opened out in front of her, rows of empty gondolas bobbing on the rain-splashed water, there was only one more bridge to cross.

The station was just opening, its coffee shops shuttered and heavy pallets of newspapers still being unloaded. A sleepy-looking clerk raised the blind at his kiosk as Nancy appeared looking like something dragged from the lagoon, but he batted not an eyelid as he took her sodden lire from her and gave her a ticket, which she tucked in her handbag.

So that was it. She had done it. By lunchtime she would be on a train, racing north-west through Europe and towards Calais.

She stopped to buy fresh ciabatta rolls straight from the baker's oven and a bag of Pamela's favourite clementines from a market stall: Pea had been eating the plump fruits like sweets ever since she'd discovered them a couple of days ago. It didn't seem so long ago that oranges were impossible to find at home, and a satsuma in your Christmas stocking was a treat to be looked forward to all year.

By the time she ducked back inside the low doorway, it was still too early for the Cavendishes to be up, so she set the table for breakfast and made a pot of stovetop Italian coffee. It was the least she could do before she left, and it distracted her from how much she would miss Pamela. Would Peter know where to go to buy the clementines? Would he make Pamela brush her hair a hundred times each evening, and wash her face as Nancy had shown her, with cold cream and then rosewater? And who would bring Peter the cup of Earl Grey that fuelled his afternoon painting session? Or find his glasses, which he misplaced somewhere different each day?

Don't be silly, Nancy: they all managed perfectly well before you arrived, she told herself. But they had been three then, and now they were two.

She was surprised by the strength of feelings she had for these people who had been strangers to her until so recently, but the itch that had plagued her for six months was unbearable, and she would rather slip quietly under the smooth surface of the murky Venetian waters than resist doing what she had planned. It was crazy: she knew that. But she needed her baby, more than she needed air to breathe and water to irrigate her burning veins. Staying away was impossible, even though it would come at a horrible price.

She had a few hours until her train left: maybe she could snatch an hour's sleep once she'd packed. She was so tired, and she needed a clear head if she was to go through with this.

The house was quiet when she awoke from her nap. Pamela and Peter must have gone out. She felt crushed: she had so wanted to say goodbye, to explain why she had to go, and that they would meet again, on the other side of the chaos she was about to unleash. She was kidding herself: if she went through with this, she would never see them, or anyone else she cared about, ever again.

She checked her watch. It was later than she'd thought, and she had less than an hour until her train left. She quickly washed her face with the jug of cold water that stood on the marble-topped dressing table.

'You forgot these.'

She jumped at the voice behind her and turned around quickly, her heart pounding.

Pamela was standing in the doorway, a silk jewellery roll in her hand.

'What are you doing there?'

'You were holding these so tightly last night after I put you to bed. I wanted to know what was so precious, so I looked in your case while you were asleep just now.'

Nancy took a step closer. 'You took them out? Pamela, those aren't yours. Give them back.' She could see that Pamela had been crying.

'So they *are* yours?' She took a step back.

'I didn't say that. Just give them to me.'

'What? Or you'll tell Pa?' Her eyes were wide with anger now, and Nancy hesitated.

'Pamela, please . . .'

'Or shall *I* tell him?'

Nancy looked at the suitcase, tucked by the doorway next to Pamela.

'You can't go, Nancy, I won't let you.'

She felt her own tears begin to swell and sting at her eyes. 'Pamela, I have to. You don't understand.'

'Yes, I do.' Her voice was rising, and bright spots had appeared on her cheeks.

Nancy held her hands out to pacify her. 'Shh, please.'

Pamela unfolded the roll and took out the tiny white crocheted booties. 'You had a baby, didn't you?'

Nancy shook her head, tears pouring down her cheeks.

'You had a baby and you gave it away. That's why you were so weird in the square yesterday, with that woman's baby.'

'No . . .'

'And now you want to leave me and take your baby back, don't you?'

'I don't want to leave you, I don't,' Nancy cried.

'You do!' Pamela screamed, and took a step further back. 'It's Charlie's, isn't it? I found the letter.' She pulled the crumpled page out of her pocket, and held it out for Nancy to see. 'You're so stupid,' Pamela spat at her.

'You don't mean that.'

'Yes, I do.' She stared at Nancy. 'You don't know, do you?'

'Know what?'

'About Charlie?'

Nancy looked at her through a smear of tears.

'He's engaged. He's getting married next month. You didn't think he'd want *you*, did you?' And she laughed. 'Little Nancy Moon from the slums? Little Nancy Moon the *slut*.'

Nancy couldn't help herself. She lunged at Pamela and they fought over the little boots, so close that Nancy could smell the younger girl's sweat, could almost taste her tears.

Eventually Pamela shrank back, leaving Nancy to cradle the boots. When the girl spoke again, it was so quietly that Nancy could barely hear her. 'Don't leave me, please, Nancy. Don't leave me,' she sobbed. 'Not you as well.'

Nancy opened the suitcase and dropped the boots inside, then lifted it by its handle, squaring up to Pamela, who stood blocking her exit.

'You have to let me go. I don't care about Charlie. I just need my daughter.'

Pamela gripped her arm. 'But I need you, Nancy. Please.' She fell to her knees and clutched at Nancy's skirt.

Nancy hadn't heard such an animal howl since the same

sound had been wrenched from deep inside her as the baby she'd carried for nine months, and had nursed for four short hours, was taken from her and placed in the arms of another.

'I'm sorry,' she sobbed, yanking her skirt away and hurrying towards the stairs.

She sat on the platform, drenched in rain and tears and sweat, oblivious to the fast-paced announcements and the scurrying commuters. She looked down at her skirt, wondering that Pamela's tears and fingerprints had left no mark on the pretty forget-me-nots.

It had come full circle, this dress. It had borne her from Wandsworth to Paris, with the promise of a new Nancy Moon, one who wouldn't be destroyed by grief and jealousy. And for a while it had worked: she had found friends and been gifted love, from a kind man who treated her as his own daughter, and from a young girl who needed a mother.

Of course she'd known Charlie wasn't her future, even if his blood would always play a part in it. There was only one person she was going back for.

And when she arrived home? How did she actually expect to get her baby back? Was she going to steal her? Take her in the dead of night? And where would they go?

She shook her head, trying to untangle the jumble of thoughts that all reached the same dead end.

There was no way this could end without lives being torn apart. Not least that of the innocent baby, who now knew its adopted mother as its real one, who wouldn't know Nancy, and who would scream in terror at her like the baby in the square had done. Could she do that, when she'd already promised to let them all get on with their lives?

It was madness.

Her train drew noisily towards the platform, and the short gnocchi-shaped guard made his way along the carriages, ushering in the last of the passengers and preparing to blow his whistle.

Nancy stood up and lifted her suitcase, its handle still slippy with rainwater.

'*Signora, il treno parte tra due minuti.*' He gesticulated to her, pointing to the large station clock. 'Two minutes.'

She took a deep breath and stepped forward. She knew what she had to do.

24

'You look incredible.'

'Really?' Flo said, but for once, she let herself believe the compliment. Seamus was so free with his flattery, whether she had a bright-red snotty nose or had just woken up the morning after a long night in the pub, and she'd forgotten to trust anything nice anyone said about her.

She wondered whether the thick brocade wasn't a little too much or a little too hot, but she loved this dress above all the others. The heavy platinum-coloured fabric had been a pig to work: fraying, catching in the teeth of the machine, so that cornering had been a bulky, awkward operation, and lining it had not been much easier. A straight-down sheath, caught with a belt at the waist, it had been deceptively tricky to make, and the round-necked jacket no simpler. The back, cut as one piece, joined to the front panels with gently sloping seams that travelled along the shoulders to just below the elbow. The three huge horn buttons Flo had found in her button box worked perfectly. It was indeed an amazing outfit, and she was pleased that Ben had also made an effort, wearing a soft cream linen suit that offset his suntan and gradually lightening hair. And wasn't paired with the Genesis T-shirt that she'd hidden at the back of the wardrobe.

'Thanks, Mr S. You look pretty good yourself. And thanks for wangling the invitation,' Flo said.

'Easy really,' he replied. 'Friend of a friend of my sister. Sort of thing.' He stopped suddenly. 'We should have a picture of us. You've got all those pictures of Nancy and her friends – you need one of your journey.'

She smiled. 'You're right.' She reached into her bag for her phone, and they pressed their faces together as they smiled at the screen.

'Look at us,' Ben said, as they admired the image of themselves against the beautiful backdrop of the old city.

'Couple of swells,' Flo said. 'I'll send it to you later.'

'Would you?' he said.

'Of course. As long as you don't show your mother.' She took his arm. 'Come on, let's get going. I think we're nearly there.'

They turned a corner and found themselves in a square dominated by a soft-pink palace, its windows white-trimmed gothic arches the height of a small Brighton house.

'Is this it?' Ben said.

Flo looked again at the stiff card invitation, then at the discreet iron letters that ran down the side of the entrance doorway. 'Palazzo Fiorentina. This is it.'

'We should have come by water taxi,' Ben said. 'Done it the stylish way.'

'Don't think we're quite the Clooneys, are we?' she said, smiling.

A set of wide marble steps led to a peaceful green courtyard bursting with overripe roses. There was something about this place that made Flo feel closer to Nancy than she had any-where else on the tour. If her great-aunt had turned the corner and greeted her, she wouldn't have been surprised.

'This way.' Ben beckoned her over, and she hurried through the shade of the colonnaded cloisters to join him.

A young woman dressed entirely in black smiled at them with murder-scene red lips as she took their invitation. '*Buena sera, e bienvenuto*.'

'Thank you,' Flo said, then hesitated. 'I wonder if it would be possible to meet with the owner of the gallery this evening?'

'Signor d'Angelo? *Si*, you will find him inside.'

Inside the palazzo, high vaulted ceilings of intricate rose-pink brickwork and striding plasterwork limbs offset plain white walls that provided the perfect background to . . . what? Flo wasn't sure how to describe the scene in front of her, which was punctuated by an echoing soundtrack of childbirth-like sounds.

She and Ben took a glass of Prosecco from a serious-looking waitress with black kohl-smudged eyes and a centimetre-long black fringe, and wandered the series of plinths of different heights, each displaying a loose variation on Disney-bright shiny genitalia.

'Well,' Flo said. 'Not sure what the Doge would make of this lot.'

Ben peered closely at one of the sculptures, a visceral study in red and blue plastic. 'Bloody hell,' he exclaimed. 'This one's got teeth.'

Flo looked around. 'I don't know about you – and don't get me wrong: I went to art college – but this is just bloody awful.'

'Good evening.'

A voice behind them made them turn around quickly.

'I'm sorry, I didn't mean to make you jump. My colleague tells me you would like to speak with me?' The man smiled at them through oversized black-rimmed glasses and held out a long, smooth hand. 'Please, I am Michele d'Angelo. This is my gallery. You like the show?'

'Um, it's . . . well—'

'It is pretty awful, no?' He laughed quietly at Flo's awkwardness. 'But it pay the bills. These people, they love this stuff.' He shrugged. 'Next month I put on something better. So, what can I do for you? I am guessing you don't want to buy anything?'

Flo laughed. 'No, I mean . . . well, no. I actually wanted to talk to you about an exhibition that was held here back in nineteen sixty-two.'

He raised his eyebrows. 'Sixty-two? That was well before my time.'

'Oh.' Flo should have realised. Whoever had been in charge back then would be well into their seventies by now at least. 'Wait,' she said, and dug around in her handbag until she produced an envelope. 'Maybe these will help.'

He took the envelope from her and pulled out a black and white photograph and an old invitation for a private view. He looked closely at the yellowed card and smiled. 'How could I forget this one?' he said.

'Why's that?'

'This was one of the gallery's most successful exhibitions ever. A collection of landscapes by artists from all over Europe. After that, it ran annually, right up until the eighties.'

'This is a long shot, but was one of the artists called Peter, by any chance? I'm afraid I don't know his surname.'

He looked up at her. 'Peter? That would have to be Peter Cavendish. Of course. He was a great friend of my uncle, Lorenzo Vitari, who used to own this gallery. Peter studied here with Lorenzo's father, Luigi, one of Italy's finest artists and teachers. I bought the gallery from Lorenzo many years ago.'

'Cavendish,' Flo said quietly, and turned to Ben. 'That's it,' she said. 'We've found him.'

'Peter Cavendish was a very fine artist,' Michele went on. 'He began by doing society portraits, but his talent went much further than that, and he became a great landscape painter.'

'Do you know what happened to him after he exhibited here?'

Michele smiled. 'My uncle bought a large property in Tuscany around the same time as this exhibition. He turned it into a kind of artist colony, if you like. Peter spent many years there. I think he may even have died there. It wasn't that long ago.' He smiled at the photo. 'Yes, that is Peter. And there is Lorenzo Vitari. The two ladies, I am not sure. I think maybe that is Peter's daughter Pamela?'

'And the other?' Flo said hopefully. 'Do you recognise her? That's my great-aunt.'

He shook his head. 'Is hard to say. She's looking away from the camera. I cannot see her face. I'm sorry.'

'Thank you so much. You've been incredibly helpful.' Flo shook his hand.

He bowed his head. 'You are welcome.' He reached into his jacket pocket and took out his card, scribbling something on the back. 'This is the address and phone number of my uncle's place. You should go and stay. It's beautiful down there.' He held it out to her, then paused. 'May I ask why you want to know about Peter?'

'He was a friend of my great-aunt, and I hope he will lead me to finding out what happened to her.'

He smiled. 'In that case, I wish you luck in finding her.' He glanced across Flo's shoulder. 'In the meantime, you must excuse me. Signora Grassi looks like she might want to buy that large yellow arse.'

Flo sat up in bed in the slightly shabby apartment she had rented, still reeling from the euphoria of finding Peter, and from the several Bellinis they had drunk after the exhibition, while Ben could be heard snoring in the other bedroom.

There had been a point as they were walking home when she had lost her footing and nearly fallen, and Ben had grabbed her arm, pulling her up so that their faces almost touched. The near miss in Capri had become a thing that needed to be dealt with: he was waiting for her permission to move things on, and while she was flattered, she just wasn't sure. It still felt treacherous to think about anyone else. If events hadn't turned out how they had, she and Seamus would have been planning a first birthday party by now, and they would have been happy: there had been nothing wrong with the relationship other than grief.

Had Seamus worried about her when he'd slept with the woman who'd been waiting for her chance? And oh yes, she had been waiting. Flo had seen her biding her time for months, if not longer. She remembered a department party, when she was still glowing with pregnant health, where her wifely instincts had bristled at the disingenuous attention of the pretty young PhD student with the Jersey-cow eyes, and the embarrassment of Seamus, who kept Flo at his side for the rest of the evening.

Maybe she had made it too easy for him. Maybe he'd been lonely too, and she'd pushed him into his infidelity. It hadn't made him happy, that was for sure. That one night of misplaced passion had taken its toll on her husband, who'd hidden his shame in a bottle of Jameson's as he tried to work out how to save his marriage. Had she asked what was wrong? Had she tried to share whatever was tearing away at him? When they lay in bed and he tried to pull her towards him, seeking only the warmth of a fellow soul who understood his pain, what had she done?

She'd pulled the duvet tightly around herself and turned her back on him.

A chasm had opened up between them that night, so that when she'd found him in what should have been the little nursery a few days later, hands cupped around the wooden toy that was never finished, instead of going to him, putting her arms around him, she'd quietly pulled the door closed and walked silently down the stairs, leaving him to his solitary grief. And when she'd opened the kitchen bin later that evening and found the toy discarded amongst dirty wrappers, she never said a word. How could she have done that, she now wondered, when there were so many words that needed to be said? Words that she now felt would drown her if she didn't let them out and say them to him.

She picked up her phone from the bedside table, and

scrolled down through her texts. Seamus. It had been weeks since she'd heard anything, and she suddenly felt the lack of him like a punch to her stomach. Her thumb hovered over the screen.

I'm sorry too. x

They sat outside a little café in a square set back from the main drag and the thick throng of early-morning tourists who were already piling out of the floating hotels moored beyond the Doge's Palace.

Flo drained her coffee and laid her hands flat on the table. 'So this is it. The last packet. Are you ready?'

Ben nodded. 'Do it.'

She took a deep breath. The dress pattern she knew all too well; she was now wearing the result of a somewhat fraught weekend trying to line up the off-centre button placket that ran down the front of the dress, and match the broad seersucker stripes that resembled Nancy's fabric as closely as possible. She'd managed to find almost identical buttons to the grey glass sample Nancy had popped into the packet.

A small brown envelope fell out, and she removed its contents. One of the items was a calling card, with an address they googled and found to be in a small town thirty kilometres from Venice. Nothing was written on the back, and there was no clue as to why Nancy had kept it.

The other slip of paper was a receipt.

'Let's see,' Ben said.

'What is it?' Flo asked, seeing his worried expression.

'It's a receipt for a train journey.'

'Does it say where to?'

Ben swallowed. 'Paris.'

Paris. Why was her heart thumping and her palms sweating?

'Oh my God. The plane. The one Tony was on. It flew from Paris, didn't it?' She snatched the receipt from him. 'What's the date on that?' She looked up. 'Twenty-first of June. Ben, she could have been going to catch the plane.'

'I'm sure there's another explanation. Maybe she was going home? She'd have had to go to Paris to get the boat train, wouldn't she?'

'I suppose so.'

He pointed at the card. 'This might help us. Let's see if the Bartoli family are still in residence.'

The small town was a short train journey out of the city, and it was still not even lunchtime as they climbed out of the stuffy carriage and onto the weed-strewn platform. Here was Venice's ugly sister, with all her warts, ruined by poverty and neglect. They hurried past the ageless black-clad women huddled outside the station, their pretty, dirty children holding out plastic cups. Flo dropped a few euros in one of these before Ben dragged her away and into the main square. There were no charming al fresco cafés here, only benches where old men in shiny anoraks gathered to smoke, and gaggles of bored youths colonised the periphery of the defunct fountain.

The address they were looking for wasn't far, so they ignored the curious stares of residents unused to visitors and ploughed on, through washing-festooned streets guarded by old ladies who sat, arms folded, in chairs outside their front doors, watching the tourists who must have got lost.

'Here we are.' Ben compared the address on the card with the wonky number hanging next to the open door, its interior hidden behind a beaded curtain.

There was no doorbell as such, so he pushed aside the strings of plastic beads and called inside. A television was playing loudly, and they tiptoed along the hallway, tapping at the open door of a kitchen.

An old lady sat hunched at the oilskin-covered table, shelling beans while watching a live stream of some kind of Catholic pilgrimage, complete with chanting and incense and priests in full regalia. She turned round at the interruption, and launched immediately into full-scale defence mode, holding up the shelling knife and yelling at the top of her voice.

'It's OK,' Flo said, holding her hands out. '*Amici?* Friends?'

The woman stood up, although no taller now than when she had been seated, and lowered her voice into a menacing growl, the grey hairs on her chin trembling as she muttered.

'*Che succede, Mamma?*' A middle-aged man appeared in the hallway behind them, breathless from running down the stairs.

'I'm sorry,' Flo said, struggling to find any vocabulary beyond that needed to order lunch.

'*Inglese?*' the man said, rubbing at his vest and glaring at the intruders. 'Why you in my mamma's house?'

'We came to ask her something.' Flo fumbled in her bag, and pulled out the card. 'Here. Are you Signor Bartoli?'

The man scratched his grey-stubbled chin. He showed the card to his mother, who slowly sat down as he explained that the English people were not trying to rob her, but wanted to talk to her. 'This was my father's card,' he said. 'How did you get it?'

Although the man's English was good, it was hard to explain how the card had ended up back here after several decades.

'I think it was given to my great-aunt. She was in Venice. In June nineteen sixty-two.'

With a combination of physical gestures and fast-paced Italian, the man explained as much as he could to his mother. The muscles in her face worked in tandem with the layers of memory Flo could see her trying to unravel.

They waited what seemed an age in the tiny, stuffy kitchen, the incessant incantations from the television and the overpowering smell of the tomato sauce bubbling away on the hob hammering at Flo, who could feel herself overheating. She took a hairband from her wrist and tied her hair into a loose ponytail, to cool the sweat pouring from the nape of her neck.

All of a sudden the old woman let out a howl, and pointed a finger at her. Her son knelt next to her, trying to pacify her.

'What's the matter?' Flo said. 'What did I do? Ben, what's happening?'

'I don't know,' he said, 'but she looks like she's just seen a ghost.'

Words flowed freely from the wild-eyed old woman as she jabbered at her son, but Flo couldn't understand them. She thought she caught the word *bambina*, but it was impossible to tell. 'Please,' she said to the man, 'what's she saying?'

He kissed his mother on the cheek and stood up. 'I'm sorry. You remind her of someone.'

'Who? Who do I remind her of?'

He sighed. 'It was a long time ago. Around the time you say your aunt was given this card.' He put his hand on his mother's shoulder; she was now slumped, sniffing quietly into an old lace handkerchief.

'What happened?' Flo asked.

'It was when I was a little boy. We were in Venice. I had a balloon. It blew away and I followed. Mamma ask a lady to look after my baby sister while she and my father try to find me.' He looked at his mother. 'When my parents come back, the woman had taken the baby from her pram. She was rocking her, you know? But when Mamma try to take the baby back again, the woman would not let her go. Mamma was frightened. The woman held my sister tightly, she made the baby cry. She was crazy, you know?' he said, screwing his forefinger against his temple. 'Mamma thought she would hurt the baby.'

'But why did your mother look at me like that?' Flo said, her heart thumping in her chest.

The man sighed. 'She say you wear the same dress, have the same hair. You look like her. She never forgotten. She think you are the crazy lady.'

'I'm sorry,' Ben said. 'That was hard to listen to.'

She stirred her Aperol with the long black straw. 'Poor Nancy.' She looked up at him. 'She must have had a baby, Ben. And then lost it somehow – adopted, given away, or worse. I just can't imagine.' She pressed the palms of her hands against the bridge of her nose, trying to hold back her tears for the woman who knew as well as Flo what it was to lose something you loved so much.

'I know. I'm sorry, Flo. This must be a horrible shock to you.'

She sighed and sat up straight. 'I'll be fine. I just wish I knew what happened to her after that awful meeting with the Bartolis.'

'Maybe she went back to England?'

'I don't know. Or maybe she went to Tuscany with Peter and Pamela, but then there's the train ticket. Maybe she was on that plane – I can't bear to think about it. I have to go to Tuscany next, whatever, now we've come this far. If Nancy did go back to England to try to find her baby, presumably it had been adopted by then. Or maybe she got rid of it. I'm not sure which is worse.'

'Are you OK?'

She wasn't, but she didn't want to make a scene in front of the cool crowd who frequented this little bar tucked down a side street next to the old fish market, laughing and smoking on tall stools around barrel tables.

'I'm fine.'

'You don't seem it.'

'I said I'm fine,' she snapped.

He sat back and breathed out heavily. 'OK.' He took a cigarette out of a packet and leant over towards the smokers on the next table to ask for a light.

'I didn't know you smoked. I thought the Gauloises were for effect.'

'I don't. Usually. Only when I'm stressed.'

'What have you got to be stressed about?'

He took a long drag on the cigarette and tried to cover up

a small choke. 'I don't know. Being here with you. And not with you.'

'What do you mean?'

'I mean, we've been doing this thing for a week or so, right? And don't get me wrong, I love helping you. It's been fun. Apart from that last bit. But it's our final night here, and I just can't work out where I stand.'

'You're my friend, aren't you? I thought we'd dealt with . . . well, you know. Capri.'

He looked at her. 'Yes, I am. But I'm not sure we did deal with Capri. I'm sorry, Flo, and I can't help it. But I really like you. I mean, *really* like you. And I suppose I just hope you feel the same.'

What was she waiting for? He was a handsome, sweet man who had been a good friend to her. They both deserved some happiness. So why not?

'I'm sorry to push. It's just I need to know where I stand. My last girlfriend . . . well, and the one before . . . she kind of crushed me, and I swore I'd never let myself get used again.'

'I haven't used you,' Flo said. 'You wanted to come along.'

'Haven't you?' He shook his head. 'I'm not sure.'

'Things have been hard for me recently, you know.'

'The baby? The cheating husband? Don't look surprised: I asked Jem to fill me in.'

Thanks, Jem. I owe you.

He leant over and took her hand. 'We're in Venice, it's our last night here, and I know we said that we were cool, but . . .'

Go on, Flo, just say yes.

'. . . well, I'd like to be with you.'

She could see what that had cost him, as he concentrated on tracing lines in the condensation on his glass.

'I don't know, Ben. I just need more time,' she said, pulling her hand away.

He looked up and stared her directly in the eyes. 'You still love your husband.'

'God, no. Absolutely not. I'm just not ready.'

'You do, Flo. You absolutely do. It's written all over you. Everything I do, I'm thinking "Flo knows Seamus wouldn't do that" or "Seamus would have said this". And I'm not ready to be a substitute for someone else. If you ever get over him, then sure, let me know, but until then, don't toy with me.'

'Ben, you've got it wrong,' she said, but as she spoke, she knew he was right. All the time they'd spent together, it had been the ghost of Seamus at her side, not the reality of Ben. She couldn't believe how cruelly she'd behaved. Poor Ben.

He put his hand over hers, seeing he had upset her. 'Look, Flo, I get it. No one can make themselves unlove someone, whatever they've done to us. However awful.'

She looked at him. 'Melanie?' His face crumpled as he nodded. 'I'm sorry, Ben. I should have realised you never get over something like that. I should have been . . .'

Shame flooded through her. God, Flo, you can be an insensitive cow, she said to herself. Of course he'd been through his own stuff – who hadn't? She could see now the dangerous game she'd unwittingly played with the feelings of this nice, kind man, who deserved someone who could love him in the way Flo had always loved Seamus: for being him, and not just for being there.

'I'm so sorry,' she said.

He shrugged. 'You can't help how you feel. And I can't make you feel something you don't.'

She smiled. 'I wish I could. It would make life a lot simpler.'

'Not in the end,' he said, smiling sadly at her.

'I wish I could be what you're looking for, Ben. I wish I could be your Mrs Simpson, but I'm not. And even if I could be, maybe happiness isn't just about finding someone. Maybe you need more too.'

'What do you mean?'

She shook her head. 'I dunno. For a start, you need to tell your mother to back off.' She held a hand up. 'No, I mean it. She's not helping you. And maybe you need to really get away. Not just Paris, but the proper travelling we were talking about the other day. All those places you said you wanted to go. Forget meeting someone, and just get to know yourself.' She had read between the lines of Ben's Paris life and found the story of someone who couldn't fit in, and yet who couldn't give in. It was so easy to see what other people needed, she knew, even if you couldn't sort your own life out, and she had a feeling he would fly if he just took a chance and escaped.

'I do know myself actually,' he replied, 'and I know what myself wants.'

'Do you?'

'You know I do. And you know what it is I want. It just seems I can't have it.'

She reached across the table for him, but he stuffed his hands in his pockets, and her hand lay there alone. Sensing the change in mood, she instead tucked her arms around her waist.

'Thanks, Flo.'

'What for?'

'For being honest.'

'Now you're just being kind.'

'And stupid. Because I'm about to tell you to find your husband and explain how you feel. Don't waste it.' He stood up, throwing his jacket over his shoulder.

'Where are you going?' she said.

'I'm going to head back to the apartment and get my stuff. I'll find a hotel tonight, and I'll be off first thing.'

'You don't have to do that.'

'I do. I won't come to Tuscany with you. You don't need me.'

'But Ben . . .'

'It's fine,' he said, kissing her lightly on the cheek. 'I'll live. I hope you find her,' he added as he walked away. 'And I hope she was happy.'

'I'm sorry,' she whispered as she watched him slouch away into the Venetian night. She seemed to be saying that a lot lately.

25

'You missed lunch. And supper.' Peter filled the kettle and put it on the stove to boil. 'Goodness,' he said, looking at Nancy, 'you're soaked through. Where've you been?'

She tucked her suitcase out of sight behind the kitchen door. 'Just for a walk.' She tugged at the skirt of her dress, which clung to her legs and dripped onto the floor.

'Good for you. I love a walk in the rain.' He held up a mug. 'Tea?'

She shook her head. 'I'm fine, thanks.'

'Righto. It'll probably be horrible anyway. I can't get the hang of making it over here.' He sighed. 'I suppose there's a few things I'm going to have to get the hang of now.'

He looked down and began picking absent-mindedly at a streak of blue on the sleeve of his old painting jumper.

'Where's Pamela?'

'She's been shut in her room all day. I thought it best to leave her, given what's happened.'

'Are you all right?' Nancy said.

'Hmm?' He looked up. 'Oh, yes, I expect so.'

'Perhaps I'll have that tea after all.' She came and sat at the table while he pottered about and eventually presented her with a mug of steaming pale-grey liquid. 'Thanks.' Even if she couldn't drink it, it at least warmed her hands; the house was freezing suddenly, without the warmth of the sun. 'Have you heard anything from Caro?'

He shook his head. 'Don't suppose I will now. Until she gets a lawyer.'

'I'm sorry,' Nancy said. 'Was it a shock?'

'Not really. Writing's been on the walls for months, if not years. Surprised she's stuck around this long.' He smiled sadly. 'She was all right, you know, underneath it all. She could be prickly, but she's a good sort, and it's been hard for her over the last few years, with work and what have you. She had a terrifically difficult upbringing, which must do things to one, I suppose.' He sighed. 'She really tried, and we were happy once, believe it or not. I only wish she and Pea had got on better. They were just too different, I suppose.'

'I'm sorry. You'll miss her.'

'I'll miss the old Caro. Loved her to bits, you know. She changed my life after Alice died. Pamela was just a baby, and for better or worse I sent her away to live with my parents. Didn't know what else to do. And then Caro came along, and she made everything better. I just hope Tony looks after her and makes her happy. He'll need to get his finances sorted when they get over there, though. She's not cheap to run, my wife. Ex-wife,' he added.

'What will you do now?' Nancy asked, fearful that now she had decided to stay, she would be sent away.

'Well, I don't know about you, but I've had enough of being on the road, and Venice has rather lost its charm. It's either go back to London or, I don't know, take Lorenzo up on his offer. To be honest, the London house will probably have to be sold anyway. It's mortgaged to the hilt.'

She bit her lip gently, knowing that at some point she would have to face the music, and that since Peter had opened up to her, this was as good a time as any to tell the truth.

'You all right, Nancy?'

She looked up at him, at his kind eyes that were so like Pamela's and at the flecks of paint smearing his cheek. 'Peter, I have to tell you something.'

Her heart was going to burst as she felt her cheeks burn. 'I don't know how to say it, and once I have, you'll never want me near Pea again.'

'Nancy . . .'

'I had a baby.' There, it was out, and there was no taking it back.

She had dreaded disappointing him, but the look on his face was worse than anything she had imagined.

'Please, say something.' Why couldn't he look angry? It would be so much easier.

He came over and knelt next to her, taking her hand in his. 'I know,' he said, smiling sadly.

'You know? How do you know?'

He shrugged. 'I might be an old duffer, but I can put two and two together. Most of the time. I suppose I guessed when Charlie turned up and you were so out of sorts. I knew he'd got a girl pregnant back in London, and the timing worked out, I suppose. And when I saw you making that little bib thing—'

'Oh, no, that was for my niece.'

'Oh. Well, as I say, two and two.'

'When do you want me to leave? I can be gone within the hour. I just want to say goodbye to Pea.'

Please ask me to stay with you, please don't send me away.

'Oh, you silly girl,' he said, hugging her to him. 'You don't have to go anywhere. You've already been through hell, I can tell, and we all make mistakes. Anyway, you can't leave. Pea adores you, and I feel like I've got myself another daughter. One who won't whinge every time I take her to an exhibition!'

She couldn't believe what she was hearing. 'Really?'

'Really.' He patted her on the back and went back to his tea. 'Let's have a quiet night, gather ourselves a bit, and then the three of us can do something nice tomorrow – put today behind us. How about that?'

'That sounds perfect.'

'Go on, you get some rest. I've got some painting to finish, and Pea's probably asleep by now. I'll see you at breakfast, yes?'

'Thanks,' Nancy said. 'For everything.'

She passed Pamela's door on the way to her own, and tapped lightly. The tray of supper that Peter had left for her was now crawling with ants, the black grapes a writhing mass and the soft cheese dotted with busy black bodies. 'Pea?' she said quietly while she waited for the door to open. 'I'm sorry. I came back.'

Silence. So Pamela was punishing her. She couldn't blame her. It had been a pretty horrible row, and she felt sick at some of the things that had been said.

'It's me. Nancy. Let me in.'

Still nothing. Nancy hadn't the energy for another row. She'd let Pamela have her sulk, and tomorrow they could be friends again.

Part Seven

TUSCANY

26

The little roads stretched interminably past wide swathes of sunflowers, then ducked under cool woodland shade and knifed past waterfalls and gorges. The scenery could have been English, were it not for the cypress trees reaching out from the green canopy, the warm-gold medieval villages perched precariously on the cliffs and hilltops, and the dark, Christmassy pines offset by clouds of grey-green olive trees and splashes of rust-brown scrubby earth.

Flo stopped the rental car in a dusty lay-by and took out her road map, enjoying the opportunity to take a break from driving. Never the most confident of drivers, after negotiating the hell that was the Bologna ring road, she had almost abandoned the tiny left-hand-drive Fiat and walked the rest of the way.

She was nearly there. She only had about three days' worth of money and energy left, so she hoped the trail would end soon. Any further searching would have to be done from the kitchen table back at home.

She smiled. That table was the first thing she and Seamus had bought together, at a back-street auction over a decade ago, with its worn Formica surface that Peggy had tutted at, unable to understand why Florence's generation were so keen to snap up the old rubbish that hers had been glad to get rid of. What would become of it now? she wondered. Would she take it with her to wherever she ended up next? And where would that be? Another flat share? She'd thought she was done with those a long while ago. Stop fretting, Flo, she told herself. These next few days are about Nancy, not you.

She waited a moment, delaying leaving the tranquil spot. Now that she was so close to the end of her journey, the chances of there not being a happy ending suddenly seemed more real. So much was against Nancy: her lost baby, the breakdown in Venice, the fact that her very existence had been kept secret for so long, and of course the whole story might yet end on a South American mountainside, if Nancy had decided to make a fresh start on the other side of the world.

Flo couldn't bear to think about it: she had to focus on Tuscany for now, and the hope that finding Peter would lead her to a happy outcome for the woman she now felt so close to. She had worn her clothes, trodden in her footsteps, discovered the tragedy that had driven her away from home, to who knew where. There was no doubt about it: in the words of Jem, she had definitely become 'more Nancy'.

She took a long slug of cool water from her bottle, and climbed back into the car. In only a few more kilometres, she might finally know what had happened to her great-aunt.

It would have been more accurate to describe the collection of huge stone buildings as a hamlet rather than a farm, and as Flo parked the car and walked around the complex, the air full of urgent birdsong and the whickering of horses, she could see that each of the buildings was divided into a combination of workshops and accommodation. Potters, artists – the whole place was a hive of industry.

'Can I help you?' A young woman in a thin cotton forties-style dress, her dark-blonde curls scrunched up in a headscarf, appeared from round a corner, drying her hands on her apron.

'Oh, yes, I've a room booked for a couple of nights. Florence Connelly – Flo.'

'Of course. Nice to meet you, Flo. I'm Emilia – I look after the place,' she said in perfect English, decorated with a touch of Italianate vowels.

Flo was grateful not to have to make herself understood in her severely limited Italian. 'You speak excellent English – I'm impressed. And embarrassed!' she added.

Emilia shrugged and smiled. 'There are lots of English members of our extended family. I had no choice!' She smiled warmly, and Flo quickly forgot the trauma of the morning's journey.

They made their way through a vine-covered courtyard and into a cool tiled hallway, where Emilia reached behind a desk and produced a key. 'Here, this is for you. Lunch is at one, dinner at seven, and for breakfast you can help yourself from the kitchen any time until ten. We're pretty relaxed here. Everyone eats together. We have a mixture of resident artists and those coming for retreats. Plus the odd holidaymaker like yourself,' she added, smiling. 'The conversation is rarely dull. There's lots to do, but let me know if you'd like to go out painting, or come to the market with me, or even ride. We have a lot of horses here.'

Flo was more exhausted than usual, and the thought of getting on a horse, let alone having a conversation with strangers over dinner, was less than tempting, but she tried to look enthusiastic. 'Thanks, I will.' She took the heavy key. 'I understand there's a gallery here? I'm doing some research on an artist who used to live here.' She had instantly warmed to the young woman who had made her feel so welcome, but it felt too early to share family secrets, and to explain Nancy's part in Peter's life. There would be a moment, perhaps, when she would want to tell Emilia more, enlist her help in finding out what had happened to Nancy, but for now, it suited her to remain low key.

Emilia's face brightened. 'Ah, Peter Cavendish, I expect?'

'How did you guess?'

Emilia smiled. 'Peter was something of a celebrity around here – we have lots of visitors who come purely because of his connection with the place. There's a collection of his work on display in the main gallery. It's not huge, but I think you might enjoy it. Give me a shout when you've settled in and I'll show you around if you like. I'll probably be in the kitchen.'

'I'd like that very much.'

Emilia frowned at her. 'Are you OK?' she asked.

Did she look that bad? Flo wondered. Yes, she was shattered, and she wasn't wearing any make-up, but did it show that much? 'I'm fine, thanks,' she said. 'I just need some rest.'

'Well, let me know if I can get you anything. Your room is number four, straight across the courtyard there.' Emilia smiled and walked away, stopping to pat one of the dogs that wandered happily around the place, then to sniff at the long bed of rosemary and basil sprouting along one side of the courtyard. Flo had missed female company, she realised, and she had a feeling that she and Emilia would get on well.

She was surprised how much she had missed Ben, and how often she had looked at the photo of their smiling faces back in Venice. She'd never sent the picture to him, and guessed it would be the last thing he wanted to see, but she couldn't quite bring herself to delete it. She hoped he was all right, and that he would eventually come to see that she had tried to do the right thing.

She felt herself yawning, the exhaustion and emotion of the last couple of days finally overwhelming her. She needed to sleep, and then she would be ready to take the last few steps of her journey.

27

Pamela didn't appear at breakfast, so Nancy made up a tray of clementines and fresh juice and a squidgy pastry oozing with berries.

She tapped lightly on her door. 'Wakey wakey, lazybones. Breakfast is served.'

She sighed. Pamela's bad mood must have continued overnight, although it was unusual for her to maintain it for this long. She turned the handle and pushed the door open. The room looked the same as usual: clothes dumped on the floor, bed unmade, new make-up strewn, lidless, on the dressing table.

Pamela's book had disappeared, however, and a quick search in the wardrobe and under the bed showed that although she'd forgotten her toothbrush, her small overnight bag and handbag were missing, along with her favourite chunky wool sweater that she had filched from her father's studio.

Nancy ran down the wide, shallow marble stairs two at a time, and found Peter sketching next to the open sitting-room window, capturing the canal scene in a concise series of charcoal markings.

'What's the matter?' he said, looking up from his sketchbook.

'It's Pamela,' she said breathlessly. 'She's gone.'

'What do you mean, gone?'

'Her room's empty, and she's taken an overnight bag.'

'Good God,' he said. 'When did she go?'

Nancy was close to tears. 'I don't know. She didn't answer last night when I knocked on her door, but I just assumed she was angry with me. Have you seen her at all?'

He ran his hand across his mouth, his eyes darting around. 'No, not since lunch yesterday. I took her some supper up, but, like you, I didn't get an answer. She'd been in a filthy mood most of the day, and I just thought she was sulking.'

'She could have been gone since yesterday,' Nancy said, trying not to panic. Panicking would help no one right now. Especially Pea.

'We need to look for her. Where do you think she might have gone?'

Nancy shook her head. 'I don't know. I'd say the ice-cream shop, but even Pea couldn't spend eighteen hours there. We need to retrace everywhere she's been since we arrived.'

'Oh God, Pea. What have you done?' Peter stood with his hands on his hips, biting his lower lip.

'Come on,' Nancy said. 'We need to get looking.'

They must have made a curious sight as they marched their way grimly along the tourist trail, pushing through the day trippers without so much as a glance at the Byzantine splendour of St Mark's, or the dainty charm of the Rialto Bridge. They ignored Titian in the Gallerie and left empty-handed Pamela's favourite *gelateria*. They scowled at street artists who got in their way and pushed past gondoliers offering them a good deal for a canal trip.

'I don't know where else to suggest,' Nancy said as they rehydrated with freshly squeezed orange juice at a back-street café. 'We've been everywhere.'

They'd been out for hours, and even though evening was fast approaching, they hadn't eaten a thing, nor could they.

'You don't think she went to follow Caro, do you?' Peter said.

It seemed highly likely to Nancy, now that he had said it. Why wouldn't she run after Caro, having been rejected by the woman she had begged to stay with her? 'You think she might be trying to get to the airport at Paris? But didn't Caro's flight leave today? She'll miss her, surely.'

'Yes, but if she got the night train, she might have made it.'

'Maybe we should go to Paris?' Nancy said, wondering how on earth they would find an English needle in the Parisian haystack. That was, if Pamela wasn't already on a flight to South America. How could she have left the poor girl? She would never forgive herself.

Peter put his head in his hands. 'I don't know, Nancy, I just don't know. If she managed to get to Paris, if she managed to get to the airport, if she managed to find Caro, if she managed to get on that plane . . . So many ifs. I just can't see it.'

Nancy looked at her watch. 'But if she did manage all that, she'd be arriving almost on the other side of the world right now.'

The waiter began to bustle around the tables, laying out starched white tablecloths and setting down hurricane lamps.

'I think we'd better move on unless we want to find ourselves staying for dinner,' Peter said. 'There's got to be somewhere else.'

Nancy suddenly sat up. 'I know. What about Lorenzo's gallery? We completely forgot to look there.'

'Of course,' Peter said. 'It'll be closed now, but I'll telephone him. He might have seen her.' He stood up and pulled on his jacket. 'Come on, let's head back to the house. We can use the phone there.'

Nancy struggled to keep up with his long-legged strides as he swallowed up the ground before him. All around them, tourists now dressed in their evening best mingled with locals reclaiming the city as the day trippers disappeared. Nancy sidestepped a couple dressed for dinner and almost crashed into a newspaper vendor tucked around a street corner.

'I'm so sorry,' she said, picking up the copies of the evening edition she had knocked to the ground.

Her heart almost stopped as she looked at the front page. Her Italian was limited, to say the least, but no words were needed to translate the violent image of the plane wreckage spread in front of her.

She looked desperately around, and grabbed the arm of a businessman walking past. 'Please,' she said. '*Parlo inglesi?* Can you tell me what this means?' She pointed at the headline.

He took the paper from her and whistled slowly. 'The flight from Paris to Santiago has crashed in Guadeloupe.'

'Guadeloupe?' He may as well have said Timbuctoo.

'In South America,' he went on. 'No survivors.'

'Thank you,' she said quietly as he gave it back to her and continued on his way. She handed the vendor a few lire and tucked the paper under her arm.

She ran blindly, barely looking where she was going. Caro and Tony were dead. She thought of poor, desperate Caro, who had given up everything, only to die a horrible death on the other side of the world. And maybe Pamela, too. It was Nancy's fault: she should never have tried to leave. How could she not have cherished the love that Pea offered her? After everything she had been through, she was still capable of pushing away a young girl who needed her. Twice she had managed to give away something precious, and she would have to live with the pain for the rest of her life.

By the time she arrived back at the apartment, she had calmed down a little, and was wondering if she had jumped to conclusions. Maybe there were two Santiago flights that day? They would phone the airline straight away, and Peter would be told not to worry, because Caro was on the next flight, and then they could all go back to being cross with her and furious with Tony. Pamela would appear any minute now, with ice-cream stains down her skirt, and it would all be fine.

As she slipped through the small doorway at the back of the house, she heard Peter's soft voice in the dark hallway, illuminated only by rippled reflections bouncing off the water outside. She had to show him the paper – at least then he could telephone the airline to see whether Caro and Pamela had been on the flight. And when she'd done that, and was sure that Pamela was safe, she would pack her things and go. She had no idea where, but she would leave this family alone before she did any more damage.

He replaced the receiver with a click.

She held the newspaper out towards him. 'I'm so sorry,' she said. 'Caro . . .'

He took it from her and placed it on the hall table. 'It's all right,' he said. 'I know. Lorenzo told me. I was speaking to the airline just now.'

'Was Caro on that flight?'

Peter pinched the bridge of his nose, and Nancy took a step towards him, waiting to see whether she needed to offer words of comfort or relief. He looked up, and even in the dimness of the hallway, she could see the tears in his eyes as he nodded slowly.

'I'm so sorry, Peter. That's just dreadful. Poor Caro. And Pea? Does anyone know where she is? Was she on the plane?'

Peter stood in front of her and held her shoulders. 'Pea is fine,' he said. 'Lorenzo drove her down to Tuscany last night. She went to the gallery yesterday and told him I'd asked him to take her there and would be following on later. Little monkey.' He shook his head. 'She's there with him now, and has been out riding all day.' He looked at her and smiled with relief. 'She's fine. Pea is fine.'

Nancy felt her knees collapse and she fell to the floor. 'Thank God,' she said, finally allowing her tears to flow freely, holding her shaking hands to her face. There was nothing anyone could do to help poor Caro now, but at least Pamela was safe.

They were there by mid morning. Lorenzo had arranged a car for them, and it took Peter three very long hours to drive the tiny Fiat across the plains of the Veneto and then through the vineyards and rugged hills of the fringes of the Tuscan countryside.

'I'm so sorry about Caro,' Nancy said. 'It's just awful. I can't bear to think what it must have been like for her.'

He stared ahead, chewing on his lip. 'Me too. It's such a waste. Wouldn't wish that even on bloody Tony.'

'Does Pea know?'

'No – Lorenzo's promised not to say anything before we arrive.'

'How do you think she'll react?' Nancy said as they slowed down to look for the tiny sign that would point them towards the village.

'I don't know. She's very good at covering up her feelings, that one. When she wants to.' Peter sighed. 'It won't be easy for her, but we just have to show her that we're here for her, and that we won't leave her. She's had enough upheaval in her life already.' He looked across at Nancy. 'I'm sorry. I was making a huge assumption in hoping that you would still be with us. You have your own life to lead. I can't expect you to stay with us for ever.'

'I'll be wherever you and Pea need me, don't worry,' she said, then sat up and pointed to the side of the road. 'Oh, stop, there it is.' Peter braked suddenly at the sight of the small roadside sign. 'It's only a kilometre from here, however far that is.'

'About half a mile, I think,' he said, turning slowly into the bumpy lane.

Nancy had never seen anywhere quite so beautiful as the little collection of rustic stone buildings huddled in front of them, balanced on a gentle mound and surrounded by a patchwork of vines and olives groves and paddocks.

'It's heaven,' she said, astonished that something so tranquil could exist alongside the crushing news that they had received only a few hours earlier.

They pulled up in front of the buildings in a cloud of dust, to be greeted by two lolloping, tail-wagging hounds, who skittered about Nancy and tried to lick her hands.

'Where do you think she'll be?' Nancy said.

Peter sighed. 'Do you need to ask?'

'Are you ready?'

He nodded. 'As I'll ever be.'

It was not hard to find the stables: they simply followed the sound of whinnying and the pungent smell of horse that drifted across the courtyard.

Three dusty, well-fed animals were tethered to a bar inside one of the outbuildings, happily tucking into fresh hay as they flicked their tails to dismiss the persistent flies. One of them lifted its large chestnut head wearily and whickered at them, a saddle-shaped area of sweat steaming across its back.

'Here you go,' said a voice from inside the building, and a girl appeared in riding breeches, carrying a large sloshing bucket of water.

She stopped in her tracks and stared at them.

'Pa,' she said. 'Nancy.'

She was flushed from her ride, her hair sweaty and littered with straw and her hands filthy. Nancy thought she had never looked prettier.

'Pea,' Peter said, and she dropped the bucket, splashing water all over the ground, and making the horses flinch as she rushed towards the newcomers.

The three of them held each other close, and Nancy couldn't tell whether each of them was laughing or crying.

'I'm sorry,' she said when they eventually pulled apart, taking Pamela's grubby hands in her own. 'I'm so sorry.'

'No, I'm sorry. I was beastly.'

'You weren't, you were just frightened.'

Peter shuffled, embarrassed at the excess of emotion. 'Well, let's just agree that we're all sorry, and we're all friends.'

'Agreed.' Pamela looked from one to the other. 'So what's next?'

Nancy and Peter exchanged a glance. It wasn't the right moment quite yet. She could see that Peter wanted to enjoy the excitement of the reunion for just a little while longer before he broke the news.

'Well,' he said, 'I haven't exactly had a chance to look around yet, but I reckon I'm ready to spend some time here. I certainly don't want to go back to London.'

'And Nancy?' Pamela said, biting her bottom lip.

Nancy looked from father to daughter and smiled. 'If you'll have me, I'd love to stay here with you.'

'Splendid! Then that's settled. We'll talk to Lorenzo and work out the logistics.' Peter suddenly frowned. 'I don't know, I feel I should carry on paying you to stay with us, Nancy. But that feels strange: you're not just an employee any more. You're family.'

'You're my big sister,' Pamela said playfully.

Nancy smiled, nudging her gently. 'Peter, you haven't paid me at all yet. So yes, big sister will do just fine.'

'Pa!' Pamela said, shocked. She took Nancy and the embarrassed Peter by the arm. 'Come on then, sis. I'll show you your room.'

They headed back across the courtyard, where Lorenzo was waiting for them. He hugged Peter to him, patting him on the back, and the two men exchanged a few whispered words in Italian, glancing across at Pamela, before releasing each other.

'Nancy, it's good to see you again,' Lorenzo said, and they both hesitated briefly before exchanging a light embrace. 'Even if the circumstances . . .'

'I know,' she said quietly. Strangely, she felt herself reluctant to leave the gentle circle of his arms. She barely knew him, and was surprised at the happy familiarity of his company, sensing that he recognised it too.

'Come, my friends,' he said, stepping back. 'I have lunch waiting for you.' He looked at Peter. 'And then maybe you and Pamela can go for a walk? You must have lots to catch up on.'

Peter smiled, but Nancy could see he was struggling to maintain the charade. The sooner Pamela knew, the better.

As they followed Lorenzo into the house, Pamela took Nancy's arm and whispered in her ear, 'Somebody's sweet on you,' before Nancy cuffed her gently across the top of her head and forced a smile to her lips. Peter was being so brave; it was the least she could do to keep up the pretence for a little longer.

There was a tricky conversation to be had very soon, and Nancy's heart bled for the father and daughter who would have to rebuild everything they had known for the last fifteen years, but for now they would just eat good food and enjoy being reunited. Nancy could only be grateful that she would be there to support Peter and Pamela through the difficult times to come, as part of her new family.

28

By the time Flo was woken by the tapping on her bedroom door, the starlings had started their evening roosting chorus and the Tuscan light was as golden as the ancient stone buildings. She sat up, and shook out her sleep-dented hair and rubbed her gluey eyes. Perhaps she was coming down with something after all. She couldn't remember the last time she'd felt so lethargic.

She opened the bedroom door, her head still swimming with the faint trails of her scrambled dreams, which had swerved between the vivid sensation of being inside a rapidly descending plane, and trying to rescue a baby from a Venetian lagoon. She must be more stressed about the conclusion to Nancy's story than she had realised.

'I didn't want to wake you – you seemed so tired earlier.' Emilia stood bearing a tray of supper: a plate of prosciutto, fresh olives and pungent cheese. She had lost the apron and headscarf, and her sun-tinted blonde hair hung loose about her shoulders, her delicate features accentuated by a whisper of pale lipstick.

Flo spotted a dark curly head tucked behind her legs. 'Ciao,' she said, smiling at the child, who barely came to the top of his mother's legs.

Emilia ruffled his hair. 'Say hello to Flo, Luca,' she said.

'I'm sorry,' she added, 'he's very shy. He speaks perfect English, but only when he wants to.'

'That's OK.' Flo shifted her head to the side as the boy hid again, slowly enticing him into a game of hide-and-seek that finally brought a reluctant smile to his face, his grey eyes beaming back at her and helping to dissolve the last threads of her nightmare.

Emilia placed the tray on the little table next to the window. 'You don't have to eat it,' she said. 'But you might feel better if you do.'

'Thanks. You're very kind.'

'Not at all.' She hesitated. 'I don't know if you were planning a quiet evening in your room, but we're not too busy tonight, and if you wanted, I could show you Peter's work.'

'I'd love that,' Flo said. 'Give me ten minutes to freshen up . . .' she looked at the plate of food, so beautifully arranged, 'and eat something.'

'Perfect. I'll meet you in the courtyard.'

She was still wearing her travelling clothes, and quickly changed into the pretty blue and white flowers that had started her trip almost a continent away. Where else had Nancy worn this dress? she wondered. Did it come here? Maybe it went back to England and found itself on the doorstep of an adoptive mother whose world fell apart at the sight of it. Maybe it boarded a plane in Paris. She couldn't think about that yet.

For the sake of politeness, she forced down some of the food, handing some of the meat to the little white dog that had found its way into her room and was turning tight circles as it settled itself in for a good sleep on her pile of discarded clothes.

She found Emilia in the courtyard with Luca and a little girl a couple of years older than him, who was busy scratching lines in the dust with a stick. She turned as she heard Flo, and for a moment Flo thought she was looking at a photograph of herself as a child, complete with straggly hair and the short, stocky legs she had hated, but which had slimmed and lengthened over time.

'Are you OK?' Emilia said, picking up Luca's toy that he'd dropped and handing it back to him.

'Oh. Yes, sorry. Just still a bit tired.'

Emilia knelt down and chattered to the children in Italian, sending them home across the courtyard, then stood and said to Flo, 'Come, let me show you.'

She led her around the side of the house, past a swimming pool still littered with damp towels, where a group of grey-haired women in floaty tunics and jewel-coloured scarves sat drinking red wine around a low table, laughing and shouting as the wine lubricated their conversation. 'The residential pottery class,' Emilia explained, waving at them. 'Help yourself to more wine from the kitchen,' she called, and they toasted her.

They continued along the edge of a paddock, where two white horses grazed, looking as though they had had a fight with a brown paint pot.

'My grandfather loved horses,' Emilia explained as they stopped briefly to lean on the rough wooden rail and watch the animals, so close Flo could hear their teeth ripping at the scrubby grass and the soft blowing of their warm breath. 'And of course my English aunt. She couldn't keep away from them when she came to visit from London. Still can't, although she doesn't ride these days.'

'So is this your family home?' Flo asked, her brain full of questions fighting to be asked.

'Yes. I grew up here. Nonno and Nonna had their children here, and Papa stayed on to run the business. He and Mamma are retired now and live in the town, and I took it over. It suits us here,' she said. 'My husband Francesco is a writer, and loves the peace and quiet.'

'Has it always been an artists' centre?'

Emilia nodded. 'That's why Nonno came here: he was tired of city life, but couldn't bear to be away from the artistic scene. So he bought this place when it was still a ruin, restored it with the help of friends, and soon the artistic scene came to him.'

Flo could see the attraction: who wouldn't feel inspired by such a beautiful setting?

'At one time, as well as the pottery, we had printmakers and paper makers, and Nonna had a studio. And of course, there was Peter.' Emilia stood back from the rail. 'Let's go and see, shall we?'

The gallery was housed in a large barn, screaming swifts diving in and out of the gaps beneath its terracotta-tiled roof. Emilia opened the heavy wooden door and flicked a few light switches. 'Oh, I like your dress,' she said. 'I didn't notice it properly outside. It suits you.'

'Thanks,' Flo said. 'I made it. Long story.'

Emilia laughed. 'You would have got on with my nonna!' She led Flo up some narrow wooden stairs to a wide mezzanine, its walls covered in canvases of all sizes and palettes: Tuscany, Venice, the unmistakable blue of the French Riviera, the little *gozzo* boats of Capri bobbing in the harbour, and the parks of Paris, their symmetry softened by the wide, generous strokes of the artist. Flo smiled as she took in the scenes that were now so familiar to her, and that she had seen with her own eyes, and wondered if Nancy had watched Peter create this beautiful visual memory of that long-gone summer.

'Of course, this is just some of his work. We only keep landscapes here, not his portraits. He used to say he would burn one if he ever set eyes on it!'

Flo remembered the portrait that Ben had shown her, and the good-humoured lack of prettification bestowed on its subject. His boredom with portraiture was clear for anyone to see. But these paintings were executed with love, and she moved closer to examine one of the Tuscan scenes, seeing how each brushstroke was just perfect, no effort wasted, the colours blending naturally on the canvas. What a shame Peter hadn't helpfully added a few little figures, to show her who he had brought here with him.

'Tell me,' she said, wondering how to begin asking the questions she needed to. 'Was Peter still married when he lived here?'

Emilia came to stand next to her. 'He had been.'

'What happened?' Flo was confused for a moment: she'd assumed Caro had followed him here, but maybe that wasn't the case.

'His wife died in a plane crash shortly before he moved here.'

'In South America? Guadeloupe, I think?'

Emilia looked surprised. 'You knew about that?'

'I must have read about it somewhere,' she said vaguely. She stared at the painting, its colours swirling as her head spun with the realisation of what had been under her nose all this time. It was Caro, not Nancy, on the plane with Tony. Of course: the affair was obvious to anyone who saw the photo from the Lido de Paris. Flo herself had assumed that Tony and Caro were a couple when she had first found the image, so much so that it had taken her a while to realise who Peter was. The unfolding drama felt as fresh as though it were happening in real time: all through that summer of 1962, Caro must have been torn between two men, only to make the decision that ended with her life snuffed out in the most dreadful of circumstances. Poor Peter and Pamela: to lose a wife and mother so horrifically.

'And what about their daughter?' she asked.

'Pamela? Well, Caro was actually her stepmother, but she stayed here with Peter for a while, until she outgrew the place.'

Just ask her about Nancy, a voice inside Flo told her, but it was too soon: she needed to let the story unfold at its own pace. Already she had discovered more than she had ever hoped to.

'And did Peter ever marry again?' she asked Emilia.

'Peter? No. He was happy just being left to paint, and anyway, I don't think he ever really got over losing Caro. He used to say he'd had enough of women for one lifetime. No one quite believed him, though: he had a twinkle in his eye right up until he died in nineteen ninety-eight. Used to pester some of the poor old ladies who came here for a painting holiday!' She sighed. 'We still miss him. He was part of the fabric of the place, and literally helped Nonno build it into what it is today.'

'Are there any photos of him here?'

'Yes, of course. We have a sort of family gallery down-stairs. I'll show you.'

Flo followed Emilia into a side room set back from the rest of the building.

'Here.' She flicked on the lights, revealing a wall covered in black-framed photographs, from black and white through to Polaroids and prints of her children.

Flo started on the left, seeing the happy images of Lorenzo and a tanned Peter working in the midst of what was still a building site, sleeves rolled up. She recognised Pamela as a young woman, riding one of Emilia's grandfather's horses and looking as though she had been born in the saddle. There was Emilia as a young child, with wild blonde dreadlocks, and again on her wedding day, the whole of the courtyard swathed in flowers as she stood pressed up against her new husband.

The pictures were in no particular order, and as Flo slowly worked her way along the wall, Emilia quietly explained each one to her, proudly revealing her family tree.

Suddenly her throat caught and she could barely breathe. She found herself face to face with a photograph of Lorenzo with his arm around a woman, a small boy, barely more than a toddler, pinned in front of her legs and a slightly older boy holding her other hand.

'Who is this?' she said quietly, trying to work out the complex family tree and unsettled by the sight of the woman beside Lorenzo.

'That's Nonno and Nonna, and my father when he was tiny. And Uncle Stanley.' Emilia laughed. 'Hey, she has a dress like yours!'

Flo looked more closely. She would know that dress anywhere. She ought to: she had spent an entire night making it, and an entire summer looking for it.

The woman stared right through the lens and into Flo's eyes, a little older now than in the last photo in which she had seen her, but her smile was unmistakable: brighter than the Tuscan sunlight that shone on her pretty, tousled blonde hair, and as warm as the smile of the man who had turned his face adoringly towards her.

She felt tears spring to her eyes as she realised that she had come to the end of her journey. Tears of relief, but also of happiness.

Here was Nancy, with a beautiful life and a man who clearly worshipped her, and of course her two little boys. Had she found her baby and brought him back here with her? And if so, what had it cost her?

'Are you OK?' Emilia stood back and studied her. 'You look like you've seen a ghost.'

'I think I just have.'

'I don't understand. I thought you were here to research Peter? What did you see in that photo of my grandparents?'

There was so much to tell Emilia, not least of which was the incredible discovery that they appeared to be related. She had no idea what to say or where to start, until it dawned on her that there was only one way to begin Nancy's story, which was exactly the same way she had begun it all those weeks ago.

'Wait there,' she said suddenly.

She ignored the confusion on Emilia's face as she ran out of the great barn and back to her room. She hadn't yet unpacked, but it was easy to find the packets, tied together with a long ribbon. She tucked them under her arm and dashed the short distance back to her new friend.

'Here,' she said breathlessly, and handed the first one to Emilia.

'A dress pattern?' she said, confused.

'Yes, but there's more. Look inside.'

Emilia opened the packet and pulled out the photograph of Nancy at the station, staring at it for what seemed like minutes. 'This looks like Nonna,' she said. 'How did you get it? And who are those people with her?'

'I know this sounds crazy, and I can't quite believe it myself, but I'm pretty certain that your nonna was my great-aunt Nancy,' Flo said, her heart racing.

'I don't understand. How do you know Nonna?'

'I'm sorry, Emilia. I wasn't completely straight with you when I arrived. I *was* researching Peter – that's all true – but only because he might have brought my great-aunt here with him.' She dragged Emilia over to the photograph of Nancy and Lorenzo, and they stood examining the smiling faces that beamed from it. 'You see?' She pointed at the photo in Emilia's hands. 'And that's her sister Peggy, my grandmother, and two of their friends.' She hadn't imagined how it would feel finally to find Nancy, but she would never have guessed it would push her this close to tears, and laughter, and utter joy, all at once. She looked at Emilia. 'It is her, isn't it? Tell me you can see it too.'

Emilia shook her head in disbelief. 'I don't know what to say. Other than, well, yes, it has to be. But why didn't she ever tell us she had a sister?'

'Exactly what I wondered about my own grandmother. I only found out after she died earlier this year.'

'I wonder what they were trying to hide.'

There was so much to tell Emilia, but Flo was exhausted now, and desperate to sit down. 'Shall we go back inside? I'll tell you what I know.'

Emilia took her arm. 'Of course.' She picked up the straggly ends of Flo's dark-blonde hair, looked at her grey eyes, so like her own. 'It's obvious now I see you properly. I'm so happy you came here, Flo. I can't believe I have a new second . . . or is it first cousin? I don't know!'

'Me neither,' said Flo, and they both burst out laughing, so that the poor gentleman who had come to ask Emilia for some aspirin, as he had overdone the sunshine on the watercolour field trip that day, wasn't sure what had come over his hostess and her new guest.

Emilia sat with Flo in her little sitting room, trying to explain to her nonplussed husband about Nancy's patterns and the story of how Flo made it here.

'There's more,' Flo said, unsure how to tell them the most important part of the story.

Francesco shook his head as Flo came to the end of the trail, to the little town outside Venice where she had discovered Nancy's secret. 'I always knew your nonna had a story,' he said to Emilia. 'But she would tell no one. Your great-aunt was a wonderful lady,' he told Flo. 'Maybe I turn her story into one of my novels?'

'Absolutely not,' Emilia said. 'Your novels are full of murders and creepy detectives.'

He shrugged. 'I'm a crime writer. What can I say? Anyway, perhaps I can offer you both some wine before I get the children back into bed?' They all listened to the running feet and shrieks in the distance.

Flo felt too sick with adrenalin for wine, so she declined.

'Probably just as well,' Emilia said, accepting a glass before he ran off, roaring, towards the noise.

'You're right. I am a bit exhausted.' Flo flopped into the old armchair with its embroidered antimacassar.

'Well, yes, but you shouldn't anyway,' Emilia said.

Flo was surprised: the place seemed to be flowing with wine, so why was Emilia suddenly putting the lid on it?

'You know.' She looked at Flo's belly. 'When are you due?'

'Due for what?' she said, puzzled.

'The baby.'

'But I'm not . . .'

Emilia put her hand to her mouth. 'Oh, I'm so sorry. I assumed you knew. Francesco is always telling me off: he says I can tell a woman is pregnant before she's even had sex.'

'I can't be. My husband and I split up a few months ago, and there's been no one else.'

'But when did you last . . . you know?'

Flo had to think back. Her life had been a sexual desert for so long that it was almost impossible to recall any intimacy with Seamus. Apart from . . .

'Oh my God. The nostalgia sex,' she said, counting back. 'Four months ago probably.'

Emilia held her hands up. 'There you go. Doesn't have to be good sex to do the job.'

Shit. Shit shit shit.

Flo leant forward, pushing her fist into her closed lips. This was not the plan. She couldn't do this on her own.

Emilia sat next to her. 'Hey, it'll be fine. Worse things have happened to women than having a baby.'

'But you don't understand. I had a baby. It died just before it was due. What if that happens again?'

'And what if it doesn't? You have to be positive.' Emilia stood up. 'I have an idea that will distract you.'

Flo looked up at her, panic gradually becoming curiosity.

'You say Nancy had a baby, right? And maybe it was my father. I don't know, and I might be completely wrong, but I want to show you something. Wait one moment.'

Flo took the opportunity to glance around while she was gone: full of books and artefacts, its furnishings a mixture of antique, mid century and modern, Emilia's home was a terracotta-tiled version of her own.

Emilia came back carrying a box very similar to the one Flo had found in Peggy's wardrobe. She put it down on the coffee table, and they both knelt on the floor next to it. 'Nonna loved sewing,' Emilia said. 'It was all she wanted to do, when she wasn't chasing the boys around, or collecting Aunty Pea from the airport, or helping Lorenzo and Peter with one of their exhibitions.' She pushed the box towards Flo. 'Go on.'

Flo took off the lid, and there, just as before, was a neat row of pattern packets. She took the first one out. It was for a little baby dress, again with the fabric swatch, and contained a photo of a chubby baby who looked nine or ten months old, sitting up and smiling at the camera. The next was a toddler's coat, with a piece of navy-blue wool pinned to the instructions, and a picture of a little girl running in what looked like a London park. There were more: party dresses, playsuits, beach clothes, on and on, and each time a photo of the same girl, with missing front teeth, blowing ten candles out on her birthday cake, wearing wide-legged trousers and a Bay City Rollers scarf. Why did she look so familiar?

'Didn't Nancy have two sons?' she asked.

'She did.'

'But these are girls' clothes.'

They stared at each other.

'Look,' Flo said, digging at the bottom of the box.

Her hands shook as she opened the manila envelope and took out a pair of crocheted newborn baby booties, the pink silk ribbon threaded around the ankles now yellowed, but otherwise in perfect condition. 'There's something else in here,' she said, trying to control the tears that were in danger of erupting: for her own baby or for Nancy's, she wasn't sure, but in that moment, it all felt the same.

'Let me,' said Emilia, taking out the little paper bracelet tucked at the bottom of the envelope. '"Baby Moon",' she read quietly. '"Girl, seven pounds two ounces, twentieth of December nineteen sixty-one, four twenty a.m."'

'She must have made all these clothes for her baby,' Flo said. 'The baby she had to give away. Why would she do that? Surely she wouldn't have been able to trace her?'

Emilia shook her head, looking as shaken as Flo. 'I don't know,' she said. 'Somehow she must have stayed in touch with whoever adopted her daughter. That's heartbreaking. Poor Nonna.'

'There are still two more packets,' Flo said, looking at the box. 'Maybe they'll tell us.'

One of the patterns was for a short-skirted dress in bold psychedelic swathes of colour, worn by the same girl, this time at a holiday camp with her parents, who stood proudly on either side of her, her familiar bored-teenager expression easily outshone by their pride and love as they huddled around her and smiled for the camera.

She didn't need to open the final packet – everything had been laid bare in that snapshot of the seventies – but she had a feeling that Nancy had wanted this box to tell the whole story, and so she gently pulled it out.

Inside, she found instructions for making a teddy bear. She turned over the photograph hidden with it: of the same girl, not much older than in the previous picture, but this time looking tired and frightened as she awkwardly held her own baby girl, who clutched the pink teddy with the worn-away paw that Flo knew so well.

29

Nancy stood barefoot on the stone floor and breathed a puff of warm air onto the frosted windowpane, rubbing at the circle of melted ice with the sleeve of her dressing gown. She gazed through the porthole she had made, at the icing-sugar dusting of white that coated the skeletal trees and the sweep of grass leading down to the river.

The sky was iron grey as it waited for the sun to bleed into the horizon. She remembered learning at school about the Greek goddess whose rose-tipped fingers brought the dawn with her as she circled the earth with her horse-drawn chariot. Surely she would hold back today, and keep the new day from coming.

She felt a quick, staggered intake of air against her neck, followed by the warm, milky breath that quickly condensed and left her flesh and the tiny cheek pressed against it bonded wetly together. She pressed her face against the baby's downy crown, feeling with her fingers the little indentations on her scalp, marvelling that something so fragile could survive such a brutal entrance into the world.

She wondered that either of them had survived. How did animals do this in the wild? This tearing, bloody, dirty ritual that somehow ensured that life would go on, the pain that she had forgotten so quickly, so that she could stand here peacefully, the bloodied sheets gone and her baby wrapped and fed, rocking gently from foot to foot. 'You are my sunshine, my only sunshine,' she sang in a cracked whisper into her daughter's perfect miniature ear.

The silence outside was broken by the sound of a car driving along the lane that led to the big old house. It couldn't be. Not yet. They had promised it wouldn't happen for hours.

Sensing her mother's agitation, the tiny child stiffened, her fists balling and her little rosebud mouth trembling.

'Don't cry, my sweet,' she said, and walked slowly back to the bed. She couldn't bear to see the car arrive, to watch the nervous, excited passengers as they walked up the steps to the front door.

She sat up against the rough linen pillows, shushing the fractious child as she slipped the bow on her nightshirt and let it fall open. The baby's cries changed suddenly from anxious hiccups to hunger, and she shook her head desperately from side to side, mouth open like a baby bird's as she looked for her feed.

Nancy felt the pain as her breasts swelled with milk, and then the bittersweet, eye-watering agony as the infant clamped her strong jaws around her swollen nipple, angrily tugging until it yielded the stream of thick colostrum that would protect her for the rest of her life, and that brought a dazed happiness to her unfocusing eyes as they wrestled between gazing at her devoted mother and closing in blissful half-sleep. Nancy smiled as her daughter's little feet kicked contentedly in the booties she had made that winter as she'd sat in this very room, waiting, always waiting.

A tap at the door startled the child, who wrenched away from the red-raw elongated nipple and turned her head, looking for the source of the new voices that had broken quietly into her tiny world.

Nancy pulled the baby closer to her. She wasn't ready. They said she would have today: one short day to last a lifetime. No one could take that from her.

'Hello, dear.' Sister Ignatia stood at the door.

'Not yet, please,' Nancy said.

The woman framed within the stiff white mantle was barely older than Nancy herself. Surely she would understand: she wasn't like some of the older nuns, who treated the girls like they were sluts and whores. No matter that some of them had been raped and abused; it was all the same to the nuns. Sister Ignatia was different, however, and they had even become friends of sorts, spending evenings together over embroidery frames and needles, as Nancy shared her knowledge with her new pupil. She had even fantasised that the kindly nun might help her escape with her baby.

But as she looked at the two terrified faces in the shadows behind the young woman, she knew that could never happen. Nancy had made a promise. A promise to her baby, and to the couple who stood awkwardly in the doorway.

Sister Ignatia sat on her bed. 'You know it's best, Nancy. The longer you have her, the harder it will be,' she said softly, struggling to keep her voice even.

Nancy began rocking the baby, gently kissing her daughter's

face. 'You are my sunshine . . .' she sang shakily, her hot tears spreading across the child's cheek and soaking into the soft white blanket.

The woman knelt next to the bed, her husband hanging back in the doorway as he anxiously played with the brim of his hat, turning it around and around in his shaking hands.

'Nancy,' she said, 'you know we'll love her and look after her, don't you?'

But Nancy kept singing. 'My only sunshine . . .'

'We can't go back now, can we?' the woman said, looking anxiously at the nun, and at her husband, who slowly shook his head.

Sister Ignatia stroked Nancy's forehead. 'It's time, my dear.'

She stood up and let the other woman take her place on the bed beside Nancy, who shrank back into the pillows, pulling her nightie up around her neck and staring wildly from face to face as she gripped her baby to her. 'No, I've changed my mind. I can't do it.'

'You have to, I'm sorry.' The nun looked at the other woman, who was trying to stifle her sobs in a lace handkerchief. 'So many people will be hurt if you don't, including your baby. You want her to have the best possible life, don't you?'

Nancy looked down at the dear little face, gently snuffling as she smacked her tiny pink lips and stared lazily at her mother with her glassy-blue eyes. The woman who sat beside her held out her arms, slowly, carefully.

'Please?' she said.

Nancy closed her eyes, trying to imagine what it would be like if she said no: with no husband, no job, no home, what could she offer this little girl, except her undying love, which was already guaranteed? She had nothing, whereas this woman could give the baby a future, a father, security. Everything Nancy didn't have.

'Oh, my darling,' she said, kissing the child's velvety forehead, the bridge of her nose, each of her cheeks, and then the tiny fists, with their flexing, starfish-like fingers. She slipped off the little booties, covering the baby's feet with the blanket, and put them in her dressing gown pocket, then took a deep breath and passed the warm bundle into the other woman's waiting arms.

'Look after her. Please? Both of you?'

'You know we will. We'll love her like she's our own.' The woman stood, cradling the baby, then bent over and kissed Nancy's cheek. 'Thank you. Thank you so much.' She wiped a tear from her cheek with her arm, then attempted a thin smile. 'Onwards and sideways?'

Nancy forced her mouth into what she knew should be a smile. 'Onwards and sideways.'

And as Donald followed Peggy and their little daughter out and closed the door quietly behind him, Nancy stared at the window and the weak rays of light that broke through the spidery outlines of the trees outside.

'Please don't take my sunshine away,' she sang quietly as she listened to the crunch of tyres moving away down the gravel drive, and the diminuendo of the car engine as it headed along the narrow lane and finally became nothing.

Part Eight

LONDON AND BRIGHTON

30

'I'm going to miss you . . .' Flo smiled at Emilia, 'cousin!' She knelt down and pulled Luca to her, planting an unwelcome kiss on his cheek. 'And you too, Nancy,' she said, ruffling the little girl's hair and smiling.

'But you'll be coming back soon, won't you?'

'Of course. I need to meet your father, apart from anything else.' She put her hand to her belly. 'Anyway, this one will have to come and meet the family too.'

'And don't forget this.' Emilia handed her an envelope, which Flo tucked in her handbag.

'I won't. Thanks.'

'She means it, you know,' Francesco said, as he tried to wrestle a large stick out of his son's hand. 'The studio is empty. We don't have time to run it, and, well, it could be just what you need.'

Flo smiled. 'I'll think about it.'

Emilia took her hand and squeezed it. 'Nancy would be so pleased that someone had taken it over. And it would mean we got to see lots of you. Both of you,' she added with a smile.

Flo couldn't deny she wasn't tempted. Nancy's studio was perfect: full of light and space, and still kitted out with four workspaces and machines, even if they needed a bit of an overhaul. It was only ten years since Nancy herself had been in there every day, supervising the three local women who had been the backbone of Nancy Vitari Design. Everything was as she had left it, down to the dusty bolts of fabric and the long rails, shrouded in plastic sheeting, that housed thirty years' worth of samples from the tiny but sought-after range of classic women's clothing.

Flo had taken one last look in there that morning. There was something incredibly peaceful about the space, as though Nancy were still there, about to appear around a corner with a length of tulle across her arms, pins clasped between her lips. It was heartbreaking to have missed by a few slender years the woman who had never let go, who had remembered birthdays for all those years, and who had watched her daughter and then her granddaughter grow up a thousand miles away. It was all catalogued in the little photo album Emilia had shown her, full of images sent by Peggy or Dorothy, so that Nancy could feel some closeness to the family she had entrusted to another woman and promised to remain apart from. So much love had been invested in the clothes that found their way back to England every few months with Pamela, and so much love remained between the two sisters who had grown up together, and grown old apart. Flo had always envied her friends who had sisters, a guaranteed companion through life. She smiled at the young woman standing opposite her, suspecting she had just found the next best thing.

'Maybe,' she said. 'I have one or two things to sort out first, though.'

Emilia smiled. 'Of course. But please, just come back whenever you like. We'll miss you.'

As Flo pulled away and watched them wave through the

cloud of dust, she smiled. She would be back. Again and again. This was her family, and after just a couple of weeks, the old farmstead already felt like home. Francesco and Emilia had even given her her own apartment for whenever she visited: one of the prettiest, away from the chatter and histrionics of the visiting artistic community, and with a private veranda that provided a ringside seat for the nightly spectacle of the Tuscan sunset. It had been Peter's, they told her, and was barely used any more. Pamela used to stay there with him when she visited from England, but she was busy with her own life in London and came infrequently these days. Flo had enjoyed inhabiting the space, planning which of her belongings she might bring with her next time, and spending hours staring at the framed sketches and miniature oils that remained on its walls.

But for now, it was time to go home – to feed the cat, drink tea with Dorothy and Phyllis, prove to Jem that she really had done it, get in touch with Pamela, and book a doctor's appointment.

It was also time to talk to Seamus.

London hid beneath a layer of dirty grey cloud as the aeroplane began its descent. Flo had almost forgotten that there was such a thing as British weather, having basked beneath clear blue skies for weeks on end, and it would take some getting used to. The plane bumped a little, and she anxiously held her belly as the seat belt dug into her, but then they were below the clouds, and the silvery Thames snaked beneath them, punctuated by the familiar landmarks of the London Eye, the Shard, London Bridge.

Somewhere below, within the scramble of streets that lay

beyond the four sentinel chimneys of Battersea Power Station, four girls had played hopscotch, talked about boys, swapped lipsticks and magazines, and promised to be friends for ever. Anxious as she was to dip her tired body into a bath of hot scented water, Flo knew she couldn't go home before visiting the quiet Wandsworth street where Dorothy had promised to have the kettle on and to spill the beans.

The plane banked steeply, and the map of London zoomed in, impossibly close, as they began their final descent.

31

'Come in, girl. You look exhausted.'

Flo kissed Dorothy's powdery cheek, despite the sickly cloud of White Diamonds that enveloped her.

Did Dorothy seem a bit stiffer, she wondered, as she followed her along the narrow hallway? Time had to take its toll even on this old fighter, and it saddened her to see the black velvet lounge pants hanging a little more loosely on the Amazonian queen of south London.

'Hi, Phyllis.'

'Hello, dear.' Peggy's old friend eased herself up out of her chair and held her arms out.

Flo smiled, accepting and returning the embrace, which as usual was like being cuddled by a violet-scented beanbag.

'So,' Dorothy said as she clattered about with mugs and tea bags, 'cat's out of the bag, eh?'

'I suppose it is.' Flo smiled. 'It's OK, Phyllis,' she said. 'Don't look so worried. There's no one left to tell you off. It's not a secret any more.'

Phyllis deflated as she breathed out. 'Lord, you have no idea how hard it was all these years.'

'Specially as that one's like a human bloody newsreel,' Dorothy muttered.

Phyllis instantly coloured. 'That's not fair, Dot.'

'She's just teasing you,' Flo said, instantly falling into the role of referee that came so naturally when she was with these two. It always astounded her that their friendship was so strong, when they bickered like siblings.

Dorothy put three mugs down on the table, ignoring Phyllis, who frowned as she rubbed away at a lipstick stain on hers. 'So,' she said, 'what do you want to know?'

Almost an entire afternoon disappeared as the two old women unloaded years' worth of secrets: trips to Italy to visit Nancy, how Phyllis had met her Marco at Nancy and Lorenzo's wedding, and how she had never told her mother that he was a waiter there, not a guest. Flo looked at a picture of the four friends reunited, the glowing, tanned bride in her beautiful sleeveless empire-line wedding dress, made in the Tuscan studio out of the finest duchess satin from a pattern Flo had found in Nancy's archive. There was Peggy, in a sun-drenched recreation of her own wedding photograph, while Stanley and Beryl had babysat for their three-year-old granddaughter.

'That was the last time your gran ever saw Nancy,' Dorothy said. 'They agreed it was best, but it broke their hearts.'

'Do you remember trying to get Peggy away at the end of that trip?' Phyllis dabbed at her eyes with a delicate hanky. 'Oh, it was terrible.'

'So Nancy never came back to England?' Flo asked.

Dorothy shook her head. 'Never. She couldn't bear to be on the same soil as little Maddie, poor love.'

'And what about the father? Did either of you know him?'

Dorothy snorted and took a long puff from the sickly scented vape. 'Oh, I knew him all right.'

'You knew who my grandfather was?'

Phyllis looked nervously at her old friend. 'Do you think you should—'

'What's the difference?' Dorothy said. 'He's dead now, isn't he? They're all dead. No harm telling the girl the truth.'

'So who was he?'

Dorothy hesitated. 'Charlie Blake,' she said. 'Good family, seemed a nice young chap, but turned out he was just like all the rest of them posh boys. Slummed it with a south London girl, then broke her heart.'

Phyllis put her hand on Flo's. 'She adored him. He was handsome – oh my, he was handsome – and he whisked her off her feet. She wasn't a bad girl, you know.'

Flo had never for a moment thought she had been: if Nancy had become pregnant even a decade later, her story might have been completely different.

'And did he look for her too?'

'Did he hell. The minute he heard she was in the club, he was off like a shot. We never heard a peep from him again. Mummy and Daddy made sure of that. Not that it did him any good in the end.'

'Why's that?'

'Married some society girl and ended up being a lawyer, just like his dad, then drank himself into an early grave. Serve him right.'

Flo wondered whether Dorothy was being harsh; perhaps it had been difficult for Charlie to break free of his expectations. 'Did he have any other children?' she asked.

Phyllis shook her head, seeing that Dorothy was too incensed still to answer. 'No, he was the end of the line there.'

It didn't matter. Charlie was almost an irrelevance in this story of the women of Victoria Street. Nancy had been happy in the end, and that was what mattered.

'There's one other thread I wanted to talk to you about,' Flo said. The two older women looked at one another.

'What's that, then?' Dorothy said.

'Pamela.'

'Ah, I wondered when you'd get around to her.'

'She must have been so close to Nancy, and younger too. Emilia gave me her email address. I thought I might track her down.'

'Did you now?' Dorothy said, but she was interrupted as the Big Ben chimes of the doorbell broke into the tiny kitchen. 'Jackson, get that, will you, you lazy lump?' she shouted. 'Bloody kids,' she muttered. 'Don't know where they all get it from. My Denzel would have sorted them out. Couldn't bear to see idleness, that man, especially in his own grandkids.'

Flo smiled, remembering the respect that Dorothy's husband used to command, and the soft heart that was hidden close to the surface of the gentle giant as he sneaked sweets to her behind his wife's back.

The front door banged closed, and the sounds of gunfire and incendiary devices resumed as the theatre of war began its next act in the sitting room.

Flo turned around as someone joined them in the kitchen. 'Oh, hi, Aunty Bean. I didn't know you'd be here.'

'I heard you were coming back. Thought I'd surprise you,' she said, leaning down and kissing Flo on the cheek. As usual, she looked as though she had dressed blindfolded at a WI jumble sale, her tights laddered, the sleeves of her tweed jacket three inches too short, and her blouse buttoned up wrong. It was one of the things they all loved about her: she just didn't care.

'Pull up a chair,' Dorothy said. 'And help yourself to tea.'

Aunty Bean pottered around the kitchen, finding tea bags and a mug. 'Ought to know my way around here,' she said. She looked at Flo. 'You know I used to lodge with your great-grandparents up the road years ago, when I was a student nurse?'

Flo nodded. She'd heard many times from the increasingly forgetful Peggy about how the young nurse had filled the gap in Stanley and Beryl's lives, providing them with one more young girl to look after, and how Aunty Bean had given so much back to the elderly couple in their later years when ill-health had beset them. From her little flat in north London, so handy for the hospital that had been her second home, it was often easier for Bean to get over to visit them than it had been for Peggy.

Bean sat down at the table. 'So how are you, Flo? I haven't seen you since Peggy's funeral. You're looking well. When's it due?'

Flo blushed. 'Not you as well!' She glanced around the table. All the women were smiling conspiratorially at each other.

'Didn't think we wouldn't guess, did you?' Dorothy said.

'I think it's just lovely,' said Phyllis, pressing her hand around Flo's.

'Well, thanks. I mean, it's early days, and obviously it's a bit complicated . . .'

'Pah.' Dorothy waved her hand in the air, setting her heavy

gold charm bracelet jingling. 'You'll sort it out. You Moon girls are good at that.'

Flo felt uncomfortable talking about the baby before she'd even had a chance to tell Seamus. She'd only just managed not to blurt it out to Jem, when she'd called to say she would be back in a few days. 'Anyway,' she said, to change the subject, 'I was asking you about Pamela.'

'What do you want to know?' Aunty Bean said, tucking her faded sandy hair behind her ears.

The three women looked at each another, then one by one they began laughing, first quietly, then uproariously, until Flo banged her hand loudly on the table, irritated at seeming to be the butt of a joke she hadn't realised had been told. 'What's so funny?'

'Do you want to tell her, Pea? Or shall I?' Dorothy looked across the table.

Flo frowned. 'Did you say Pea?'

Aunty Bean sighed. 'It was your mum who got it wrong when she was tiny. Aunty Pea became Aunty Bean, and . . . well, it was funny, so we never corrected her. And by the time you came along, it had stuck.'

Flo looked at her. How had she not seen it? The freckles, the hair that was never quite tidy, and as age had changed her, there was Peter in her features, as Flo had seen him in the photographs.

For all those years, Pamela had been right under her nose, and she listened rapt as Aunty Bean described how she had held the two sides of the family together as she flitted from England to Italy and back again, bringing her precious cargo of photographs and hand-made gifts, so that Nancy could watch her little girl grow up and become a mother herself, and Peggy could dress Maddie in the beautiful clothes that had been made with love in a studio in far-off Tuscany.

Flo's head was spinning. There was so much she wanted to ask Pamela, but she was shattered. There would be plenty of opportunity once she had digested everything in a few days. For now, though, it was time to go home, back to the little terraced house that Jem had been looking after.

Before she could go anywhere, however, there was one more thing she had promised to do. She reached into her handbag and removed the envelope Emilia had given her. She took out the photograph inside, and watched the jaws of the three older women drop as one.

'I don't bloody believe it,' Dorothy said.

'But how . . . ?' Phyllis shook her head.

Pamela picked up the photo, smiling as she looked at the two faces. 'So you still had a secret up your sleeve, Nancy,' she said.

'I have no idea how it happened, but there they are. Who'd have thought it?' And Flo joined the others in looking at the two faces that smiled out from the photograph: Nancy, now middle-aged and still perfectly groomed, her hair in an immaculate French pleat, arm in arm with the young woman whose hippyish appearance was the antithesis of her mother's. Nancy and Maddie.

'Was that before you were born?' Phyllis said to Flo.

Pamela smiled. 'I wonder if that's why she called you Florence – the capital of Tuscany. It probably wasn't because of *The Magic Roundabout*.'

'Maybe. I suspect there's another story there,' Flo said.

'If you ever track that mother of yours down, maybe you can ask her one day,' Dorothy said.

It was late now, and Flo made her farewells, hugging each of the three women tight. She was ready to go home and work out what on earth she would do next.

Jem was waiting to greet her at Willow Terrace, bag packed and ready to vacate.

'Hey, stranger,' she said, hugging Flo to her. 'Missed you.' She looked down at the growling cat. 'So did he.'

'Great. It's still alive.'

Jem stood back and looked at her friend. 'You look amazing. Travelling suits you.' She frowned. 'There's something different about you. Eaten too much pasta, maybe?'

Flo felt herself blush, furious that she had given herself away so easily.

Jem threw her hands to her mouth as she looked at the gentle swell of Flo's stomach. 'Oh my God. I don't believe it!'

'You mustn't tell anyone. Promise! I need to talk to Seamus first, once I've found him.'

Jem smiled. 'Cross my heart.'

'You haven't heard anything from him, have you?' It seemed an age since she had sent that text off, and the lack of a response was beginning to unnerve her.

'Me? Nah, not for ages.' Jem squeezed her hand. 'Don't fret, babe. I'm sure he'll turn up sooner or later.'

'I hope you're right. I don't want to do this without him.'

'Don't worry for now. Things have a way of working themselves out in the end.'

'I hope so.' Flo dropped her bag on the stairs. 'God, it's good to be home. Does feel a bit weird, though.'

'You'll get used to it.'

'You don't have to go, you know? You can stay as long as you like.'

'Nah, you're all right. Our place is fixed now, and Clare moved back in last week. Besides,' she added, 'you need a bit of space. It's been a mad few weeks.'

Flo nodded. 'I suppose so.' Suddenly she wanted nothing more than to wave Jem goodbye. There was plenty of time for a proper catch-up, and she'd be back in the shop soon enough. Well, maybe. Suddenly anything was up for grabs, and she couldn't begin to guess what the next few months would bring, apart from the little life that was growing inside her, all being well.

'OK, babe, I'm off. There's milk and a few bits in the fridge for you. See you soon.' Jem kissed her on the cheek, and Flo rubbed at what she knew was a huge red lipstick mark.

'See you.' She was just closing the door, when Jem called back to her from the end of the path.

'Oh, by the way, I left something else in the kitchen for you. I'd go and look now before it gets cold.' She smiled and waved, and Flo watched through the stained glass of the front door as she disappeared from sight.

She was desperate to get the bath running, but she'd be mad not to eat whatever Jem had left for her, when she was starving hungry all of a sudden.

She heard a ping from the direction of the stairs, and saw the blue light of her phone glowing from her handbag. She pulled it out, praying it would be her husband, as she remembered those three brave words she had sent him: *I'm sorry too* . . .

And there he was, her Seamus at last:

That means a lot, Flossie. Thank you x

It was the first she had heard from him in months. She'd almost begun to believe that he had forgotten her. Those few words didn't tell her much, but they were a start. Maybe there was hope. If nothing else, at least they finally had a channel of communication. God knew, there was enough to talk about.

She dropped the phone on the hall table and headed towards the kitchen, wondering why she couldn't smell cooking. Not more bloody cold food, please: much as she'd loved it, she'd be happy not to see another slice of salami for a good while yet.

'Hi, Floss.'

She stood rooted to the spot, one hand on the kitchen door handle. It couldn't be.

But there he was, putting his phone down on the table and looking like the last few months had never happened.

'Keep an old eejit company?' he said quietly.

'Seamus. How did you get here?' she said, walking slowly towards him.

'Great big machine with wings and an engine.'

She couldn't help a laugh escaping. 'You know what I mean.'

'Wee Jem there told me you were coming back.'

'Jem told you?'

'Aye, she's a shite friend, that one. I wouldn't tell her anything again if I were you.'

'So,' she said hesitantly, 'why are you here?'

'It's my home. You're my home, Flo. I missed you. I had to come back.' He chewed on his bottom lip. 'If you'll have me.' He looked uncertainly at her. 'Will you, Floss? Will you have me back?'

She looked at him. It was the old Seamus, full of hope, full of love, the wreckage of their break-up left behind on the other side of the ocean. And she knew that she was back too; that the fractured, angry Flo who had refused to see what she was losing was gone for good.

Five paces lay between them, five paces that could determine the rest of their lives.

'Seamus,' she said, her voice breaking, 'I'm sorry . . . for not listening to you, for pushing you out, for everything.'

He smiled as he stood and walked towards her. 'Me too, Floss. I should never have put you in that position. I deserved everything I got.'

They took each other's hands and smiled.

'Fresh start?' he said.

She nodded. 'Come here, eejit,' she said and opened her arms.

The smell of him, the feel of his arms around her again, the love that she allowed to wrap her up and squeeze her tightly intoxicated her so completely that she nearly forgot for a moment.

She drew back and looked into his eyes.

'Seamus,' she said, 'I've got something to tell you.'

He looked anxious for a moment, then questioning, until he caught the smile in her eyes and on her lips. 'My clever wee girl,' he laughed, picking her up and spinning her around.

'Takes two.' She smiled as he dropped her back to the ground, pressing her hands to his rough cheeks as she stood on tiptoe to reach him. 'And now I think it's time you kissed your wife.'

Epilogue

'You're sure you'll be all right?' Flo looked anxiously at the sleeping child.

'Florence, I was a nurse for thirty years. Your baby will be fine. Now go on. You'll miss your table.'

Sometimes there really was no arguing with Pea, so Flo surrendered and let Seamus lead her out of the nursery and down the stairs.

'Come on, missus,' he said. 'When's the last time you and I got out of the house together? That wee baby has taken over our lives.'

She smiled, knowing that he was as anxious as she about leaving little Peter, but he was right: it was their wedding anniversary, and it felt good to be dressed up, made up and with not a single nappy in her handbag. In a few weeks' time, Seamus would break up for the Easter holidays and they would be packing up the car for a month in Italy: they needed to get used to leaving the house, and a celebratory dinner was a good start. She had a last look around the kitchen to make sure she hadn't forgotten anything, and stopped when she saw that Ben's postcard had dropped from its magnet on the fridge door. She picked it up, looking at the image of Ayers Rock and smiling as she read the short message: *Is this far enough away*

*from my mother? Best thing I ever did! In haste – off trekking
with the guys tomorrow. Mr Simpson x*

'Come on, Floss, we'll miss our table,' Seamus shouted
from the hallway.

'Coming,' she replied, pinning the card back on the fridge
then banging the front door closed behind her as she followed
him out onto the pavement.

'What are they like?' Pamela said, stroking little Peter's soft
cheek and listening to their chatter as they disappeared along
the street.

He smiled up at her with huge grey eyes.

'You're going to be a charmer like your pa, aren't you?' she
said, smiling. 'Your great-granny Nancy would have adored
you, little fellow.' It was lovely to be with a baby again, and
she was thrilled that Flo had asked her. It seemed so many
years since she'd helped Nancy and Lorenzo with their little
boys. She supposed babies must be in her blood: from the
neonatal ward she had run like a ship for all those years, to
the *bambini* in Italy, she loved being around them. She'd never
needed or even wanted her own; she had a rich life populated
by friends and family and of course her beloved dogs. This
one was a poppet, however, and there was definitely a bit of
Nancy in him.

She missed Nancy desperately; in the end, she had been
more of a mother than a sister to her, and she had looked after
Pa in his dotage. It was down to Nancy that Peter had eventually been persuaded to let Pamela go to London and take up
her studies, if only to get her out of the stables. And he'd been

proud in the end, even travelling to London to see her gradu-
ate from the teaching hospital, winning the gold medal for her
year. She wished Nancy could have been there too, but nothing
could make her visit England ever again, and so Pamela had
made sure she brought lots of photos of the ceremony back
with her when she next went to Tuscany.

It was good at last to be able to share so many happy
memories with Flo, who couldn't get enough of hearing about
their trip through Europe, how Nancy and Lorenzo eventually
married after three years of his asking her, and how loved and
happy she had been in her new life. She was glad that Flo
and Seamus would be part of that world now, if only for a
few months a year. And who knew? Once Flo had settled into
motherhood, maybe she would take over Nancy's studio, as
she kept saying she would.

The baby thrashed his fists happily against the mattress,
gurgling and looking at the little music box that hung from
the bars of his cot.

'You want this again? I swear, young man, you would listen
to this all night, wouldn't you?'

She pulled the cord on the box, and the sweet chimes
played the tune that made him smile every time, the same tune
that had soothed Nancy's baby boys when they were tiny.

Pamela hummed along as the cord retracted into the box,
and she was forced to pull it again, lest he cry.

'You are my sunshine,' she sang quietly as she stroked his
warm cheek, 'my only sunshine . . .'

*

Nancy sat up straight and stretched her back: years of hunching over a machine were beginning to take their toll. Maybe she should listen to Lorenzo and take it easy. Now that Luigi had taken over the day-to-day running of the gallery and the workshops and Stanley was settled in his new job at the university, they were free to spend more time together, take some of the trips they had always promised each other. Perhaps they would go to stay at the Villa du Cap Bleu and drink champagne as the sun set, or sip coffee at a Parisian pavement café.

She lifted the little dress and held it up to examine it. It really was adorable. She just needed to press the little Peter Pan collar and perhaps tuck in an extra stitch at the bottom of the zip, but otherwise it was ready. She would wrap it in tissue and Pamela could take it back with her tomorrow. The holidays together always seemed so short, and Pamela had little time off, but she loved her job and they were all very proud of her. They'd have supper together tonight: she, Lorenzo, Pamela and Peter, and hopefully Luigi and Angela would bring little Emilia over with them. What an angel that child was, bringing so much joy to her grandmother. Maybe Stanley and Eduardo would be able to make it too – she loved hearing their stories about the city, now that she spent so much time tucked away in the countryside. They led such a glamorous life, the art historian and the magazine editor, and always indulged her with sweet treats and vintage accessories that they found for her in the more expensive Florentine streets.

She leant across the sewing table and picked up an identical little dress. One for Emilia and one for Florence. How funny that they were almost the same age. She wondered whether they would ever meet. Perhaps one day, when the old stories and the old secrets didn't matter any more; perhaps then the families could find one another.

It was getting dark outside, the starlings roosting in the olive grove outside her window. She listened carefully to the avian lullaby, and for a moment thought she heard something else: a snatch of music, a melody from years ago. Yes, there it was. Maybe it was just a memory, her mind playing tricks on her, but it was clear enough for her to find herself singing quietly along.

'. . . my only sunshine . . .'

She felt a cold rush of air, like a winter's morning blown in from the English countryside. Foolish old woman, she told herself, standing up and folding the little dresses. It was time to pack up for the night.

She looked around the studio once more just before she switched out the lights, its walls glowing as the Tuscan sunset reached in through the windows. She hoped one day someone would want to take it over. So much love had gone into creating it, but she knew she was becoming tired, and that soon she would have to stop.

'Onwards and sideways, Nancy,' she said, as she flicked the light switch. 'Onwards and sideways.'

Acknowledgements

The few hundred pages contained within the beautiful cover of this book are so much more than the sum of words printed here. At risk of this author's thankyou sounding like an indulgent awards speech, there are many people I want to thank for being part of the lifelong process of Nancy's creation, but I will try to be succinct.

My need to get words out of my head and onto the page no doubt had its nascence in the home I grew up in, which was always full of books: children's books, reference books, classics and moderns, cookery books, music books. Thanks, Dad, for all those Saturday mornings in the public library, where you let us spend hours choosing our armfuls of books every week, and for the bookshop trips where you guided us towards the books you grew up loving and helped us find our own treasures. Listening to you reading to my own children when they were tiny has been one of my great joys.

Nancy was partly born of my own love of dressmaking, and I have to thank Mum for her patient hours being my own Miss Nightingale, showing me how to use the old Singer sewing machine, how to make peg dollies, how (less successfully) to knit, and how to turn a packet of tissue paper into increasingly more wearable items of clothing. Thank you for all the wavy scarves you taught your grandchildren to knit and for the happy, messy hours spent at the kitchen table with them.

Writing is a joyous, agonising, frustrating way to spend one's time, and I thank all the music teachers I had over the years, who taught me that creativity is nothing without hours of hard, lonely work, and that the visible part of any artist's craft is the briefest glimpse of years of graft. I try to remember that when I stare into a void, waiting for the words to come, or looking at a page full of the right words, but in the wrong order. It is all worth it for those giddy moments riding the wave, that can turn into hours if you're lucky, or be gone in the time it takes to reach for a thesaurus.

I am fortunate in having my own community of writing friends, who all understand this, and have inspired and humbled me over the years with their talent and generosity: Kate Hicks Beach, Christine Kidney, Tom Kane, Emma Cuthbert, Katja Sass, Geraldine Terry, Deb Jess Kermode, Deb Dooley, Antoinette Whittingham, I love and admire you more than words can say. An extra-special thanks has to go to my dear friend and fellow writer Clare Palmer, who gave Nancy, Flo and me a quiet space to get to know each other away from home, providing me with a desk to work at and the adorable Squeeks [sic] the cat as distraction.

Nancy's arrival on the Continent was but a latter stage in her journey, and she would never have made it there had the incredibly talented Gill Paul not encouraged me to take Nancy out from the back of the wardrobe and introduce her to the world. I still have to pinch myself that the completely brilliant Gaia Banks scooped us up and brought us into the Sheil Land family, and thank her for the hours she happily spends chatting with me about our shared vintage-clothing habit. This really was a match made in heaven's atelier. Thanks too to Alba Arnau of SLA, who does a great job of looking after me and easing my natural antipathy to paperwork.

Enormous and heartfelt thanks go to Sherise Hobbs and Eleanor Dryden of Headline Review, who fell in love with my book and made me cry with the beautiful letter they wrote to me. Nancy couldn't be in better or more caring hands. Thank you to Siobhan Hooper for the beautiful jacket design, Rosie Margesson and Ellie Morley for working so hard to launch Nancy even in the midst of a pandemic, and to Faith Stoddard for helping the editorial process run so smoothly. Thanks, too, to Jane Selley for her meticulous and sensitive copy-edit. My first job ever was as assistant to Carole Welch at Hodder & Stoughton, and to be an author within the Hachette umbrella feels like a very happy and privileged homecoming.

And of course I thank my patient, slightly neglected family, who have had to sit at the dinner table listening to their mother raving about a plot twist that meant nothing to them, or celebrating another wordcount goal. Kate, Molly and Gus, I promise to listen attentively from now on.

Questions for discussion

1. What do you think Nancy's life would have been like if she had changed her mind at the last minute, and did she realistically have a choice? How much has society changed in that respect since 1962?

2. What is it about a homemade garment that makes it feel so special to wear? Do we still value dressmaking and 'domestic' crafts in the same way that we did back in 1962? Without fast fashion, many women back then made their own clothes out of necessity – have we lost something in being able to shop cheaply on the high street and the Internet when we want a new outfit?

3. Seamus did a terrible thing to Flo, but is it understandable that he made a mistake? And was Flo right to allow herself to be attracted to Ben and treat him as she did, in the wake of her marriage breakdown? It is common for families to unravel after a tragedy, but what is it that pushes them apart rather than the shared experience bringing them together?

4. If you could choose one decade in which to dress, which would it be, and why? And how do you think the fashion of that decade, particularly for women, was influenced by the ethics and expectations of society at the time?

5. Which character in the book do you consider to be the best parent, regardless of biology, and what makes a good parent? How much of being 'family' is about blood?

6. Would or should Dorothy and Phyllis have told Flo the truth about her family, had she not discovered it for herself? Do you think Peggy wanted it to remain a secret, and does anyone have the right to tell the secrets of those who have died?

7. Was Maddie right to leave her daughter behind? Do you think it was an act of selfishness or sacrifice?

8. Do you think Pamela had a more privileged upbringing than the Wandsworth girls? What is it that makes a 'good' childhood?

9. 1962 was a fascinating year: the first man was propelled into space; the Beatles were born and Marilyn Monroe died; women's fashion was just about to morph from Grace Kelly elegance to the short skirts of Mary Quant; the contraceptive pill had just become available in the UK, and televisions were gradually becoming more common in households. What do you think were the changes for better or worse in the 1960s?